THE W

TALES O
BLACKWO

Blackwood's Edinburgh Magazine was founded by William Blackwood (1776–1834) in October 1817, after a six-month false start as the dull and directionless *Edinburgh Monthly Magazine*. Blackwood himself became editor when he changed the name and, with the help of John Wilson and J. G. Lockhart, quickly turned it into a highly marketable blend of slander, sensationalism, erudition, buffoonery, and truculent High Toryism. The magazine featured reviews and original fiction, as well as articles on travel, the military, economics, architecture, art, philosophy, astrology, and much else. Samuel Taylor Coleridge, Walter Scott, James Hogg, Mary Shelley, Charles Lamb, Thomas De Quincey, and John Galt were all contributors at this time, and when Blackwood's son Alexander took over in 1834 he continued to attract important writers, including Elizabeth Barrett Browning and Edward Bulwer-Lytton. In the second half of the century the magazine maintained its diversity and its place as the leading representative of Tory thought, though the recklessness of the early years was replaced by moderation. George Eliot's *Scenes of Clerical Life* (1857–8), Margaret Oliphant's *Miss Marjoribanks* (1865–6), Anthony Trollope's *John Caldigate* (1878–9), and Joseph Conrad's *Heart of Darkness* (1899) were all published in *Blackwood's*, as were shorter pieces by Arthur Conan Doyle, Thomas Hardy, Oscar Wilde, and many others. *Blackwood's* reputation remained high in the twentieth century, partly because of contributors like John Buchan and Alfred Noyes, and partly because its Toryism greatly enhanced its popularity in wartime. The magazine began to decline in the 1950s, when its reactionary politics and dated storylines failed to attract new readers. *Blackwood's* ceased publication in December 1980 after nearly 164 years of continuous publication and ten Blackwood editors, all directly descended from the founder.

ROBERT MORRISON is Assistant Professor of English at Acadia University, Nova Scotia. He is the editor of three volumes of *The Works of Thomas De Quincey* (forthcoming).

CHRIS BALDICK is Professor of English at Goldsmiths' College, University of London. He has edited *The Oxford Book of Gothic Tales* (1992) and is the author of *In Frankenstein's Shadow* (1987) and other works of literary history.

THE WORLD'S CLASSICS

Tales of Terror from Blackwood's Magazine

Edited with an Introduction by
ROBERT MORRISON
and
CHRIS BALDICK

Oxford   New York
OXFORD UNIVERSITY PRESS
1995

Oxford University Press, Walton Street, Oxford OX2 6DP
Oxford New York
Athens Auckland Bangkok Bombay
Calcutta Cape Town Dar es Salaam Delhi
Florence Hong Kong Istanbul Karachi
Kuala Lumpur Madras Madrid Melbourne
Mexico City Nairobi Paris Singapore
Taipei Tokyo Toronto
and associated companies in
Berlin Ibadan

Oxford is a trade mark of Oxford University Press

British Library Cataloguing in Publication Data
Data available

Library of Congress Cataloging-in-Publication Data
Tales of terror from Blackwood's magazine / edited with an
introduction by Robert Morrison and Chris Baldick.
p.   cm. — (The World's classics)
Includes bibliographical references (p.   ).
1. Horror tales, English.   2. English fiction—19th century.
I. Morrison, Robert.   II. Baldick, Chris.   III. Blackwood's
magazine.   IV. Series.
PR1309.H6T34   1995   823'.0873808—dc20   95-3676
ISBN 0-19-282366-3

1 3 5 7 9 10 8 6 4 2

Typeset by Graphicraft Typesetters Ltd., Hong Kong
Printed in Great Britain by
BPC Paperbacks Ltd.
Aylesbury, Bucks

CONTENTS

INTRODUCTION

> A man who does not contribute his quota of grim
> stories now-a-days seems hardly to be free of the repub-
> lic of letters. He is bound to wear a death's head, as part
> of his insignia. If he does not frighten every body, he is
> nobody.
>
> Leigh Hunt, 1819[1]

IN a letter of 1832, Samuel Taylor Coleridge told William
Blackwood that '"Blackwood's Magazine" is an unprec-
ented Phenomenon in the world of letters', and he praised its
irony, variety, and 'sustained wisdom'.[2] Coleridge's enthusiasm of 1832 stands in marked contrast to his reaction of 1817,
when a scabrous review of *Biographia Literaria* led him to
consider legal action against *Blackwood's*. Yet his two very
different responses are understandable for, like several others,
he was both slandered and praised by a magazine that achieved
notoriety for its inconsistency and bile. As Coleridge's 1832
comment suggests, *Blackwood's* was also an exciting blend
of raucous humour, penetrating intelligence, arrogant ultra-
Toryism, and Gothic terror. There was nothing else like it,
and it secured enormous popularity and influence.

William Blackwood was an increasingly successful Edinburgh bookseller and publisher when he determined to found
a magazine in 1817. His immediate aim was to challenge the
Scots Magazine, an ailing miscellany published by his Edinburgh rival Archibald Constable; less directly, he hoped to
establish a spirited Tory monthly that would challenge the
influence of the Whiggish *Edinburgh Review* and comple-
ment the ponderous Toryism of the *Quarterly Review*. Blackwood seems to have realized that the magazine format itself,
which had remained essentially unaltered since Edward Cave
introduced his *Gentleman's Magazine* in 1731, was now ripe

[1] 'A Tale for a Chimney Corner' in *The Indicator*, 10, 73.
[2] *Collected Letters of Samuel Taylor Coleridge*, ed. E. L. Griggs (6 vols;
Oxford, 1956–71), vi. 912.

for change; and he saw the potential of exploiting the rich literary and cultural climate of Edinburgh. A generation earlier it had been one of the centres of the European Enlightenment as the home of such men as the historian and philosopher David Hume and the economist Adam Smith. It was still a lively intellectual centre for philosophy, history, and literature, its reputation maintained by writers like Dugald Stewart, Professor of Moral Philosophy at Edinburgh University, Francis Jeffrey, editor of the *Edinburgh*, and Walter Scott, then in the middle of his career as a novelist.

Initially, Blackwood's plans went badly. The first issue of his *Edinburgh Monthly Magazine*, which appeared in April 1817, was dull, unfocused, and, worse, began with an article praising Francis Horner, arch-Whig and one of the founders of the *Edinburgh*. Blackwood soon served notice on his two editors, Thomas Pringle and James Cleghorn, and took over the position himself, gathering John Wilson and J. G. Lockhart around him as prize contributors and advisers. The reconstituted effort appeared as *Blackwood's Edinburgh Magazine* in October 1817, and Blackwood never looked back. In the first issue of the new magazine Wilson delivered his vicious personal assault on Coleridge; Lockhart began his series on the 'Cockney School of Poetry', which included scurrilous attacks on Leigh Hunt, William Hazlitt, and John Keats; and Wilson, Lockhart, and James Hogg combined to produce the 'Chaldee Manuscript', an allegorical attack on Constable and other notable Edinburgh Whigs that left many gasping and others threatening legal action. Blackwood pacified some, paid off others, and compromised to the extent of issuing a second printing in which the 'Chaldee Manuscript' was expunged and Lockhart's attack on Leigh Hunt slightly mitigated. But the magazine had made its mark.

In the months that followed, *Blackwood's* maintained its reputation for the outrageous and controversial, yet it was always much more than a scandal sheet. Blackwood's objectives in founding the magazine were realized in full: it quickly drove Constable's *Scots Magazine* from the field and, while never acquiring (or seeking) the authority of the two major reviews, it was a powerful alternative. It provided a more flamboyant expression of Toryism than the *Quarterly* and incessantly, often effectively, mocked the *Edinburgh*. *Blackwood's* established a new pattern for magazines by removing all the formal departments, mixing together fiction, reviews, correspondence, and essays, and infusing exuberance throughout; and finally, it drew deeply on its Edinburgh context for writers, topics, settings, and political attitudes.

Blackwood's quickly spawned imitators, most notably the *New Monthly* and the *London*, but neither of these magazines was able to keep pace. In 1822, only two years after its founding, Charles Lamb warned the proprietors of the *London* that they were getting 'too serious' and that their magazine 'wanted the personal note too much'.[3] Meanwhile, *Blackwood's* was convincingly proclaiming itself as 'a real Magazine of mirth, misanthropy, wit, wisdom, folly, fiction, fun, festivity, theology, bruising and thingumbob'.[4] It was able to blend authority and élitism with frankness and bravado, claiming the approval of the aristocracy while repeatedly championing the breadth of its own popular appeal. It was read and discussed by everyone from Byron and Wordsworth to John Wilson Croker and the Duke of Wellington, and influenced, among others, Poe, Hawthorne, Browning, Dickens, and Charlotte and Emily Brontë. Only with the founding of *Fraser's* in 1830, with the former *Blackwood's* contributor William Maginn as editor, was its dominance as a magazine seriously challenged.

Politically speaking, *Blackwood's* was on the extreme right, espousing a narrow version of High Church Tory bigotry that truculently opposed all forms of Whiggery and any faintheartedness in the Tory ranks. Catholic Emancipation and the Reform Bill of 1832 were fiercely derided, and 'Cockneys' like Hunt and Keats were condemned on the basis of social class. 'All the great poets of our country have been men of some rank in society', Lockhart sneered, 'and there is no vulgarity in any of their writings; but Mr. Hunt cannot utter a dedication, or even a note, without betraying the *Shibboleth*

---

[3] *The Letters of Charles and Mary Lamb*, ed. E. V. Lucas (3 vols; London, 1935), ii. 323.
[4] *Blackwood's Magazine*, 12 (1822), 105–6.

of low birth and low habits'.[5] *Blackwood's* political rhetoric had its roots in Edmund Burke, but it was a good deal less discriminating and more vituperative, and on many occasions became as overwrought as anything in its sensation fiction. When events in France in 1830 led anxious Tory hearts to fear revolution, De Quincey's heated exclamations and nervous questions were characteristic of the *Blackwood's* style:

REVOLUTION!—French Revolution!—Dread watchword of mystery and fear!—Augury of sorrow to come!—Record of an Iliad of woes!— Is it then indeed true that another French Revolution has dawned? That its laurels are already mingled with cypress? That its victims are again seeking their old asylum in England?[6]

In 1833 Thomas Carlyle labelled De Quincey 'one of the most irreclaimable Tories now extant',[7] but he could just as easily have been speaking of *Blackwood's* political writers as a whole.

Yet, while unwavering in its politics, *Blackwood's* was often keenly alive to the literary spirit of the age, and was capable of praising those whose religious and political views were diametrically opposite to its own. Walter Scott's review of Mary Shelley's *Frankenstein* (1818) was the most discerning of the early reviews, and De Quincey's appraisal of Shelley's *The Revolt of Islam* (1818) the most intelligent assessment of the poet's genius to appear during his lifetime. Byron was on occasion treated roughly but he himself praised Wilson's review of *Manfred* (1817) and an 1823 'letter' of Lockhart's has been called 'the best of all the accounts of the spirit and status of *Don Juan* printed in any periodical of the time'.[8] *Blackwood's* treatment of Wordsworth and Coleridge was sometimes slanderous but most of its comments on them were positive and perceptive. Wordsworth was described as 'the first man that stripped thought and passion of all vain or foolish disguises, and shewed them in their just proportions and unencumbered

[5] *Blackwood's Magazine*, 2 (1817), 39.

[6] Ibid. 28 (1830), 542.

[7] *The Collected Letters of Thomas and Jane Welsh Carlyle*, ed. C. R. Sanders, *et al.* (21 vols; Durham, NC, 1970–), vi. 371.

[8] Theodore Redpath, *The Young Romantics and Critical Opinion* (London, 1973), 48.

power'; and Coleridge 'has perhaps the finest superstitious vein of any person alive'. R. P. Gillies and Lockhart published a ground-breaking series on German writers like Goethe and the Schlegels, while John Neal provided the most thorough and provocative contemporary survey of American literature. William Cullen Bryant and Fenimore Cooper were given short shrift, but Washington Irving had 'great power—original power' and Charles Brockden Brown the ability 'to impress his pictures upon the human heart, with such unexampled vivacity, that no time can obliterate them'.[9] For many *Blackwood's* meant blackguard, but some of the most perceptive assessments of contemporary genius appeared in its pages. No other magazine or review of the time can boast a comparable record.

Fiction was a part of *Blackwood's* from the beginning and became more central as the magazine evolved. Several novels were serialized in the early years, including John Galt's *The Ayrshire Legatees* (1820–1), Douglas Moir's *The Autobiography of Mansie Wauch* (1824–8), and Michael Scott's *Tom Cringle's Log* (1829–33). Popular tales of the pathetic, such as Wilson's own *Lights and Shadows from Scottish Life* (1820–1) were featured, as were adventure tales by John Howison, William Mudford, and several others. John Wain calls *Blackwood's* 'the cradle of Victorian fiction'[10] and indeed, George Eliot, Trollope, and Conrad later published there. *Blackwood's* was particularly interested in the ghastly and macabre. Novels of terror and sensation like William Godwin's *Mandeville* (1817), Charles Maturin's *Melmoth the Wanderer* (1820), and Galt's *The Omen* (1825) were reviewed, complete with lengthy excerpts, while Lockhart's and Gillie's critique of E. T. A. Hoffmann's *The Devil's Elixir* (1824) had a profound effect on Poe.[11] Seminal tales of the fantastic like Robert MacNish's 'The Metempsychosis' (1826) appeared, as did De Quincey's

---

[9] *Blackwood's Magazine*, 12 (1822), 175; 3 (1818), 649; 17 (1825), 67; 16 (1824), 421.

[10] *Contemporary Reviews of Romantic Poetry*, ed. John Wain (London, 1953), 25.

[11] Margaret Alterton, *Origins of Poe's Critical Theory* (Iowa City, 1925), 13–15.

satire 'On Murder Considered as one of the Fine Arts' (1827) and David Lyndsay's 'Sacred Drama' on 'The First Murder; or, the Rejection of the Sacrifice' (1821). Terror was also woven into a number of seemingly innocuous articles such as 'Hints for the Jurymen' (1823), where a consideration of medical jurisprudence leads to a gruesomely detailed discussion of the symptoms of death.[12]

Blackwood's often blurred the distinction between fact and fiction. The 'Chaldee Manuscript' (1817) is an allegory in mock-biblical language, in which Whig enemies and Tory friends appear in the fictional guise of birds and beasts;[13] while in the imaginary conversations of the *Noctes Ambrosianae* (1822–35) several *Blackwood's* contributors, including De Quincey, Hogg, and Wilson (as *Blackwood's* notional editor, 'Christopher North'), are dressed up in fictional titles.[14] *Blackwood's* also found it profitable and cruelly effective to use fictions and pseudonyms to persecute their enemies, so that an account of the first few years of the magazine reads like a Gothic tale of violence and revenge. When Lockhart as 'Z' attacked Hunt in the 'Cockney' poets series, the result was a tale of paranoia and persecution. Lockhart called himself Hunt's 'avenging shadow' and menaced, 'I shall probe you to the core. I shall prove you to be ignorant of all you pretend to understand.' The literary war that erupted between *Blackwood's* and the *London* led eventually to the shooting to death of the *London's* editor, John Scott, by Lockhart's ally, James Christie. The incident provoked outrage, but *Blackwood's* was unrepentant: less than two months after Scott's death it cheerfully referred to 'Z' as 'wet with the blood of the Cockneys' and cited Christopher North as a man who had 'slain' many with his 'trenchant and truculent falchion'. Later, *Blackwood's* announced that it had 'been looking about for some person or other to immolate to our fury—some victim to break upon the wheel, and to whom we might give, with soft reluctant

---

[12] Alterton, *Origins of Poe's Critical Theory*, 19.
[13] 'The Chaldee Manuscript' in F. D. Tredrey, *The House of Blackwood* (Edinburgh, 1954), 244–58.
[14] See Introduction to J. H. Alexander, *The Tavern Sages: A Selection from the Noctes Ambrosianae* (Aberdeen, 1992), pp. vii–xv.

amorous delay, the coup-de-grace'.[15] Such rhetoric is designed
to sell magazines but it is also indicative of *Blackwood's* pre-
occupation with bloodshed, persecution, and hysteria.

Intemperate in political polemic and feared for its literary
assassinations, *Blackwood's* became just as notorious for the
shocking power of its fictional offerings. The tales it published in its first fifteen years set a new standard of concen-
trated dread and precisely calculated alarm. A distinctive style
of hair-raising sensationalism took shape in its tales of terror
and guilt, one that was astutely recognized, parodied, and re-
worked by Edgar Allan Poe, with momentous consequences
for the tradition of the short story in English. Poe grasped
that there was a common principle of exaggerated intensity at
work in several of *Blackwood's* more successful tales, and that
its further exploitation had a real cash value for an aspiring
magazine writer like himself. Writing from Baltimore to the
proprietor of the *Southern Literary Messenger* in 1835 to justify the gruesome bad taste of his tale 'Berenice'—in which
the hero extracts all thirty-two of his female cousin's teeth
while she is in a coma—Poe asserted that good or bad taste
was irrelevant: all that mattered in the desperately competitive
modern magazine boom was that one's stories should be read.
The most celebrated and sought-after articles, he claimed,
citing William Maginn's *Blackwood's* tale, 'The Man in the
Bell', and other recent successes, were those that displayed 'the
ludicrous heightened into the grotesque: the fearful coloured
into the horrible: the witty exaggerated into the burlesque: the
singular wrought out into the strange and mystical'.[16] It is a
useful summary both of the typically overheated effects of a
Blackwood's tale and of Poe's own literary manner, so often
indebted to his precursors in Edinburgh.

Three years later, in 1838, Poe defined at greater length, and
in the light-hearted spirit of burlesque, his view of the singular
contribution of the *Blackwood's* tale to modern literature in

---

[15] *Blackwood's Magazine*, 3 (1818), 199, 201; 9 (1821), 62; 13 (1822),
321.
[16] *The Letters of Edgar Allan Poe*, ed. John Ward Ostrom (2 vols; New
York, 1966), i. 57–8.

'How to Write a Blackwood Article', written for the Baltimore *American Museum*. Here the fictional narrator, Signora
Psyche Zenobia, seeks advice from Mr Blackwood himself on
how to compose 'a genuine Blackwood article of the sensation
stamp',[17] learns that she must undergo some frightening ordeal
like an earthquake or a balloon disaster in order to record her
sensations, and accordingly succeeds in having herself decapitated by the minute-hand of an Edinburgh church clock, as
both her eyes pop out into the gutter. The comic exaggeration
highlights a genuinely observable pattern in the most celebrated
shorter tales published in the 'Maga', and Poe cites real examples to support his parody, all of them first-person accounts
of terrifying ordeals: John Galt's 'The Buried Alive' (1821),
Maginn's 'The Man in the Bell' (1821), in which the narrator
is stuck within inches of a huge bell as it tolls deafeningly over
him, and the later story (not reprinted in the present selection), 'The Involuntary Experimentalist' (1837), in which a
doctor finds himself trapped in an empty copper boiler during
a fire in a distillery, suffering terrible extremes of heat. Poe
makes his 'Mr Blackwood' refer to these as exemplary models
for Signora Zenobia to follow, adding: 'Sensations are the great
things, after all. Should you ever be drowned or hung, be sure
and make a note of your sensations—they will be worth to
you ten guineas a sheet.'[18] He could have cited many more
Blackwood's pieces as examples of the same formula: Henry
Thomson's 'Le Revenant' (1827) recounts the experiences of a
condemned man who survives his hanging; Daniel Keyte
Sandford's 'A Night in the Catacombs' (1818) gives us the
terrors of a narrator accidentally locked into the underground
tombs without a light; and, most famously, William Mudford's
'The Iron Shroud' (1830)—raided by Poe himself for his own
story, 'The Pit and the Pendulum' (1843)—offers the account
of a prisoner trapped in an increasingly confined cell. In each
case, the special intensity noted by Poe is achieved by presenting the recorded 'sensations' of a first-person narrator

[17] *Collected Works of Edgar Allan Poe*, ed. T. O. Mabbott (3 vols;
Cambridge, Mass., 1978), ii. 340.
[18] Ibid.

witnessing his own responses to extreme physical and psychological pressures.

There had been reputable literary precedents for such effects, in the fully documented sufferings of Samuel Richardson's heroines in *Pamela* (1740) and *Clarissa* (1747–8), and in the anxious narrative of the eponymous hero in William Godwin's *Adventures of Caleb Williams* (1794); but these works were very far from attempting the pointed condensation achieved by the best magazine stories of the early nineteenth century. The same is true of the suspense and unease cultivated in the Gothic novels of Ann Radcliffe, protracted as these are through the leisurely three-volume form. Certain kinds of 'terror', or at least of anxiety, were developed in quite sophisticated ways by Radcliffe and other Gothicists in the late eighteenth century, primarily through ominous suggestion and the careful evocation of 'atmosphere'. The *Blackwood's* authors differ markedly from the Gothicists not just in their concise scope but also in their sharper and more explicit rendering of terror. As H. P. Sucksmith has remarked, the vague suggestions of Radcliffean Gothic give way in *Blackwood's* to a greater precision of description in scenes of terror and horror, reaching an almost scientific degree of accuracy.[19] The usual tone in these stories is one of clinical observation (although without the customary detachment) rather than of genteel trepidation, and for the most part the terrors are unflinchingly 'witnessed', not ambiguously evoked: here there are fewer phantoms or rumours of phantoms than actual drownings, suicides, murders, executions, and death agonies, veiled by only the thinnest layer of euphemism and moralizing.

The more direct realism of *Blackwood's* terror fiction seems to be derived partly from the popular traditions of sensational 'true crime' narrative often found in broadsheet, chapbook, and newspaper publications. The narrator of Thomson's 'Le Revenant' seems to indicate as much when he confesses that

[19] H. P. Sucksmith, 'The Secret of Immediacy: Dickens' Debt to the Tale of Terror in *Blackwood's*' in *Nineteenth-Century Fiction*, 26 (Sept. 1971), 146–7.

My greatest pleasure, through life, has been the perusal of extra-ordinary narratives of fact. An account of a shipwreck in which hundreds have perished; of a plague which has depopulated towns or cities; anecdotes and inquiries connected with the regulation of prisons, hospitals, lunatic receptacles; nay, the very police reports of a common newspaper—as relative to matters of reality; have always excited a degree of interest in my mind which cannot be produced by the best invented tale of fiction.[20]

The efforts of *Blackwood's* storytellers were often devoted to rivalling the strangeness of fact, in tales of miraculous survival or outlandish crime, often enough in 'prisons, hospitals, lunatic receptacles'—in short, in those inscrutable institutions in which the extremes of human experience were, increasingly, being shut away out of sight. Several of these storytellers feed upon the unhealthy public curiosity provoked by the sequestration of madness, disease, and criminality into enclosed realms now penetrable only by such experts as the physician, the minister of religion, or the executioner. Such tales as John Wilson's 'Extracts from Gosschen's Diary' and William Godwin the Younger's 'The Executioner' satisfy their readers' curiosity by placing them on the 'inside' of secret events—with the priest at the condemned murderer's last-minute confession, or on the gallows itself. Similarly, the long-running series of *Passages from the Diary of a Late Physician* (1830–7), written anonymously by the former medical student Samuel Warren, let us into the intimate confidences of the diseased and the insane, and permit us to hear the ravings of the deathbed. Warren presented a clear enough view of the 'rich mine of incident and sentiment' that he was about to exploit, when he claimed in a preface to the series' first instalment that 'The bar, the church, the army, the navy, and the stage, have all of them spread the secret volumes of their history to the prying gaze of the public; while that of the medical profession has remained hitherto—with scarcely an exception—a sealed book'.[21] Although there was at least one indignant letter to the *Lancet* protesting against the breach of medical confidentiality, the

[20] *Blackwood's Magazine*, 21 (1827), 409.
[21] Ibid. 28 (1830), 322.

result was a striking success among *Blackwood's* readers, at home and abroad.

Warren's focusing of the public's 'prying gaze' upon disease and madness in these tales was widely recognized as an excursion beyond the bounds of good taste, and his pretentious habit of quoting from Greek and Latin sources was mocked by Poe, whose Psyche Zenobia carries on alluding to classical authors even after her head has been sliced off. Aiming, as he put it, 'to furnish both instruction and amusement to the public',[22] Warren tends to disguise the sensational and prurient basis of the amusement under a cloak of sermonizing instruction and obtrusive erudition, thus maintaining at least the pretence of offering us 'improving' fiction. Wherever possible, he set up deathbed scenes in order to contrast the despairing exit of the dissipated rake with the peaceful departure of the virtuous maiden. Several of his longer tales are laborious and too obviously padded out, but at his best, as in 'A "Man About Town"', 'The Spectre-Smitten', and 'The Thunder-Struck', he orchestrates his melodramatic and horrific material to startling effect, holding us under the spell of his contrived hysteria for several pages at a time. Few readers will forget, for instance, the physician's tense battle with the naked, razor-wielding lunatic in 'The Spectre-Smitten'.

The early tales of Samuel Warren represent the strengths of *Blackwood's* in the more extended story, by contrast with Galt's 'The Buried Alive' or Michael Scott's 'Heat and Thirst', which concentrate their impact within three or four pages. For the most part, the shortest stories published in the early years of the 'Maga' were tales of claustrophobic confinement such as 'The Iron Shroud', while the longer stories showed a greater variety of subject-matter and tone, including the sentimental, the historical, and the folkloric. James Hogg, the 'Ettrick Shepherd', contributed several tales making use of supernatural legends of fairies and witches; of these, 'The Mysterious Bride' comes closest to the uncanny effects of the tale of terror. Strangely, given the continuing vogue for Gothic fiction at this time, there are in the early volumes of

[22] Ibid.

Blackwood's scarcely any short stories that one could plausibly describe as Gothic. There are, however, some approxima-
tions: ghost stories, such as those of Hogg, on one side and,
on the other, some powerful tales of accursed, guilt-ridden
families. The most remarkable story in the latter category is
'The Executioner' (1832), by William Godwin the Younger,
son of the novelist and philosopher. Readers who are familiar
with the elder Godwin's *Caleb Williams*, or with the *Frankenstein* (1818) of the younger Godwin's half-sister Mary Shelley,
will find that the tale takes them back to familiar territory,
drawing heavily on both those novels and even matching them
in the evocation of the outcast's guilt.

This is the first collection of the early *Blackwood's* tales
since the nineteenth century. In making our selection of stories
for inclusion in this volume, we have decided to limit ourselves
to the first sixteen years (1817–32) of the magazine's life, these
being the years in which its short fiction made the most distinctive impact upon the world of letters. We have also confined our choices to tales of terror, both because these represent
the most remarkable of *Blackwood's* specialities, and because
the sentimental and comical fiction of that period is almost
entirely unpalatable to modern readers. We have tried to
balance the claims of the shorter tales against those of the
longer, and to encompass the widest variety of contributors,
so that only Samuel Warren is represented here by more than
one story. The tales are presented here in chronological order,
with the unexpected but convenient result that this collection
begins with thirteen relatively short tales illustrating the variety of morbid invention exhibited in the phase from 1817 to
1830, and ends with four substantially longer tales published
between 1830 and 1832, three of these coming from Warren's
Passages from the Diary of a Late Physician. The most important principle governing our selections, however, has been the
hope that these tales, many of them having been overlooked
for more than a century, will still have the power to startle,
disconcert, and fascinate new generations of readers.

NOTE ON THE TEXT

In the course of preparing this edition, we came across the hitherto unnoticed problem of different versions of *Blackwood's Magazine*. It appears that many of the early volumes were reprinted in their entirety, with inevitable minor variations. This problem has not yet been subjected to full scholarly analysis, so that it is not yet possible to establish which of the two available texts is the original. A comparison between the texts of several of the tales in this volume revealed only minor variations, mostly in punctuation and typography.

We have modernized the text in a number of ways: for example, rows of asterisks employed to subdivide the text have been eliminated, double quotation marks have been changed to single, square brackets have been changed to round, and a standard format has been adopted for the headings of the tales. We have silently corrected obvious errors in spelling and punctuation. Some of Samuel Warren's own footnotes have been incorporated into our explanatory notes, and a long footnote on the etymology of the word 'epilepsy' has been removed from 'The Spectre-Smitten'. Prefatory letters or statements have been omitted from the front of some of the tales and, wherever possible, signatures have been removed from the end of tales. Details of the signatures appear in the explanatory notes.

SELECT BIBLIOGRAPHY

THE best contemporary accounts of the early years of *Blackwood's Magazine* are the letters, essays, and reminiscences of Samuel Taylor Coleridge, Leigh Hunt, John Scott, John Keats, Thomas Carlyle, and Edgar Allan Poe. See also the essays and letters of William Blackwood and of *Blackwood's* contributors like J. G. Lockhart, Thomas De Quincey, John Galt, James Hogg, and John Wilson. Good introductions to the early years of *Blackwood's* are still Alexander Shand, 'Magazine Writers' in *Blackwood's Magazine*, 125 (1879), 225–47, and George Saintsbury's essays on Hogg, Wilson, Lockhart, and Maginn in *The Collected Letters and Papers of George Saintsbury* (4 vols; London, 1923), i. 26–52, 184–209; ii. 1–30, 168–76. Margaret Oliphant, *Annals of a Publishing House* (Edinburgh, 1897) and F. D. Tredrey, *The House of Blackwood* (Edinburgh, 1954) are sympathetic accounts of the history of the magazine.

More recent discussions of *Blackwood's* include the following: J. H. Alexander, '*Blackwood's*: Magazine as Romantic Form' in *The Wordsworth Circle*, 15 (1984), 57–68; J. H. Alexander, *The Tavern Sages: A Selection from the Noctes Ambrosianae* (Aberdeen, 1992); Maurice Milne, 'The Veiled Editor Unveiled: William Blackwood and his Magazine' in *Publishing History*, 16 (1984), 87–103; Emily Lorraine de Montluzin, 'William Blackwood: The Human Face Behind the Mask of "Ebony"' in *Keats–Shelley Journal*, 36 (1987), 158–89; Robert Morrison, '*Blackwood's* under William Blackwood' in *Scottish Literary Journal*, 22 (1995), 61–5; George Pottinger, *Heirs of the Enlightenment: Edinburgh Reviewers and Writers 1800–1830* (Edinburgh, 1992); and Roger Wallins, 'Blackwood's Edinburgh Magazine' in *British Literary Magazines: The Romantic Age*, ed. Alvin Sullivan (London, 1983), 45–53.

For individual authors and their relationship with *Blackwood's*, see: Michael Allen, *Poe and the British Magazine Tradition* (New York, 1969); George Douglas, *The Blackwood Group* (Edinburgh, 1897), 134–50, for Michael Scott; Winifred Gérin, *Emily Brontë* (Oxford, 1971); Ian Gordon, *John Galt: The Life of a Writer* (Edinburgh, 1972); Lewis Simpson, *James Hogg: A Critical Study* (Edinburgh, 1962); Lockhart's *Letter to Lord Byron*, ed. A. L. Strout (Oklahoma, 1947); H. P. Sucksmith, 'The Secret of Immediacy: Dickens' Debt to the Tale of Terror in *Blackwood's*' in *Nineteenth-Century Fiction*, 26 (1971), 151–7; Elsie Swann, *Christopher North [John Wilson]*

(Edinburgh, 1934); M. M. H. Thrall, *Rebellious Fraser's* (New York, 1934), for William Maginn; and A. Wood, 'Sir W. Scott and "Maga"' in *Blackwood's Magazine*, 232 (1932), 1–15.

Surprisingly, there has been no full-length study of the tale of terror in *Blackwood's*. For background discussion, see Edith Birkhead, *The Tale of Terror* (London, 1921); Terry Heller, *The Delights of Terror* (Urbana, Ill., 1987); R. D. Mayo, 'The Gothic Short Story in the Magazines' in *Modern Literary Review*, 37 (1942), 448–54; David Punter, *The Literature of Terror* (London, 1980); and Donald Ringe, *American Gothic* (Lexington, Ky., 1982).

CHRONOLOGY OF
BLACKWOOD'S MAGAZINE

1817   Apr. *Edinburgh Monthly Magazine* established, published by William Blackwood, edited by James Cleghorn and Thomas Pringle.

Oct. Cleghorn and Pringle are fired; the magazine is renamed *Blackwood's Edinburgh Magazine*, with William Blackwood as editor; Lockhart's 'On the Cockney School of Poetry' (eight instalments ending in Aug. 1825, with some by Wilson); Hogg's 'The Chaldee Manuscript' (with Lockhart and Wilson).

1818   Mar. Scott's 'Remarks on *Frankenstein*'.

Sept. Wilson's 'The Preternatural in Works of Fiction'.

1819   Apr. Hogg's *The Shepherd's Calendar* (thirteen instalments ending in Apr. 1828).

1820   June. Galt's *The Ayrshire Legatees* (eight instalments ending in Feb. 1821).

1821   Feb. John Scott, editor of the *London Magazine*, is shot in a duel by Lockhart's second, James Christie, after weeks of feuding between *Blackwood's* and the *London*. Galt's *The Steam-Boat* (eight instalments ending in Dec. 1821).

1822   Mar. Lockhart's *Noctes Ambrosianae* (seventy-one instalments ending in Feb. 1835; most written by Wilson, with help from several others).

1824   Oct. Douglas Moir's *The Autobiography of Mansie Wauch* (twelve instalments ending in Dec. 1828).

1825   Oct. Lockhart leaves *Blackwood's* to become editor of the *Quarterly Review*.

1827   Feb. De Quincey's 'On Murder Considered as one of the Fine Arts' (second instalment Nov. 1839).

June. Thomas Hamilton's *Letters from the Peninsula* (five instalments ending in Aug. 1830).

1829   Feb. William Mudford's *First and Last* (seven instalments ending in Nov. 1830).

Sept. Michael Scott's *Tom Cringle's Log* (twenty-three instalments ending in Aug. 1833).

1830   Aug. Samuel Warren's *Passages from the Diary of a Late Physician* (eighteen instalments ending in Aug. 1837).

ACKNOWLEDGEMENTS

WE would like to thank the following people for their help with the production of this book: J. H. Alexander, Roy Bishop, Geoffrey Carnall, Graeme Ching, Graham Hogg, Allister Mac-Donald, Bruce Matthews, Carole Morrison, Glenn Parsons, Sue Rauth, Blair Ross, Ralph Stewart, and Beert Verstraete. We also wish to thank the staffs of the Acadia University Library, the Cambridge University Library, and the National Library of Scotland, as well as the Acadia University Faculty Association for their generous research grant.

TALES OF TERROR FROM
BLACKWOOD'S MAGAZINE

SKETCH OF A TRADITION RELATED BY A MONK IN SWITZERLAND

Patrick Fraser-Tytler

MR EDITOR,

IN the course of an excursion, during the autumn of last year, through the wildest and most secluded parts of Switzerland, I took up my residence, during one stormy night, in a convent of Capuchin Friars, not far from Altorf,* the birth-place of the famous William Tell. In the course of the evening, one of the fathers related a story, which, both on account of the interest which it is naturally calculated to excite, and the impressive manner in which it was told, produced a very strong effect upon my mind. I noted it down briefly in the morning, in my journal, preserving as much as possible the old man's style, but it has no doubt lost much by translation.

Having just read Lord Byron's drama, 'Manfred,'* there appears to me such a striking coincidence in some characteristic features, between the story of that performance and the Swiss tradition, that without further comment, I extract the latter from my journal, and send it for your perusal. It relates to an ancient family, now extinct, whose names I neglected to write down, and have now forgotten, but that is a matter of little importance.

'His soul was wild, impetuous, and uncontrollable. He had a keen perception of the faults and vices of others, without the power of correcting his own; alike sensible of the nobility, and of the darkness of his moral constitution, although unable to cultivate the one to the exclusion of the other.

'In extreme youth, he led a lonely and secluded life in the solitude of a Swiss valley, in company with an only brother, some years older than himself, and a young female relative, who had been educated along with them from her birth. They lived under the care of an aged uncle, the guardian of those extensive domains which the brothers were destined jointly to inherit.

'A peculiar melancholy, cherished and increased by the utter seclusion of that sublime region, had, during the period of their infancy, preyed upon the mind of their father, and finally produced the most dreadful result. The fear of a similar tendency in the minds of the brothers, induced their protector to remove them, at an early age, from the solitude of their native country. The elder was sent to a German university, and the youngest completed his education in one of the Italian schools.

'After the lapse of many years, the old guardian died, and the elder of the brothers returned to his native valley; he there formed an attachment to the lady with whom he had passed his infancy; and she, after some fearful forebodings, which were unfortunately silenced by the voice of duty and of gratitude, accepted of his love, and became his wife.

'In the meantime, the younger brother had left Italy, and travelled over the greater part of Europe. He mingled with the world, and gave full scope to every impulse of his feelings. But that world, with the exception of certain hours of boisterous passion and excitement, afforded him little pleasure, and made no lasting impression upon his heart. His greatest joy was in the wildest impulses of the imagination.

'His spirit, though mighty and unbounded, from his early habits and education naturally tended to repose; he thought with delight on the sun rising among the Alpine snows, or gilding the peaks of the rugged hills with its evening rays. But within him he felt a fire burning for ever, and which the snows of his native mountains could not quench. He feared that he was alone in the world, and that no being, kindred to his own, had been created; but in his soul there was an image of angelic perfection, which he believed existed not on earth, but without which he knew he could not be happy. Despairing to find it in populous cities, he retired to his paternal domain. On again entering upon the scenes of his infancy, many new and singular feelings were experienced,—he is enchanted with the surpassing beauty of the scenery, and wonders that he should have rambled so long and so far from it. The noise and the bustle of the world were immediately forgotten on contemplating

'The silence that is in the starry sky,
The sleep that is among the lonely hills.'*

A light, as it were, broke around him, and exhibited a strange and momentary gleam of joy and of misery mingled together. He entered the dwelling of his infancy with delight, and met his brother with emotion. But his dark and troubled eye betokened a fearful change, when he beheld the other playmate of his infancy. Though beautiful as the imagination could conceive, she appeared otherwise than he expected. Her form and face were associated with some of his wildest reveries,—his feelings of affection were united with many undefinable sensations,—he felt as if she was not the wife of his brother, although he knew her to be so, and his soul sickened at the thought.

'He passed the night in a feverish state of joy and horror. From the window of a lonely tower he beheld the moon shining amid the bright blue of an Alpine sky, and diffusing a calm and beautiful light on the silvery snow. The eagle owl uttered her long and plaintive note from the castellated summits which overhung the valley, and the feet of the wild chamois were heard rebounding from the neighbouring rocks; these accorded with the gentler feelings of his mind, but the strong spirit which so frequently overcame him, listened with intense delight to the dreadful roar of an immense torrent, which was precipitated from the summit of an adjoining cliff, among broken rocks and pines, overturned and uprooted, or to the still mightier voice of the avalanche, suddenly descending with the accumulated snows of a hundred years.

'In the morning he met the object of his unhappy passion. Her eyes were dim with tears, and a cloud of sorrow had darkened the light of her lovely countenance.

'For some time there was a mutual constraint in their manner, which both were afraid to acknowledge, and neither was able to dispel. Even the uncontrollable spirit of the wanderer was oppressed and overcome, and he wished he had never returned to the dwelling of his ancestors. The lady is equally aware of the awful peril of their situation, and without the knowledge of her husband, she prepared to depart from the castle, and take the veil in a convent situated in a neighbouring valley.

'With this resolution she departed on the following morning; but in crossing an Alpine pass, which conducted by a nearer route to the adjoining valley, she was enveloped in mists and vapour, and lost all knowledge of the surrounding country. The clouds closed in around her, and a tremendous thunder-storm took place in the valley beneath. She wandered about for some time, in hopes of gaining a glimpse through the clouds, of some accustomed object to direct her steps, till exhausted by fatigue and fear, she reclined upon a dark rock, in the crevices of which, though it was now the heat of summer, there were many patches of snow. There she sat, in a state of feverish delirium, till a gentle air dispelled the dense vapour from before her feet, and discovered an enormous chasm, down which she must have fallen, if she had taken another step. While breathing a silent prayer to Heaven for this providential escape, strange sounds were heard, as of some disembodied voice floating among the clouds. Suddenly she perceived, within a few paces, the figure of the wanderer tossing his arms in the air, his eye inflamed, and his general aspect wild and distracted—he then appeared meditating a deed of sin,—she rushed towards him, and, clasping him in her arms, dragged him backwards, just as he was about to precipitate himself into the gulph below.

'Overcome by bodily fatigue, and agitation of mind, they remained for some time in a state of insensibility. The brother first revived from his stupor; and finding her whose image was pictured in his soul lying by his side, with her arms resting upon his shoulder, he believed for a moment that he must have executed the dreadful deed he had meditated, and had wakened in heaven. The gentle form of the lady is again reanimated, and slowly she opened her beautiful eyes. She questioned him regarding the purpose of his visit to that desolate spot—a full explanation took place of their mutual sensations, and they confessed the passion which consumed them.

'The sun was now high in heaven—the clouds of the morning had ascended to the loftiest Alps—and the mists, "into their airy elements resolved, were gone."* As the god of day advanced, dark vallies were suddenly illuminated, and lovely lakes brightened like mirrors among the hills—their waters sparkling with the fresh breeze of the morning. The most beautiful clouds were sailing in the air—some breaking on the mountain tops, and others resting on the sombre pines, or slumbering on the surface of the unilluminated vallies. The shrill whistle of the marmot was no longer heard, and the chamois had bounded to its inaccessible retreat. The vast range of the neighbouring Alps was next distinctly visible, and presented, to the eyes of the beholders, "glory beyond all glory ever seen."*

'In the meantime a change had taken place in the feelings of the mountain pair, which was powerfully strengthened by the glad face of nature. The glorious hues of earth and sky seemed indeed to sanction and rejoice in their mutual happiness. The darker spirit of the brother had now fearfully overcome him. The dreaming predictions of his most imaginative years appeared realised in their fullest extent, and the voice of prudence and of nature was inaudible amidst the intoxication of his joy. The object of his affection rested in his arms in a state of listless happiness, listening with enchanted ear to his wild and impassioned eloquence, and careless of all other sight or sound.

'She too had renounced her morning vows, and the convent was unthought of, and forgotten. Crossing the mountains by wild and unfrequented paths, they took up their abode in a deserted cottage, formerly frequented by goatherds and the hunters of the roe. On looking down, for the last time, from the mountain top, on that delightful valley in which she had so long lived in innocence and peace, the lady thought of her departed mother, and her heart would have died within her, but the wild glee of the brother again rendered her insensible to all other sensations, and she yielded to the sway of her fatal passion.

'There they lived, secluded from the world, and supported, even through evil, by the intensity of their passion for each other. The turbulent spirit of the brother was at rest—he had found a being endowed with virtues like his own, and, as he thought, destitute of all his vices. The day dreams of his fancy had been realized, and all that he had imagined of beauty, or affection, was embodied in that form which he could call his own.

'On the morning of her departure the dreadful truth burst upon the mind of her wretched husband. From the first arrival of the dark-eyed stranger, a gloomy vision of future sorrow had haunted him by day and by night. Despair and misery now made him their victim, and that awful malady which he inherited from his ancestors was the immediate consequence. He was seen, for the last time, among some stupendous cliffs which overhung the river, and his hat and cloak were found by the chamois hunters at the foot of an ancient pine.

'Soon too was the guilty joy of the survivors to terminate. The gentle lady, even in felicity, felt a load upon her heart. Her spirit had burned too ardently, and she knew it must, ere long, be extinguished. Day after day the lily of her cheek encroached upon the rose, till at last she assumed a monumental paleness, unrelieved save by a transient and hectic glow. Her angelic form wasted away, and soon the flower of the valley was no more.

'The soul of the brother was dark, dreadfully dark, but his body wasted not, and his spirit caroused with more fearful strength. "The sounding cataract haunted him like a passion."* He was again alone in the world, and his mind endowed with more dreadful energies. His wild eye sparkled with unnatural light, and his raven hair hung heavy on his burning temples. He wandered among the forests and the mountains, and rarely entered his once beloved dwelling, from the windows of which he had so often beheld the sun sinking in a sea of crimson glory.

'He was found dead in that same pass in which he had met his sister among the mountains; his body bore no marks of external violence, but his countenance was convulsed by bitter insanity.'

NARRATIVE OF A FATAL EVENT

Walter Scott

I F it could alleviate in the smallest degree the intense sufferings that have preyed upon my mind, and blasted my hope, during a period now of almost seven-and-thirty years, I would account the pain I may feel, during the time I am attempting to narrate the following occurrence, of no more consequence than the shower of sleet that drives in my face while I am walking home from the parish church to my parlour fire.

I already remarked, it is within a few months of being thirty-seven years since I left the university of Glasgow, in company with a young person of my own age, and from the same part of the country. I shall speak of him by the name of Campbell; it can interest few but myself now, to say that it is not his real name. We had been intimately acquainted for years before we came together to the college, and a predilection for the same studies, a strong bias for general literature, and more especially for those courses of inquiry, which are the amusement rather than the task of minds given to the pursuit of knowledge, had, in the course of four swift years, bound us together in one of those friendships which young men are apt to persuade themselves can never possibly be dissolved, while no sooner are they separated for a time, than every event they meet with in the course of common life tends insensibly to obliterate this youthful union; as the summer showers so imperceptibly melt the wreath of snow upon the mountain, that the evening on which the last speck disappears passes unnoticed.

But our friendship was not destined to be subjected to this slow and wasting process: it was suddenly and fearfully broken off. It is now seven-and-thirty years, next June, since the event I allude to; and I still flatter myself, that had I had the courage to have saved Campbell's life when probably it was in my power, our mutual regard would have suffered no diminution, wherever our future lots might have been cast.

The teachers of youth, in the university of the western capital of the kingdom, had fallen, about that time, into the great and presumptuous error of letting their pupils loose in a desert and boundless field, as if the truth could be found every where by searching the wilderness; and error was only to be stumbled upon by chance, and immediately detected and avoided. Wiser surely it had been to consider truth and error as at least equally obvious to the youthful mind, and therefore to rein in the minds of their pupils, and oblige them to conform to the safe and long established modes of reasoning and thinking.

One lamentable consequence of this presumptuous system was, the effect it had upon the young men of my own age, in arousing in our minds a disregard for the standards of our faith in religion; for instead of studying nature by the help of revelation, we reversed the order of induction, and pretending to follow the works of the Deity as our principal guide, endeavoured to illustrate the revealed will of God by the analogy of nature. This may appear somewhat foreign to the subject, but a similar train of thought always mingles with my recollections, and it is not the least cause of my unceasing regret, that I should, in the pride and rashness of youthful enthusiasm, have encouraged Campbell, and even often lead the way in these dangerous speculations. It was our last year at Principal ——'s[†] class: and alas! I have to endure the remembrance that my friend was snatched to a premature death, while he was yet an unbeliever in some of the most sublime mysteries of our holy faith.

As I said already, Campbell and I, after a winter of hard study, proposed to ourselves, and set out on, a journey of six weeks, in order to indulge our predilection for natural history, among the mountains and isles of the Highlands.

We had one morning ascended a high mountain in Knapdale.* Many objects were either new to us or unobserved before, or we saw them under new views. Poor Campbell's spirits seemed to rise, and his mind to take wilder flights, in proportion as he looked to the barometer that he carried, and observed the sinking of the mercury. 'This *Cannach*,'* said

[†] Last year of attendance on the course of Theology (*Editor*).

he, 'that blooms here on the mountains of Scotland, unseen, save by the deer, and the ptarmagan, is not it more delicately beautiful than the *gloriosa* of Siam, or the rose of Cashmere; and if, as philosophers assert, there is an analogy through all the works of nature, and the meaner animals proceed from the parent as slumbering embryos, and the more perfect are produced nearly as they afterwards exist, why do we meet here in this cold and stormy region with the *Festuca vivipara*, which has flowers and seeds in the warmer valleys below? Does this puny grass adapt its economy to its circumstances, and finding that the cold and the winds render its flowers abortive, does it resolve to continue its species by these buds and little plants, which it is observed to shake off, when they can provide for themselves?' These and similar speculations enlivened our botanical labours.

The day was calm, the sky resplendent, and a view of the sea and the islands, from the point of Cantyre,* on the south to Tiree and Coll on the N. West, (the most picturesque and singular portion of our native country) was pourtrayed on the expanse before us. The scene had its full effect upon the mind of my friend, fitted alike to concentrate itself upon the most minute, and expand itself to grasp the most magnificent, objects in nature; he had not been more charmed with the most diminutive plants than now, when he took a rapid review of the vast ocean, with all its mighty movements of tides and currents; of the joint and contending influence of the sun and moon; of the agency of a mass of matter, inert in itself, revolving at a distance, and with a velocity alike inconceivable, and even moving, as by a mysterious cord, the vast pivot around which it rolled; and of the progressive power of man, originally fixed below his tree, and comparatively ignorant, listless, and blind, who had formed unto himself new senses, and new powers and instruments of thought, until he at last weighed the sun as in a balance, and seemed to have gained a view of the infinitude of space, and was lost in the fearful extent of his own discoveries.*

We descended towards the shore of what is called the Sound of Jura, through many a dell and bosky wood, sometimes loitering as we stopped to examine the objects of our study, sometimes gaily walking over the barren moor.

The sea-shore presented us with a new field of inquiry, and a new class of objects; many curious and beautiful species of *fuci* grow on these shores, and of several of the smaller and finer kinds we were enabled to acquire specimens, with the view of enriching our common herbarium. 'On the summit of Knockmordhu,' said Campbell, 'we were talking of the wonderful adaptation of plants, but is there not something in the economy of these algae, that shews a wise and intelligent provision, as clearly as does the conformation of any part of the human body? How comes it that the invisible seed of the lichens should be of the same specific weight, or lighter than the air, so that the most precipitous rock that the wind blows upon is furnished with them in abundance? And their sister tribe, these *fuci*, that thrive only within reach of the wave, the seeds of these are almost equally minute, that they too may be fitted to lodge in the asperities of the rock, and they are of the same weight of the sea water, and float about in it continually; so that every dash of the spray is full of them, and they fix upon every fragment that is detached from the cliff.'

As the ebbing tide began to discover to us the black side of the rocky islets, we procured a boat at a small hamlet that overhung a little bay, and went on a mimic voyage of discovery. While we returned again to the mainland, the warmth of the day, and the beautiful transparency of the water, which, as the whole extent of the west coast is rocky shore, is highly remarkable, tempted Campbell to propose that we should amuse ourselves with swimming. Owing to a horror I had acquired when a boy, from an exaggerated description of the danger of the convulsive grasp of a person drowning, or *dead grip* as it is called, I always felt an involuntary repugnance to practise this exercise in company with others. However, we now indulged in it, so long that I began to feel tired, and was swimming towards the rocky shore, which was at no great distance. Campbell, who had now forgot his philosophical reveries, in the pleasure of a varied and refreshing amusement, was sporting in all the gaiety of exuberant spirits, when I heard a sudden cry of fear. I turned, and saw him struggling violently, as if in the act of sinking. I immediately swam towards him. He had been seized with cramp, which suspends all power of regular exertion, while at the same time it commonly deprives its victim of presence of mind; and as poor Campbell alternately sunk and rose, his wild looks as I approached him, and convulsed cries for assistance, struck me with a sudden and involuntary panic, and I hesitated to grasp the extended hand of my drowning friend. After a moment's struggle he sunk, exclaiming, My God! with a look at me of such an expression, that it has ten thousand times driven me to wish my memory was a blank. A dreadful alarm now struck my heart, like the stab of a dagger, and with almost a similar sensation of pain; I rushed to the place where he disappeared, the boiling of the water, caused by his descending body, prevented a distinct view, but on looking down, I thought I saw three or four corpses, struggling with each other, while, at the same moment, I heard a loud and melancholy cry from the bushes on the steep bank that overhung the shore. As the boiling of the water settled, I was partly relieved from extreme horror; but I had the misery to see Campbell again; for the water was as clear as the air. He stood upright at the bottom among the large sea-weeds,—he even reached up his arms and exerted himself, as if endeavouring fruitlessly to climb to the surface. I looked in despair towards the shore, and all around. The feeling of hopeless loneliness was dreadful. I again distinctly heard the same melancholy cry. A superstitious dread came over me as before, for a few seconds; but I observed an old gray goat, which had advanced to the jutting point of a rock; he had perhaps been alarmed from the unusual appearance in the sea below, and was bleating for his companions. I now recollected the boat, and swam exhausted to the shore, while every moment I imagined I saw before me the extended hand of my friend which I should never more grasp. I rowed back more than half distracted. The water, when Campbell had sunk, was between twelve and fourteen feet deep, and, as I said before, remarkably transparent. Some people are capable of sustaining life under water far longer than others, and poor Campbell was of an extremely vigorous constitution. I saw him again more distinctly, and his appearance was in the utmost degree affecting. He seemed to be yet alive, for he sat upright, and grasped with one hand the stem of a large tangle;

the broad frond of which waved sometimes over him as it was moved by the tide, while he moved convulsively his other arm and one of his legs.[†] I remember well, I cried out in agony, O if I had a rope! With great exertion, and by leaning over the boat with my arm and face under water, I tried to arouse his attention, by touching his hands with the oar. I was convinced that, had there been a length of rope in the boat, I could have saved him. He evidently was not quite insensible, for upon repeatedly touching his hand, he let go his hold of the tangle, and after feebly and ineffectually grasping at the oar, I saw him once more stretch up his hand, as if conscious that some person was endeavouring to assist him. He then fell slowly on his back, and lay calm, and still, among the sea weed.

Unconnected ravings, and frantic cries, could alone express the unsufferable anguish I endured.—His stretched out hand!—I often, often see it still! yet it is nearly thirty-seven years ago. But the heart that would not save his friend, that saw him about to perish, yet kept aloof in his last extremity, perhaps deserves that suffering which time seems rather to increase than alleviate.

It is in vain that I reason with myself,—that I say, 'all this is too true,—I hesitated to save him,—I kept aloof from him, —I answered not his last cry for help,—I refused his out-stretched hand, and saw him engulfed in the cruel waters,— but yet surely this did not spring from selfish or considerate care for my own safety. Before and since I have hazarded my life, with alertness and enthusiasm, to rescue others,—no cold calculating prudence kept me back; it was an instinctive and involuntary impulse, originating from a strong early impression, and on finding myself suddenly placed in circumstances which had been long dreaded in imagination!'

But all this reasoning avails nothing. I still recollect the inestimable endowments and amiable disposition of my early and only friend,—memory still dwells upon our taking leave of the city,—our passage of the Clyde,—our researches and walks in the woodlands and sequestered glens of Cowal,—our

---

[†] This appearance might arise from the refraction of the agitated water, as well as from the excited imagination of the narrator (*Editor*).

moonlight sail on Lochfine,*—our ascent of the mountain,—the splendid view of the sea and islands,—and our conversation on the summit,—the first cry of alarm,—the out-stretched hand and upbraiding look,—the appearance of the sinking body,—the bleating of the goat,—my friend's dying efforts among the sea-weed!

It is nearly seven and thirty years now; yet, day or night, I may almost say, a waking hour has not passed in which I have not felt part of the suffering that I witnessed convulsing the body of my poor friend, under the agonies of a strangely protracted death. Why then, will the reader say, does the writer of this melancholy story now communicate his miseries to the public? This natural question I will endeavour to answer. The body of Campbell was found, but the distracting particulars of his fate were unknown. They were treasured in my own bosom, with the same secrecy with which a catholic bigot conceals the *discipline*, or whip of wire, which, in execution of his private penance, is so often dyed in his blood. I avoided every allusion to the subject, when the ordinary general inquiries had been answered, and it was too painful a subject for any one to press upon me for particulars. It was soon forgotten by all but me; and a long period has passed away, if not of secret guilt, at least of secret remorse. Accident led me about a month since, to disclose the painful state of my mind to a friend in my neighbourhood, who pretends to some philosophy and knowledge of the human heart. I hardly knew how I was surprised into the communication of feelings which I had kept so long secret. The discourse happened to turn upon such moods of the mind as that under which I have suffered. I was forced into my narrative almost involuntarily, and might apply to myself the well-known lines:

> Forthwith this frame of mine was wrenched
>   With a strange agony,
> Which forc'd me to begin my tale,
>   And then it left me free.*

My friend listened to the detail of my feelings with much sympathy. 'I do not,' he said, when my horrid narrative was closed, 'attempt by reasoning to eradicate from your mind feelings so painfully disproportioned to the degree of blame which justly attaches to your conduct. I do not remind you, that your involuntary panic palsied you as much as the unfortunate sufferer's cramp, and that you were in the moment as little able to give him effectual assistance, as he was to keep afloat without it. I might add in your apology, that the instinct of self-preservation is uncommonly active in cases where we ourselves are exposed to the same sort of danger with that in which we see others perishing. I once witnessed a number of swimmers amusing themselves in the entrance of Leith harbour, when one was seized with the cramp and went down. In one instant the pier was crowded with naked figures, who had fled to the shore to escape the supposed danger; and in the next as many persons, who were walking on the pier, had thrown off part of their clothes and plunged in to assist the perishing man. The different effect upon the bystanders, and on those who shared the danger, is to be derived from their relative circumstances, and from no superior benevolence of the former, or selfishness of the latter. Your own understanding must have often suggested these rational grounds of consolation, though the strong impression made on your imagination by circumstances so deplorable, has prevented your receiving benefit from them. The question is, how this disease of the mind (for such it is) can be effectually removed?'

I looked anxiously in his face, as if in expectation of the relief he spoke of. 'I was once,' said he, 'when a boy, in the company of an old military officer, who had been, in his youth, employed in the service of apprehending some outlaws, guilty of the most deliberate cruelties. The narrative told by one so nearly concerned with it, and having all those minute and circumstantial particulars, which seize forcibly on the imagination, placed the shocking scene as it were before my very eyes. My fancy was uncommonly lively at that period of my life, and it was strongly affected. The tale cost me a sleepless night, with fervor and tremor on the nerves. My father, a man of uncommonly solid sense, discovered, with some difficulty, the cause of my indisposition. Instead of banishing the subject which had so much agitated me, he entered upon the discussion, shewed me the volume of the state trials which contained the case of the outlaws, and, by enlarging repeatedly upon the narrative, rendered it familiar to my imagination, and of consequence more indifferent to it. I would advise you, my friend, to follow a similar course. It is the secrecy of your sufferings which goes far to prolong them. Have you never observed, that the mere circumstance of a fact, however indifferent in itself, being known to one, and one only, gives it an importance in the eyes of him who possesses the secret, and renders it of much more frequent occurrence as the progress of his thoughts, than it could have been from any direct interest which it possesses. Shake these fetters therefore from your mind, and mention this event to one or two of our common friends; hear them, as you now hear me, treat your remorse, relatively to its extent and duration, as a mere disease of the mind, the consequence of the impressive circumstances of that melancholy event over which you have suffered your fancy to brood in solemn silence and secrecy. Hearing it thus spoken of by others, their view of the case will end by becoming familiar and habitual to you, and you will then get rid of the agonies which have hitherto operated like a night-mare to hagride your imagination.'

Such was my friend's counsel, which I heard in silence, inclined to believe his deductions, yet feeling abhorrent to make the communications he advised. I had been once surprised into such a confession, but to tell my tale again deliberately, and face to face,—to avow myself guilty of something approaching at once to cowardice and to murder,—I felt myself incapable of the resolution necessary to the disclosure. As a middle course I send you this narrative; my name will be unknown, for the event passed in a distant country from that in which I now live. I shall hear, perhaps, the unfortunate survivor censured, or excused; the wholesome effect may be produced in my mind which my friend expects from the narrative becoming the theme of public discussion; and to him who can best pity and apologise for my criminal weakness, I may perhaps find courage to whisper, 'the unhappy object of your compassion is now before you.'

EXTRACTS FROM GOSSCHEN'S DIARY

John Wilson

NEVER had a murder so agitated the inhabitants of this city as that of Maria von Richterstein. No heart could be pacified till the murderer was condemned. But no sooner was his doom sealed, and the day fixed for his execution, than a great change took place in the public feeling. The evidence, though conclusive, had been wholly circumstantial. And people who, before his condemnation, were as assured of the murderer's guilt as if they had seen him with red hands, began now to conjure up the most contradictory and absurd reasons for believing in the possibility of his innocence. His own dark and sullen silence seemed to some, an indignant expression of that innocence which he was too proud to avow,—some thought they saw in his imperturbable demeanour, a resolution to court death, because his life was miserable, and his reputation blasted,—and others, the most numerous, without reason or reflection, felt such sympathy with the criminal, as almost amounted to a negation of his crime. The man under sentence of death was, in all the beauty of youth, distinguished above his fellows for graceful accomplishments, and the last of a noble family. He had lain a month in his dungeon, heavily laden with irons. Only the first week he had been visited by several religionists, but he then fiercely ordered the jailor to admit no more 'men of God,'—and till the eve of his execution, he had lain in dark solitude, abandoned to his own soul.

It was near midnight when a message was sent to me by a magistrate, that the murderer was desirous of seeing me. I had been with many men in his unhappy situation, and in no case had I failed to calm the agonies of grief, and the fears of the world to come. But I had known this youth—had sat with him at his father's table—I knew also that there was in him a strange and fearful mixture of good and evil—I was aware that there were circumstances in the history of his progenitors not generally known—nay, in his own life—that made him an object of awful commiseration—and I went to his cell with an agitating sense of the enormity of his guilt, but a still more agitating one of the depth of his misery, and the wildness of his misfortunes.

I entered his cell, and the phantom struck me with terror. He stood erect in his irons, like a corpse that had risen from the grave. His face, once so beautiful, was pale as a shroud, and drawn into ghastly wrinkles. His black-matted hair hung over it with a terrible expression of wrathful and savage misery. And his large eyes, which were once black, glared with a light in which all colour was lost, and seemed to fill the whole dungeon with their flashings. I saw his guilt—I saw what was more terrible than his guilt—his insanity—not in emaciation only—not in that more than death-like whiteness of his face—but in *all* that stood before me—*the figure*, round which was gathered the agonies of so many long days and nights of remorse and phrenzy—and of a despair that had no fears of this world or its terrors, but that was plunged in the abyss of eternity.

For a while the figure said nothing. He then waved his arm, that made his irons clank, motioning me to sit down on the iron frame-work of his bed; and when I did so, the murderer took his place by my side.

A lamp burned on a table before us—and on that table there had been drawn by the maniac—for I must indeed so call him—a decapitated human body—the neck as if streaming with gore—and the face writhed into horrible convulsions, but bearing a resemblance not to be mistaken to that of him who had traced the horrid picture. He saw that my eyes rested on this fearful mockery—and, with a recklessness fighting with despair, he burst out into a broken peal of laughter, and said, 'to-morrow will you see that picture drawn in blood!'

He then grasped me violently by the arm, and told me to listen to his confession,—and then to say what I thought of God and his eternal Providence.

'I have been assailed by idiots, fools, and drivellers, who could understand nothing of me nor of my crime,—men who came not here that I might confess before God, but reveal myself to them,—and I drove the tamperers with misery and guilt out of a cell sacred to insanity. But my hands have played in infancy, long before I was a murderer, with thy gray hairs, and now, even that I am a murderer, I can still touch them with love and with reverence. Therefore my lips, shut to all beside, shall be opened unto thee.

'I murdered her. Who else loved her so well as to shed her innocent blood? It was I that enjoyed her beauty—a beauty surpassing that of the daughters of men,—it was I that filled her soul with bliss, and with trouble,—it was I alone that was privileged to take her life. I brought her into sin—I kept her in sin—and when she would have left her sin, it was fitting that I, to whom her heart, her body, and her soul belonged, should suffer no divorcement of them from my bosom, as long as there was blood in her's,—and when I saw that the poor infatuated wretch was resolved—I slew her;—yes, with this blessed hand I stabbed her to the heart.

'Do you think there was no pleasure in murdering her? I grasped her by that radiant, that golden hair,—I bared those snow-white breasts,—I dragged her sweet body towards me, and, as God is my witness, I stabbed, and stabbed her with this very dagger, ten, twenty, forty times, through and through her heart. She never so much as gave one shriek, for she was dead in a moment,—but she would not have shrieked had she endured pang after pang, for she saw my face of wrath turned upon her,—she knew that my wrath was just, and that I did right to murder her who would have forsaken her lover in his insanity.

'I laid her down upon a bank of flowers,—that were soon stained with her blood. I saw the dim blue eyes beneath the half-closed lids,—that face so changeful in its living beauty was now fixed as ice, and the balmy breath came from her sweet lips no more. My joy, my happiness, was perfect. I took her into my arms—madly as I did on that night when first I robbed her of what fools called her innocence—but her innocence has gone with her to heaven—and there I lay with her bleeding breasts prest to my heart, and many were the thousand kisses that I gave those breasts, cold and bloody as they were, which I had many million times kissed in all the warmth of their loving loveliness, and which none were ever to kiss again but the husband who had murdered her.

'I looked up to the sky. There shone the moon and all her stars. Tranquillity, order, harmony, and peace, glittered throughout the whole universe of God. "Look up, Maria, your favourite star has arisen." I gazed upon her, and death had begun to change her into something that was most terrible. Her features were hardened and sharp,—her body stiff as a lump of frozen clay,—her fingers rigid and clenched,—and the blood that was once so beautiful in her thin blue veins was now hideously coagulated all over her corpse. I gazed on her one moment longer, and, all at once, I recollected that we were a family of madmen. Did not my father perish by his own hand? Blood had before been shed in our house. Did not that warrior ancestor of ours die raving in chains? Were not those eyes of mine always unlike those of other men? Wilder— at times fiercer—and oh! father, saw you never there a melancholy, too woful for mortal man, a look sent up from the darkness of a soul that God never visited in his mercy?

'I knelt down beside my dead wife. But I knelt not down to pray. No: I cried unto God, if God there be—"Thou madest me a madman! Thou madest me a murderer! Thou foredoomedst me to sin and to hell! Thou, thou, the gracious God whom we mortals worship. There is the sacrifice! I have done thy will,—I have slain the most blissful of all thy creatures;— am I a holy and commissioned priest, or am I an accursed and infidel murderer?"

'Father, you start at such words! You are not familiar with a madman's thoughts. Did I make this blood to boil so? Did I form this brain? Did I put that poison into my veins which flowed a hundred years since in the heart of that lunatic, my heroic ancestor? Had I not my being imposed, forced upon me, with all its red-rolling sea of dreams; and will you, a right holy and pious man, curse me because my soul was carried away by them as a ship is driven through the raging darkness of a storm? A thousand times, even when she lay in resigned love in my bosom, something whispered to me, "Murder her!" It may have been the voice of Satan—it may have been the voice of God. For who can tell the voice of heaven from that of hell? Look on this blood-crusted dagger—look on the hand that drove it to her heart, and then dare to judge of me and of my crimes, or comprehend God and all his terrible decrees!

'Look not away from me. Was I not once confined in a madhouse? Are these the first chains I ever wore? No. I remember things of old, that others may think I have forgotten. Dreams will disappear for a long, long time, but they will return again. It may have been some one like me that I once saw sitting chained, in his black melancholy, in a madhouse. I may have been only a stranger passing through that wild world. I know not. The sound of chains brings with it a crowd of thoughts, that come rushing upon me from a dark and far-off world. But if it indeed be true, that in my boyhood I was not as other happy boys, and that even then the clouds of God's wrath hung around me,—that God may not suffer my soul everlastingly to perish.

'I started up. I covered the dead body with bloody leaves, and tufts of grass, and flowers. I washed my hands from blood—I went to bed—I slept—yes, I slept—for there is no hell like the hell of sleep, and into that hell God delivered me. I did not give myself up to judgment. I wished to walk about with the secret curse of the murder in my soul. What could men do to me so cruel as to let me live? How could God curse me more in black and fiery hell than on this green and flowery earth? And what right had such men as those dull heavy-eyed burghers to sit in judgment upon me, in whose face they were afraid to look for a moment, lest one gleam of it should frighten them into idiocy? What right have they, who are not as I am, to load me with their chains, or to let their villain executioner spill my blood? If I deserve punishment—it must rise up in a blacker cloud under the hand of God in my soul.

'I will not kneel—a madman has no need of sacraments. I do not wish the forgiveness nor the mercy of God. All that I wish is the forgiveness of her I slew; and well I know that death cannot so change the heart that once had life, as to obliterate from THINE the merciful love of me! Spirits may in heaven have beautiful bosoms no more; but thou, who art a spirit, wilt save him from eternal perdition, whom thou now knowest God created subject to a terrible disease. If there be

mercy in heaven, it must be with thee. Thy path thither lay
through blood: so will mine. Father! thinkst thou that we
shall meet in heaven. Lay us at least in one grave on earth.'

In a moment he was dead at my feet. The stroke of the
dagger was like lightning, and—

A NIGHT IN THE CATACOMBS

Daniel Keyte Sandford

MY DEAR S——,

THERE is nothing more baneful than the influence which privileged nurses and other attendants upon young children exercise over their untutored imaginations, through the medium of superstitious dread. You know that there are few who have suffered more from such cruelty than myself; that for the prime years of my youth I was the victim of a distempered fancy, which I in vain attempted to chasten or correct; and that it was only by a most singular and unexpected accident, that I was freed from the reign of terror. But I believe you have never been made acquainted with the full detail of that accident; and I therefore send you this account of it, impressed with the deepest gratitude to the providence which turned to so much benefit in my own case, that which, considering the peculiar state and temper of my mind, might have caused insanity or death, and wishing it to become, if possible, as useful to others. Superstition is not indeed an epidemic of the present age; yet there may be individuals, who cast their eyes upon my tale, that will thank me for its lesson.

I never knew the fostering care of a father; and my mother, except by the boundless affection which I remember in my solitary tears, did not well supply his place. Inheriting a large domain in the wildest district of Wales, I was early taught to attach notions of dignity and importance to myself, and entertained a long train of more interesting thoughts than usually occupy the breast of boyhood. From the indulgence of my guardians to an only son, I was never sent to school, and thus had no opportunity of acquiring the prompt and active spirit that is generated in a public seminary, or that hard yet brilliant polish of the world, that repels from its surface all assaults of sanguine and romantic feeling. My domestic tutor enriched my mind with an extensive knowledge of the classics, and imbued it with the deepest admiration of their beauties; but he did not apply himself to correct the wild tissue of absurd and superstitious notions, which an accurate observer must have detected in my bosom, or the greedy taste for fiction, and nervous sensibility, of which I myself perceived and lamented the excess. Ever since I could walk, I had been under the superintendence of an old nurse attached to the family, whose memory, like that of most of her countrywomen, was well stored with legend and tradition, and who had secretly acquired an absolute authority over me. While I was a mere child, she used to frighten me into obedience, if refractory, by threats of supernatural interference, and sometimes by devices of so horrible and extraordinary a nature, that I can hardly now recollect them without a shudder. The earnestness and emphasis, moreover, with which she told me tales in which she more than half believed, gave her gradually an entire dominion over my fears and fancy, which she could rouse and regulate at will. Even after I had emerged from the nursery, it used to be my great delight to steal to her apartment in the evening, and sit listening for hours to her ghostly narratives, till my knees shook, and every nerve in my body trembled, in the agitation and over-excitement she produced. It was then almost too much for my courage to hurry through the long passage, lighted by a single central lamp, to the library in our gothic mansion; and there, when I entered breathless and with a beating heart, I used to find my mother alone, weeping over the correspondence of my poor father in silence, and yielding to the sorrow that finally bowed her to the grave. My sole amusement every night, while thus sitting in the room with her (for we saw no company at all), was in poring with a perpetually-increasing interest, over all that could most tend to nourish the deleterious passion of my soul. My mother was too much absorbed in her own recollections to pay much attention to my employments or my studies; and her own mind was too much weakened by affliction to have suggested any salutary restoratives for mine.

The agonies I felt at my beloved parent's death, and for many a wakeful night after she was committed to the tomb, are too sacred to my remembrance, to be even now unravelled.

I shortly after came of age, and one of the first acts of my majority was a visit to Paris, during the short interval of war afforded by the peace of Amiens,* in the hopes of alleviating my anguish. Here indeed I saw something of life; but I was too reserved to enter into intimacy with any of those to whose acquaintance my guardians introduced me. Proud, shy, and sensitive, I was fearful of their penetrating into the weaknesses of my character, which I felt were far from harmonizing with the general opinions of mankind; and I fancy they perceived something unfashionably cold and sombre about me, which mutually prevented our knowledge of each other. To the value of even your friendship, my dear S——, I was then insensible, —but you cannot say I have remained so.

In one of my lonely rambles about the wonderful and interesting capital I was now visiting, I joined a crowd of twenty or thirty persons, waiting at the outer door that leads to the upper entrance of the Catacombs.* I had heard of these extraordinary vaults, but not having passed before the Barrière d'Enfer,* I had not inspected them in person. Though I could not help conjecturing that a subterraneous cemetery, where the relics of ten centuries reposed, must be a sight too congenial with the morbid temper of my mind, I had no notion of the actual horrors of that mansion for the dead, or in my then distempered state of feeling, I should not have trusted my nerves with the spectacle to be expected. How will the curious tourist of the present day smile as he peruses this confession, if you give my story to the public!—but a few perhaps will understand and pity what *were* my follies. As it was, I provided myself, like the rest, with a waxen taper, and we waited with impatience for the appearance of the guide from below, with the party that had preceded us. It was about three o'clock of a sultry afternoon, and we were detained so long, that when the door opened at last, we all rushed in, and hurried old Jerome to the task of conducting us, without giving him time for the necessary precaution of counting our number. I was an utter stranger to all present, and felt at first, as if I should have wished to view the sight, towards which we hurried our conductor, with him alone, or at least with fewer and less vociferous companions: but when we had descended many steps into the bowels of the earth, and the cold air from the dwellings of mortality smote my brow, I owned a sensible relief from the presence of the living around me, and was cheered by the sound of their various exclamations. Even with these accompaniments, however, it was with more than astonishment that I gazed upon the opening scene, and ever and anon, wrapped up in my thoughts, I anticipated with secret forebodings, the horrors I was doomed to undergo.

It would be superfluous to describe what has been described so often,* yet none can have received, from a survey of the catacombs, such impressions as my mind was prepared to admit; and few can have retained so vivid and distinct a picture of their appearance, as has been branded on my soul in characters not to be effaced. Alas! I entered them with little of that fine exalting spirit so divinely eulogized by Virgil, in the motto that is inscribed upon their walls:

> 'Felix qui potuit rerum cognoscere causas,
> Atque metus omnes, et inexorabile fatum
> Subjecit pedibus, strepitumque Acherontis avari!'*

The interminable rows of bare and blackening skulls—the masses interposed of gaunt and rotting bones, that once gave strength and symmetry to the young, the beautiful, the brave, now mildewed by the damp of the cavern, and heaped together in indiscriminate arrangement—the faint mouldering and deathlike smell that pervaded these gloomy labyrinths, and the long recesses in the low-roofed rock, to which I dared not turn my eyes except by short and fitful glances, as if expecting something terrible and ghastly to start from the indistinctness of their distance,—all had associations for my thoughts very different from the solemn and edifying sentiments they must rouse in a well regulated breast, and, by degrees, I yielded up every faculty to the influence of an ill-defined and mysterious alarm. My eyesight waxed gradually dull to all but the fleshless skulls that were glaring in the yellow light of the tapers—the hum of human voices was stifled in my ears, and I thought myself alone, already with the dead. The guide thrust the light he carried into a huge skull that was lying separate in a niche; but I marked not the action or the man, but only the fearful glimmering of the transparent bone, which I thought a smile of triumphant malice from the presiding spectre of the place, while imagined accents whispered, in my hearing, 'Welcome to our charnel-house, for THIS shall be your chamber!' Dizzy with indescribable emotions, I felt nothing but a painful sense of oppression from the presence of others, as if I could not breathe for the black shapes that were crowding near me; and turning unperceived, down a long and gloomy passage of the catacombs, I rushed as far as I could penetrate, to feed in solitude the growing appetite for horror, that had quelled for the moment, in my bosom, the sense of fear, and even the feeling of identity. To the rapid whirl of various sensations that had bewildered me ever since I left the light of day, a season of intense abstraction now succeeded. I held my burning eyeballs full upon the skulls in front, till they almost seemed to answer my fixed regard, and claim a dreadful fellowship with the being that beheld them. How long I stood motionless in this condition I know not—my taper was calculated to last a considerable time, and I was wakened from my trance by the scorching heat of its expiring in my hand. Still insensible of what I was about, I threw it to the ground; and gleaming once more, as if to shew the darkness and solitude to which I was consigned, it was speedily extinguished. But, by the strong impression on my brain, the whole scene remained distinct; and it was not for some time that my fit of abstraction passed away, and the horrific conviction came upon me, that I was left deserted, as I fancied in my first confusion, by faithless friends, and abandoned to the mercy of a thousand demons. All the ideal terrors I had cherished from my childhood, exalted to temporary madness by the sense and certainty of the horrid objects that surrounded me, rushed at once upon my soul; and in an agony of impatient consternation, I screamed and shouted, loud and long, for assistance. Not an answer was returned, but the dreary echoes of this dreadful tomb. I saw that my cries for succour were hopeless and in vain, and my voice failed me for very fear—my jaws were fixed and open, my palate dry— a cold sweat distilled from every pore, and my limbs were chill and powerless as death. Their vigour at length revived, and I rushed in a delirium through the passages, struggling through their various windings to retrace my path, and plunged at every step in more inextricable error, till, running with the speed of lightning along one of the longest corridors, I came with violence in full and loathsome contact with the skeleton relics at the end. The shock was like fire to my brain—I wept tears of rage and despair; and thrusting my fingers in the sockets of the empty skulls, to wrench them from the wall, I clutched their bony edges till the blood sprung from my lacerated hand. In short, I cannot paint to you the extravagancies I acted, or the wild alternation of my feelings that endured for many hours. Sometimes excited to phrenzy, I imagined I know not what of horrid and appalling, and saw, with preternatural acuteness, through the darkness as clear as noon,—while grisly visages seemed glaring on me near, and a red and bloody haze enveloped the more fearful distance. Then, when reason was on the point of going, an interval of terrible collection would succeed. I felt in my very soul how I was left alone—perhaps not to be discovered, at any rate for what appeared to me an endless period, in which I should perhaps expire of terror, and I longed for deep deep sleep, or to be as cold and insensate as the things around me. I tried to recollect the courage, that only on one point had ever failed me, but judgment missed her stays, and the whispers of the subterraneous wind, or the stealthy noises I seemed to hear in concert with the audible beatings of my heart, overcame me irresistibly. Sometimes I thought I could feel silence palpable, like a soft mantle on my ear—I figured dreadful hands within a hair-breadth of my body, ready to tear me if I stirred, and in desperation flung myself upon the ground. Then would I creep close to the mouldering fragments at the bottom of the wall, and try to dig with my nails, from the hard rock, something to cover me. Oh! how I longed for a cloak to wrap and hide me, though it had been my mother's winding sheet, or a grave-flannel animate with worms. I buried my head in the skirts of my coat and prayed for slumber; but a fearful train of images forced me again to rise and stumble on, shivering in frame with unearthly cold, and yet internally fevered with a tumult of agonizing thoughts. Any one must have suffered somewhat in such a situation; but no one's sufferings could resemble mine, unless he carried to the scene a mind so hideously prepared. Part of these awful excavations are said to have been once haunted by banditti; but I had no fears of them, and should have swooned with transport to have come upon their fires at one of the turnings in the rock, though my appearance had been the instant signal for their daggers.

In my wanderings I recovered for a moment the path taken by the guides, and found myself in a sort of cell within the rock, where particular specimens of mortality were preserved. My arm rested on the table, where two or three loosened skulls, and a thigh-bone of extravagant dimensions, were lying, and a new fit of madness seized me. My heart beat with redoubled violence, while I brandished the enormous bone, and hoarsely called for its original possessor to come in all the terrors of the grave, and there would I wrestle with him for the relic of his own miserable carcase. I struck repeatedly, and hard, the hollow-sounding sides of the cell, shouting my defiance; then throwing myself with violence towards the opening, I missed my balance, and, snatching at the wall round the corner to save myself, I jammed my hand in an aperture among the bones, and fancied that the grisly adversary I invoked had grasped my arm in answer to my challenge. My shrieks of agony rang through the caverns, and, staggering back into the cell, I fell upon my face, hardly daring to respire, and expecting unimagined horrors or speedy dissolution.

How my feelings varied for a space of time, I know not; but sleep insensibly fell upon me. In my dream, I did not seem to change the scene, but still reclining in the cell, I fancied the skulls upon the wall same in number, but magnified to a terrific size, with black jetty eyes imbedded in their naked sockets, and rivetted with malicious earnestness on me. A dim recess seemed opened beyond one side of the cell, and each spectral eye turning with a sidelong glance towards it, drew mine the same direction by an uncontrollable fascination. Still appearing to gaze determinedly upon them, I had power, as I dreamed, to obey their impulse simultaneously, and to perceive a dreadful figure, black, bony, and skull-headed, with similar terrific eyes, whom they seemed to hail as their minister of cruelty, while with slow and silent paces, it drew near to clasp me in its hideous arms. Closer and closer it advanced,—but, thanks and praise to the all-gracious Power that stills the tempests of the soul!—the limit of suffering was reached, and the force of terror was exhausted. My nerves, so long weak, and prone to agitation, were recovered, by the over-violence of their momentum,—and, instead of losing reason in the shock, or waking in the extremity of fear,—the vision was suddenly changed,—the scenery of horror melted into light, and a calm and joyful serenity took possession of my bosom. My animal powers must have been nearly worn out, for long—long I slept in this delightful tranquillity,—and when I awakened, it was, for the first time of my life, in a peaceful and healthy state of mind, unfettered, and released for ever from all that had enfeebled and debased my nature. I had passed in that celestial sleep from death to life, from the dreams of weakness, and lapses of insanity, to the full use and animation of my faculties,—and I felt as if a cemented load had broken and crumbled off my soul, and left me fearless and serene. I was never happy,—I was never worthy the stile* of Man till then; and, as I lay, I faultered out my thanks in ecstasy to Heaven, for all that had befallen me.

My limbs were numbed by the cold and damp of the floor on which I had been lying; but, rising from it, a new being in all that is essential to existence, I entered the passage, and walked briskly up and down, to recover the play and vigour of my frame. I found the thigh-bone on the ground where I had dropped it,—and no longer tortured by the fears that were gone for ever, replaced it quietly in its former situation. I kept near the entrance of the cell, that the first guide who descended might not miss me; and it could not be more than two hours, before Jerome, whose hair stood on end when he heard where I had passed the night, came down with an early party of visitors, and freed me from my dungeon.—There was no straggling among the company for that day.

You well know, my dear friend, what have been my habits and employments since that night; and I could summon you with confidence, to give your testimony, that few persons are now less slaves of superstitious terror than myself. By a strange and singular anomaly of circumstances, the wild fancies I had imbibed in the free air of my native hills, and among the cheerful scenes of romantic nature, I unlearned in the dreary catacombs of Paris. If I still am fanciful, you will not charge me with extravagance; if I still have sensibility, I trust it does not verge on weakness;—and, as I have proved my personal courage on more than a single trial, I may be allowed to smile, when I hear in future some boisterous relater of my narrative condemn me for a coward.

THE BURIED ALIVE

John Galt

I HAD been for some time ill of a low and lingering fever. My strength gradually wasted, but the sense of life seemed to become more and more acute as my corporeal powers became weaker. I could see by the looks of the doctor that he despaired of my recovery; and the soft and whispering sorrow of my friends, taught me that I had nothing to hope.

One day towards the evening, the crisis took place.—I was seized with a strange and indescribable quivering,—a rushing sound was in my ears,—I saw around my couch innumerable strange faces; they were bright and visionary, and without bodies. There was light, and solemnity, and I tried to move, but could not.—For a short time a terrible confusion overwhelmed me,—and when it passed off, all my recollection returned with the most perfect distinctness, but the power of motion had departed.—I heard the sound of weeping at my pillow—and the voice of the nurse say, 'He is dead.'—I cannot describe what I felt at these words.—I exerted my utmost power of volition to stir myself, but I could not move even an eyelid. After a short pause my friend drew near; and sobbing, and convulsed with grief, drew his hand over my face, and closed my eyes. The world was then darkened, but I still could hear, and feel, and suffer.

When my eyes were closed, I heard by the attendants that my friend had left the room, and I soon after found, the undertakers were preparing to habit me in the garments of the grave. Their thoughtlessness was more awful than the grief of my friends. They laughed at one another as they turned me from side to side, and treated what they believed a corpse, with the most appalling ribaldry.

When they had laid me out, these wretches retired, and the degrading formality of affected mourning commenced. For three days, a number of friends called to see me.—I heard them, in low accents, speak of what I was; and more than one touched me with his finger. On the third day, some of them talked of the smell of corruption in the room.

The coffin was procured—I was lifted and laid in—My friend placed my head on what was deemed its last pillow, and I felt his tears drop on my face.

When all who had any peculiar interest in me, had for a short time looked at me in the coffin, I heard them retire; and the undertaker's men placed the lid on the coffin, and screwed it down. There were two of them present—one had occasion to go away before the task was done. I heard the fellow who was left begin to whistle as he turned the screw-nails; but he checked himself, and completed the work in silence.

I was then left alone,—every one shunned the room.— I knew, however, that I was not yet buried; and though darkened and motionless, I had still hope;—but this was not permitted long. The day of interment arrived—I felt the coffin lifted and borne away—I heard and felt it placed in the hearse.—There was a crowd of people around; some of them spoke sorrowfully of me. The hearse began to move—I knew that it carried me to the grave. It halted, and the coffin was taken out—I felt myself carried on shoulders of men, by the inequality of the motion—A pause ensued—I heard the cords of the coffin moved—I felt it swing as dependent by them— It was lowered, and rested on the bottom of the grave—The cords were dropped upon the lid—I heard them fall.—Dreadful was the effort I then made to exert the power of action, but my whole frame was immoveable.

Soon after, a few handfuls of earth were thrown upon the coffin—Then there was another pause—after which the shovel was employed, and the sound of the rattling mould, as it covered me, was far more tremendous than thunder. But I could make no effort. The sound gradually became less and less, and by a surging reverberation in the coffin, I knew that the grave was filled up, and that the sexton was treading in the earth, slapping the grave with the flat of his spade. This too ceased, and then all was silent.

I had no means of knowing the lapse of time; and the silence continued. This is death, thought I, and I am doomed to remain in the earth till the resurrection. Presently the body will fall into corruption, and the epicurean worm, that is only satisfied with the flesh of man, will come to partake of the banquet that has been prepared for him with so much solicitude and care. In the contemplation of this hideous thought, I heard a low and under-sound in the earth over me, and I fancied that the worms and the reptiles of death were coming—that the mole and the rat of the grave would soon be upon me. The sound continued to grow louder and nearer. Can it be possible, I thought, that my friends suspect they have buried me too soon? The hope was truly like light bursting through the gloom of death.

The sound ceased, and presently I felt the hands of some dreadful being working about my throat. They dragged me out of the coffin by the head. I felt again the living air, but it was piercingly cold; and I was carried swiftly away—I thought to judgment, perhaps perdition.

When borne to some distance, I was then thrown down like a clod—it was not upon the ground. A moment after I found myself on a carriage; and, by the interchange of two or three brief sentences, I discovered that I was in the hands of two of those robbers who live by plundering the grave, and selling the bodies of parents, and children, and friends. One of the men sung snatches and scraps of obscene songs, as the cart rattled over the pavement of the streets.

When it halted, I was lifted out, and I soon perceived, by the closeness of the air, and the change of temperature, that I was carried into a room; and, being rudely stripped of my shroud, was placed naked on a table. By the conversation of the two fellows with the servant who admitted them, I learnt that I was that night to be dissected.

My eyes were still shut, I saw nothing; but in a short time I heard, by the bustle in the room, that the students of anatomy were assembling. Some of them came round the table, and examined me minutely. They were pleased to find that so good a subject had been procured. The demonstrator himself at last came in.

Previous to beginning the dissection, he proposed to try on me some galvanic experiment*—and an apparatus was arranged for that purpose. The first shock vibrated through all my nerves: they rung and jangled like the strings of a harp. The students expressed their admiration at the convulsive effect. The second shock threw my eyes open, and the first person I saw was the doctor who had attended me. But still I was as dead: I could, however, discover among the students the faces of many with whom I was familiar; and when my eyes were opened, I heard my name pronounced by several of the students, with an accent of awe and compassion, and a wish that it had been some other subject.

When they had satisfied themselves with the galvanic phenomena, the demonstrator took the knife, and pierced me on the bosom with the point. I felt a dreadful crackling, as it were, throughout my whole frame—a convulsive shuddering instantly followed, and a shriek of horror rose from all present. The ice of death was broken up—my trance ended. The utmost exertions were made to restore me, and in the course of an hour I was in the full possession of all my faculties.

THE FLOATING BEACON

John Howison

ONE dark and stormy night, we were on a voyage from Bergen to Christiansand* in a small sloop. Our captain suspected that he had approached too near the Norwegian coast, though he could not discern any land, and the wind blew with such violence, that we were in momentary dread of being driven upon a lee-shore. We had endeavoured, for more than an hour, to keep our vessel away; but our efforts proved unavailing, and we soon found that we could scarcely hold our own. A clouded sky, a hazy atmosphere, and irregular showers of sleety rain combined to deepen the obscurity of night, and nothing whatever was visible, except the sparkling of the distant waves, when their tops happened to break into a wreath of foam. The sea ran very high, and sometimes broke over the deck so furiously, that the men were obliged to hold by the rigging, lest they should be carried away. Our captain was a person of timid and irresolute character, and the dangers that environed us made him gradually lose confidence in himself. He often gave orders, and countermanded them in the same moment, all the while taking small quantities of ardent spirits at intervals. Fear and intoxication soon stupified him completely, and the crew ceased to consult him, or to pay any respect to his authority, in so far as regarded the management of the vessel.

About midnight our main-sail was split, and shortly after we found that the sloop had sprung a leak. We had before shipped a good deal of water through the hatches, and the quantity that now entered from below was so great, that we thought she would go down every moment. Our only chance of escape lay in our boat, which was immediately lowered. After we had all got on board of her, except the captain, who stood leaning against the mast, we called to him, requesting that he would follow us without delay. 'How dare you quit the sloop without my permission?' cried he, staggering forwards. 'This is not fit weather to go a-fishing. Come back—back with you all!'—'No, no,' returned one of the crew, 'we don't want to be sent to the bottom for your obstinacy. Bear a hand there, or we'll leave you behind.'—'Captain, you are drunk,' said another; 'you cannot take care of yourself. You must obey *us* now.'—'Silence! mutinous villain,' answered the captain. 'What are you all afraid of? This is a fine breeze—Up main-sail, and steer her right in the wind's eye.'

The sea knocked the boat so violently and constantly against the side of the sloop, that we feared the former would be injured or upset, if we did not immediately row away; but, anxious as we were to preserve our lives, we could not reconcile ourselves to the idea of abandoning the captain, who grew more obstinate the more we attempted to persuade him to accompany us. At length, one of the crew leapt on board the sloop, and having seized hold of him, tried to drag him along by force; but he struggled resolutely, and soon freed himself from the grasp of the seaman, who immediately resumed his place among us, and urged that we should not any longer risk our lives for the sake of a drunkard and a madman. Most of the party declared they were of the same opinion, and began to push off the boat; but I entreated them to make one effort more to induce their infatuated commander to accompany us. At that moment he came up from the cabin, to which he had descended a little time before, and we immediately perceived that he was more under the influence of ardent spirits than ever. He abused us all in the grossest terms, and threatened his crew with severe punishment, if they did not come on board, and return to their duty. His manner was so violent, that no one seemed willing to attempt to constrain him to come on board the boat; and after vainly representing the absurdity of his conduct, and the danger of his situation, we bid him farewell, and rowed away.

The sea ran so high, and had such a terrific appearance, that I almost wished myself in the sloop again. The crew plied the oars in silence, and we heard nothing but the hissing of the enormous billows as they gently rose up, and slowly subsided again, without breaking. At intervals, our boat was elevated far above the surface of the ocean, and remained, for a few moments, trembling upon the pinnacle of a surge, from which it would quietly descend into a gulf, so deep and awful, that we often thought the dense black mass of waters which formed its sides, were on the point of over-arching us, and bursting upon our heads. We glided with regular undulations from one billow to another; but every time we sunk into the trough of the sea, my heart died within me, for I felt as if we were going lower down than we had ever done before, and clung instinctively to the board on which I sat.

Notwithstanding my terrors, I frequently looked towards the sloop. The fragments of her main-sail, which remained attached to the yard, and fluttered in the wind, enabled us to discern exactly where she lay, and shewed, by their motion, that she pitched about in a terrible manner. We occasionally heard the voice of her unfortunate commander, calling to us in tones of frantic derision, and by turns vociferating curses and blasphemous oaths, and singing sea-songs with a wild and frightful energy. I sometimes almost wished that the crew would make another effort to save him, but, next moment, the principle of self-preservation repressed all feelings of humanity, and I endeavoured, by closing my ears, to banish the idea of his sufferings from my mind.

After a little time the shivering canvas disappeared, and we heard a tumultuous roaring and bursting of billows, and saw an unusual sparkling of the sea about a quarter of a mile from us. One of the sailors cried out that the sloop was now on her beam ends, and that the noise, to which we listened, was that of the waves breaking over her. We could sometimes perceive a large black mass heaving itself up irregularly among the flashing surges, and then disappearing for a few moments, and knew but too well that it was the hull of the vessel. At intervals, a shrill and agonized voice uttered some exclamations, but we could not distinguish what they were, and then a long-drawn shriek came across the ocean, which suddenly grew more furiously agitated near the spot where the sloop lay, and, in a few moments, she sunk down, and a black wave formed itself out of the waters that had engulfed her, and swelled gloomily into a magnitude greater than that of the surrounding billows.

The seamen dropped their oars, as if by one impulse, and looked expressively at each other, without speaking a word. Awful forebodings of a fate similar to that of the captain, appeared to chill every heart, and to repress the energy that had hitherto excited us to make unremitting exertions for our common safety. While we were in this state of hopeless inaction, the man at the helm called out that he saw a light ahead. We all strained our eyes to discern it, but, at the moment, the boat was sinking down between two immense waves, one of which closed the prospect, and we remained in breathless anxiety till a rising surge elevated us above the level of the surrounding ocean. A light like a dazzling star then suddenly flashed upon our view, and joyful exclamations burst from every mouth. 'That,' cried one of the crew, 'must be the floating beacon which our captain was looking out for this afternoon. If we can but gain it, we'll be safe enough yet.' This intelligence cheered us all, and the men began to ply the oars with redoubled vigour, while I employed myself in baling out the water that sometimes rushed over the gunnel of the boat when a sea happened to strike her.

An hour's hard rowing brought us so near the light-house that we almost ceased to apprehend any further danger; but it was suddenly obscured from our view, and, at the same time, a confused roaring and dashing commenced at a little distance, and rapidly increased in loudness. We soon perceived a tremendous billow rolling towards us. Its top, part of which had already broke, overhung the base, as if unwilling to burst until we were within the reach of its violence. The man who steered the boat, brought her head to the sea, but all to no purpose, for the water rushed furiously over us, and we were completely immersed. I felt the boat swept from under me, and was left struggling and groping about in hopeless desperation, for something to catch hold of. When nearly exhausted, I received a severe blow on the side from a small cask of water which the sea had forced against me. I immediately twined my arms round it, and, after recovering myself a little, began to look for the boat, and to call to my companions; but I could not discover any vestige of them, or of their vessel. However, I still had a faint hope that they were in existence, and that the intervention of the billows concealed them from my view. I continued to shout as loud as possible, for the sound of my own voice in some measure relieved me from the feeling of awful and heart-chilling loneliness which my situation inspired; but not even an echo responded to my cries, and, convinced that my comrades had all perished, I ceased looking for them, and pushed towards the beacon in the best manner I could. A long series of fatiguing exertions brought me close to the side of the vessel which contained it, and I called out loudly, in hopes that those on board might hear me and come to my assistance, but no one appearing, I waited patiently till a wave raised me on a level with the chains, and then caught hold of them, and succeeded in getting on board.

As I did not see any person on deck, I went forwards to the sky-light, and looked down. Two men were seated below at a table, and a lamp, which was suspended above them, being swung backwards and forwards by the rolling of the vessel, threw its light upon their faces alternately. One seemed agitated with passion, and the other surveyed him with a scornful look. They both talked very loudly, and used threatening gestures, but the sea made so much noise that I could not distinguish what was said. After a little time, they started up, and seemed to be on the point of closing and wrestling together, when a woman rushed through a small door and prevented them. I beat upon the deck with my feet at the same time, and the attention of the whole party was soon transferred to the noise. One of the men immediately came up the cabin stairs, but stopped short on seeing me, as if irresolute whether to advance or hasten below again. I approached him, and told my story in a few words, but instead of making any reply, he went down to the cabin, and began to relate to the others what he had seen. I soon followed him, and easily found my way into the apartment where they all were. They appeared to feel mingled sensations of fear and astonishment at my presence, and it was some time before any of them entered into conversation with me, or afforded those comforts which I stood so much in need of.

After I had refreshed myself with food, and been provided with a change of clothing, I went upon deck, and surveyed the singular asylum in which Providence had enabled me to take refuge from the fury of the storm. It did not exceed thirty feet long, and was very strongly built, and completely decked over, except at the entrance to the cabin. It had a thick mast at midships, with a large lantern, containing several burners and reflectors, on the top of it; and this could be lowered and hoisted up again as often as required, by means of ropes and pullies. The vessel was firmly moored upon an extensive sandbank, the beacon being intended to warn seamen to avoid a part of the ocean where many lives and vessels had been lost in consequence of the latter running aground. The accommodations below decks were narrow, and of an inferior description; however, I gladly retired to the berth that was allotted me by my entertainers, and fatigue and the rocking of billows combined to lull me into a quiet and dreamless sleep.

Next morning, one of the men, whose name was Angerstoff, came to my bedside, and called me to breakfast in a surly and imperious manner. The others looked coldly and distrustfully when I joined them, and I saw that they regarded me as an intruder and an unwelcome guest. The meal passed without almost any conversation, and I went upon deck whenever it was over. The tempest of the preceding night had in a great measure abated, but the sea still ran very high, and a black mist hovered over it, through which the Norwegian coast, lying at eleven miles distance, could be dimly seen. I looked in vain for some remains of the sloop or boat. Not a bird enlivened the heaving expanse of waters, and I turned shuddering from the dreary scene, and asked Morvalden, the youngest of the men, when he thought I had any chance of getting ashore. 'Not very soon, I'm afraid,' returned he. 'We are visited once a month by people from yonder land, who are appointed to bring us supply of provisions and other necessaries. They were here only six days ago, so you may count how long it will be before they return. Fishing boats sometimes pass us during fine weather, but we won't have much of that this moon at least.'

No intelligence could have been more depressing to me than this. The idea of spending perhaps three weeks in such a place was almost insupportable, and the more so, as I could not hasten my deliverance by any exertions of my own, but would be obliged to remain, in a state of inactive suspense, till good fortune, or the regular course of events, afforded me the means of getting ashore. Neither Angerstoff nor Morvalden seemed to sympathize with my distress, or even to care that I should have it in my power to leave the vessel, except in so far as my departure would free them from the expence of supporting me. They returned indistinct and repulsive answers to all the questions I asked, and appeared anxious to avoid having the least communication with me. During the greater part of the forenoon, they employed themselves in trimming the lamps, and cleaning the reflectors, but never conversed any. I easily perceived that a mutual animosity existed between them, but was unable to discover the cause of it. Morvalden seemed to fear Angerstoff, and, at the same time, to feel a deep resentment towards him, which he did not dare to express. Angerstoff apparently was aware of this, for he behaved to his companion with the undisguised fierceness of determined hate, and openly thwarted him in every thing.

Marietta, the female on board, was the wife of Morvalden. She remained chiefly below decks, and attended to the domestic concerns of the vessel. She was rather good-looking, but so reserved and forbidding in her manners, that she formed no desirable acquisition to our party, already so heartless and unsociable in its character.

When night approached, after the lapse of a wearisome and monotonous day, I went on deck to see the beacon lighted, and continued walking backwards and forwards till a late hour. I watched the lantern, as it swung from side to side, and flashed upon different portions of the sea alternately, and sometimes fancied I saw men struggling among the billows that tumbled around, and at other times imagined I could discern the white sail of an approaching vessel. Human voices seemed to mingle with the noise of the bursting waves, and I often listened intently, almost in the expectation of hearing articulate sounds. My mind grew sombre as the scene itself, and strange and fearful ideas obtruded themselves in rapid succession. It was dreadful to be chained in the middle of the deep—to be the continual sport of the quietless billows—to be shunned as a fatal thing by those who traversed the solitary ocean. Though within sight of the shore, our situation was more dreary than if we had been sailing a thousand miles from it. We felt not the pleasure of moving forwards, nor the hope of reaching port, nor the delights arising from favourable breezes and genial weather. When a billow drove us to one side, we were tossed back again by another; our imprisonment had no variety or definite termination; and the calm and the tempest were alike uninteresting to us. I felt as if my fate had already become linked with that of those who were on board the vessel. My hopes of being again permitted to mingle with mankind died away, and I anticipated long years of gloom and despair in the company of these repulsive persons into whose hands fate had unexpectedly consigned me.

Angerstoff and Morvalden tended the beacon alternately during the night. The latter had the watch while I remained upon deck. His appearance and manner indicated much perturbation of mind, and he paced hurriedly from side to side, sometimes muttering to himself, and sometimes stopping suddenly to look through the sky-light, as if anxious to discover what was going on below. He would then gaze intently upon the heavens, and next moment take out his watch, and contemplate the motions of its hands. I did not offer to disturb these reveries, and thought myself altogether unobserved by him, till he suddenly advanced to the spot where I stood, and said, in a loud whisper,—'There's a villain below—a desperate villain—this is true—he is capable of any thing—and the woman is as bad as him.'—I asked what proof he had of all this.—'Oh, I know it,' returned he; 'that wretch Angerstoff, whom I once thought my friend, has gained my wife's affections. She has been faithless to me—yes, she has. They both wish I were out of the way. Perhaps they are now planning my destruction. What can I do? It is very terrible to be shut up in such narrow limits with those who hate me, and to have no means of escaping, or defending myself from their infernal machinations.'—'Why do you not leave the beacon,' inquired I, 'and abandon your companion and guilty wife?'—'Ah, that is impossible,' answered Morvalden; 'if I went on shore I would forfeit my liberty. I live here that I may escape the vengeance of the law, which I once outraged for the sake of her who has now withdrawn her love from me. What ingratitude! Mine is indeed a terrible fate, but I must bear it. And shall I never again wander through the green fields, and climb the rocks that encircle my native place? Are the weary dashings of the sea, and the moanings of the wind, to fill my ears continually, all the while telling me that I am an exile?—a hopeless despairing exile. But it won't last long,' cried he catching hold of my arm; 'they will murder me!—I am sure of it—I never go to sleep without dreaming that Angerstoff has pushed me overboard.'

'Your lonely situation, and inactive life, dispose you to give way to these chimeras,' said I; 'you must endeavour to resist them. Perhaps things aren't so bad as you suppose.'—'This is not a lonely situation,' replied Morvalden, in a solemn tone. 'Perhaps you will have proof of what I say before you leave us. Many vessels used to be lost here, and a few are wrecked still; and the skeletons and corpses of those who have perished lie all over the sand-bank. Sometimes, at midnight, I have seen crowds of human figures moving backwards and forwards upon the surface of the ocean, almost as far as the eye could reach. I neither knew who they were, nor what they did there. When watching the lantern alone, I often hear a number of voices talking together, as it were, under the waves; and I twice caught the very words they uttered, but I cannot repeat them—they dwell incessantly in my memory, but my tongue refuses to pronounce them, or to explain to others what they meant.'

'Do not let your senses be imposed upon by a distempered imagination,' said I; 'there is no reality in the things you have told me.'—'Perhaps my mind occasionally wanders a little, for it has a heavy burden upon it,' returned Morvalden. 'I have been guilty of a dreadful crime. Many that now lie in the deep below us, might start up, and accuse me of what I am just going to reveal to you. One stormy night, shortly after I began to take charge of this beacon, while watching on deck, I fell into a profound sleep; I know not how long it continued, but I was awakened by horrible shouts and cries—I started up, and instantly perceived that all the lamps in the lantern were extinguished. It was very dark, and the sea raged furiously;

but notwithstanding all this, I observed a ship a-ground on the bank, a little way from me, her sails fluttering in the wind, and the waves breaking over her with violence. Half frantic with horror, I ran down to the cabin for a taper, and lighted the lamps as fast as possible. The lantern, when hoisted to the top of the mast, threw a vivid glare on the surrounding ocean, and shewed me the vessel disappearing among the billows. Hundreds of people lay gasping in the water near her. Men, women, and children, writhed together in agonizing struggles, and uttered soul-harrowing cries; and their countenances, as they gradually stiffened under the hand of death, were all turned towards me with glassy stare, while the lurid expression of their glistening eyes upbraided me with having been the cause of their untimely end. Never shall I forget these looks. They haunt me wherever I am—asleep and awake—night and day. I have kept this tale of horror secret till now, and do not know if I shall ever have courage to relate it again. The masts of the vessel projected above the surface of the sea for several months after she was lost, as if to keep me in recollection of the night on which so many human creatures perished, in consequence of my neglect and carelessness. Would to God I had no memory! I sometimes think I am getting mad. The past and present are equally dreadful to me; and I dare not anticipate the future.'

I felt a sort of superstitious dread steal over me, while Morvalden related his story, and we continued walking the deck in silence, till the period of his watch expired. I then went below, and took refuge in my berth, though I was but little inclined for sleep. The gloomy ideas, and dark forebodings, expressed by Morvalden, weighed heavily upon my mind, without my knowing why; and my situation, which had at first seemed only dreary and depressing, began to have something indefinitely terrible in its aspect.

Next day, when Morvalden proceeded as usual to put the beacon in order, he called upon Angerstoff to come and assist him, which the latter peremptorily refused. Morvalden then went down to the cabin, where his companion was, and requested to know why his orders were not obeyed. 'Because I hate trouble,' replied Angerstoff.—'I am master here,' said

Morvalden, 'and have been entrusted with the direction of every thing. Do not attempt to trifle with me.'—'Trifle with you!' exclaimed Angerstoff, looking contemptuously. 'No, no; I am no trifler; and I advise you to walk up stairs again, lest I prove this to your cost.'—'Why, husband,' cried Marietta, 'I believe there are no bounds to your laziness. You make this young man toil from morning to night, and take advantage of his good-nature in the most shameful manner.'—'Peace, infamous woman!' said Morvalden; 'I know very well why you stand up in his defence; but I'll put a stop to the intimacy that exists between you. Go to your room instantly! You are my wife, and shall obey me.'—'Is this usage to be borne?' exclaimed Marietta. 'Will no one step forward to protect me from his violence?'—'Insolent fellow!' cried Angerstoff, 'don't presume to insult my mistress.'—'Mistress!' repeated Morvalden. 'This to my face!' and struck him a severe blow. Angerstoff sprung forward, with the intention of returning it, but I got between them, and prevented him. Marietta then began to shed tears, and applauded the generosity her paramour had evinced in sparing her husband, who immediately went upon deck, without speaking a word, and hurriedly resumed the work that had engaged his attention previous to the quarrel.

Neither of the two men seemed at all disposed for a reconciliation, and they had no intercourse during the whole day, except angry and revengeful looks. I frequently observed Marietta in deep consultation with Angerstoff, and easily perceived that the subject of debate had some relation to her injured husband, whose manner evinced much alarm and anxiety, although he endeavoured to look calm and cheerful. He did not make his appearance at meals, but spent all his time upon deck. Whenever Angerstoff accidentally passed him, he shrunk back with an expression of dread, and intuitively, as it were, caught hold of a rope, or any other object to which he could cling. The day proved a wretched and fearful one to me, for I momentarily expected that some terrible affray would occur on board, and that I would be implicated in it. I gazed upon the surrounding sea almost without intermission, ardently hoping that some boat might approach near enough to afford me an opportunity of quitting the horrid and dangerous abode to which I was imprisoned.

It was Angerstoff's watch on deck till midnight; and as I did not wish to have any communication with him, I remained below. At twelve o'clock, Morvalden got up and relieved him, and he came down to the cabin, and soon after retired to his berth. Believing, from this arrangement, that they had no hostile intentions, I lay down in bed with composure, and fell asleep. It was not long before a noise overhead awakened me. I started up, and listened intently. The sound appeared to be that of two persons scuffling together, for a succession of irregular footsteps beat the deck, and I could hear violent blows given at intervals. I got out of my berth, and entered the cabin, where I found Marietta standing alone, with a lamp in her hand. 'Do you hear that?' cried I.—'Hear what?' returned she; 'I have had a dreadful dream—I am all trembling.'—'Is Angerstoff below?' demanded I.—'No—Yes, I mean,' said Marietta. 'Why do you ask that? He went upstairs.'—'Your husband and he are fighting. We must part them instantly.'— 'How can that be?' answered Marietta; 'Angerstoff is asleep.'— 'Asleep! Didn't you say he went up stairs?'—'I don't know,' returned she; 'I am hardly awake yet—Let us listen a moment.'

Every thing was still for a few seconds; then a voice shrieked out, 'Ah! that knife! You are murdering me! Draw it out! No help! Are you done? Now—now—now!'—A heavy body fell suddenly along the deck, and some words were spoken in a faint tone, but the roaring of the sea prevented me from hearing what they were.

I rushed up the cabin stairs, and tried to push open the folding doors at the head of them, but they resisted my utmost efforts. I knocked violently and repeatedly, to no purpose. 'Some one is killed,' cried I. 'The person who barred these doors on the outside is guilty.'—'I know nothing of that,' returned Marietta. 'We can't be of any use now.—Come here again!—How dreadfully quiet it is.—My God!—A drop of blood has fallen through the sky-light.—What faces are yon looking down upon us?—But this lamp is going out.— We must be going through the water at a terrible rate.—How it rushes past us!—I am getting dizzy.—Do you hear these bells ringing? and strange voices——'

The cabin doors were suddenly burst open, and Angerstoff next moment appeared before us, crying out, 'Morvalden has fallen overboard. Throw a rope to him!—He will be drowned.' His hands and dress were marked with blood, and he had a frightful look of horror and confusion. 'You are a murderer!' exclaimed I, almost involuntarily.—'How do you know that?' said he, staggering back; 'I'm sure you never saw—' 'Hush, hush,' cried Marietta to him; 'Are you mad?—Speak again! —What frightens you?—Why don't you run and help Morvalden?'—'Has any thing happened to him?' inquired Angerstoff, with a gaze of consternation.—'You told us he had fallen overboard,' returned Marietta. 'Must my husband perish?'—'Give me some water to wash my hands,' said Angerstoff, growing deadly pale, and catching hold of the table for support.

I now hastened upon deck, but Morvalden was not there. I then went to the side of the vessel, and put my hands on the gunwale, while I leaned over, and looked downwards. On taking them off, I found them marked with blood. I grew sick at heart, and began to identify myself with Angerstoff the murderer. The sea, the beacon, and the sky, appeared of a sanguine hue; and I thought I heard the dying exclamations of Morvalden sounding a hundred fathom below me, and echoing through the caverns of the deep. I advanced to the cabin door, intending to descend the stairs, but found that some one had fastened it firmly on the inside. I felt convinced that I was intentionally shut out, and a cold shuddering pervaded my frame. I covered my face with my hands, not daring to look around; for it seemed as if I was excluded from the company of the living, and doomed to be the associate of the spirits of drowned and murdered men. After a little time I began to walk hastily backwards and forwards; but the light of the lantern happened to flash on a stream of blood that ran along the deck, and I could not summon up resolution to pass the spot where it was a second time. The sky looked black and threatening—the sea had a fierceness in its sound and motions—and the wind swept over its bosom with melancholy sighs. Every thing was sombre and ominous; and I looked in vain for some object that would, by its soothing aspect, remove the dark impressions which crowded upon my mind.

While standing near the bows of the vessel, I saw a hand and arm rise slowly behind the stern, and wave from side to side. I started back as far as I could go in horrible affright, and looked again, expecting to behold the entire spectral figure of which I supposed they formed a part. But nothing more was visible. I struck my eyes till the light flashed from them, in hopes that my senses had been imposed upon by distempered vision—however it was in vain, for the hand still motioned me to advance, and I rushed forwards with wild desperation, and caught hold of it. I was pulled along a little way notwithstanding the resistance I made, and soon discovered a man stretched along the stern-cable, and clinging to it in a convulsive manner. It was Morvalden. He raised his head feebly, and said something, but I could only distinguish the words 'murdered—overboard—reached this rope—terrible death'.—I stretched out my arms to support him, but at that moment the vessel plunged violently, and he was shaken off the cable, and dropped among the waves. He floated for an instant, and then disappeared under the keel.

I seized the first rope I could find, and threw one end of it over the stern, and likewise flung some planks into the sea, thinking that the unfortunate Morvalden might still retain strength enough to catch hold of them if they came within his reach. I continued on the watch for a considerable time, but at last abandoned all hopes of saving him, and made another attempt to get down to the cabin—the doors were now unfastened, and I opened them without any difficulty. The first thing I saw on going below, was Angerstoff stretched along the floor, and fast asleep. His torpid look, flushed countenance, and uneasy respiration, convinced me that he had taken a large quantity of ardent spirits. Marietta was in her own apartment. Even the presence of a murderer appeared less terrible than the frightful solitariness of the deck, and I lay down upon a bench, determining to spend the remainder of the night there. The lamp that hung from the roof soon went out, and left me in total darkness. Imagination began to conjure up a thousand appalling forms, and the voice of Angerstoff, speaking in his sleep, filled my ears at intervals— 'Hoist up the beacon!—the lamps won't burn—horrible!— they contain blood instead of oil.—Is that a boat coming?—Yes, yes, I hear the oars.—Damnation!—why is that corpse so long of sinking?—If it doesn't go down soon they'll find me out— How terribly the wind blows!—We are driving ashore—See! see! Morvalden is swimming after us—How he writhes in the water!'—Marietta now rushed from her room, with a light in her hand, and seizing Angerstoff by the arm, tried to awake him. He soon rose up with chattering teeth and shivering limbs, and was on the point of speaking, but she prevented him, and he staggered away to his berth, and lay down in it.

Next morning, when I went upon deck, after a short and perturbed sleep, I found Marietta dashing water over it, that she might efface all vestige of the transactions of the preceding night. Angerstoff did not make his appearance till noon, and his looks were ghastly and agonized. He seemed stupified with horror, and sometimes entirely lost all perception of the things around him for a considerable time. He suddenly came close up to me, and demanded, with a bold air, but quivering voice, what I had meant by calling him a murderer?—'Why, that you are one,' replied I, after a pause.—'Beware what you say,' returned he fiercely,—'you cannot escape my power now—I tell you, sir, Morvalden fell overboard.'—'Whence, then, came that blood that covered the deck?' inquired I.—He grew pale, and then cried, 'You lie—you lie infernally—there was none!'— 'I saw it,' said I—'I saw Morvalden himself—long after midnight. He was clinging to the stern-cable, and said'—'Ha, ha, ha—devils!—curses!'—exclaimed Angerstoff—'Did you hear me dreaming?—I was mad last night—Come, come, come!— We shall tend the beacon together—Let us make friends, and don't be afraid, for you'll find me a good fellow in the end.' He now forcibly shook hands with me, and then hurried down to the cabin.

In the afternoon, while sitting on deck, I discerned a boat far off, but I determined to conceal this from Angerstoff and Marietta, lest they should use some means to prevent its approach. I walked carelessly about, casting a glance upon the sea occasionally, and meditating how I could best take advantage of the means of deliverance which I had in prospect. After the lapse of an hour, the boat was not more than half a mile distant from us, but she suddenly changed her course, and bore away towards the shore. I immediately shouted, and waved a handkerchief over my head, as signals for her to return. Angerstoff rushed from the cabin, and seized my arm, threatening at the same time to push me overboard if I attempted to hail her again. I disengaged myself from his grasp, and dashed him violently from me. The noise brought Marietta upon deck, who immediately perceived the cause of the affray, and cried, 'Does the wretch mean to make his escape? For Godsake, prevent the possibility of that!'—'Yes, yes,' returned Angerstoff; 'he never shall leave the vessel—He had as well take care, lest I do to him what I did to—' 'To Morvalden, I suppose you mean,' said I.—'Well, well, speak it out,' replied he ferociously; 'there is no one here to listen to your damnable falsehoods, and I'll not be fool enough to give you an opportunity of uttering them elsewhere. I'll strangle you the next time you tell these lies about—' 'Come,' interrupted Marietta, 'don't be uneasy—the boat will soon be far enough away—If he wants to give you the slip, he must leap overboard.'

I was irritated and disappointed beyond measure at the failure of the plan of escape I had formed, but thought it most prudent to conceal my feelings. I now perceived the rashness and bad consequences of my bold assertions respecting the murder of Morvalden; for Angerstoff evidently thought that his personal safety, and even his life, would be endangered, if I ever found an opportunity of accusing and giving evidence against him. All my motions were now watched with double vigilance. Marietta and her paramour kept upon deck by turns during the whole day, and the latter looked over the surrounding ocean, through a glass, at intervals, to discover if any boat or vessel was approaching us. He often muttered threats as he walked past me, and, more than once, seemed waiting for an opportunity to push me overboard. Marietta and he frequently whispered together, and I always imagined I heard my name mentioned in the course of these conversations.

I now felt completely miserable, being satisfied that

Angerstoff was bent upon my destruction. I wandered, in a state of fearful circumspection, from one part of the vessel to the other, not knowing how to secure myself from his designs. Every time he approached me, my heart palpitated dreadfully; and when night came on, I was agonized with terror, and could not remain in one spot, but hurried backwards and forwards between the cabin and the deck, looking wildly from side to side, and momentarily expecting to feel a cold knife entering my vitals. My forehead began to burn, and my eyes dazzled; I became acutely sensitive, and the slightest murmur, or the faintest breath of wind, set my whole frame in a state of uncontrollable vibration. At first, I sometimes thought of throwing myself into the sea; but I soon acquired such an intense feeling of existence, that the mere idea of death was horrible to me.

Shortly after midnight I lay down in my berth, almost exhausted by the harrowing emotions that had careered through my mind during the past day. I felt a strong desire to sleep, yet dared not indulge myself; soul and body seemed at war. Every noise excited my imagination, and scarcely a minute passed, in the course of which I did not start up, and look around. Angerstoff paced the deck overhead, and when the sound of his footsteps accidentally ceased at any time, I grew deadly sick at heart, expecting that he was silently coming to murder me. At length I thought I heard some one near my bed—I sprung from it, and, having seized a bar of iron that lay on the floor, rushed into the cabin.—I found Angerstoff there, who started back when he saw me, and said, 'What is the matter? Did you think that—I want you to watch the beacon, that I may have some rest.—Follow me upon deck, and I will give you directions about it.' I hesitated a moment, and then went up the gangway stairs behind him. We walked forward to the mast together, and he shewed how I was to lower the lantern when any of the lamps happened to go out, and bidding me beware of sleep, returned to the cabin. Most of my fears forsook me the moment he disappeared. I felt nearly as happy as if I had been set at liberty, and, for a time, forgot that my situation had any thing painful or alarming connected with it. Angerstoff resumed his station in about three hours, and I again took refuge in my berth, where I enjoyed a short but undisturbed slumber.

Next day while I was walking the deck, and anxiously surveying the expanse of ocean around, Angerstoff requested me to come down to the cabin. I obeyed his summons, and found him there. He gave me a book, saying it was very entertaining and would serve to amuse me during my idle hours; and then went above, shutting the doors carefully behind him. I was struck with his behaviour, but felt no alarm, for Marietta sat at work near me, apparently unconscious of what had passed. I began to peruse the volume I held in my hand, and found it so interesting that I paid little attention to any thing else, till the dashing of oars struck my ear. I sprung from my chair, with the intention of hastening upon deck, but Marietta stopped me, saying, 'It is of no use. The gangway doors are fastened.' Notwithstanding this information, I made an attempt to open them, but could not succeed. I was now convinced, by the percussion against the vessel, that a boat lay alongside, and I heard a strange voice addressing Angerstoff. Fired with the idea of deliverance, I leaped upon a table which stood in the middle of the cabin, and tried to push off the sky-light, but was suddenly stunned by a violent blow on the back of my head. I staggered back and looked round. Marietta stood close behind me, brandishing an axe, as if in the act of repeating the stroke. Her face was flushed with rage, and, having seized my arm, she cried, 'Come down instantly, accursed villain! I know you want to betray us, but may we all go to the bottom if you find a chance of doing so.' I struggled to free myself from her grasp, but, being in a state of dizziness and confusion, I was unable to effect this, and she soon pulled me to the ground. At that moment, Angerstoff hurriedly entered the cabin, exclaiming, 'What noise is this? Oh, just as I expected! Has that devil—that spy—been trying to get above boards? Why haven't I the heart to despatch him at once? But there's no time now. The people are waiting—Marietta, come and lend a hand.' They now forced me down upon the floor, and bound me to an iron ring that was fixed in it. This being done, Angerstoff directed his female accomplice to prevent me from speaking, and went upon deck again.

While in this state of bondage, I heard distinctly all that passed without. Some one asked Angerstoff how Morvalden did.—'Well, quite well,' replied the former; 'but he's below, and so sick that he can't see any person.'—'Strange enough,' said the first speaker, laughing. 'Is he ill and in good health at the same time? he had as well be overboard as in that condition.'—'Overboard!' repeated Angerstoff, 'what!—how do you mean?—all false!—but listen to me.—Are there any news stirring ashore?'—'Why,' said the stranger, 'the chief talk there just now is about a curious thing that happened this morning. A dead man was found upon the beach, and they suspect, from the wounds on his body, that he hasn't got fair play. They are making a great noise about it, and government means to send out a boat, with an officer on board, who is to visit all the shipping round this, that he may ascertain if any of them has lost a man lately. 'Tis a dark business; but they'll get to the bottom of it, I warrant ye.—Why you look as pale as if you knew more about this matter than you choose to tell.'—'No, no, no,' returned Angerstoff; 'I never hear of a murder, but I think of a friend of mine who—but I won't detain you, for the sea is getting up—We'll have a blowy night, I'm afraid.'—'So you don't want any fish today?' cried the stranger. 'Then I'll be off—Good morning, good morning. I suppose you'll have the government boat alongside by and bye.' I now heard the sound of oars, and supposed, from the conversation having ceased, that the fishermen had departed. Angerstoff came down to the cabin soon after, and released me without speaking a word.

Marietta then approached him, and, taking hold of his arm, said, 'Do you believe what that man has told you?'—'Yes, by the eternal hell!' cried he vehemently; 'I suspect I will find the truth of it soon enough.'—'My God!' exclaimed she, 'what is to become of us?—How dreadful! We are chained here, and cannot escape.'—'Escape what?' interrupted Angerstoff; 'girl, you have lost your senses. Why should we fear the officers of justice? Keep a guard over your tongue.'—'Oh,' returned Marietta, 'I talk without thinking, or understanding my own words; but come upon deck, and let me speak with you there.' They now went up the gangway stairs together, and continued in deep conversation for some time.

Angerstoff gradually became more agitated as the day advanced. He watched upon deck almost without intermission, and seemed irresolute what to do, sometimes sitting down composedly, and at other times hurrying backwards and forwards, with clenched hands and bloodless cheeks. The wind blew pretty fresh from the shore, and there was a heavy swell; and I supposed, from the anxious looks with which he contemplated the sky, that he hoped the threatening aspect of the weather would prevent the government boat from putting out to sea. He kept his glass constantly in his hand, and surveyed the ocean through it in all directions.

At length he suddenly dashed the instrument away, and exclaimed, 'God help us! they are coming now!' Marietta, on hearing this, ran wildly towards him, and put her hands in his, but he pushed her to one side, and began to pace the deck, apparently in deep thought. After a little time, he started, and cried, 'I have it now!—It's the only plan—I'll manage the business—yes, yes—I'll cut the cables, and off we'll go—that's settled!'—He then seized an axe, and first divided the hawser at the bows, and afterwards the one attached to the stern.

The vessel immediately began to drift away, and having no sails or helm to steady her, rolled with such violence, that I was dashed from side to side several times. She often swung over so much, that I thought she would not regain the upright position, and Angerstoff all the while unconsciously strengthened this belief, by exclaiming, 'She will capsize! shift the ballast, or we must go to the bottom!' In the midst of this, I kept my station upon deck, intently watching the boat, which was still several miles distant. I waited in fearful expectation, thinking that every new wave against which we were impelled would burst upon our vessel, and overwhelm us, while our pursuers were too far off to afford any assistance. The idea of perishing when on the point of being saved was inexpressibly agonizing.

As the day advanced, the hopes I had entertained of the boat making up with us gradually diminished. The wind blew violently, and we drifted along at a rapid rate, and the weather grew so hazy that our pursuers soon became quite undistinguishable. Marietta and Angerstoff appeared to be stupified with terror. They stood motionless, holding firmly by the bulwarks of the vessel; and though the waves frequently broke over the deck, and rushed down the gangway, they did not offer to shut the companion door, which would have remained open, had not I closed it. The tempest, gloom, and danger, that thickened around us, neither elicited from them any expressions of mutual regard, nor seemed to produce the slightest sympathetic emotion in their bosoms. They gazed sternly at each other and at me, and every time the vessel rolled, clung with convulsive eagerness to whatever lay within their reach.

About sunset our attention was attracted by a dreadful roaring, which evidently did not proceed from the waves around us; but the atmosphere being very hazy, we were unable to ascertain the cause of it, for a long time. At length we distinguished a range of high cliffs, against which the sea beat with terrible fury. Whenever the surge broke upon them, large jets of foam started up to a great height, and flashed angrily over their black and rugged surfaces, while the wind moaned and whistled with fearful caprice among the projecting points of rock. A dense mist covered the upper part of the cliffs, and prevented us from seeing if there were any houses upon their summits, though this point appeared of little importance, for we drifted towards the shore so fast that immediate death seemed inevitable.

We soon felt our vessel bound twice against the sand, and, in a little time after, a heavy sea carried her up the beach, where she remained imbedded and hard a-ground. During the ebb of the waves there was not more than two feet of water round her bows. I immediately perceived this, and watching a favourable opportunity, swung myself down to the beach, by means of part of the cable that projected through the hawse-hole. I began to run towards the cliffs, the moment my feet touched the ground, and Angerstoff attempted to follow me, that he might prevent my escape; but, while in the act of descending from the vessel, the sea flowed in with such violence, that he was obliged to spring on board again to save himself from being overwhelmed by its waters.

I hurried on and began to climb up the rocks, which were very steep and slippery; but I soon grew breathless from fatigue, and found it necessary to stop. It was now almost dark, and when I looked around, I neither saw any thing distinctly, nor could form the least idea how far I had still to ascend before I reached the top of the cliffs. I knew not which way to turn my steps, and remained irresolute, till the barking of a dog faintly struck my ear. I joyfully followed the sound, and, after an hour of perilous exertion, discovered a light at some distance, which I soon found to proceed from the window of a small hut.

After I had knocked repeatedly, the door was opened by an old man, with a lamp in his hand. He started back on seeing me, for my dress was wet and disordered, my face and hands had been wounded while scrambling among the rocks, and fatigue and terror had given me a wan and agitated look. I entered the house, the inmates of which were a woman and a boy, and having seated myself near the fire, related to my host all that had occurred on board the floating beacon, and then requested him to accompany me down to the beach, that we might search for Angerstoff and Marietta. 'No, no,' cried he, 'that is impossible. Hear how the storm rages! Worlds would not induce me to have any communication with murderers. It would be impious to attempt it on such a night as this. The Almighty is surely punishing them now! Come here, and look out.'

I followed him to the door, but the moment he opened it, the wind extinguished the lamp. Total darkness prevailed without, and a chaos of rushing, bursting, and moaning sounds swelled upon the ear with irregular loudness. The blast swept round the hut in violent eddyings, and we felt the chilly spray of the sea driving upon our faces at intervals. I shuddered, and the old man closed the door, and then resumed his seat near the fire.

My entertainer made a bed for me upon the floor, but the noise of the tempest, and the anxiety I felt about the fate of Angerstoff and Marietta, kept me awake the greater part of the night. Soon after dawn my host accompanied me down to the beach. We found the wreck of the floating beacon, but were unable to discover any traces of the guilty pair whom I had left on board of it.

THE MAN IN THE BELL

William Maginn

IN my younger days, bell-ringing was much more in fashion among the young men of ——, than it is now. Nobody, I believe, practises it there at present except the servants of the church, and the melody has been much injured in consequence. Some fifty years ago, about twenty of us who dwelt in the vicinity of the Cathedral, formed a club, which used to ring every peal that was called for; and, from continual practice and a rivalry which arose between us and a club attached to another steeple, and which tended considerably to sharpen our zeal, we became very Mozarts on our favourite instruments. But my bell-ringing practice was shortened by a singular accident, which not only stopt my performance, but made even the sound of a bell terrible to my ears.

One Sunday, I went with another into the belfry to ring for noon prayers, but the second stroke we had pulled shewed us that the clapper of the bell we were at was muffled. Some one had been buried that morning, and it had been prepared, of course, to ring a mournful note. We did not know of this, but the remedy was easy. 'Jack,' said my companion, 'step up to the loft, and cut off the hat;' for the way we had of muffling was by tying a piece of an old hat, or of cloth (the former was preferred) to one side of the clapper, which deadened every second toll. I complied, and mounting into the belfry, crept as usual into the bell, where I began to cut away. The hat had been tied on in some more complicated manner than usual, and I was perhaps three or four minutes in getting it off; during which time my companion below was hastily called away, by a message from his sweetheart I believe, but that is not material to my story. The person who called him was a brother of the club, who, knowing that the time had come for ringing for service, and not thinking that any one was above, began to pull. At this moment I was just getting out, when I felt the bell moving; I guessed the reason at once—it was a moment of terror; but by a hasty, and almost convulsive effort, I succeeded in jumping down, and throwing myself on the flat of my back under the bell.

The room in which it was, was little more than sufficient to contain it, the bottom of the bell coming within a couple of feet of the floor of lath. At that time I certainly was not so bulky as I am now, but as I lay it was within an inch of my face. I had not laid myself down a second, when the ringing began.—It was a dreadful situation. Over me swung an immense mass of metal, one touch of which would have crushed me to pieces; the floor under me was principally composed of crazy laths, and if they gave way, I was precipitated to the distance of about fifty feet upon a loft, which would, in all probability, have sunk under the impulse of my fall, and sent me to be dashed to atoms upon the marble floor of the chancel, an hundred feet below. I remembered—for fear is quick in recollection—how a common clock-wright, about a month before, had fallen, and bursting through the floors of the steeple, driven in the ceilings of the porch, and even broken into the marble tombstone of a bishop who slept beneath. This was my first terror, but the ringing had not continued a minute, before a more awful and immediate dread came on me. The deafening sound of the bell smote into my ears with a thunder which made me fear their drums would crack.—There was not a fibre of my body it did not thrill through: it entered my very soul; thought and reflection were almost utterly banished; I only retained the sensation of agonizing terror. Every moment I saw the bell sweep within an inch of my face; and my eyes—I could not close them, though to look at the object was bitter as death—followed it instinctively in its oscillating progress until it came back again. It was in vain I said to myself that it could come no nearer at any future swing than it did at first; every time it descended, I endeavoured to shrink into the very floor to avoid being buried under the down-sweeping mass; and then reflecting on the danger of pressing too weightily on my frail support, would cower up again as far as I dared.

At first my fears were mere matter of fact. I was afraid the pullies above would give way, and let the bell plunge on me. At another time, the possibility of the clapper being shot out in some sweep, and dashing through my body, as I had seen a ramrod glide through a door, flitted across my mind. The dread also, as I have already mentioned, of the crazy floor, tormented me, but these soon gave way to fears not more unfounded, but more visionary, and of course more tremendous. The roaring of the bell confused my intellect, and my fancy soon began to teem with all sort of strange and terrifying ideas. The bell pealing above, and opening its jaws with a hideous clamour, seemed to me at one time a ravening monster, raging to devour me; at another, a whirlpool ready to suck me into its bellowing abyss. As I gazed on it, it assumed all shapes; it was a flying eagle, or rather a roc of the Arabian story-tellers, clapping its wings and screaming over me. As I looked upward into it, it would appear sometimes to lengthen into indefinite extent, or to be twisted at the end into the spiral folds of the tail of a flying-dragon. Nor was the flaming breath, or fiery glance of that fabled animal, wanting to complete the picture. My eyes inflamed, bloodshot, and glaring, invested the supposed monster with a full proportion of unholy light.

It would be endless were I to merely hint at all the fancies that possessed my mind. Every object that was hideous and roaring presented itself to my imagination. I often thought that I was in a hurricane at sea, and that the vessel in which I was embarked tossed under me with the most furious vehemence. The air, set in motion by the swinging of the bell, blew over me, nearly with the violence, and more than the thunder of a tempest; and the floor seemed to reel under me, as under a drunken man. But the most awful of all the ideas that seized on me were drawn from the supernatural. In the vast cavern of the bell hideous faces appeared, and glared down on me with terrifying frowns, or with grinning mockery, still more appalling. At last, the devil himself, accoutred, as in the common description of the evil spirit, with hoof, horn, and tail, and eyes of infernal lustre, made his appearance, and called on me to curse God and worship him, who was powerful to save me. This dread suggestion he uttered with the full-toned clangour of the bell. I had him within an inch of me, and I thought on the fate of the Santon Barsisa.* Strenuously and desperately I defied him, and bade him be gone. Reason, then, for a moment, resumed her sway, but it was only to fill me with fresh terror, just as the lightning dispels the gloom that surrounds the benighted mariner, but to shew him that his vessel is driving on a rock, where she must inevitably be dashed to pieces. I found I was becoming delirious, and trembled lest reason should utterly desert me. This is at all times an agonizing thought, but it smote me then with tenfold agony. I feared lest, when utterly deprived of my senses, I should rise, to do which I was every moment tempted by that strange feeling which calls on a man, whose head is dizzy from standing on the battlement of a lofty castle, to precipitate himself from it, and then death would be instant and tremendous. When I thought of this, I became desperate. I caught the floor with a grasp which drove the blood from my nails; and I yelled with the cry of despair. I called for help, I prayed, I shouted, but all the efforts of my voice were, of course, drowned in the bell. As it passed over my mouth, it occasionally echoed my cries, which mixed not with its own sound, but preserved their distinct character. Perhaps this was but fancy. To me, I know, they then sounded as if they were the shouting, howling, or laughing of the fiends with which my imagination had peopled the gloomy cave which swung over me.

You may accuse me of exaggerating my feelings; but I am not. Many a scene of dread have I since passed through, but they are nothing to the self-inflicted terrors of this half hour. The ancients have doomed one of the damned, in their Tartarus, to lie under a rock, which every moment seems to be descending to annihilate him,*—and an awful punishment it would be. But if to this you add a clamour as loud as if ten thousand furies were howling about you—a deafening uproar banishing reason, and driving you to madness, you must allow that the bitterness of the pang was rendered more terrible. There is no man, firm as his nerves may be, who could retain his courage in this situation.

In twenty minutes the ringing was done. Half of that time passed over me without power of computation,—the other half appeared an age. When it ceased, I became gradually more quiet, but a new fear retained me. I knew that five minutes would elapse without ringing, but, at the end of that short time, the bell would be rung a second time for five minutes more. I could not calculate time. A minute and an hour were of equal duration. I feared to rise, lest the five minutes should have elapsed, and the ringing be again commenced, in which case I should be crushed, before I could escape, against the walls or frame-work of the bell. I therefore still continued to lie down, cautiously shifting myself, however, with a careful gliding, so that my eye no longer looked into the hollow. This was of itself a considerable relief. The cessation of the noise had, in a great measure, the effect of stupifying me, for my attention, being no longer occupied by the chimeras I had conjured up, began to flag. All that now distressed me was the constant expectation of the second ringing, for which, how-ever, I settled myself with a kind of stupid resolution. I closed my eyes, and clenched my teeth as firmly as if they were screwed in a vice. At last the dreaded moment came, and the first swing of the bell extorted a groan from me, as they say the most resolute victim screams at the sight of the rack, to which he is for a second time destined. After this, however, I lay silent and lethargic, without a thought. Wrapt in the de-fensive armour of stupidity, I defied the bell and its intona-tions. When it ceased, I was roused a little by the hope of escape. I did not, however, decide on this step hastily, but, putting up my hand with the utmost caution, I touched the rim. Though the ringing had ceased, it still was tremulous from the sound, and shook under my hand, which instantly recoiled as from an electric jar.* A quarter of an hour prob-ably elapsed before I again dared to make the experiment, and then I found it at rest. I determined to lose no time, fearing that I might have lain then already too long, and that the bell for evening service would catch me. This dread stimulated me, and I slipped out with the utmost rapidity, and arose. I stood, I suppose, for a minute, looking with silly wonder on the place of my imprisonment, penetrated with joy at escaping, but then rushed down the stony and irregular stair with the velocity of lightning, and arrived in the bell-ringer's room.

This was the last act I had power to accomplish. I leant against the wall, motionless and deprived of thought, in which posture my companions found me, when, in the course of a couple of hours, they returned to their occupation.

They were shocked, as well they might, at the figure before them. The wind of the bell had excoriated my face, and my dim and stupified eyes were fixed with a lack-lustre gaze in my raw eye-lids. My hands were torn and bleeding; my hair dishevelled; and my clothes tattered. They spoke to me, but I gave no answer. They shook me, but I remained insensible. They then became alarmed, and hastened to remove me. He who had first gone up with me in the forenoon, met them as they carried me through the church-yard, and through him, who was shocked at having, in some measure, occasioned the accident, the cause of my misfortune was discovered. I was put to bed at home, and remained for three days delirious, but gradually recovered my senses. You may be sure the bell formed a prominent topic of my ravings, and if I heard a peal, they were instantly increased to the utmost violence. Even when the delirium abated, my sleep was continually disturbed by imagined ringings, and my dreams were haunted by the fancies which almost maddened me while in the steeple. My friends removed me to a house in the country, which was sufficiently distant from any place of worship, to save me from the apprehensions of hearing the church-going bell; for what Alexander Selkirk, in Cowper's poem,* complained of as a misfortune, was then to me as a blessing. Here I recovered; but, even long after recovery, if a gale wafted the notes of a peal towards me, I started with nervous apprehension. I felt a Mahometan hatred to all the bell tribe, and envied the subjects of the Commander of the Faithful the sonorous voice of their Muezzin.* Time cured this, as it does the most of our follies; but, even at the present day, if, by chance, my nerves be un-strung, some particular tones of the cathedral bell have power to surprise me into a momentary start.

THE LAST MAN

Anonymous

I AWOKE as from a long and deep sleep. Whether I had been in a trance, or asleep, or dead, I knew not; neither did I seek to inquire. With that inconsistency that may often be remarked in dreams, I took the whole as a matter of course, and awoke with the full persuasion that the long sleep or trance in which I had been laid, had nothing in it either new or appalling. That it *had* been of long continuance I doubted not; indeed I thought that I knew that months and years had rolled over my head while I was wrapped in mysterious slumbers. Yet my recollection of the occurrences that had taken place before I had been lulled to sleep was perfect; and I had the most accurate remembrance of the spot on which I lay, and the plants and flowers that had been budding around me. Still there was all the mistiness of a vision cast over the time, and the cause of my having laid myself down. It was one of the vagaries of a dream, and I thought on it without wondering.

The spot on which I was lying was just at the entrance of a cave, that I fancied had been the scene of some of my brightest joys and my deepest sorrows. It was known to none save me, and to me it had been a place of refuge and a defence, for in the wildness of my dream I thought that I had been persecuted and hunted from the society of man; and that in that lone cave, and that romantic valley, I had found peace and security.

I lay with my back on the ground, and my head resting on my arm, so that when I opened my eyes, the first objects that I gazed on were the stars and the full moon; and the appearance that the heavens presented to me was so extraordinary, and at the same time so awful, because so unlike the silvery brightness of the sky on which I had last gazed, that I raised my head on my hand, and, leaning on my elbow, looked with a long and idiot stare on the moon and the stars, and the black expanse of ether.*

There was a dimness in the air—an unnatural dimness—not a haze or a thin mantle of clouds stretching over and obscuring the atmosphere—but a darkness—a broad shadow—spreading over, yet obscuring nothing, as if above the heavenly bodies had been spread an immense covering of clouds, that hid from them the light in which they moved and had their being.*

The moon was large and dark. It seemed to have approached so near the earth, that had it shone with its usual lustre, the seas, and the lands, and the forests, that I believed to exist in it, would have been all distinctly visible. As it was, it had no longer the fair round shape that I had so often gazed on with wonder.* The few rays of light that it emitted seemed thrown from hollow and highland—from rocks and from rugged declivities. It glared on me like a monstrous inhabitant of the air, and, as I shuddered beneath its broken light, I fancied that it was descending nearer and nearer to the earth, until it seemed about to settle down and crush me slowly and heavily to nothing. I turned from that terrible moon, and my eyes rested on stars and on planets, studded more thickly than imagination can conceive. They too were larger, and redder, and darker than they had been, and they shone more steadily through the clear darkness of the mysterious sky. They did not twinkle with varying and silvery beams—they were rather like little balls of smouldering fire, struggling with a suffocating atmosphere for existence.

I started up with a loud cry of despair,—I saw the whole reeling around me,—I felt as if I had been delirious,—mad,—I threw myself again on the flat rock, and again closed my eyes to shut out the dark fancies that on every side seemed to assail me,—a thousand wild ideas whirled through my brain,—I was dying,—I was dead,—I had perished at the mouth of that mossy cave,—I was in the land of spirits,—myself a spirit, and waiting for final doom in one of the worlds that I had seen sparkling around me. No, no,—I had not felt the pangs of dissolution, and my reason seemed to recall unto me all that I had suffered, and all that I had endured,—I repeated the list of my miseries,—it was perfect, but Death was not there.

I was delirious,—in a mad fever,—I felt helpless and weak, and the thought flashed across my mind that there I was left to die alone, and to struggle and fight with death in utter desolation,—the cave was known to none save me, and—as I imagined in my delirium—to one fair being whom I had loved, and who had visited my lonely cave as the messenger of joy and gladness. Then all the unconnected imaginations of a dream came rushing into my mind, and overwhelming me with thoughts of guilt and sorrow,—indistinctly marked out, and darkly understood, but pressing into my soul with all the freshness of a recent fact,—and I shrieked in agony; for I thought that I had murdered her, my meek and innocent love, and that now with my madness I was expiating the foulness of my crime.—No, no, no,—these visions passed away, and I knew that I had not been guilty,—but I thought—and I shook with a strong convulsion as I believed it to be true—I thought that I had sunk to sleep in her arms, and that the last sounds that I heard were the sweet murmurs of her voice.—Merciful heavens! she too is dead,—or she too has deserted me,—my shrieks, my convulsive agony, would else have aroused her. But *no*—I shook off these fancies with a strong effort, and again I hoped. I prayed that I might still be asleep, and still only suffering from the pressure of an agonizing dream. I roused myself—I called forth all my energies, and I again opened my eyes, and again saw the moon and the stars, and the unnatural heaven glaring on me through the darkness of the night, and again overpowered with the strong emotions that shook my reason, I fell to the ground in a swoon.

When I recovered, the scene was new. The moon and the stars had set, and the sun had arisen,—but still the same dark atmosphere, and the same mysterious sky. As yet, I saw not the sun, for my face was not in the direction of his rising. My courage was, however, revived, and I began to hope that all had been but one of the visions of the night. But when I raised my head, and looked around, I was amazed,—distracted,—I had lain down in a woody and romantic glen,—I looked around for the copse and hazel that had sheltered me,—I looked for the clear wild stream that fell in many a cascade from the rocks,—I listened for the song of the birds, and strained my ear to catch one sound of life or animation; no tree reared its green boughs to the morning sun,—all was silent, and lone, and gloomy,—nothing was there but grey rocks, that seemed fast hastening to decay, and the old roots of some immense trees, that seemed to have grown, and flourished, and died there.

I raised myself until I sat upright. Horrible was the palsy that fell on my senses when I saw the cave—the very cave that I had seen covered with moss, and the wild shrubs of the forest, standing as grim and as dark as the grave, without one leaf of verdure to adorn it, without one single bush to hide it; there it was, grey and mouldering; and there lay the beautiful vale, one dreadful mass of rocky desolation, with a wide, dry channel winding along what had once been the foot of a green valley.

I looked around on that inclosed glen as far as my eye could reach, but all was dark and dreary, all seemed alike hastening to decay. The rocks had fallen in huge fragments, and among these fragments appeared large roots and decayed trunks of trees, not clothed with moss, or with mushrooms, springing up from the moist wood, but dry, and old, and wasted. I well remembered, that in that valley no tree of larger growth than the hazel, or the wild rose, had found room or nourishment, yet there lay large trees among the black masses of rock, and it was evident that there they had grown and died.

Some dreadful convulsion must have taken place—yet it was not the rapid devastation of an earthquake. The slow finger of time was there, and every object bore marks of the lapse of years—ay, of centuries. Rocks had mouldered away—young trees and bushes had grown up, and come to maturity, and perished, while I was wrapped in oblivion. And yet, now that I saw, and knew that it was only through many a year having passed by, that all these changes had been effected, even now my senses recovered in some measure from the delirious excitement of the first surprise, and, such is the inconsistency of a dream, I almost fancied that all this desolation had been a thing to be looked for and expected, for *then*, for the first time, I remembered that during my long sleep I thought that I knew, that days and months, and years, were rolling over me in rapid and noiseless succession.

No sooner had this idea seized my mind—no sooner did I

conceive that I had indeed slept—that I had indeed lain in silent insensibility, until wood, and rock, and river, had dried up, or fallen beneath the hand of time—that the moon and the stars—and, prepared as I was for wonders, I started, as at that instant I instinctively turned towards that part of the heavens in which the sun was to make his appearance; prepared as I was, I started when I beheld his huge round bulk heaving slowly above the barrier of rocks that surrounded me. His was no longer the piercing ray, the dazzling, the pure and colourless light, that had shed glory and radiance on the world on which I had closed my eyes—he was now a dark round orb of reddish flame. He had sunk nearer the earth as he approached nearer the close of his career, and he too seemed to share with the heaven and the earth the symptoms of decay and dissolution.

When I saw universal nature thus worn out and exhausted—thus perishing from old age, and expiring from the sheer want of renewing materials, then I thought that surely my frail body must likewise have waxed old and infirm—surely I too must be bowed down with age and weariness.

I raised myself slowly and fearfully from the earth, and at length I stood upright. There I stood unscathed by time—fresh and vigorous as when last I walked on the surface of a green and beautiful world—my frame as firmly knit, and my every limb as active as if a few brief hours, instead of many and long years, had witnessed me extended on that broad platform of rock.

At first a sudden gleam of joy broke on my soul, when I thought that here I stood unharmed by time—that I at least had lost nothing of life by the wonderful visitation that had befallen me.

I felt as if I could fly away from this scene of devastation, and in other climes seek for fresher skies and more verdant vales. Alas! alas! I soon and easily gained the top of the rising bank, and fixed my eyes on the wide landscape of a desolate and unpeopled world. Desolation! Desolation! I knew that it was to be dreaded as a fearful and a terrible thing, and I had felt the sorrows of a lone and helpless spirit—but never, never had I conceived the full misery that is contained in that one awful word, until I stood on the brow of that hill, and looked on the wide and wasted world that lay stretched in one vast desert before me.

Then despair and dread indeed laid hold of me—then dark visions of woe and of loneliness rose indistinctly before me—thoughts of nights and days of never-ending darkness and cold—and then the miseries of hunger and of slow decay and starvation, and hopeless destitution—and then the hard struggle to live, and the still harder struggle of youth and strength to die——Dark visions of woe, where fled ye? before what angel of light hid ye your diminished heads? The sum of my miseries seemed to overwhelm me—a loud sound, as of one universal crash of dissolving nature, rung in my ears—I gave one wild shriek—one convulsive struggle—and—*awoke*——and there stood my man John, with my shaving-jug in the one hand, and my well-cleaned boots in the other—his mouth open, and his eyes rolling hideously at thus witnessing the frolics of his staid and quiet master.

By his entrance were these visions dispelled, else Lord knows how long I might have lingered out my existence in that dreary world, or what woes and unspeakable miseries had been in store for χ^{β}.

LE REVENANT*

Henry Thomson

'There are but two classes of persons in the world—
those who are hanged, and those who are not hanged;
and it has been my lot to belong to the former.'

THERE are few men, perhaps, who have not a hundred times
in the course of life, felt a curiosity to know what their sensations would be if they were compelled to lay life down. The
very impossibility, in all ordinary cases, of obtaining any approach to this knowledge, is an incessant spur pressing on the
fancy in its endeavours to arrive at it. Thus poets and painters
have ever made the estate of a man condemned to die, one of
their favourite themes of comment or description. Footboys
and 'prentices hang themselves almost every other day, con-
clusively—missing their arrangement for slipping the knot half
way—out of a seeming instinct to try the secrets of that fate,
which—less in jest than earnest—they feel an inward moni-
tion may become their own. And thousands of men, in early
life, are uneasy until they have mounted a breach, or fought a
duel, merely because they wish to know, experimentally, that
their nerves are capable of carrying them through that peculiar
ordeal. Now *I* am in a situation to speak, from experience,
upon that very interesting question—the sensations attendant
upon a passage from life to death. I have been HANGED, and
am ALIVE—perhaps there are not three other men, at this
moment, in Europe, who can make the same declaration. Before
this statement meets the public eye, I shall have quitted England for ever; therefore I have no advantage to gain from its
publication. And, for the vanity of knowing, when I shall be
a sojourner in a far country, that my name—for good or ill—
is talked about in this,—such fame would scarcely do even my
pride much good, when I dare not lay claim to its identity.
But the cause which excites me to write is this—My greatest

pleasure, through life, has been the perusal of any extraordinary narratives of fact. An account of a shipwreck in which hundreds have perished; of a plague which has depopulated towns or cities; anecdotes and inquiries connected with the regulation of prisons, hospitals, or lunatic receptacles; nay, the very police reports of a common newspaper—as relative to matters of reality; have always excited a degree of interest in my mind which cannot be produced by the best invented tale of fiction. Because I believe, therefore, that, to persons of a temper like my own, the reading that which I have to relate will afford very high gratification;—and because I know also, that what I describe can do mischief to no one, while it may prevent the symptoms and details of a very rare consummation from being lost;—for these reasons I am desirous, as far as a very limited education will permit me, to write a plain history of the strange fortunes and miseries to which, during the last twelve months, I have been subjected.

I have stated already, that I have *been* hanged and *am* alive. I can gain nothing now by misrepresentation—I was GUILTY of the act for which I suffered. There are individuals of respectability whom my conduct already has disgraced, and I will not revive their shame and grief by publishing my name. But it stands in the list of capital convictions in the Old Bailey Calendar for the Winter Sessions 1826; and this reference, coupled with a few of the facts which follow, will be sufficient to guide any persons who are doubtful, to the proof that my statement is a true one. In the year 1824, I was a clerk in a Russia broker's house, and fagged between Broad Street Buildings and Batson's Coffeehouse, and the London Docks, from nine in the morning to six in the evening, for a salary of fifty pounds a-year. I did this—not contentedly—but I endured it; living sparingly in a little lodging at Islington for two years; till I fell in love with a poor, but very beautiful girl, who was honest where it was very hard to be honest; and worked twelve hours a-day at sewing and millinery, in a mercer's shop in Cheapside, for half a guinea a-week. To make short of a long tale—this girl did not know how poor I was; and, in about six months, I committed seven or eight forgeries, to the amount of near two hundred pounds. I was seized one morning—I

expected it for weeks,—as regularly as I awoke—every morning; and carried, after a very few questions, for examination
before the Lord Mayor. At the Mansion-House I had nothing
to plead. Fortunately my motions had not been watched; and
so no one but myself was implicated in the charge—as no one
else was really guilty. A sort of instinct to try the last hope
made me listen to the magistrate's caution, and remain silent;
or else, for any chance of escape I had, I might as well have
confessed the whole truth at once. The examination lasted
about half an hour; when I was fully committed for trial, and
sent away to Newgate.*

The shock of my first arrest was very slight indeed; indeed
I almost question if it was not a relief, rather than a shock, to
me. For months, I had known perfectly that my eventual discovery was certain. I tried to shake the thought of this off; but
it was of no use—I dreamed of it even in my sleep; and I never
entered our counting-house of a morning, or saw my master
take up the cash-book in the course of the day, that my heart
was not up in my mouth, and my hand shook so that I could
not hold the pen—for twenty minutes afterwards, I was sure
to do nothing but blunder. Until, at last, when I saw our chief
clerk walk into the room, on New Year's morning, with a
police officer, I was as ready for what followed, as if I had had
six hours' conversation about it. I do not believe I showed—
for I am sure I did not feel it—either surprise or alarm. My
'fortune,' however, as the officer called it, was soon told. I was
apprehended on the 1st of January; and the Sessions being
then just begun, my time came rapidly round. On the 4th of
the same month, the London Grand Jury found three Bills
against me for forgery; and, on the evening of the 5th, the
Judge exhorted me to 'prepare for death;' for 'there was no
hope, that, in this world, mercy could be extended to me.'

The whole business of my trial and sentence, passed over as
coolly and formally, as I would have calculated a question of
interest or summed up an underwriting account. I had never,
though I lived in London, witnessed the proceedings of a
Criminal Court before; and I could hardly believe the composure, and indifference—and yet civility—for there was no show
of anger or ill temper—with which I was treated; together

with the apparent perfect insensibility of all the parties round me, while I was rolling on—with a speed which nothing could check and which increased every moment—to my ruin! I was called suddenly up from the dock, when my turn for trial came, and placed at the bar; and the Judge asked, in a tone which had neither severity about it, nor compassion—nor carelessness, nor anxiety—nor any character or expression whatever that could be distinguished—'If there was any counsel appeared for the prosecution?' A barrister then, who seemed to have some consideration—a middle aged, gentlemanly looking man —stated the case against me—as he said he would do—very 'fairly and forbearingly;' but, as soon as he read the facts from his brief, that only—I heard an officer of the gaol, who stood behind me, say—'put the rope about my neck.' My master then was called to give his evidence; which he did very temperately—but it was conclusive; a young gentleman, who was my counsel, asked a few questions in cross-examination, after he had carefully looked over the indictment: but there was nothing to cross-examine upon—I knew that well enough— though I was thankful for the interest he seemed to take in my case. The Judge then told me, I thought more gravely than he had spoken before, 'That it was time for me to speak in my defence, if I had anything to say.' I had nothing to say. I thought one moment to drop down upon my knees, and beg for mercy;—but, again—I thought it would only make me look ridiculous; and I only answered—as well as I could— 'That I would not trouble the Court with any defence.' Upon this, the Judge turned round with a more serious air still, to the Jury, who stood up all to listen to him as he spoke. And I listened too—or tried to listen attentively—as hard as I could; and yet—with all I could do—I could not keep my thoughts from wandering! For the sight of the Court—all so orderly, and regular, and composed, and formal, and well satisfied— spectators and all—while I was running on with the speed of wheels upon smooth soil downhill, to destruction—seemed as if the whole trial were a dream, and not a thing in earnest! The barristers sat round the table, silent, but utterly unconcerned, and two were looking over their briefs, and another was reading a newspaper; and the spectators in the galleries looked on and listened as pleasantly, as though it were a matter not of death going on, but of pastime or amusement; and one very fat man, who seemed to be the clerk of the Court, stopped his writing when the Judge began, but leaned back in his chair with his hands in his breeches' pockets, except once or twice that he took a snuff; and not one living soul seemed to take notice—they did not seem to know the fact—that there was a poor, desperate, helpless, creature—whose days were fast running out—whose hours of life were even with the last grains in the bottom of the sand glass—among them! I lost the whole of the Judge's charge thinking of I know not what—in a sort of dream—unable to steady my mind to anything, and only biting the stalk of a piece of rosemary that lay by me. But I heard the low, distinct whisper of the Foreman of the Jury, as he brought in the verdict—'GUILTY,'—and the last words of the Judge, saying—'that I should be hanged by the neck until I was dead;' and bidding me 'prepare myself for the next life, for that my crime was one that admitted of no mercy in this.' The gaoler then, who had stood close by me all the while, put his hand quickly upon my shoulder, in an under voice, telling me, to 'Come along!' Going down the hall steps, two other officers met me; and, placing me between them, without saying a word, hurried me across the yard in the direction back to the prison. As the door of the court closed behind us, I saw the Judge fold up his papers, and the Jury being sworn in the next case. Two other culprits were brought up out of the dock; and the crier called out for—'The prosecutor and witnesses against James Hawkins, and Joseph Sanderson, for burglary!'

I had no friends, if any in such a case could have been of use to me—no relatives but two; by whom—I could not complain of them—I was at once disowned. On the day after my trial, my master came to me in person, and told me, that 'he had recommended me to mercy, and should try to obtain a mitigation of my sentence.' I don't think I seemed very grateful for this assurance—I thought, that if he had wished to spare my life he might have made sure, by not appearing against me. I thanked him; but the colour was in my face—and the worst feelings that ever rose in my heart in all my life were at this visit. I thought he was not a wise man to come into my cell at that time—though he did not come alone.—But the thing went no farther.

There was but one person then in all the world that seemed to belong to me; and that one was Elizabeth Clare! And, when I thought of her, the idea of all that was to happen to myself was forgotten—I covered my face with my hands, and cast myself on the ground; and I wept, for I was in desperation. While I was being examined, and my desk searched for papers at home, before I was carried to the Mansion-house, I had got an opportunity to send one word to her,—'That if she wished me only to try for my life, she should not come, nor send, nor be known in any way in my misfortune.' But my scheme was to no purpose. She had gone wild as soon as she had heard the news of my apprehension—never thought of herself, but confessed her acquaintance with me. The result was, she was dismissed from her employment—and it was her only means of livelihood.

She had been every where,—to my master—to the judge that tried me—to the magistrates—to the sheriffs—to the aldermen—she had made her way even to the Secretary of State! My heart did misgive me at the thought of death; but, in despite of myself, I forgot fear when I missed her usual time of coming, and gathered from the people about me how she was employed. I had no thought about the success or failure of her attempt. All my thoughts were,—that she was a young girl, and beautiful—hardly in her senses, and quite unprotected—without money to help, or a friend to advise her—pleading to strangers—humbling herself perhaps to menials, who would think her very despair and helpless condition, a challenge to infamy and insult. Well, it mattered little! The thing was no worse, because I was alive to see and suffer from it. Two days more, and all would be over; the demons that fed on human wretchedness would have their prey. She would be homeless—pennyless—friendless,—she would have been the companion of a forger and a felon; it needed no witchcraft to guess the termination.

We hear curiously, and read every day, of the visits of friends and relatives to wretched criminals condemned to die. Those who read and hear of these things the most curiously, have little impression of the sadness of the reality. It was six days after my first apprehension when Elizabeth Clare came, for the last time, to visit me in prison! In only these short six days her beauty, health, strength—all were gone; years upon years of toil and sickness could not have left a more worn-out wreck. Death—as plainly as ever death spoke—sat in her countenance—she was broken-hearted. When she came, I had not seen her for two days. I could not speak, and there was an officer of the prison with us too: I was the property of the law now; and my mother, if she had lived, could not have blest, or wept for me, without a third person, and that a stranger, being present. I sat down by her on my bedstead, which was the only place to sit on in my cell, and wrapped her shawl close round her, for it was very cold weather, and I was allowed no fire; and we sat so for almost an hour without exchanging a word. She had no good news to bring me; I knew that; all I wanted to hear was about herself. I did hear! She had not a help—nor a hope—nor a prop left, upon the earth! The only creature that sheltered her—the only relative she had—was a married sister, whose husband I knew to be a villain. What would she do—what could she attempt? She 'did not know that;' and 'it was not long that she should be a trouble to any body.' But 'she should go to Lord S—— again that evening about me. He had treated her kindly; and she felt certain she should still succeed. It was her fault—she had told every body this—all that had happened: if it had not been for meeting her, I should never have gone into debt, and into extravagance.' I listened—and I could only listen! I would have died—coward as I was—upon the rack, or in the fire, so I could but have left her safe. I did not ask so much as to leave her happy! Oh then I did think, in bitterness of spirit, if I had but shunned temptation, and staid poor and honest! If I could only have placed her once more in the hard laborious poverty where I had first found her! It was my work, and she never could be there again! How long this vain remorse might have lasted, I cannot tell. My head was light and giddy! I understood the glance of the turnkey, who was watching me—'That Elizabeth must be got away;' but I had not strength even to attempt it. The thing had been arranged for me. The master of the gaol entered. She went—it was then the afternoon; and she was got away, on the pretence that she might make one more effort to save me, with a promise that she should return again at night. The master was an elderly man, who had daughters of his own; and he promised—for he saw I knew how the matter was—to see Elizabeth safe through the crowd of wretches among whom she must pass to quit the prison. She went, and I knew that she was going for ever. As she turned back to speak as the door was closing, I knew that I had seen her for the last time. The door of my cell closed. We were to meet no more on earth. I fell upon my knees—I clasped my hands—my tears burst out afresh—and I called on God to bless her.

It was four o'clock in the afternoon when Elizabeth left me; and when she departed, it seemed as if my business in this world was at an end. I could have wished, then and there, to have died upon the spot; I had done my last act, and drank my last draught in life. But, as the twilight drew in, my cell was cold and damp; and the evening was dark and gloomy; and I had no fire, nor any candle, although it was in the month of January, nor much covering to warm me; and by degrees my spirits weakened, and my heart sunk at the desolate wretchedness of everything about me; and gradually—for what I write now shall be the truth—the thoughts of Elizabeth, and what would be her fate, began to give way before a sense of my own situation. This was the first time—I cannot tell the reason why—that my mind had ever fixed itself fully upon the trial that I had, within a few hours, to go through; and, as I reflected on it, a terror spread over me almost in an instant, as though it were that my sentence was just pronounced, and that I had not known, really and seriously, that I was to die, before. I had eaten nothing for twenty-four hours. There was food, which a religious gentleman who visited me had sent from his own table, but I could not taste it; and when I looked at it, strange fancies came over me. It was dainty food—not such as was served to the prisoners in the gaol. It was sent to me because I was to die to-morrow! and I thought of the beasts of the field, and the fowls of the air, that were pampered for slaughter. I felt that my own sensations were not as they ought to be at this time; and I believe that, for a while, I was insane. A sort of dull humming noise, that I could not get rid of, like the buzzing of bees, sounded in my ears. And though it was dark, sparks of light seemed to dance before my eyes; and I could recollect nothing. I tried to say my prayers, but could only remember a word here and there; and then it seemed to me as if these were blasphemies that I was uttering;— I don't know what they were—I cannot tell what it was I said; and then, on a sudden, I felt as though all this terror was useless, and that I would not stay there to die; and I jumped up, and wrenched at the bars of my cell window with a force that bent them—for I felt as if I had the strength of a lion. And I felt all over the lock of my door; and tried the door itself with my shoulder—though I knew it was plated with iron, and heavier than that of a church; and I groped about the very walls, and into the corners of my dungeon—though I knew very well, if I had had my senses, that it was all of solid stone three feet thick; and that, if I could have passed through a crevice smaller than the eye of a needle, I had no chance of escaping. And, in the midst all this exertion, a faintness came over me as though I had swallowed poison; and I had just power to reel to the bed-place, where I sank down, as I think, in a swoon: but this did not last,—for my head swam round, and the cell seemed to turn with me; and I dreamed—between sleeping and waking—that it was midnight, and that Elizabeth had come back as she had promised, and that they refused to admit her. And I thought that it snowed heavily, and that the streets were all covered with it as if with a white sheet, and that I saw her dead—lying in the fallen snow—and in the darkness—at the prison gate! When I came to myself, I was struggling and breathless. In a minute or two, I heard St Sepulchre's clock go ten; and I knew it was a dream that I had had; but I could not help fancying that Elizabeth really had come back. And I knocked loudly at the door of my cell; and, when one of the turnkeys came, I begged of him, for mercy's sake, to go down to the gate and see; and moreover, to take a small bundle, containing two shirts—which I pushed to him through the grate—for I had no money; and—if he would have my blessing—to bring me but one small cup of brandy to keep my heart alive; for I felt that I had not the strength of a man, and should never be able to go through my trial like one. The turnkey shook his head at my request, as he went away; and said that he had not the brandy, even if he dared run the risk to give it me. But, in a few minutes, he returned, bringing me a glass of wine, which he said the master of the gaol had sent me, and hoped it would do me good,—however, he would take nothing for it. And the chaplain of the prison, too, came, without my sending; and—for which I shall ever have cause to thank him—went himself down to the outer gates of the gaol, and pledged his honour as a man and a Christian clergyman, that Elizabeth was not there, nor had returned; and moreover, he assured me that it was not likely she would come back, for her friends had been told privately that she could not be admitted: but nevertheless, he should himself be up during the whole night; and if she should come, although she could not be allowed to see me, he would take care that she should have kind treatment and protection; and I had reason afterwards to know that he kept his word. He then exhorted me solemnly 'to think no more of cares or troubles in this world, but to bend my thoughts upon that to come, and to try to reconcile my soul to Heaven; trusting that my sins, though they were heavy, under repentance, might have hope of mercy.' When he was gone, I did find myself, for a little while, more collected; and I sat down again on the bed, and tried seriously to commune with myself, and prepare myself for my fate. I recalled to my mind, that I had but a few hours more at all events to live—that there was no hope on earth of escaping—and that it was at least better that I should die decently and like a man. Then I tried to recollect all the tales that I had ever heard about death by hanging—that it was said to be the sensation of a moment—to give no pain— to cause the extinction of life instantaneously—and so on, to twenty other strange ideas. By degrees, my head began to wander and grow unmanageable again. I put my hands tightly to my throat, as though to try the sensation of strangling. Then I felt my arms at the places where the cords would be tied. I went through the fastening of the rope—the tying of the hands together: the thing that I felt most averse to, was the having the white cap muffled over my eyes and face. If I could avoid that, the rest was not so very horrible! In the midst of these fancies, a numbness seemed to creep over my senses. The giddiness that I had felt, gave way to a dull stupor, which lessened the pain that my thoughts gave me, though I still went on thinking. The church clock rang midnight: I was sensible of the sound, but it reached me indistinctly—as though coming through many closed doors, or from a far distance. By and by, I saw the objects before my mind less and less clearly—then only partially—then they were gone altogether. I fell asleep.

I slept until the hour of execution. It was seven o'clock on the next morning, when a knocking at the door of my cell awoke me. I heard the sound, as though in my dreams, for some moments before I was fully awake; and my first sensation was only the dislike which a weary man feels at being roused: I was tired, and wished to doze on. In a minute after, the bolts on the outside of my dungeon were drawn; a turnkey, carrying a small lamp, and followed by the master of the gaol and the chaplain, entered: I looked up—a shudder like the shock of electricity—like a plunge into a bath of ice—ran through me—one glance was sufficient: Sleep was gone as though I had never slept: even as I never was to sleep again— I was conscious of my situation! 'R——,' said the master to me, in a subdued, but steady tone, 'It is time for you to rise.' The chaplain asked me how I had passed the night? and proposed that we should join in prayer. I gathered myself up, and remained seated on the side of the bed-place. My teeth chattered, and my knees knocked together in despite of myself. It was barely daylight yet; and, as the cell door stood open, I could see into the small paved court beyond: the morning was thick and gloomy; and a slow, but settled, rain was coming down. 'It is half-past seven o'clock, R——!' said the master. I just mustered an entreaty to be left alone till the last moment. I had thirty minutes to live.

I tried to make another observation when the master was leaving the cell; but, this time, I could not get the words out: my tongue stuck to the roof of my mouth, and my speech seemed gone: I made two desperate efforts; but it would not do—I could not utter. When they left me, I never stirred from my place on the bed. I was benumbed with the cold, probably from the sleep and the unaccustomed exposure; and I sat crouched together, as it were, to keep myself warmer, with my arms folded across my breast, and my head hanging down, shivering; and my body felt as if it were such a weight to me that I was unable to move it, or stir. The day now was breaking, yellow,—and heavily; and the light stole by degrees into my dungeon, showing me the damp stone walls and desolate dark paved floor; and, strange as it was—with all that I could do, I could not keep myself from noticing these trifling things—though perdition was coming upon me the very next moment. I noticed the lamp which the turnkey had left on the floor, and which was burning dimly, with a long wick, being clogged with the chill and bad air, and I thought to myself—even at that moment—that it had not been trimmed since the night before. And I looked at the bare, naked, iron bedframe that I sat on; and at the heavy studs on the door of the dungeon; and at the scrawls and writing upon the wall, that had been drawn by former prisoners; and I put my hand to try my own pulse, and it was so low that I could hardly count it:—I could not feel—though I tried to make myself feel it—that I was going to DIE. In the midst of this, I heard the chime of the chapel clock begin to strike; and I thought—Lord take pity on me, a wretch!—it could not be the three quarters after seven yet! The clock went over the three quarters—it chimed the fourth quarter, and struck eight. They were in my cell before I perceived them. They found me in the place, and in the posture, as they had left me.

What I have farther to tell will lie in a very small compass: my recollections are very minute up to this point, but not at all so close as to what occurred afterwards. I scarcely recollect very clearly how I got from my cell to the press-room. I think two little withered men, dressed in black, supported me. I know I tried to rise when I saw the master and his people come into my dungeon; but I could not.

In the press-room were the two miserable wretches that were to suffer with me; they were bound, with their arms behind them, and their hands together; and were lying upon a bench hard by, until I was ready. A meagre-looking old man, with thin white hair, who was reading to one of them, came up, and said something—'That we ought to embrace,'— I did not distinctly hear what it was.

The great difficulty that I had was to keep from falling. I had thought that these moments would have been all of fury and horror, but I felt nothing of this; but only a weakness, as though my heart—and the very floor on which I stood—was sinking under me. I could just make a motion, that the old white-haired man should leave me; and some one interfered, and sent him away. The pinioning of my hands and arms was then finished; and I heard an officer whisper to the chaplain that 'all was ready.' As we passed out, one of the men in black held a glass of water to my lips; but I could not swallow: and Mr W——, the master of the gaol, who had bid farewell to my companions, offered me his hand. The blood rushed into my face once more for one moment! It was too much—the man who was sending me to execution, to offer to shake me by the hand!

This was the last moment—but one—of full perception, that I had in life. I remember our beginning to move forward, through the long arched passages which led from the press-room to the scaffold. I saw the lamps that were still burning, for the day-light never entered here: I heard the quick tolling of the bell, and the deep voice of the chaplain reading as he walked before us—

'I am the resurrection and the life, saith the Lord; he that believeth in me, though he were dead, shall live. And though after my skin worms destroy this body, yet in my flesh shall I see God!'

It was the funeral service—the order for the grave—the office for those that were senseless and dead—over us, the quick and the living.

I felt once more—and saw! I felt the transition from these dim, close, hot, lamp-lighted subterranean passages, to the open platform, and steps, at the foot of the scaffold, and to day. I saw the immense crowd blackening the whole area of the street below me. The windows of the shops and houses opposite, to the fourth story, choaked with gazers. I saw St Sepulchre's church through the yellow fog in the distance, and heard the pealing of its bell. I recollect the cloudy, misty morning; the wet that lay upon the scaffold—the huge dark mass of building, the prison itself, that rose beside, and seemed to cast a shadow over us—the cold, fresh breeze, that as I emerged from it, broke upon my face. I see it all now—the whole horrible landscape is before me. The scaffold—the rain—the faces of the multitude—the people clinging to the house-tops—the smoke that beat heavily downwards from the chimneys—the waggons filled with women, staring in the inn-yards opposite—the hoarse low roar that ran through the gathered crowd as we appeared. I never saw so many objects at once, so plainly and distinctly, in all my life, as at that one glance; but it lasted only for an instant.

From that look, and from that instant, all that followed is a blank. Of the prayers of the Chaplain; of the fastening the fatal noose; of the putting on of the cap which I had so much disliked; of my actual *execution* and *death*, I have not the slightest atom of recollection. But that I know such occurrences must have taken place, I should not have the smallest consciousness that they ever did so. I read in the daily newspapers, an account of my behaviour at the scaffold—that I conducted myself decently, but with firmness—Of my death—that I seemed to die almost without a struggle. Of any of these events I have not been able, by any exertion, to recall the most distant remembrance. With the first view of the scaffold, all my recollection ceases. The next circumstance, which—to my perception—seems to follow, is the having awoke, as if from sleep, and found myself in a bed, in a handsome chamber; with a gentleman—as I first opened my eyes—looking attentively at me. I had my senses perfectly, though I did not speak at once. I thought directly, that I had been reprieved at the scaffold, and had fainted. After I knew the truth, I thought that I had an imperfect recollection, of having found, or fancied, myself—as in a dream—in some strange place lying naked, and with a mass of figures floating about before me: but this idea certainly never presented itself to me until I was informed of the fact that it had occurred.

The accident to which I owe my existence, will have been

divined! My condition is a strange one! I am a living man; and I possess certificates both of my death and burial. I know that a coffin filled with stones, and with my name upon the plate, lies buried in the churchyard of St Andrew's, Holborn: I saw, from a window, the undressed hearse arrive that carried it: I was a witness to my own funeral: these are strange things to see. My dangers, however, and I trust, my crimes, are over for ever. Thanks to the bounty of the excellent individual, whose benevolence has recognised the service which he did me for a claim upon him, I am married to the woman, whose happiness and safety proved my last thought—so long as reason remained with me—in dying. And I am about to sail upon a far voyage, which is only a sorrowful one—that it parts me for ever from my benefactor. The fancy that this poor narrative—from the singularity of the facts it relates—may be interesting to some people, has induced me to write it: perhaps at too much length; but it is not easy for those who write without skill, to write briefly. Should it meet the eye of the few relatives I have, it will tell *one* of them—that, to his jealousy of being known in connexion with me—even *after death*—I owe my *life*. Should my old master read it, perhaps, by this time, he may have thought I suffered severely for yielding to a first temptation; at least—while I bear him no ill will—I will not believe that he will learn my deliverance with regret. For the words are soon spoken, and the act is soon done, which dooms a wretched creature to an untimely death; but bitter are the pangs—and the sufferings of the body are among the least of them—that he must go through before he arrives at it!

THE MURDER HOLE

Catherine Sinclair

Ah, frantic Fear!
I see, I see thee near;
I know thy hurried step, thy hagard eye!
Like thee I start, like thee disorder'd fly!

Collins*

In a remote district of country belonging to Lord Cassillis, between Ayrshire and Galloway, about three hundred years ago, a moor of apparently boundless extent stretched several miles along the road, and wearied the eye of the traveller by the sameness and desolation of its appearance; not a tree varied the prospect—not a shrub enlivened the eye by its freshness —nor a native flower bloomed to adorn this ungenial soil. One 'lonesome desert'* reached the horizon on every side, with nothing to mark that any mortal had ever visited the scene before, except a few rude huts that were scattered near its centre; and a road, or rather pathway, for those whom business or necessity obliged to pass in that direction. At length, deserted as this wild region had always been, it became still more gloomy. Strange rumours arose, that the path of unwary travellers had been beset on this 'blasted heath,'* and that treachery and murder had intercepted the solitary stranger as he traversed its dreary extent. When several persons, who were known to have passed that way, mysteriously disappeared, the inquiries of their relatives led to a strict and anxious investigation; but though the officers of justice were sent to scour the country, and examine the inhabitants, not a trace could be obtained of the persons in question, nor of any place of concealment which could be a refuge for the lawless or desperate to horde in. Yet, as inquiry became stricter, and the disappearance of individuals more frequent, the simple inhabitants of the neighbouring hamlet were agitated by the most fearful

apprehensions. Some declared that the death-like stillness of
the night was often interrupted by sudden and preternatural
cries of more than mortal anguish, which seemed to arise in
the distance; and a shepherd one evening, who had lost his
way on the moor, declared he had approached three mysterious figures, who seemed struggling against each other with
supernatural energy, till at length one of them, with a frightful
scream, suddenly sunk into the earth.

Gradually the inhabitants deserted their dwellings on the
heath, and settled in distant quarters, till at length but one of
the cottages continued to be inhabited by an old woman and
her two sons, who loudly lamented that poverty chained them
to this solitary and mysterious spot. Travellers who frequented
this road now generally did so in groups to protect each other;
and if night overtook them, they usually stopped at the humble
cottage of the old woman and her sons, where cleanliness compensated for the want of luxury, and where, over a blazing fire
of peat, the bolder spirits smiled at the imaginary terrors of
the road, and the more timid trembled as they listened to the
tales of terror and affright with which their hosts entertained
them.

One gloomy and tempestuous night in November, a pedlar
boy hastily traversed the moor. Terrified to find himself involved in darkness amidst its boundless wastes, a thousand
frightful traditions, connected with this dreary scene, darted
across his mind—every blast, as it swept in hollow gusts over
the heath, seemed to teem with the sighs of departed spirits—
and the birds, as they winged their way above his head, appeared, with loud and shrill cries, to warn him of approaching
danger. The whistle with which he usually beguiled his weary
pilgrimage died away into silence, and he groped along with
trembling and uncertain steps, which sounded too loudly in
his ears. The promise of Scripture occurred to his memory,
and revived his courage. 'I will be unto thee as a rock in the
desert, and as an hiding-place in the storm.'* *Surely*, thought
he, *though alone, I am not forsaken*; and a prayer for assistance hovered on his lips.

A light now glimmered in the distance which would lead
him, he conjectured, to the cottage of the old woman; and

towards that he eagerly bent his way, remembering as he hastened along, that when he had visited it the year before, it was in company with a large party of travellers, who had beguiled the evening with those tales of mystery which had so lately filled his brain with images of terror. He recollected, too, how anxiously the old woman and her sons had endeavoured to detain him when the other travellers were departing; and now, therefore, he confidently anticipated a cordial and cheering reception. His first call for admission obtained no visible marks of attention, but instantly the greatest noise and confusion prevailed within the cottage. They think it is one of the supernatural visitants of whom the old lady talks so much, thought the boy, approaching a window, where the light within shewed him all the inhabitants at their several occupations; the old woman was hastily scrubbing the stone floor, and strewing it thickly over with sand, while her two sons seemed with equal haste to be thrusting something large and heavy into an immense chest, which they carefully locked. The boy, in a frolicsome mood, thoughtlessly tapped at the window, when they all instantly started up with consternation so strongly depicted on their countenances, that he shrunk back involuntarily with an undefined feeling of apprehension; but before he had time to reflect a moment longer, one of the men suddenly darted out at the door, and seizing the boy roughly by the shoulder, dragged him violently into the cottage. 'I am not what you take me for,' said the boy, attempting to laugh, 'but only the poor pedlar who visited you last year.' 'Are you *alone*?' inquired the old woman, in a harsh deep tone, which made his heart thrill with apprehension. 'Yes,' said the boy, 'I am alone *here*; and alas!' he added, with a burst of uncontrollable feeling, 'I am alone in the wide world also! Not a person exists who would assist me in distress, or shed a single tear if I died this very night.' '*Then* you are welcome!' said one of the men with a sneer, while he cast a glance of peculiar expression at the other inhabitants of the cottage.

It was with a shiver of apprehension, rather than of cold, that the boy drew towards the fire, and the looks which the old woman and her sons exchanged, made him wish that he had preferred the shelter of any one of the roofless cottages which were scattered near, rather than trust himself among persons of such dubious aspect. Dreadful surmises flitted across his brain; and terrors which he could neither combat nor examine imperceptibly stole into his mind; but alone, and beyond the reach of assistance, he resolved to smother his suspicions, or at least not increase the danger by revealing them. The room to which he retired for the night had a confused and desolate aspect; the curtains seemed to have been violently torn down from the bed, and still hung in tatters around it—the table seemed to have been broken by some violent concussion, and the fragments of various pieces of furniture lay scattered upon the floor. The boy begged that a light might burn in his apartment till he was asleep, and anxiously examined the fastenings of the door; but they seemed to have been wrenched asunder on some former occasion, and were still left rusty and broken.

It was long ere the pedlar attempted to compose his agitated nerves to rest; but at length his senses began to 'steep themselves in forgetfulness,'* though his imagination remained painfully active, and presented new scenes of terror to his mind, with all the vividness of reality. He fancied himself again wandering on the heath, which appeared to be peopled with spectres, who all beckoned to him not to enter the cottage, and as he approached it, they vanished with a hollow and despairing cry. The scene then changed, and he found himself again seated by the fire, where the countenances of the men scowled upon him with the most terrifying malignity, and he thought the old woman suddenly seized him by the arms, and pinioned them to his side. Suddenly the boy was startled from these agitated slumbers, by what sounded to him like a cry of distress; he was broad awake in a moment, and sat up in bed,— but the noise was not repeated, and he endeavoured to persuade himself it had only been a continuation of the fearful images which had disturbed his rest, when, on glancing at the door, he observed underneath it a broad red stream of blood silently stealing its course along the floor. Frantic with alarm, it was but the work of a moment to spring from his bed, and rush to the door, through a chink of which, his eye nearly dimmed with affright, he could watch unsuspected whatever might be done in the adjoining room.

His fear vanished instantly when he perceived that it was only a *goat* that they had been slaughtering; and he was about to steal into his bed again, ashamed of his groundless apprehensions, when his ear was arrested by a conversation which transfixed him aghast with terror to the spot.

'This is an easier job than you had yesterday,' said the man who held the goat. 'I wish all the throats we've cut were as easily and quietly done. Did you ever hear such a noise as the old gentleman made last night! It was well we had no neighbour within a dozen of miles, or they must have heard his cries for help and mercy.'

'Don't speak of it,' replied the other; 'I was never fond of bloodshed.'

'Ha! ha!' said the other, with a sneer, 'you say so, do you?'

'I do,' answered the first, gloomily; 'the Murder Hole is the thing for me—*that* tells no tales—a single scuffle—a single plunge—and the fellow's dead and buried to your hand in a moment. I would defy all the officers in Christendom to discover any mischief *there*.'

'Ay, Nature did us a good turn when she contrived such a place as that. Who that saw a hole in the heath, filled with clear water, and so small that the long grass meets over the top of it, would suppose that the depth is unfathomable, and that it conceals more than forty people who have met their deaths there?—it sucks them in like a leech!'

'How do you mean to dispatch the lad in the next room?' asked the old woman in an under tone. The elder son made her a sign to be silent, and pointed towards the door where their trembling auditor was concealed; while the other, with an expression of brutal ferocity, passed his bloody knife across his throat.

The pedlar boy possessed a bold and daring spirit, which was now roused to desperation; but in any open resistance the odds were so completely against him, that flight seemed his best resource. He gently stole to the window, and having by one desperate effort broke the rusty bolt by which the

casement had been fastened, he let himself down without noise
or difficulty. This betokens good, thought he, pausing an
instant in dreadful hesitation what direction to take. This
momentary deliberation was fearfully interrupted by the hoarse
voice of the men calling aloud, '*The boy has fled—let loose
the blood-hound*!' These words sunk like a death-knell on his
heart, for escape appeared now impossible, and his nerves
seemed to melt away like wax in a furnace. Shall I perish without a struggle! thought he, rousing himself to exertion, and,
helpless and terrified as a hare pursued by its ruthless hunters,
he fled across the heath. Soon the baying of the blood-hound
broke the stillness of the night, and the voice of its masters
sounded through the moor, as they endeavoured to accelerate
its speed,—panting and breathless the boy pursued his hopeless career, but every moment his pursuers seemed to gain
upon his failing steps. The hound was unimpeded by the darkness which was to him so impenetrable, and its noise rung
louder and deeper on his ear—while the lanterns which were
carried by the men gleamed near and distinct upon his vision.

At his fullest speed, the terrified boy fell with violence over
a heap of stones, and having nothing on but his shirt, he was
severely cut in every limb. With one wild cry to Heaven for
assistance, he continued prostrate on the earth, bleeding, and
nearly insensible. The hoarse voices of the men, and the still
louder baying of the dog, were now so near, that instant destruction seemed inevitable,—already he felt himself in their
fangs, and the bloody knife of the assassin appeared to gleam
before his eyes,—despair renewed his energy, and once more,
in an agony of affright that seemed verging towards madness,
he rushed forward so rapidly that terror seemed to have given
wings to his feet. A loud cry near the spot he had left arose
on his ears without suspending his flight. The hound had
stopped at the place where the pedlar's wounds bled so pro-
fusely, and deeming the chase now over, it lay down there,
and could not be induced to proceed; in vain the men beat it
with frantic violence, and tried again to put the hound on the
scent,—the sight of blood had satisfied the animal that its work
was done, and with dogged resolution it resisted every in-
ducement to pursue the same scent a second time. The pedlar

boy in the meantime paused not in his flight till morning dawned—and still as he fled, the noise of steps seemed to pursue him, and the cry of his assassins still sounded in the distance. Ten miles off he reached a village, and spread instant alarm throughout the neighbourhood—the inhabitants were aroused with one accord into a tumult of indignation—several of them had lost sons, brothers, or friends on the heath, and all united in proceeding instantly to seize the old woman and her sons, who were nearly torn to pieces by their violence. Three gibbets were immediately raised on the moor, and the wretched culprits confessed before their execution to the destruction of nearly fifty victims in the Murder Hole which they pointed out, and near which they suffered the penalty of their crimes. The bones of several murdered persons were with difficulty brought up from the abyss into which they had been thrust; but so narrow is the aperture, and so extraordinary the depth, that all who see it are inclined to coincide in the tradition of the country people that it is unfathomable. The scene of these events still continues nearly as it was 300 years ago. The remains of the old cottage, with its blackened walls, (haunted of course by a thousand evil spirits,) and the extensive moor, on which a more modern *inn* (if it can be dignified with such an epithet) resembles its predecessor in every thing but the character of its inhabitants; the landlord is deformed, but possesses extraordinary genius; he has himself manufactured a violin, on which he plays with untaught skill,—and if any *discord* be heard in the house, or any *murder* committed in it, *this* is his only instrument. His daughter (who has never travelled beyond the heath) has inherited her father's talent, and learnt all his tales of terror and superstition, which she relates with infinite spirit; but when you are led by her across the heath to drop a stone into that deep and narrow gulf to which our story relates,—when you stand on its slippery edge, and (parting the long grass with which it is covered) gaze into its mysterious depths,—when she describes, with all the animation of an *eye-witness*, the struggle of the victims grasping the grass as a last hope of preservation, and trying to drag in their assassin as an expiring effort of vengeance,—when you are told that for 300 years the clear waters in this diamond of the desert have remained untasted by mortal lips, and that the solitary traveller is still pursued at night by the howling of the blood-hound,—it is *then only* that it is possible fully to appreciate the terrors of THE MURDER HOLE.

HEAT AND THIRST,—A SCENE
IN JAMAICA

Michael Scott

THE Torch was lying at anchor in Bluefields Bay. It was between eight and nine in the morning. The land wind had died
away, and the sea-breeze had not set in—there was not a breath
stirring. The pennant from the mast-head fell sluggishly down,
and clung amongst the rigging like a dead snake, whilst the
folds of the St George's ensign that hung from the mizen-
peak, were as motionless as if they had been carved in marble.

The anchorage was one unbroken mirror, except where its
glasslike surface was shivered into sparkling ripples by the
gambols of a skipjack, or the flashing stoop of his enemy the
pelican; and the reflection of the vessel was so clear and steady,
that at the distance of a cable's length you could not distinguish the water-line, nor tell where the substance ended and
shadow began, until the casual dashing of a bucket overboard
for a few moments broke up the phantom ship; but the waver-
ing fragments soon reunited, and she again floated double, like
the swan of the poet.* The heat was so intense, that the iron
stancheons of the awning could not be grasped with the hand,
and where the decks were not screened by it, the pitch boiled
out from the seams. The swell rolled in from the offing in long
shining undulations, like a sea of quicksilver, whilst every now
and then a flying fish would spark out from the unruffled
bosom of the heaving water, and shoot away like a silver arrow,
until it dropped with a flash into the sea again. There was not
a cloud in the heavens, but a quivering blue haze hung over
the land, through which the white sugar-works and overseers'
houses on the distant estates appeared to twinkle like objects
seen through a thin smoke, whilst each of the tall stems of
the cocoa-nut trees on the beach, when looked at steadfastly,
seemed to be turning round with a small spiral motion, like so
many endless screws. There was a dreamy indistinctness about

the outlines of the hills, even in the immediate vicinity, which increased as they receded, until the blue mountains in the horizon melted into sky. The crew were listlessly spinning oakum, and mending sails, under the shade of the awning; the only exceptions to the general languor were Johncrow the black, and Jackoo the monkey. The former (who was an *improvisatore* of a rough stamp) sat out on the bowsprit, through choice, beyond the shade of the canvas, without hat or shirt, like a bronze bust, busy with his task, whatever that might be, singing at the top of his pipe, and between whiles confabulating with his hairy ally, as if he had been a messmate. The monkey was hanging by the tail from the dolphin-striker, admiring what Johncrow called 'his own dam ogly face in the water.'—'Tail like yours would be good ting for a sailor, Jackoo, it would leave his two hands free aloft—more use, more hornament too, I'm sure, den de piece of greasy junk dat hangs from de Captain's taffril.*—Now I shall sing to you, how dat Corromantee* rascal, my fader, was sell me on de Gold Coast.

> '"Two red nightcap, one long knife,
>   All him get for Quackoo,
>   For gun next day him sell him wife—
>   You tink dat good song, Jackoo?"'

'Chocko, chocko,' chattered the monkey, as if in answer. 'Ah, you tink so—sensible honimal!—What is dat? shark?— Jackoo, come up, sir: don't you see dat big shovel-nosed fish looking at you? Pull your hand out of the water, Garamighty!' The negro threw himself on the gammoning* of the bowsprit to take hold of the poor ape, who, mistaking his kind intention, and ignorant of his danger, shrunk from him, lost his hold, and fell into the sea. The shark instantly sank to have a run, then dashed at his prey, raising his snout over him, and shooting his head and shoulders three or four feet out of the water, with poor Jackoo shrieking in his jaws, whilst his small bones crackled and crunched under the monster's triple row of teeth.

Whilst this small tragedy was acting—and painful enough it was to the kind-hearted negro—I was looking out towards the eastern horizon, watching the first dark-blue ripple of the sea-breeze, when a rushing noise passed over my head.

I looked up and saw a *gallinaso*, the large carrion-crow of the tropics, sailing, contrary to the habits of its kind, seaward over the brig. I followed it with my eye, until it vanished in the distance, when my attention was attracted by a dark speck far out in the offing, with a little tiny white sail. With my glass I made it out to be a ship's boat, but I saw no one on board, and the sail was idly flapping about the mast.

On making my report, I was desired to pull towards it in the gig; and as we approached, one of the crew said he thought he saw some one peering over the bow. We drew nearer, and I saw him distinctly. 'Why don't you haul the sheet aft, and come down to us, sir?'

He neither moved nor answered, but, as the boat rose and fell on the short sea raised by the first of the breeze, the face kept mopping and mowing at us over the gunwale.

'I will soon teach you manners, my fine fellow! give way, men'—and I fired my musket, when the crow that I had seen rose from the boat into the air, but immediately alighted again, to our astonishment, vulture-like with outstretched wings, *upon the head.*

Under the shadow of this horrible plume, the face seemed on the instant to alter like a hideous change in a dream. It appeared to become of a deathlike paleness, and anon streaked with blood. Another stroke of the oar—the chin had fallen down, and the tongue was hanging out. Another pull—the eyes were gone, and from their sockets, brains and blood were fermenting, and flowing down the cheeks. It was the face of a putrefying corpse. In this floating coffin we found the body of another sailor, doubled across one of the thwarts, with a long Spanish knife sticking between his ribs, as if he had died in some mortal struggle, or, what was equally probable, had put an end to himself in his frenzy; whilst along the bottom of the boat, arranged with some shew of care, and covered by a piece of canvass stretched across an oar above it, lay the remains of a beautiful boy, about fourteen years of age, apparently but a few hours dead. Some biscuit, a roll of jerked beef, and an earthen water-jar, lay beside him, shewing that hunger at least could have had no share in his destruction,—*but the pipkin was dry, and the small water-cask in the bow was staved, and empty.*

We had no sooner cast our grappling over the bow, and begun to tow the boat to the ship, than the abominable bird that we had scared settled down into it again, notwithstanding our proximity, and began to peck at the face of the dead boy. At this moment we heard a gibbering noise, and saw something like a bundle of old rags roll out from beneath the stern-sheet, and apparently make a fruitless attempt to drive the gallinaso from its prey. Heaven and earth, what an object met our eyes! It was a full-grown man, but so wasted, that one of the boys lifted him by his belt with one hand. His knees were drawn up to his chin, his hands were like the talons of a bird, while the falling in of his chocolate-coloured and withered features gave an unearthly relief to his forehead, over which the horny and transparent skin was braced so tightly that it seemed ready to crack. But in the midst of this desolation, his deep-set coal-black eyes sparkled like two diamonds with the fever of his sufferings; there was a fearful fascination in their flashing brightness, contrasted with the deathlike aspect of the face, and rigidity of the frame. When sensible of our presence he tried to speak, but could only utter a low moaning sound. At length—'Aqua, aqua'—we had not a drop of water in the boat. 'El muchacho esta moriendo de sed—Aqua.'*

We got on board, and the surgeon gave the poor fellow some weak tepid grog. It acted like magic. He gradually uncoiled himself, his voice, from being weak and husky, became comparatively strong and clear. 'El hijo—Aqua para mi pedrillo—No le hace para mi—Oh la noche pasado, la noche pasado!' He was told to compose himself, and that his boy would be taken care of. 'Dexa me verlo entonces, oh Dios, dexa me verlo'*—and he crawled, grovelling on his chest, like a crushed worm across the deck, until he got his head over the port-sill, and looked down into the boat. He there beheld the pale face of his dead son; it was the last object he ever saw— 'Ay de mi!' he groaned heavily, and dropped his face against the ship's side—He was dead.

THE IRON SHROUD

William Mudford

THE castle of the Prince of Tolfi was built on the summit of
the towering and precipitous rock of Scylla, and commanded
a magnificent view of Sicily in all its grandeur.* Here, during
the wars of the middle ages, when the fertile plains of Italy
were devastated by hostile factions, those prisoners were confined, for whose ransom a costly price was demanded. Here,
too, in a dungeon, excavated deep in the solid rock, the miserable victim was immured, whom revenge pursued,—the dark,
fierce, and unpitying revenge of an Italian heart.

Vivenzio—the noble and the generous, the fearless in battle,
and the pride of Naples in her sunny hours of peace—the
young, the brave, the proud, Vivenzio fell beneath this subtle
and remorseless spirit. He was the prisoner of Tolfi, and he
languished in that rock-encircled dungeon, which stood alone,
and whose portals never opened twice upon a living captive.

It had the semblance of a vast cage, for the roof, and floor,
and sides, were of iron, solidly wrought, and spaciously con-
structed. High above there ran a range of seven grated windows,
guarded with massy bars of the same metal, which admitted
light and air. Save these, and the tall folding doors beneath
them, which occupied the centre, no chink, or chasm, or pro-
jection, broke the smooth black surface of the walls. An iron
bedstead, littered with straw, stood in one corner: and beside it,
a vessel with water, and a coarse dish filled with coarser food.

Even the intrepid soul of Vivenzio shrunk with dismay as
he entered this abode, and heard the ponderous doors triple-
locked by the silent ruffians who conducted him to it. Their
silence seemed prophetic of his fate, of the living grave that
had been prepared for him. His menaces and his entreaties, his
indignant appeals for justice, and his impatient questioning of
their intentions, were alike vain. They listened, but spoke not.
Fit ministers of a crime that should have no tongue!

How dismal was the sound of their retiring steps! And, as their faint echoes died along the winding passages, a fearful presage grew within him, that never more the face, or voice, or tread, of man, would greet his senses. He had seen human beings for the last time! And he had looked his last upon the bright sky, and upon the smiling earth, and upon a beautiful world he loved, and whose minion he had been! Here he was to end his life—a life he had just begun to revel in! And by what means? By secret poison? or by murderous assault? No—for then it had been needless to bring him thither. Famine perhaps—a thousand deaths in one! It was terrible to think of it—but it was yet more terrible to picture long, long years of captivity, in a solitude so appalling, a loneliness so dreary, that thought, for want of fellowship, would lose itself in madness, or stagnate into idiocy.

He could not hope to escape, unless he had the power, with his bare hands, of rending asunder the solid iron walls of his prison. He could not hope for liberty from the relenting mercies of his enemy. His instant death, under any form of refined cruelty, was not the object of Tolfi, for he might have inflicted it, and he had not. It was too evident, therefore, he was reserved for some premeditated scheme of subtle vengeance; and what vengeance could transcend in fiendish malice, either the slow death of famine, or the still slower one of solitary incarceration, till the last lingering spark of life expired, or till reason fled, and nothing should remain to perish but the brute functions of the body?

It was evening when Vivenzio entered his dungeon, and the approaching shades of night wrapped it in total darkness, as he paced up and down, revolving in his mind these horrible forebodings. No tolling bell from the castle, or from any neighbouring church or convent, struck upon his ear to tell how the hours passed. Frequently he would stop and listen for some sound that might betoken the vicinity of man; but the solitude of the desert, the silence of the tomb, are not so still and deep, as the oppressive desolation by which he was encompassed. His heart sunk within him, and he threw himself dejectedly upon his couch of straw. Here sleep gradually obliterated the consciousness of misery, and bland dreams wafted his delighted spirit to scenes which were once glowing realities for him, in whose ravishing illusions he soon lost the remembrance that he was Tolfi's prisoner.

When he awoke, it was daylight; but how long he had slept he knew not. It might be early morning, or it might be sultry noon, for he could measure time by no other note of its progress than light and darkness. He had been so happy in his sleep, amid friends who loved him, and the sweeter endearments of those who loved him as friends could not, that in the first moments of waking, his startled mind seemed to admit the knowledge of his situation, as if it had burst upon it for the first time, fresh in all its appalling horrors. He gazed round with an air of doubt and amazement, and took up a handful of the straw upon which he lay, as though he would ask himself what it meant. But memory, too faithful to her office, soon unveiled the melancholy past, while reason, shuddering at the task, flashed before his eyes the tremendous future. The contrast overpowered him. He remained for some time lamenting, like a truth, the bright visions that had vanished; and recoiling from the present, which clung to him as a poisoned garment.

When he grew more calm, he surveyed his gloomy dungeon. Alas! the stronger light of day only served to confirm what the gloomy indistinctness of the preceding evening had partially disclosed, the utter impossibility of escape. As, however, his eyes wandered round and round, and from place to place, he noticed two circumstances which excited his surprise and curiosity. The one, he thought, might be fancy; but the other was positive. His pitcher of water, and the dish which contained his food, had been removed from his side while he slept, and now stood near the door. Were he even inclined to doubt this, by supposing he had mistaken the spot where he saw them over night, he could not, for the pitcher now in his dungeon was neither of the same form nor colour as the other, while the food was changed for some other of better quality. He had been visited therefore during the night. But how had the person obtained entrance? Could he have slept so soundly, that the unlocking and opening of those ponderous portals were effected without waking him? He would have said this was not possible, but that in doing so, he must admit a greater difficulty, an entrance by other means, of which he was convinced there existed none. It was not intended, then, that he should be left to perish from hunger. But the secret and mysterious mode of supplying him with food, seemed to indicate he was to have no opportunity of communicating with a human being.

The other circumstance which had attracted his notice, was the disappearance, as he believed, of one of the seven grated windows that ran along the top of his prison. He felt confident that he had observed and counted them; for he was rather surprised at their number, and there was something peculiar in their form, as well as in the manner of their arrangement, at unequal distances. It was so much easier, however, to suppose he was mistaken, than that a portion of the solid iron, which formed the walls, could have escaped from its position, that he soon dismissed the thought from his mind.

Vivenzio partook of the food that was before him, without apprehension. It might be poisoned; but if it were, he knew he could not escape death, should such be the design of Tolfi, and the quickest death would be the speediest release.

The day passed wearily and gloomily; though not without a faint hope that, by keeping watch at night, he might observe when the person came again to bring him food, which he supposed he would do in the same way as before. The mere thought of being approached by a living creature, and the opportunity it might present of learning the doom prepared, or preparing, for him, imparted some comfort. Besides, if he came alone, might he not in a furious onset overpower him? Or he might be accessible to pity, or the influence of such munificent rewards as he could bestow, if once more at liberty and master of himself. Say he were armed. The worst that could befall, if nor bribe, nor prayers, nor force prevailed, was a faithful blow, which, though dealt in a damned cause, might work a desired end. There was no chance so desperate, but it looked lovely in Vivenzio's eyes, compared with the idea of being totally abandoned.

The night came, and Vivenzio watched. Morning came, and Vivenzio was confounded! He must have slumbered without knowing it. Sleep must have stolen over him when exhausted by fatigue, and in that interval of feverish repose, he had been baffled; for there stood his replenished pitcher of water, and there his day's meal! Nor was this all. Casting his looks towards the windows of his dungeon, he counted but five! *Here* was no deception; and he was now convinced there had been none the day before. But what did all this portend? Into what strange and mysterious den had he been cast? He gazed till his eyes ached; he could discover nothing to explain the mystery. That it was so, he knew. Why it was so, he racked his imagination in vain to conjecture. He examined the doors. A simple circumstance convinced him they had not been opened.

A wisp of straw, which he had carelessly thrown against them the preceding day, as he paced to and fro, remained where he had cast it, though it must have been displaced by the slightest motion of either of the doors. This was evidence that could not be disputed; and it followed there must be some secret machinery in the walls by which a person could enter. He inspected them closely. They appeared to him one solid and compact mass of iron; or joined, if joined they were, with such nice art, that no mark of division was perceptible. Again and again he surveyed them—and the floor—and the roof—and that range of visionary windows, as he was now almost tempted to consider them: he could discover nothing, absolutely nothing, to relieve his doubts or satisfy his curiosity. Sometimes he fancied that altogether the dungeon had a more contracted appearance—that it looked smaller; but this he ascribed to fancy, and the impression naturally produced upon his mind by the undeniable disappearance of two of the windows.

With intense anxiety, Vivenzio looked forward to the return of night; and as it approached, he resolved that no treacherous sleep should again betray him. Instead of seeking his bed of straw, he continued to walk up and down his dungeon till daylight, straining his eyes in every direction through the darkness, to watch for any appearances that might explain these mysteries. While thus engaged, and as nearly as he could judge, (by the time that afterwards elapsed before the morning came in,) about two o'clock, there was a slight tremulous motion of the floors. He stooped. The motion lasted nearly a minute; but it was so extremely gentle, that he almost doubted whether it was real, or only imaginary. He listened. Not a sound could be heard. Presently, however, he felt a rush of cold air blow upon him; and dashing towards the quarter whence it seemed to proceed, he stumbled over something which he judged to be the water ewer. The rush of cold air was no longer perceptible; and as Vivenzio stretched out his hands, he found himself close to the walls. He remained motionless for a considerable time; but nothing occurred during the remainder of the night to excite his attention, though he continued to watch with unabated vigilance.

The first approaches of the morning were visible through the grated windows, breaking, with faint divisions of light, the darkness that still pervaded every other part, long before Vivenzio was enabled to distinguish any object in his dungeon. Instinctively and fearfully he turned his eyes, hot and inflamed with watching, towards them. There were FOUR! He could *see* only four: but it might be that some intervening object prevented the fifth from becoming perceptible; and he waited impatiently to ascertain if it were so. As the light strengthened, however, and penetrated every corner of the cell, other objects of amazement struck his sight. On the ground lay the broken fragments of the pitcher he had used the day before, and at a small distance from them, nearer to the wall, stood the one he had noticed the first night. It was filled with water, and beside it was his food. He was now certain, that, by some mechanical contrivance, an opening was obtained through the iron wall, and that through this opening the current of air had found entrance. But how noiseless! For had a feather almost waved at the time, he must have heard it. Again he examined that part of the wall; but both to sight and touch it appeared one even and uniform surface, while to repeated and violent blows, there was no reverberating sound indicative of hollowness.

This perplexing mystery had for a time withdrawn his thoughts from the windows; but now, directing his eyes again towards them, he saw that the fifth had disappeared in the same manner as the preceding two, without the least distinguishable alteration of external appearances. The remaining four looked as the seven had originally looked; that is, occupying, at irregular distances, the top of the wall on that side of the dungeon. The tall folding door, too, still seemed to stand beneath, in the centre of these four, as it had at first stood in the centre of the seven. But he could no longer doubt, what, on the preceding day, he fancied might be the effect of visual deception. The dungeon *was* smaller. The roof had lowered—and the opposite ends had contracted the intermediate distance by a space equal, he thought, to that over which the three windows had extended. He was bewildered in vain imaginings to account for these things. Some frightful purpose—some devilish torture of mind or body—some unheard-of device for producing exquisite misery, lurked, he was sure, in what had taken place.

Oppressed with this belief, and distracted more by the dreadful uncertainty of whatever fate impended, than he could be dismayed, he thought, by the knowledge of the worst, he sat ruminating, hour after hour, yielding his fears in succession to every haggard fancy. At last a horrible suspicion flashed suddenly across his mind, and he started up with a frantic air. 'Yes!' he exclaimed, looking wildly round his dungeon, and shuddering as he spoke—'Yes! it must be so! I see it!— I feel the maddening truth like scorching flames upon my brain! Eternal God!—support me! it must be so!—Yes, yes, *that* is to be my fate! Yon roof will descend!—these walls will hem me round—and slowly, slowly, crush me in their iron arms! Lord God! look down upon me, and in mercy strike me with instant death! Oh, fiend—oh, devil—is this your revenge?'

He dashed himself upon the ground in agony;—tears burst from him, and the sweat stood in large drops upon his face— he sobbed aloud—he tore his hair—he rolled about like one suffering intolerable anguish of body, and would have bitten the iron floor beneath him; he breathed fearful curses upon Tolfi, and the next moment passionate prayers to heaven for immediate death. Then the violence of his grief became exhausted, and he lay still, weeping as a child would weep. The twilight of departing day shed its gloom around him ere he arose from that posture of utter and hopeless sorrow. He had taken no food. Not one drop of water had cooled the fever of his parched lips. Sleep had not visited his eyes for six and thirty hours. He was faint with hunger; weary with watching, and with the excess of his emotions. He tasted of his food; he drank with avidity of the water; and reeling like a drunken man to his straw, cast himself upon it to brood again over the appalling image that had fastened itself upon his almost frenzied thoughts.

He slept. But his slumbers were not tranquil. He resisted, as long as he could, their approach; and when, at last, enfeebled nature yielded to their influence, he found no oblivion from his cares. Terrible dreams haunted him—ghastly visions harrowed up his imagination—he shouted and screamed, as if he already felt the dungeon's ponderous roof descending on him—he breathed hard and thick, as though writhing between its iron walls. Then would he spring up—stare wildly about him—stretch forth his hands, to be sure he yet had space enough to live—and, muttering some incoherent words, sink down again, to pass through the same fierce vicissitudes of delirious sleep.

The morning of the fourth day dawned upon Vivenzio. But it was high noon before his mind shook off its stupor, or he awoke to a full consciousness of his situation. And what a fixed energy of despair sat upon his pale features, as he cast his eyes upwards, and gazed upon the THREE windows that now alone remained! The three!—there were no more!—and they seemed to number his own allotted days. Slowly and calmly he next surveyed the top and sides, and comprehended all the meaning of the diminished height of the former, as well as of the gradual approximation of the latter. The contracted dimensions of his mysterious prison were now too gross and palpable to be the juggle of his heated imagination. Still lost in wonder at the means, Vivenzio could put no cheat upon his reason, as to the end. By what horrible ingenuity it was contrived, that walls, and roof, and windows, should thus silently and imperceptibly, without noise, and without motion almost, fold, as it were, within each other, he knew not. He only knew they did so; and he vainly strove to persuade himself it was the intention of the contriver, to rack the miserable wretch who might be immured there, with anticipation, merely, of a fate, from which, in the very crisis of his agony, he was to be reprieved.

Gladly would he have clung even to this possibility, if his heart would have let him; but he felt a dreadful assurance of its fallacy. And what matchless inhumanity it was to doom the sufferer to such lingering torments—to lead him day by day to so appalling a death, unsupported by the consolations of religion, unvisited by any human being, abandoned to himself, deserted of all, and denied even the sad privilege of knowing that his cruel destiny would awaken pity! Alone he was to perish!—alone he was to wait a slow coming torture, whose most exquisite pangs would be inflicted by that very solitude and that tardy coming!

'It is not death I fear,' he exclaimed, 'but the death I must prepare for! Methinks, too, I could meet even that—all horrible and revolting as it is—if it might overtake me now. But where shall I find fortitude to tarry till it come? How can I outlive the three long days and nights I have to live? There is no power within me to bid the hideous spectre hence—none to make it familiar to my thoughts; or myself, patient of its errand. My thoughts, rather, will flee from me, and I grow mad in looking at it. Oh! for a deep sleep to fall upon me! That so, in death's likeness, I might embrace death itself, and drink no more of the cup that is presented to me, than my fainting spirit has already tasted!'

In the midst of these lamentations, Vivenzio noticed that his accustomed meal, with the pitcher of water, had been conveyed, as before, into his dungeon. But this circumstance no longer excited his surprise. His mind was overwhelmed with others of a far greater magnitude. It suggested, however, a feeble hope of deliverance; and there is no hope so feeble as not to yield some support to a heart bending under despair. He resolved to watch, during the ensuing night, for the signs he had before observed; and should he again feel the gentle, tremulous motion of the floor, or the current of air, to seize that moment for giving audible expression to his misery. Some person must be near him, and within reach of his voice, at the instant when his food was supplied; some one, perhaps, susceptible of pity. Or if not, to be told even that his apprehensions were just, and that his fate *was* to be what he foreboded, would be preferable to a suspense which hung upon the possibility of his worst fears being visionary.

The night came; and as the hour approached when Vivenzio imagined he might expect the signs, he stood fixed and silent as a statue. He feared to breathe, almost, lest he might lose any sound which would warn him of their coming. While thus listening, with every faculty of mind and body strained to an agony of attention, it occurred to him he should be more sensible of the motion, probably, if he stretched himself along the iron floor. He accordingly laid himself softly down, and had not been long in that position when—yes—he was certain of it—the floor moved under him! He sprang up, and in a voice suffocated nearly with emotion, called aloud. He paused—the motion ceased—he felt no stream of air—all was hushed—no voice answered to his—he burst into tears; and as he sunk to the ground, in renewed anguish, exclaimed,—'Oh, my God! my God! You alone have power to save me now, or strengthen me for the trial you permit.'

Another morning dawned upon the wretched captive, and the fatal index of his doom met his eyes. Two windows!—and *two* days—and all would be over! Fresh food—fresh water! The mysterious visit had been paid, though he had implored it in vain. But how awfully was his prayer answered in what he now saw! The roof of the dungeon was within a foot of his head. The two ends were so near, that in six paces he trod the space between them. Vivenzio shuddered as he gazed, and as his steps traversed the narrowed area. But his feelings no longer vented themselves in frantic wailings. With folded arms, and clenched teeth, with eyes that were bloodshot from much watching, and fixed with a vacant glare upon the ground, with a hard quick breathing, and a hurried walk, he strode backwards and forwards in silent musing for several hours. What mind shall conceive, what tongue utter, or what pen describe the dark and terrible character of his thoughts? Like the fate that moulded them, they had no similitude in the wide range of this world's agony for man. Suddenly he stopped, and his eyes were riveted upon that part of the wall which was over his bed of straw. Words are inscribed there! A human language, traced by a human hand! He rushes towards them; but his blood freezes as he reads:—

'I, Ludovico Sforza, tempted by the gold of the Prince of Tolfi, spent three years in contriving and executing this accursed triumph of my art. When it was completed, the perfidious Tolfi, more devil than man, who conducted me hither one morning, to be witness, as he said, of its perfection, doomed *me* to be the first victim of my own pernicious skill; lest, as he declared, I should divulge the secret, or repeat the effort of my ingenuity. May God pardon him, as I hope he will me, that ministered to his unhallowed purpose! Miserable wretch, whoe'er thou art, that readest these lines, fall on thy knees, and invoke, as I have done, His sustaining mercy, who alone can nerve thee to meet the vengeance of Tolfi, armed with his tremendous engine which, in a few hours, must crush *you*, as it will the needy wretch who made it.'

A deep groan burst from Vivenzio. He stood, like one transfixed, with dilated eyes, expanded nostrils, and quivering lips, gazing at this fatal inscription. It was as if a voice from the sepulchre had sounded in his ears, 'Prepare!' Hope forsook him. There was his sentence, recorded in those dismal words. The future stood unveiled before him, ghastly and appalling. His brain already feels the descending horror,—his bones seem to crack and crumble in the mighty grasp of the iron walls! Unknowing what it is he does, he fumbles in his garment for some weapon of self-destruction. He clenches his throat in his convulsive gripe, as though he would strangle himself at once. He stares upon the walls, and his warring spirit demands, 'Will they not anticipate their office if I dash my head against them?' An hysterical laugh chokes him as he exclaims, 'Why should I? He was but a man who died first in their fierce embrace; and I should be less than man not to do as much!'

The evening sun was descending, and Vivenzio beheld its golden beams streaming through one of the windows. What a thrill of joy shot through his soul at the sight! It was a precious link, that united him, for the moment, with the world beyond. There was ecstasy in the thought. As he gazed, long and earnestly, it seemed as if the windows had lowered sufficiently for him to reach them. With one bound he was beneath them—with one wild spring he clung to the bars. Whether it was so contrived, purposely to madden with delight the wretch who looked, he knew not; but, at the extremity of a long vista, cut through the solid rocks, the ocean, the sky, the setting sun, olive groves, shady walks, and, in the farthest distance, delicious glimpses of magnificent Sicily, burst upon his sight. How exquisite was the cool breeze as it swept across his cheek, loaded with fragrance! He inhaled it as though it were the breath of continued life. And there was a freshness in the landscape, and in the rippling of the calm green sea, that fell upon his withering heart like dew upon the parched earth. How he gazed, and panted, and still clung to his hold! sometimes hanging by one hand, sometimes by the other, and then grasping the bars with both, as loath to quit the smiling paradise outstretched before him; till exhausted, and his hands swollen and benumbed, he dropped helpless down, and lay stunned for a considerable time by the fall.

When he recovered, the glorious vision had vanished. He was in darkness. He doubted whether it was not a dream that had passed before his sleeping fancy; but gradually his scattered thoughts returned, and with them came remembrance. Yes! he had looked once again upon the gorgeous splendour of nature! Once again his eyes had trembled beneath their veiled lids, at the sun's radiance, and sought repose in the soft verdure of the olive-tree, or the gentle swell of undulating waves. Oh, that he were a mariner, exposed upon those waves to the worst fury of storm and tempest; or a very wretch, loathsome with disease, plague-stricken, and his body one leprous contagion from crown to sole, hunted forth to gasp out the remnant of infectious life beneath those verdant trees, so he might shun the destiny upon whose edge he tottered!

Vain thoughts like these would steal over his mind from time to time, in spite of himself; but they scarcely moved it from that stupor into which it had sunk, and which kept him, during the whole night, like one who had been drugged with opium. He was equally insensible to the calls of hunger and of thirst, though the third day was now commencing since even a drop of water had passed his lips. He remained on the ground, sometimes sitting, sometimes lying; at intervals, sleeping heavily; and when not sleeping, silently brooding over what was to come, or talking aloud, in disordered speech, of his wrongs, of his friends, of his home, and of those he loved, with a confused mingling of all.

In this pitiable condition, the sixth and last morning dawned upon Vivenzio, if dawn it might be called—the dim, obscure light which faintly struggled through the ONE SOLITARY window of his dungeon. He could hardly be said to notice the melancholy token. And yet he did notice it; for as he raised his eyes and saw the portentous sign, there was a slight convulsive distortion of his countenance. But what did attract his notice, and at the sight of which his agitation was excessive, was the change his iron bed had undergone. It was a bed no longer. It stood before him, the visible semblance of a funeral couch or bier! When he beheld this, he started from the ground; and, in raising himself, suddenly struck his head against the roof, which was now so low that he could no longer stand upright. 'God's will be done!' was all he said, as he crouched his body, and placed his hand upon the bier; for such it was. The iron bedstead had been so contrived, by the mechanical art of Ludovico Sforza, that as the advancing walls came in contact with its head and feet, a pressure was produced upon concealed springs, which, when made to play, set in motion a very simple though ingeniously contrived machinery, that effected the transformation. The object was, of course, to heighten, in the closing scene of this horrible drama, all the feelings of despair and anguish, which the preceding ones had aroused. For the same reason, the last window was so made as to admit only a shadowy kind of gloom rather than light, that the wretched captive might be surrounded, as it were, with every seeming preparation for approaching death.

Vivenzio seated himself on his bier. Then he knelt and prayed fervently; and sometimes tears would gush from him. The air seemed thick, and he breathed with difficulty; or it might be that he fancied it was so, from the hot and narrow limits of his dungeon, which were now so diminished that he could neither stand up nor lie down at his full length. But his wasted spirits and oppressed mind no longer struggled within him. He was past hope, and fear shook him no more. Happy if thus revenge had struck its final blow; for he would have fallen beneath it almost unconscious of a pang. But such a lethargy of the soul, after such an excitement of its fiercest passions, had entered into the diabolical calculations of Tolfi; and the fell artificer of his designs had imagined a counteracting device.

The tolling of an enormous bell struck upon the ears of Vivenzio! He started. It beat but once. The sound was so close and stunning, that it seemed to shatter his very brain, while it echoed through the rocky passages like reverberating peals of thunder. This was followed by a sudden crash of the roof and walls, as if they were about to fall upon and close around him at once. Vivenzio screamed, and instinctively spread forth his arms, as though he had a giant's strength to hold them back. They had moved nearer to him, and were now motionless. Vivenzio looked up, and saw the roof almost touching his head, even as he sat cowering beneath it; and he felt that a farther contraction of but a few inches only must commence the frightful operation. Roused as he had been, he now gasped for breath. His body shook violently—he was bent nearly double. His hands rested upon either wall, and his feet were drawn under him to avoid the pressure in front. Thus he remained for more than an hour, when that deafening bell beat again, and again there came the crash of horrid death. But the concussion was now so great that it struck Vivenzio down. As he lay gathered up in lessened bulk, the bell beat loud and frequent—crash succeeded crash—and on, and on, and on came the mysterious engine of death, till Vivenzio's smothered groans were heard no more! He was horribly crushed by the ponderous roof and collapsing sides—and the flattened bier was his *Iron Shroud*.

THE MYSTERIOUS BRIDE

James Hogg

A GREAT number of people now-a-days are beginning broadly to insinuate that there are no such things as ghosts, or spiritual beings visible to mortal sight. Even Sir Walter Scott is turned renegade,* and, with his stories made up of half-and-half, like Nathaniel Gow's* toddy, is trying to throw cold water on the most certain, though most impalpable, phenomena of human nature. The bodies are daft. Heaven mend their wits! Before they had ventured to assert such things, I wish they had been where I have often been; or, in particular, where the Laird of Birkendelly was on St Lawrence's Eve,* in the year 1777, and sundry times subsequent to that.

Be it known, then, to every reader of this relation of facts that happened in my own remembrance, that the road from Birkendelly to the great muckle village of Balmawhapple, (commonly called the muckle town, in opposition to the little town that stood on the other side of the burn,)—that road, I say, lay between two thorn hedges, so well kept by the Laird's hedger, so close, and so high, that a rabbit could not have escaped from the highway into any of the adjoining fields. Along this road was the Laird riding on the Eve of St Lawrence, in a careless, indifferent manner, with his hat to one side, and his cane dancing a horn-pipe on the curtch* of the saddle before him. He was, moreover, chanting a song to himself, and I have heard people tell what song it was too. There was once a certain, or rather uncertain, bard, ycleped Robert Burns, who made a number of good songs; but this that the Laird sung was an amorous song of great antiquity, which like all the said bard's best songs, was sung one hundred and fifty years before he was born. It began thus:

> 'I am the Laird of Windy-wa's,
> I cam nae here without a cause,

> An' I hae gotten forty fa's
>> In coming o'er the knowe, joe!

> The night it is baith wind and weet;
> The morn it will be snaw and sleet;
> My shoon are frozen to my feet;
>> O, rise an' let me in, joe!
>>> Let me in this ae night,' &c. &c.*

This song was the Laird singing, while, at the same time, he was smudging and laughing at the catastrophe,* when, ere ever aware, he beheld, a short way before him, an uncommonly elegant and beautiful girl walking in the same direction with him. 'Aye,' said the Laird to himself, 'here is something very attractive indeed! Where the deuce can she have sprung from? She must have risen out of the earth, for I never saw her till this breath. Well, I declare I have not seen such a female figure—I wish I had such an assignation with her as the Laird of Windy-wa's had with his sweetheart.'

As the Laird was half-thinking, half-speaking this to himself, the enchanting creature looked back at him with a motion of intelligence that she knew what he was half-saying, half-thinking, and then vanished over the summit of the rising ground before him, called the Birky Brow. 'Aye, go your ways!' said the Laird; 'I see by you, you'll not be very hard to overtake. You cannot get off the road, and I'll have a chat with you before you make the Deer's Den.'

The Laird jogged on. He did not sing the 'Laird of Windy-wa's' any more, for he felt a sort of stifling about his heart; but he often repeated to himself, 'She's a very fine woman!—a very fine woman indeed—and to be walking here by herself! I cannot comprehend it.'

When he reached the summit of the Birky Brow he did not see her, although he had a longer view of the road than before. He thought this very singular, and began to suspect that she wanted to escape him, although apparently rather lingering on him before. 'I shall have another look at her, however,' thought the Laird; and off he set at a flying trot. No. He came first to one turn, then another. There was nothing of the young lady to be seen. 'Unless she take wings and fly away, I shall be up with her,' quoth the Laird; and off he set at the full gallop.

In the middle of his career he met with Mr M'Murdie of Aulton, who hailed him with, 'Hilloa! Birkendelly! where the deuce are you flying at that rate?'

'I was riding after a woman,' said the Laird, with great simplicity, reining in his steed.

'Then I am sure no woman on earth can long escape you, unless she be in an air balloon.'

'I don't know that. Is she far gone?'

'In which way do you mean?'

'In this.'

'Aha-ha-ha! Hee-hee-hee!' nichered M'Murdie, misconstruing the Laird's meaning.

'What do you laugh at, my dear sir? Do you know her, then?'

'Ho-ho-ho! Hee-hee-hee! How should I, or how can I, know her, Birkendelly, unless you inform me who she is?'

'Why, that is the very thing I want to know of you. I mean the young lady whom you met just now.'

'You are raving, Birkendelly. I met no young lady, nor is there a single person on the road I have come by, while you know, that for a mile and a half forward your way, she could not get out of it.'

'I know that,' said the Laird, biting his lip, and looking greatly puzzled. 'But confound me if I understand this; for I was within speech of her just now on the top of the Birky Brow there; and, when I think of it, she could not have been even thus far as yet. She had on a pure white gauze frock, a small green bonnet and feathers, and a green veil, which, flung back over her left shoulder, hung below her waist; and was altogether such an engaging figure, that no man could have passed her on the road without taking some note of her.—Are you not making game of me? Did you not really meet with her?'

'On my word of truth and honour, I did not. Come, ride back with me, and we shall meet her still, depend on it. She has given you the go-by on the road. Let us go; I am only going to call at the mill about some barley for the distillery, and will return with you to the big town.'

Birkendelly returned with his friend. The sun was not yet

set, yet M'Murdie could not help observing that the Laird
looked thoughtful and confused, and not a word could he
speak about any thing save this lovely apparition with the
white frock and the green veil; and lo, when they reached the
top of the Birky Brow, there was the maiden again before
them, and exactly at the same spot where the Laird first saw
her before, only walking in the contrary direction.

'Well, this is the most extraordinary thing that I ever knew!'
exclaimed the Laird.

'What is it, sir?' said M'Murdie.

'How that young lady could have eluded me,' returned the
Laird; 'see, here she is still.'

'I beg your pardon, sir, I don't see her. Where is she?'

'There, on the other side of the angle; but you are short-
sighted. See, there she is ascending the other eminence in
her white frock and green veil, as I told you—What a lovely
creature!'

'Well, well, we have her fairly before us now, and shall see
what she is like at all events,' said M'Murdie.

Between the Birky Brow and this other slight eminence,
there is an obtuse angle of the road at the part where it is
lowest, and, in passing this, the two friends necessarily lost
sight of the object of their curiosity. They pushed on at a
quick pace—cleared the low angle—the maiden was not there!
They rode full speed to the top of the eminence from whence
a long extent of road was visible before them—there was no
human creature in view! M'Murdie laughed aloud; but the
Laird turned pale as death, and bit his lip. His friend asked at
him, good-humouredly, why he was so much affected. He
said, because he could not comprehend the meaning of this
singular apparition or illusion, and it troubled him the more,
as he now remembered a dream of the same nature which he
had had, and which terminated in a dreadful manner.

'Why, man, you are dreaming still,' said M'Murdie; 'but
never mind. It is quite common for men of your complexion
to dream of beautiful maidens, with white frocks and green
veils, bonnets, feathers, and slender waists. It is a lovely image,
the creation of your own sanguine imagination, and you
may worship it without any blame. Were her shoes black or

green?—And her stockings, did you note them? The symmetry of the limbs, I am sure you did! Good-bye; I see you are not disposed to leave the spot. Perhaps she will appear to you again.'

So saying, M'Murdie rode on towards the mill, and Birkendelly, after musing for some time, turned his beast's head slowly round, and began to move towards the great muckle village.

The Laird's feelings were now in terrible commotion. He was taken beyond measure with the beauty and elegance of the figure he had seen; but he remembered, with a mixture of admiration and horror, that a dream of the same enchanting object had haunted his slumbers all the days of his life; yet how singular that he should never have recollected the circumstance till now! But farther, with the dream there were connected some painful circumstances, which, though terrible in their issue, he could not recollect, so as to form them into any degree of arrangement.

As he was considering deeply of these things, and riding slowly down the declivity, neither dancing his cane, nor singing the 'Laird of Windy-wa's,' he lifted up his eyes, and there was the girl on the same spot where he saw her first, walking deliberately up the Birky Brow. The sun was down; but it was the month of August, and a fine evening, and the Laird, seized with an unconquerable desire to see and speak with that incomparable creature, could restrain himself no longer, but shouted out to her to stop till he came up. She beckoned acquiescence, and slackened her pace into a slow movement. The Laird turned the corner quickly, but when he had rounded it, the maiden was still there, though on the summit of the Brow. She turned round, and, with an ineffable smile and curtsy, saluted him, and again moved slowly on. She vanished gradually beyond the summit, and while the green feathers were still nodding in view and so nigh, that the Laird could have touched them with a fishing-rod, he reached the top of the Brow himself. There was no living soul there, nor onward, as far as his view reached. He now trembled every limb, and, without knowing what he did, rode straight on to the big town, not daring well to return and see what he had seen for three several times; and, certain he would see it again when the shades of evening were deepening, he deemed it proper and prudent to decline the pursuit of such a phantom any farther.

He alighted at the Queen's Head, called for some brandy and water, quite forgot what was his errand to the great muckle town that afternoon, there being nothing visible to his mental sight but lovely fairy images, with white gauze frocks and green veils. His friend, Mr M'Murdie, joined him; they drank deep, bantered, reasoned, got angry, reasoned themselves calm again, and still all would not do. The Laird was conscious that he had seen the beautiful apparition, and, moreover, that she was the very maiden, or the resemblance of her, who, in the irrevocable decrees of Providence, was destined to be his. It was in vain that M'Murdie reasoned of impressions on the imagination, and

'Of fancy moulding in the mind,
Light visions on the passing wind.'*

Vain also was a story that he told him of a relation of his own, who was greatly harassed by the apparition of an officer in a red uniform, that haunted him day and night, and had very nigh put him quite distracted several times; till at length his physician found out the nature of this illusion so well, that he knew, from the state of his pulse, to an hour when the ghost of the officer would appear; and by bleeding, low diet, and emollients, contrived to keep the apparition away altogether.

The Laird admitted the singularity of this incident, but not that it was one in point; for the one, he said, was imaginary, and the other real; and that no conclusions could convince him in opposition to the authority of his own senses. He accepted of an invitation to spend a few days with M'Murdie and his family; but they all acknowledged afterwards that the Laird was very much like one bewitched.

As soon as he reached home, he went straight to the Birky Brow, certain of seeing once more the angelic phantom; but she was not there. He took each of his former positions again and again, but the desired vision would in nowise make its appearance. He tried every day, and every hour of the day, all with the same effect, till he grew absolutely desperate, and had the audacity to kneel on the spot and entreat of Heaven to see her. Yes, he called on Heaven to see her once more, whatever she was, whether a being of earth, heaven, or hell!

He was now in such a state of excitement that he could not exist; he grew listless, impatient, and sickly; took to his bed, and sent for M'Murdie and the doctor; and the issue of the consultation was, that Birkendelly consented to leave the country for a season, on a visit to his only sister in Ireland, whither we must now accompany him for a short space.

His sister was married to Captain Bryan, younger of Scoresby, and they two lived in a cottage on the estate, and the Captain's parents and sisters at Scoresby Hall. Great was the stir and preparation when the gallant young Laird of Birkendelly arrived at the cottage, it never being doubted that he had come to forward a second bond of connexion with the family, which still contained seven dashing sisters, all unmarried, and all alike willing to change that solitary and helpless state for the envied one of matrimony—a state highly popular among the young women of Ireland. Some of the Misses Bryan had now reached the years of womanhood, several of them scarcely; but these small disqualifications made no difference in the estimation of the young ladies themselves; each and all of them brushed up for the competition, with high hopes and unflinching resolutions. True, the elder ones tried to check the younger in their good-natured, forthright, Irish way; but they retorted, and persisted in their superior pretensions. Then there was such shopping in the county-town! It was so boundless, that the credit of the Hall was finally exhausted, and the old squire was driven to remark, that 'Och and to be sure it was a dreadful and tirrabell concussion, to be put upon the equipment of seven daughters all at the same moment, as if the young gentleman could marry them all! Och, then, poor dear shoul, he would be after finding that one was sufficient, if not one too many. And, therefore, there was no occasion, none at all, at all, and that there was not, for any of them to rig out more than one.'

It was hinted that the Laird had some reason for complaint at this time; but as the lady sided with her daughters, he had no chance. One of the items of his account was, thirty-seven buckling-combs, then greatly in vogue. There were black combs, pale combs, yellow combs, and gilt ones, all to suit or set off various complexions; and if other articles bore any proportion at all to these, it had been better for the Laird and all his family that Birkendelly had never set foot in Ireland.

The plan was all concocted. There was to be a grand dinner at the Hall, at which the damsels were to appear in all their finery. A ball was to follow, and note taken which of the young ladies was their guest's choice, and measures taken accordingly. The dinner and the ball took place, and what a pity I may not describe that entertainment, the dresses, and the dancers, for they were all exquisite in their way, and *outré* beyond measure. But such details only serve to derange a winter's evening tale such as this.

Birkendelly having at this time but one model for his choice among womankind, all that ever he did while in the presence of ladies, was to look out for some resemblance to her, the angel of his fancy; and it so happened, that in one of old Bryan's daughters named Luna, or more familiarly, Loony, he perceived or thought he perceived, some imaginary similarity in form and air to the lovely apparition. This was the sole reason why he was incapable of taking his eyes off from her the whole of that night; and this incident settled the point, not only with the old people, but even the young ladies were forced, after every exertion on their own parts, to 'yild the pint to their sister Loony, who certinly was nit the mist genteelest, nor mist handsomest of that guid-lucking fimily.'

The next day Lady Luna was dispatched off to the cottage in grand style, there to live hand and glove with her supposed lover. There was no standing all this. There were the two parrocked together, like a ewe and a lamb, early and late; and though the Laird really appeared to have, and probably had, some delight in her company, it was only in contemplating that certain indefinable air of resemblance which she bore to the sole image impressed on his heart. He bought her a white gauze frock, a green bonnet and feathers, with a veil, which she was obliged to wear thrown over her left shoulder; and every day after, six-times a day, was she obliged to walk over a certain eminence at a certain distance before her lover. She was delighted to oblige him; but still when he came up, he looked disappointed, and never said, 'Luna, I love you; when are we to be married?' No, he never said any such thing, for all her looks and expressions of fondest love; for, alas, in all this dalliance, he was only feeding a mysterious flame, that preyed upon his vitals, and proved too severe for the powers either of reason or religion to extinguish. Still time flew lighter and lighter by, his health was restored, the bloom of his cheek returned, and the frank and simple confidence of Luna had a certain charm with it, that reconciled him to his sister's Irish economy. But a strange incident now happened to him which deranged all his immediate plans.

He was returning from angling one evening, a little before sunset, when he saw Lady Luna awaiting him on his way home. But instead of rushing up to meet him as usual, she turned, and walked up the rising ground before him. 'Poor sweet girl! how condescending she is,' said he to himself, 'and how like she is in reality to the angelic being whose form and features are so deeply impressed on my heart! I now see it is no fond or fancied resemblance. It is real! real! real! How I long to clasp her in my arms, and tell her how I love her; for, after all, that is the girl that is to be mine, and the former a vision to impress this the more on my heart.'

He posted up the ascent to overtake her. When at the top she turned, smiled, and curtsied. Good heavens! it was the identical lady of his fondest adoration herself, but lovelier, far lovelier than ever. He expected every moment that she would vanish as was her wont; but she did not—she awaited him, and received his embraces with open arms. She was a being of real flesh and blood, courteous, elegant, and affectionate. He kissed her hand, he kissed her glowing cheek, and blessed all the powers of love who had thus restored her to him again, after undergoing pangs of love such as man never suffered.

'But, dearest heart, here we are standing in the middle of the highway,' said he; 'suffer me to conduct you to my sister's house, where you shall have an apartment with a child of nature having some slight resemblance to yourself.' She smiled, and said, 'No, I will not sleep with Lady Luna to-night. Will you please to look round you, and see where you are.' He did so, and behold they were standing on the Birky Brow, on the only spot where he had ever seen her. She smiled at his embarrassed look, and asked if he did not remember aught of his coming over from Ireland. He said he thought he did remember something of it, but love with him had long absorbed every other sense. He then asked her to his own house, which she declined, saying she could only meet him on that spot till after their marriage, which could not be before St Lawrence's Eve come three years. 'And now,' said she, 'we must part. My name is Jane Ogilvie, and you were betrothed to me before you were born. But I am come to release you this evening, if you have the slightest objection.'

He declared he had none; and, kneeling, swore the most solemn oath to be hers for ever, and to meet her there on St Lawrence's Eve next, and every St Lawrence's Eve until that blessed day on which she had consented to make him happy, by becoming his own for ever. She then asked him affectionately to exchange rings with her, in pledge of their faith and truth, in which he joyfully acquiesced; for she could not have then asked any conditions, which, in the fulness of his heart's love, he would not have granted; and after one fond and affectionate kiss, and repeating all their engagements over again, they parted.

Birkendelly's heart was now melted within him, and all his senses overpowered by one overwhelming passion. On leaving his fair and kind one, he got bewildered, and could not find the road to his own house, believing sometimes that he was going there, and sometimes to his sister's, till at length he came, as he thought, upon the Liffey, at its junction with Loch Allan; and there, in attempting to call for a boat, he awoke from a profound sleep, and found himself lying in his bed within his sister's house, and the day sky just breaking.

If he was puzzled to account for some things in the course of his dream, he was much more puzzled to account for them now that he was wide awake. He was sensible that he had met his love, had embraced, kissed, and exchanged vows and rings with her, and, in token of the truth and reality of all these, her emerald ring was on his finger, and his own away; so there was no doubt that they had met,—by what means it was beyond the power of man to calculate.

There was then living with Mrs Bryan an old Scotswoman commonly styled Lucky Black. She had nursed Birkendelly's mother, and been dry-nurse to himself and sister; and having more than a mother's attachment for the latter, when she was married, old Lucky left her country, to spend the last of her days in the house of her beloved young lady. When the Laird entered the breakfast parlour that morning, she was sitting in her black velvet hood, as usual, reading 'The Fourfold State of Man,'* and being paralytic and somewhat deaf, she seldom regarded those who went out or came in. But chancing to hear him say something about the ninth of August, she quitted reading, turned round her head to listen, and then asked, in a hoarse tremulous voice, 'What's that he's saying? What's the unlucky callant* saying about the ninth of August? Aih? To be sure it is St Lawrence's Eve, although the tenth be his day. It's ower true, ower true! ower true for him an' a' his kin, poor man! Aih? What was he saying then?'

The men smiled at her incoherent earnestness, but the lady, with true feminine condescension, informed her, in a loud voice, that Allan had an engagement in Scotland on St Lawrence's Eve. She then started up, extended her shrivelled hands, that shook like the aspen, and panted out, 'Aih, aih? Lord preserve us! whaten an engagement has he on St Lawrence's Eve? Bind him! bind him! shackle him wi' bands of steel, and of brass, and of iron!—O, may He whose blessed will was pleased to leave him an orphan sae soon, preserve him from the fate which I tremble to think on!'

She then tottered round the table, as with supernatural energy, and seizing the Laird's right hand, she drew it close to her unstable eyes, and then, perceiving the emerald ring chased in blood, she threw up her arms with a jerk, opened her skinny jaws with a fearful gape, and uttering a shriek, that made all the house yell, and every one within it to tremble, she fell back lifeless and rigid on the floor. The gentlemen both fled, out of sheer terror; but a woman never deserts her friends in extremity. The lady called her maids about her, had her old nurse conveyed to bed, where every means were used to restore animation. But, alas! life was extinct! The vital spark had fled for ever, which filled all their hearts with grief, disappointment, and horror, as some dreadful tale of mystery was now sealed up from their knowledge, which, in all likelihood, no other could reveal. But to say the truth, the Laird did not seem greatly disposed to probe it to the bottom.

Not all the arguments of Captain Bryan and his lady, nor the simple entreaties of Lady Luna, could induce Birkendelly to put off his engagement to meet his love on the Birky Brow on the evening of the 9th of August; but he promised soon to return, pretending that some business of the utmost importance called him away. Before he went, however, he asked his sister if ever she had heard of such a lady in Scotland as Jane Ogilvie. Mrs Bryan repeated the name many times to herself, and said that name undoubtedly was once familiar to her, although she thought not for good, but at that moment she did not recollect one single individual of the name. He then shewed her the emerald ring that had been the death of old Lucky Black; but the moment the lady looked at it, she made a grasp at it to take it off by force, which she had very nearly effected. 'O, burn it, burn it!' cried she; 'it is not a right ring! Burn it!'

'My dear sister, what fault is in the ring?' said he. 'It is a very pretty ring, and one that I set great value by.'

'O, for Heaven's sake, burn it, and renounce the giver!' cried she. 'If you have any regard for your peace here, or your soul's welfare hereafter, burn that ring! If you saw with your own eyes, you would easily perceive that that is not a ring befitting a Christian to wear.'

This speech confounded Birkendelly a good deal. He retired by himself and examined the ring, and could see nothing in it unbecoming a Christian to wear. It was a chased gold ring, with a bright emerald, which last had a red foil, in some lights giving it a purple gleam, and inside was engraven *'Elegit,'** much defaced, but that his sister could not see; therefore he could not comprehend her vehement injunctions concerning it. But that it might no more give her offence, or any other, he sewed it within his vest, opposite his heart, judging that there was something in it which his eyes were withholden from discerning.

Thus he left Ireland with his mind in great confusion, groping his way, as it were, in a hole of mystery, yet the passion that preyed on his heart and vitals more intense than ever. He seems to have had an impression all his life that some mysterious fate awaited him, which the correspondence of his dreams and day visions tended to confirm. And though he gave himself wholly up to the sway of one overpowering passion, it was not without some yearnings of soul, manifestations of terror, and so much earthly shame, that he never more mentioned his love, or his engagements, to any human being, not even to his friend M'Murdie, whose company he forthwith shunned.

It is on this account that I am unable to relate what passed between the lovers thenceforward. It is certain that they met at the Birky Brow that St Lawrence's Eve, for they were seen in company together; but of the engagements, vows, or dalliance, that passed between them, I can say nothing; nor of all their future meetings, until the beginning of August 1781, when the Laird began decidedly to make preparations for his approaching marriage; yet not as if he and his betrothed had been to reside at Birkendelly, all his provisions rather bespeaking a meditated journey.

On the morning of the 9th, he wrote to his sister, and then arraying himself in his new wedding suit, and putting the emerald ring on his finger, he appeared all impatience, until towards evening, when he sallied out on horseback to his appointment. It seems that his mysterious innamorata had met him, for he was seen riding through the big town before sunset, with a young lady behind him, dressed in white and green, and the villagers affirmed that they were riding at the rate of fifty miles an hour! They were seen to pass a cottage called Mosskilt, ten miles farther on, where there was no highway, at the same tremendous speed; and I could never hear that they were any more seen, until the following morning, when Birkendelly's fine bay horse was found lying dead at his own stable door; and shortly after, his master was likewise discovered lying a blackened corpse on the Birky Brow, at the very spot where the mysterious, but lovely dame, had always appeared to him. There was neither wound, bruise, nor dislocation, in his whole frame; but his skin was of a livid colour, and his features terribly distorted.

This woful catastrophe struck the neighbourhood with great consternation, so that nothing else was talked of. Every ancient tradition and modern incident were raked together, compared, and combined; and certainly a most rare concatenation of misfortunes was elicited. It was authenticated that his father had died on the same spot that day twenty years, and his grandfather that day forty years, the former, as was supposed, by a fall from his horse when in liquor, and the latter nobody knew how; and now this Allan was the last of his race,* for Mrs Bryan had no children.

It was moreover now remembered by many, and among the rest, the Rev. Joseph Taylor, that he had frequently observed a young lady, in white and green, sauntering about that spot on a St Lawrence's Eve.

When Captain Bryan and his lady arrived to take possession of the premises, they instituted a strict enquiry into every circumstance; but nothing farther than what was related to them by Mr M'Murdie could be learned of this Mysterious Bride, besides what the Laird's own letter bore. It ran thus:—

'DEAREST SISTER,

'I shall, before this time to-morrow, be the most happy, or most miserable, of mankind, having solemnly engaged myself this night to wed a young and beautiful lady, named Jane Ogilvie, to whom it seems I was betrothed before I was born. Our correspondence has been of a most private and mysterious nature; but my troth is pledged, and my resolution fixed. We set out on a far journey to the place of her abode on the nuptial eve, so that it will be long before I see you again.

                                    'Your's till death,
                                'ALLAN GEORGE SANDISON.
                        'Birkendelly, August 8th, 1781.'

That very same year, an old woman, named Marion Haw, was returned upon that, her native parish, from Glasgow. She had led a migratory life with her son—who was what he called a bell-hanger, but in fact a tinker of the worst grade—for many years, and was at last returned to the muckle town in a state of great destitution. She gave the parishioners a history of the

Mysterious Bride, so plausibly correct, but withal so romantic, that every body said of it, (as is often said of my narratives,
with the same narrow-minded prejudice and injustice,) that it
was *a made story*. There were, however, some strong testi-
monies of its veracity.

She said the first Allan Sandison, who married the great
heiress of Birkendelly, was previously engaged to a beautiful
young lady, named Jane Ogilvie, to whom he gave any thing
but fair play; and, as she believed, either murdered her, or
caused her to be murdered, in the midst of a thicket of birch
and broom, at a spot which she mentioned; that she had good
reasons for believing so, as she had seen the red blood and the
new grave, when she was a little girl, and ran home and mentioned it to her grandfather, who charged her as she valued
her life never to mention that again, as it was only the nombles
and hide of a deer, which he himself had buried there. But
when, twenty years subsequent to that, the wicked and unhappy Allan Sandison was found dead on that very spot, and
lying across the green mound, then nearly level with the surface, which she had once seen a new grave, she then for
the first time ever thought of a Divine Providence; and she
added, 'For my grandfather, Neddy Haw, he dee'd too; there's
naebody kens how, nor ever shall.'

As they were quite incapable of conceiving, from Marion's
description, any thing of the spot, Mr M'Murdie caused her to
be taken out to the Birky Brow in a cart, accompanied by Mr
Taylor, and some hundreds of the townsfolk; but whenever
she saw it, she said, 'Aha, birkies! the haill kintra's altered
now. There was nae road here than; it gaed straight ower the
tap o' the hill. An' let me see—there's the thorn where the
cushats biggit;* an' there's the auld birk that I aince fell aff an'
left my shoe stickin i' the cleft. I can tell ye, birkies, either the
deer's grave, or bonny Jane Ogilvie's, is no twa yards off the
place where that horse's hind feet are standin'; sae ye may
howk,* an' see if there be ony remains.'

The minister, and M'Murdie, and all the people, stared at
one another, for they had purposely caused the horse to stand
still on the very spot where both the father and son had been
found dead. They digged, and deep, deep below the road, they

found part of the slender bones and skull of a young female, which they deposited decently in the churchyard. The family of the Sandisons is extinct—the Mysterious Bride appears no more on the Eve of St Lawrence—and the wicked people of the great muckle village have got a lesson on Divine justice written to them in lines of blood.

THE EXECUTIONER

William Godwin the Younger

CHAPTER I

YES, I—I am an executioner—a common hangman!—These fingers, that look, as I hold them before mine eyes, as a part and parcel of humanity, have fitted the noose and strained the cord to drive forth the soul from its human mansion, and to kill the life that was within it! Oh, horror of horrors, I have stood on the public scaffold, amid the execrations of thousands, more hated than the criminal that was to die by me—more odious than the offender that tottered thither in expiation, with life half fled already—and I have heard a host of human voices join in summoning Heaven's malediction on me and my disgusting office. Well, well I deserved it; and as I listened to the piercing cry, my conscience whispered in still more penetrating accents, 'Thou guilty Ambrose, did they but know all thy meed of wickedness, they would be silent—silent in mere despair of inventing curses deep enough to answer to the depth of thy offence.'

What is it that prompts me to tell the history of my transgressions? Why sit I in my solitude, thinking and thinking till thought is madness, and trembling as I gaze on the white and unsoiled paper that is destined shortly to be so foully blotted with the annals of my crime and my misery? Alas, I know not why! I have no power to tell the impulse that compels me —I can only pronounce that the impulse has existence, and that it seems to me as if the sheet on which I write served me instead of a companion, and I could conjure from its fancied society a sort of sympathy in the entireness of my wretchedness.

As some men are born to greatness, so are some to misery. My evil genius, high heaven and the truth can witness, clutched me in my cradle, and never have I been free from the grasp that urged me onwards and onwards, as though the great sea of destruction was being lashed into tenfold speed and might for the sole purpose of overwhelming me.

Yes, if earliest memory may justify the phrase, from my very cradle was I foredoomed to sin and sorrow. The first recollection that I have of those worldly incidents that marked my daily course, takes me back to a gloomy, marshy, half-sterile spot, deep seated in the fens of Lincolnshire. May I say that I lived there? Was it life to see the same dull round of nothings encompassing me day after day—to have none to speak to, or to hear speak, save an old and withered crone, who to my young comprehension appeared to be fastened down, as it were, to the huge chimney-corner, and who seemed to exist (paradox-like) more by sleeping, than by the employment of any other function of the animal frame? The only variation of this monotonous circle of my days was the monthly arrival of my father, who used to come across the quaggy moor in a sort of farmer's cart, and on whose periodical visits we entirely depended for our provisions for the ensuing month. The parent at all times exercises mighty influence over the mind of his offspring; but were I to attempt to describe that which my father possessed over me, it would seem as if I were penning some romantic tale to make old women bless their stars and crouch nearer to the blazing Christmas log, rather than simply narrating the prime source of all those curseful events that have made me the wretch I am. Nor need I here describe his power; for each page that I have to write will more and more develope the entireness of his baneful influence over my mind, and shew how he employed it to my irretrievable undoing.

Monthly he came;—and as I grew from boyhood into the full youth-tide of my blood and vigour, it seemed to me as if I only condescended to live for the recurrence of these visits. The question in my mind was, not what day of the week, or what date of the month it was; but how many days had elapsed since my father's last visit—how many were to elapse before I should see him again. And then, after these periodical heart-aching reckonings, he would come—come but to go again, after a short tantalizing one-day stay. Once—once I ventured to press him to take me with him: my eagerness made me eloquent. I bowed to my very knees in supplication for the indulgence. But in vain—in vain; and it was then, perhaps, that I first fully ascertained the power that he had over my heart—ay, over my soul—my very soul of souls. Angry at my continued entreaties, he lost his temper, raged till his teeth gnashed in the fierceness of his ire, and bade me again ask to accompany him at the peril of his curse. To me, at that time, his passion was little less than so many dagger-thrusts in my bosom, and I shrank in exquisite anguish from the contest, tremblingly convinced that never again might I dare to urge the cherished desire of my imagination. When I remembered the height of his indignation, it almost seemed as if there must have been something heinous, in an unheard-of degree, in my request: my father, to my mind, was the wisest, the best, and the most judicious of mankind; how could it be otherwise, when he was the only one with whom I had ever held communication, save the crone who appeared to have slept away her brains, if she ever had any? and that wisdom, that goodness, that judiciousness, I had offended! Where, then, was the wonder that I myself cried shame upon the offence?

In this state of things I attained about my twenty-third year, as nearly as I can guess; and then, at last, a change arrived. Great heaven, what a change! Fool that I was, not to content myself with being at least as well off as the beast of the field, or the steed that is stalled and cared for, as far as nature and his appetite make demands upon him. But ignorant, restless, and morbid in my sensations, I must needs have change. It came; and I changed too—into a wretch—an outcast—a thing hated, despised, and hooted at!

It began with an ill omen! I might have foreseen that some deed of horrid circumstance was at hand.

The old woman was seated, as usual, in the chimney-corner. She had been sitting there from six in the morning till nine at night, without uttering a syllable—without tasting food, as far as I knew, though during some hours in the day she had been left to herself, while I was wandering my solitary round through the plashy fens. At length, our hour of nightly rest arrived, and I summoned her from her stationary posture. But she answered not—she moved not: I approached, and gently shook her: I took hold of her withered, wrinkled hand—it was cold and clammy:—I raised her head—it was expressionless—her eye was inanimate. She was dead!

It took some minutes for me to persuade myself that death had indeed been at work. I had thought of death—dreamed of death—pictured death; but now, for the first time, he presented himself to my outward observation, and I shrank with morbid instinct from the task of contemplation. Always a creature of passion—always a creature of waywardness and prejudice—without education, without instruction, without guidance, I had no philosophy to lead me but my own ignorance—no rule of conduct save the *ignes fatui** of my own imagination. I doubt whether at any time, or with any training, I could have taken my first lesson in mortality without an involuntary shuddering; but circumstanced as I then was, I almost instinctively tottered into a far-off corner of the room, and there, for a while, as I held my hands before my eyes, to shut out all visible presence of the corpse, I seemed as if I was gradually assuming its motionless rigour, and sharing in its cessation of existence.

It was a fearful night; and so the days and nights that followed. From the time of the old woman's decease, to the period of my father's next visit, was a fortnight. Flight from this scene of death was one of the first thoughts that presented itself to my mind—but whither? I had no one clew to guide me in my search for my parent; and to me, every thing beyond the cottage in the fens and its neighbourhood was a blank. As I debated this within myself, I tried to resolve to stay—I determined to confine myself to another room of the narrow dwelling—I called upon my energy to assist me in forgetting how nearly I was hand in hand with death. But the task was too much for me—my whole mental faculty succumbed under the attempt—and my brain felt as if it was under the utter dominion of the Prince of terrors; each hour added fresh visions of dismay to those which already appalled me; and when, after the lapse of three or four days, the odour of the decaying corpse spread itself through every portion of the cottage, the thoughts that seized upon my excited imagination became unbearable, and, without plan or project, I almost unwittingly rushed from the abode of my childhood, to face the perils of all that lay before me, unknowing and unknown.

My first steps were those of real flight, prompted by a desire of freeing myself from a sort of incubus that seemed to be urging me on to madness, as long as I remained within its influence. This feeling lent speed to my pace for nearly half the day, and then, when I began to consider the rate at which I had walked—or rather, when I was able to begin to consider any of the circumstances that attended my change, I gradually obtained the power of perceiving that I was by degrees releasing myself from the painful impulse that had hitherto been pressing me forward. But in proportion as I escaped from these sensations, others of a scarcely less dreary complexion took possession of my mind. Where was I?—What was I about?—Whither was I going?—And how was I to find my father, of whom I did not even so much as know his name?—With these and similar thoughts disturbing my imagination, I found the night fast gathering around me, while I was still vainly extending my gaze in every direction for the abode of man, or any practicable refuge for the destitute wanderer. Vainly, indeed, did I run my aching eyes along the farthest margin of the horizon. Nothing but a low marshy land, with here and there a stunted water-loving tree, was to be seen; and when I turned my glance upwards, the clouds that met my sight appeared as sullen and as gloomy as the prospect which a moment before the earth had presented. But even this was comfortable in the comparison to that which followed; for presently a chilly soaking rain commenced falling; the day completely closed; and I scarcely took a step without finding myself plunged knee-deep in some marish reservoir, or unexpected quagmire. Surrounded with evils, the best that I could do was to choose the least; and, feeling that it was hopeless to pursue my path when all was utter doubt and darkness, I resolved to take shelter in one of the stunted trees which I found scattered over the fens, and there to remain till the morning should begin to dawn. My project succeeded as far as mere rest was concerned, and with cramps and rheums for my bedfellows, I found that I might hope to pass through the tedious night. But though I thus escaped any farther trials of the treacherous footing that awaited me beneath, the thin and scanty foliage of my tree of refuge afforded no shelter from the pitiless storm, in which the wind and the rain seemed to be playing an alternate game, the one undertaking to dry me as fast as the other drenched me to the skin.

This, then, was my first introduction to the world. This was the 'Go on, and prosper,' that attended me on my first venturing forth from the dwelling that had hitherto sheltered me. As I sat stilted, as it were, in my dark arbour of slippery branches, amid which I felt as if couched in a morass, I could not help recalling to my mind the ominous words with which my father had, two years before, prophesied that I should most surely repent any endeavour to make the world and myself more intimately acquainted. Already did I repent! yea, even though the act of my quitting the cottage in this instance had been scarcely more than what I considered to be a sort of self-preservation.

At length morning came. It still rained—a heavy, penetrating, chilling torrent. The wind still roared, as though the northern blast was hallooing to its brother of the east to come and make dreary holyday for the nonce; a hunger, fierce and gnawing, had taken possession of me, as if that too was in cruel collusion with the elements to crush me. But still, in spite of rain, wind, and hunger, there was light—and with light came hope—with hope, a sort of artificial buoyancy and vigour, which enabled me to descend from my scrambling melancholy couch, and once again to stretch forward in search of some track of human existence.

Whither, or in what direction I wandered, I never was able to satisfy myself, though I have since, more than once, pored over the map of Lincolnshire, with a desire of tracing my first journey from the solitary cottage in the fens, to the habitation of man, and of civilized society. All that I know is, that after nearly exhausting the whole of this second day in fruitless rambling, I at length, even at the moment when I thought I must finally give up the effort, and sink in obedience to declining nature, had my heart gladdened with the sound of the barking of a dog, and by following this aural track, I was fortunate enough to reach the small village of Fairclough a little before nightfall.

How my bosom glowed as I attained this spot of human sojourn! I was like the arctic traveller, who, after wild beasts for his companions, and snow for his pillow, at last arrives at one of those godsend hunting huts, that to his longing eyes start up in the wilderness, more brilliant than the most gorgeous palace of the East to the perverted gaze of a luxurious emir. Now, thought I, is the hour at length arrived for me to be introduced to my kindred men—now is the world of humanity before—now will every one that I meet be a brother or a sister;—and my heart, too long pent-up, and compelled to be a self-devourer, will find an opportunity for that expansion for which it has so long been yearning.

As I thus communed with myself, I approached a cottage. The door stood invitingly open. 'Hail, happy omen of the heart that reigns within,' cried I; and, with an honest reverence for my own picture of human nature, I entered. The only persons that I perceived inside were a woman and a child, sickly and puling, whom the former was endeavouring to coax from its shrill crying, by the offer of a slice of bread and butter.

It was not till I had fairly crossed the threshold, and found that I was noticed by the female, that I remembered that my errand was a begging one; and the sudden recurrence of the thought threw some little embarrassment into my manner. However, I had no time for consideration; for the woman, without waiting for my address, briefly demanded—'What's your want?'

'For the sake of pity,' replied I, somewhat chilled by her words, and still more by the callous manner in which she used them—'for the sake of pity, afford me some food—this is the second day that these lips have gone without a morsel.'

'Food, quotha!' reiterated the woman—'hark ye, youngster, did you never hear of rent and taxes, and poor-rates to boot? It is not over much food that we get for ourselves—none that we have to give away. You had better try the overseer.'

'The overseer!' returned I, somewhat puzzled as to whom he might be—'alas, I have no strength left to carry me farther!

A crust of bread and half an hour's rest is all I ask.' And, as I uttered these words, I sank exhausted into a chair that stood near.

'Poor fellow!' cried the occupant of the cottage, probably moved by the too apparent condition to which I was reduced:— 'Well, God knows, bread is dear enough, and money is scarce enough, and supper is seldom enough; but if a crust will satisfy you, it shall not be wanting. But, harkye, you can't stay here to eat it; my husband will be here anon, and——'

Scarcely had she uttered the words—hardly was the proffered crust within my grasp, when he, of whom she spoke, made his appearance, with evident symptoms about him that he had not visited the village alehouse in vain.

'How now, Suky,' cried he, as he observed my presence— 'what does this chap do here?'

'Poor wretch,' replied his wife, 'it seems as if it were nearly over with him, what with fatigue and what with hunger, so he asked leave to sit down a bit, and rest his poor bones.'

'And why the devil did you let him?' surlily demanded the man:—'I'll have no bone-resting here. Am I the lord of the manor, or squire of the village, that I can afford to take in every pauper that finds his way here?—and who gave him that bread?'

The wife seemed to shrink from the question, while I mustered resolution to reply—'She—who will be blessed for it, as long as heaven blesses charity.'

'Heyday,' cried the fellow, 'why the chap is a Methodist parson in disguise, after all!—Harkye, Mr Parson-pauper, please to turn out.—Once a-week is quite enough for that sort of thing.'

'Do not force me abroad again to-night!—I have not strength to move.'

'Hoity toity,' exclaimed the drunkard, 'you have strength to eat, and pretty briskly too.—And who, do you suppose, is to find your lazy carcass a lodging for the night?—Turn out, I say.'

'For pity's sake——'

'Pity be d—d! Turn out, I say,'—and as he spoke he seized me by the collar, and whirling me round by mere brute force,

I found myself in an instant outside the cottage; while, as a token that all hope of re-entry was vain, he slammed the door violently in my face.

This was my first introduction to the benevolence of mankind:—this was the earliest welcome that awaited the wanderer from the fens.—I groaned, and tottered onwards.

But if this was my first introduction, I soon found that it was by no means a solitary specimen of what was to be presented for my acceptance. Another, and another, and another cottage was tried,—and still the same result. I was spurned by the most cruel—I was unheeded by the most humane—I was neglected by all; and one other much-begrudged crust of bread was all that my importunities were able to obtain. With this I retired to a miserable outhouse attached to a farm at the extremity of the village, and having devoured it, I endeavoured to make myself a bed in the scattered straw that lay strewed about the ground. My hunger, though not altogether appeased, had ceased to press with such torturing pain on my very vitals; and the exhaustion of my frame speedily lulled me to sleep.

Sound and refreshing were my slumbers; and it was not till I was roused by the owner of the building that I awoke from them.

'Halloo, my fine spark!' cried he; 'who gave you permission to take possession of my outhouse? Please to get up, and away; and you may think yourself well off that you escape so easily.'

This was a bad omen for begging a breakfast; and I was about to depart, without a syllable in reply, when it suddenly crossed my mind that I might at least solicit work. Heaven knows that it was never my desire to live on the bread of idleness, and with how much willingness I was ready to undertake the most menial or the most laborious employment to entitle myself to my daily food!

'Well,' cried the farmer, perceiving that I lingered, 'will you not take my advice, and disappear before I shew that I am in earnest?'

'I was hoping, sir,' replied I, 'that you would not take it amiss if I solicited you to give me some work. Indeed, indeed you will find me very willing; and I think I could be useful.'

'Useful, youngster! In what?—Can you plough? Can you thrash? Can you reap?'

A mournful negative was my reply. 'But I am ready to learn.'

'And who is to pay for your teaching? Besides, a pretty hope it would be that you will ever be good for any thing, when we find a tall strapping fellow like you, who has been too idle as yet to learn to plough or to reap. No, no, thankye, we have plenty of paupers here already, and I have no fancy to add to the number, by giving you a settlement in the parish. So, good day, my friend; and when you again offer to work, see if you cannot give yourself a better character.'

Again baffled in hope, and checked in spirit, I moved away, seeing but too clearly that the village of Fairclough was no resting-place for me.

'Oh, father, father!' cried I, with bitterness in my accent, as I paced slowly forward—'where am I to seek you? How am I to find you?'

It was a dreary day in March that again witnessed me—a wanderer—creeping along on my unpurposed journey, and tracking my weary way from spot to spot, as chance or destiny might direct. The early produce of the fields afforded me a scanty, miserable breakfast; and as I looked upwards, and saw the linnet and the finch flitting with a gay carol over my head, a sort of envy of their condition seized me, and, instead of glorying in my station, as one of the master works of nature, I mourned at the shackled unhappiness of my lot. What now had become of my fancy-decked picture of the all-receiving brotherhood of mankind? Whither had flown the friendship, the kindness, the heart-in-hand welcome that I had so fondly dreamt waited my arrival in the abodes of the world? Fictions! Empty, deceitful fictions, that had betrayed me to myself, and that, for a short moment, had taken the place of the withering, frightful truth, that for the houseless, penniless wanderer there was no sympathy, no hospitable tendering to his necessities!

Thus, for many days, strayed I through the humid atmosphere of a Lincolnshire March, now and then reaping one miserable meal, or one measured draught of milk from a whole village, but more often feeding on the vegetable productions of the hedges and the fields, and trusting to the chances of the road for a nightly shelter.

Meanwhile, I felt that my heart was gradually changing within me. I had brought it into the world of men, with its offering of love and kindness, but none would accept it—none would reciprocate to it; it was the heart of a beggar, and society cried, Out upon it! I began to ask myself gloomy and frightful questions—questions that no heart ought to be forced to ask itself. As I laboured along in solitude, misery, and neglect, I demanded of myself a thousand times, 'Why am I to have love for man, when mankind has none for me?'

At length accident conducted my steps to the little town of Okeham, the capital of Rutlandshire.* There the hedges, and the other cold cheer of nature failed me, and I was compelled to beg for my very existence. It is impossible to describe the disgust with which I contemplated this necessity. The rebuffs with which, one after another, I had met, had sickened upon my soul, and I felt that the mere act of petitioning charity was like offering my cheek to be smote, or my person to be insulted. It was nothing short of utter starvation that was able to drive me to it.

But it seemed as if my evil genius was accumulating the venom of disgrace for me. It was my ill fortune to select, as my first house of trial, the abode of one of the constables of the town; and the words of imploring charity were not cold from my mouth, ere this high official burst forth in a strain that astonished even me, accustomed as I was to rebuke and reproach, for daring to announce that hunger had on me the same effect as on the rest of mankind. According to this man's creed, I was a villain, a vagabond, and a rapscallion, and I ought to go on my knees to thank him for not instantly dragging me before a magistrate, to be dealt with as the heinousness of my presumption demanded. Alas! he might have spared his wrath, for I was too well accustomed to rejection not to take the first hint, and shrink from an encounter where all power was on one side, and all irresistance on the other.

'Come with me, my poor fellow,' exclaimed a gentle voice that was hardly audible amid the constabulary storm that I had raised. 'Come with me, and I will afford you such poor assistance as my wretched means will allow. I am your twin-brother in misery, and my ear too well knows the cry of distress.'

I looked round to see what angel it was that thus pronounced the first real words of kindness that had reached me since my secession from the cottage in the fens. He who had spoken was a thin, sickly-looking youth, about eighteen or nineteen years of age; and when his face was scanned, though only for a moment, the beholder would feel that there was no need for his confession of misery. Sorrow, and wellnigh despair, were seated there; and his thin uncoloured cheek declared the waste that grief had inflicted on his heart.

'Come with you, indeed!' cried the man of office, tauntingly. 'Why, that will be rogue to rogue with a vengeance; and I suppose we shall have a pretty account by to-morrow, of some burglary to be looked after.'

When I took my first glance at my new friend, it seemed to me as if nothing but art could have lent colour to his sallow countenance; but nature was more strong in him than I had imagined, and as he listened to the words that were uttered by this overbearing Dogberry,* the quick blood bubbled to his cheek, and he glowed with the full fire of indignation, as he replied—'I would that the law permitted me to commit a burglary on thy wicked heart, that I might break it open, and shew mankind how foul a composition may be cased in human substance. But no matter,—I speak to iron! Come, good fellow,' added he, turning to me, 'we will avoid this iniquitous libel on the species, and seek another spot for farther conversation.'

'Now that's just what you won't,' roared his brutal opponent:—'I rather suspect what you have said amounts to a threat of assault; and I shall ask Justice Goffle about it; but at all events I know that this ragged barebones, who seems to be all at once your bosom friend, has brought himself within the vagrant act; so you may go and seek your conversation by yourself, or along with your father, who is snug in the lock-up, for you know what; for as to this youngster he stirs not till Mr Goffle has had a word or two with him; and then perhaps a month at the tread-mill may put him into better condition for the high honour of your friendship.'

He suited the action to the word, for before he had finished his speech I felt myself within his nervous gripe.

The youth saw that opposition was vain. For my own part I felt no inclination to struggle or contend: the one drop of liquid tempering, with which his words of sympathy had softened my heart, was again dried up and consumed by the new cruelty that attended on my destitution; and I felt a sort of bitter satisfaction that my last week's resolve of hatred against mankind had escaped the peril of being shaken by the benevolent offer of this exception to his species.

Under the watchful custody of the constable, I was speedily conveyed to the presence of Mr Justice Goffle: my offence was too evident to admit of a moment's doubt; he who had captured me, was at once my prosecutor, my convicting witness, and my custos* to lead me, according to the sentence of the law, and of Mr Justice Goffle, to a fortnight's imprisonment and hard labour in the jail of the town. In another half hour, I was safely lodged within its gloomy walls.

The first lesson which I there learned was, that the criminal and the offender of the laws were better fed than the harmless, wretched wanderer, whose only sin was that of being hungry in obedience to nature's ordinances. I could hardly believe my senses when I had proffered to me, and without asking for it either, a substantial meal—such a one as had not gladdened my sight since I quitted the cottage in the fens: and, as I silently devoured it, I tried to account for the phenomenon, but in vain; it was too much for my philosophy. It did not, however, tend to ease the cankering hatred against mankind that was fast eating into the very core of my every sensation.

My next lesson was one still more mischievous. It was that which I received from my fellow-prisoners, and which was made up of vain-glory for the enormity of their crimes that were passed, and of wily subtle resolves for the execution of those that were to come. A week before I had held all mankind to be excellent and lovely. I now deemed the whole race wicked and pernicious.

The third morning after my initiation into Okeham jail, I

perceived an unusual bustle taking place: the turnkeys crossed the yard in which we were confined with more than their usual importance; and the head jailer rattled his keys with extraordinary emphasis. What to me would have been a long unravelled mystery, if left to my own lucubrations, was speedily explained by some of my companions. It was the day for the commencement of the assize—the judges were hourly expected—fresh prisoners were being brought in from the various locks-up, and every thing was in preparation for their reception. Presently a buzz went round among those that were already confined, anticipatory of a fresh arrival of colleagues in misfortune; and a minute afterwards the yard-gate was unlocked.

'Pass in Edward Foster, committed for horse-stealing,' shouted one of the turnkeys, outside.

'Edward Foster passed in,' echoed his brother turnkey, who stood at the yard gate; and the new prisoner, on his appearance among us, was received with a cheer by the gaping crowd of malefactors, as Lucifer might be by his kith and kin of fallen angels on his arrival at Pandemonium. After the lapse of another minute, Foster was conveyed to a solitary cell, in token of his being confined on a capital charge.

'Pass in Stephen Lockwood, king's evidence, and committed for want of sureties,' again shouted the same voice, from without.

'Stephen Lockwood passed in,' repeated he at the gate.

The crowd of prisoners gathered round the entry as nearly as they dared approach; and, on receiving this other new comer among them, saluted him with a threatening groan, that ran round the old walls of the jail, for the purpose of shewing their contempt of 'the snivelling 'peach.'*

He who was thus welcomed to his dungeon, made his way as speedily as he could through the mob of jail-birds, and approached the spot where I was standing, probably so induced, from its being the least crowded part of the yard.

Eternal Heaven! what were my horror and astonishment, on perceiving that it was my father that thus drew near!

Our mutual recognition was instantaneous; but before I could speak, he muttered hastily,—'Not a word of our relationship before these wretches.'

It was some time before the indignant criminals that surrounded my father, afforded us an opportunity of conversation. When at length we had an opportunity of exchanging a few words without being overheard, my parent demanded of me the circumstances that had made me the inmate of a prison. When they were recounted,—'It is well,' cried he, 'fate has brought us together in its own mysterious way. It is well!—it is well!—But we may yet be revenged on the world.'

My eyes gleamed with delight at the sound of the word 'revenge;' and I echoed it from the very bottom of my soul. It was easy for my father to understand the spirit in which I uttered it; for it had been with no cold-blooded suppression of manner that I had narrated to him my adventures since I had quitted the cottage in the fens.

'But you, my father,' cried I, 'why are you here?'

'Hush,' whispered he, 'this is no place to relate the tale of my wrongs and of my wretchedness. Your sentence of imprisonment will be over in twelve days; and till then we must restrain ourselves. I have a dreadful story for your ears.'

'But how soon shall you be free?'

'In four or five days, beyond all doubt:—the trial for which I am detained is expected to come on tomorrow, after which I shall be at liberty. On the day of the expiration of your imprisonment, I will wait for you outside the jail. Meanwhile, feed your heart with thoughts of vengeance—the dearest, sweetest, only worldly solace that remains for men so undone as Stephen Lockwood and his progeny.'

Dreadful was the anxiety with which I counted the hours till that of my release arrived. My father's calculation as to his own term of imprisonment proved to be correct; and for the last eight days of my confinement I was left alone to brood over my heart's wild conjectures—born of the dark and mysterious hints that he had poured into my ear.

At length the day of my restoration to liberty arrived, and, true to his word, I found my parent waiting for me in eager expectation outside the prison.

'Follow me,' cried he hastily, as soon as he perceived that I was by his side:—'follow me to the fields beyond the town; for I have those things to relate that other than you must never hear.'

I obeyed in silence, for my whole soul was so completely wrapt in expectation of that which he had to communicate, that I sickened at the thought of dwelling on any less momentous subject. He, as we strode along, was equally reserved; but I could perceive that the thoughts that were raging within him were of sufficient potency to disturb the outward man, and to give a wildness of action to his demeanour that I had never before observed, save on that one occasion when I had pressed him beyond endurance to make me his companion, by releasing me from my sojourn at the cottage in the fens.

At length we arrived at a secluded spot some distance from the town we had just quitted, and where a long, blank, nearly-untrodden moor gave promise that we might escape interruption.

'It is here, Ambrose,' cried my father, suddenly pausing in his progress, 'it is here that we will take our stand; hateful man cannot approach us without being seen—the roaring wind cannot blab our secrecies, for none are nigh to catch the whisper it conveys—trees and darkling coverts there are none to hide our foe, or permit his stealthy footstep to creep unwarily upon us:—here, then, here we may talk truths, and cry aloud for vengeance without fear or hinderance.'

I was all ear, but murmured not a sound. Like the tyro in the schools, I waited to be led to my conclusions; and with the sentiments that I entertained towards my father, his words seemed to be those of one inspired.

He himself paused as though it required some great effort to enable him to commence his tale. At length he continued—'The time is now come, Ambrose, when I have to place before you the circumstances that induced me to fix your residence in the lonely spot you have so lately quitted, in the hopes of sheltering you from the unkind treatment of that world that has used your father so bitterly. The time is come, and with it our revenge. Listen, my son, that you may learn the grudge you owe to man—that you may be taught how to resent the wrong that was inflicted on you long before you dreamt that mischief had station on the earth, or had played you false in your very earliest existence.'

'Your every word, my father, reaches the very centre of my heart. I am in your hands:—mould me to your bidding.'

'You will require no moulding, Ambrose. My tale will be sufficient to direct your course. Listen:—I was born of humble parents in the village of Ravenstoke; and though I had the misfortune to lose both my father and my mother almost before I knew the value of such beings, the evils that attend a child of poverty were averted by the kindly notice of the principal family of the place. The good man at its head, and who never made fall a tear till death took him from the world, early noticed me, and was pleased to think that he saw in me sufficient capacity and promise to befit me to be the companion of Edward, his only child, whose years were pretty nearly the same as my own. Thus in happiness and content passed away my youth; but it only seemed as if the demon that had marked me for his prey, was resting for the purpose of accumulating his whole force in order to crush me. In a neighbouring village, to which my walks had been frequently directed, there lived a maiden whose gentleness of disposition and beauty of person had won for her the affection of all who were blessed enough to be acquainted with her. In my eyes she was even more than my young fancy, ever too busy in picturing forth happiness and loveliness, had at any time conjured to the vision of my senses. Need I say that I loved—loved to distraction, and how more than mortally happy I deemed myself when I received from the fair lips of Ellen a half-whispered approval of my love? Oh, my Ambrose, I cannot recall those early days of fondness and affection, and prevent the hot tears coursing down my cheeks, there to stream as witnesses of my devotion, till the bitter recollection of the manner in which that devotion was abused dries up the liquid testimony at the very source, and leaves me even now, after the lapse of twenty years, the victim of a distorted faith—too fresh, too real, and too scathing, ever to be extinguished till this body is returned to moulder with the dust.'

As Lockwood thus spoke, his eyes gave proof of the fulness of his feelings; and some minutes elapsed before he was able to proceed.

'I must be brief, Ambrose, with the rest of my story, for I feel that my heart will scarcely allow me words to conclude it. When Ellen had confessed her affection for me, there was nought to prevent our union, and a few weeks, therefore, saw

me, as I deemed myself, the happiest of men; and our dearest
hope appeared to be that we might live and die with one
another. The hour of separation—fatal, fatal separation—
however, arrived; and to oblige Edward, who, on the death of
his father, had succeeded to the family property, which was
somewhat involved, I consented to go to the East Indies for
him, relative to an estate there on which he had a considerable
claim. This journey, and the delay which I met with abroad,
occupied two years; and it was with a heavy heart that I quitted
Ellen, who, on the eve of being brought to bed, was in no
condition to share with me the fatigues of a long sea voyage.
Well might my heart be heavy with presentiment! Could it
have anticipated all that was to happen, it would have turned
to lead, and refused to obey its nature-appointed functions. At
length the day of my return approached: each hour that the
ship neared England I stood on the deck, counting the lazy
minutes, and stretching my eyes landward, in the hope of
catching the first glimpse of the white cliffs of my native land;
and so, when I reached the shore, I reckoned each moment an
age till the happy one should arrive that was to restore me to
the arms of my wife. There was no such moment in store for
me; for just as I was quitting the metropolis for Ravenstoke,
I met an old village acquaintance, who felled my every hope
with the intelligence that my Ellen—mine—she whom I had
deemed to be the truest, the faithfullest of her sex—was living
with another as his avowed mistress—acknowledged, brazen,
barefaced before the whole world, and in defiance of the thousand vows in the face of God and man by which she had
pledged herself mine, and mine alone. You may well start with
astonishment, my son, and gaze wildly, as if in doubt of the
truth of this atrocity. So started I—so doubted I—till evidence
beyond evidence bore bitterest conviction to my soul. But the
whole is not yet told.—Ellen's falsity came not single. He
who had seduced her from her liege affections shewed with
equal perjury before high Heaven. It was Edward! Yes,
Edward—my friend, my companion;—he for whom I had
quitted my gentle wife and peaceful home—Edward, the
monster, the traitor, the fiend begot of sin essential, had taken
advantage of the opportunity, which he himself had solicited,

of my friendship, and stolen from me, by double deceit and treason, the prize that I cared for more than life or any thing on earth.'

'Gracious powers!' exclaimed I, overwhelmed by the dreadful incidents that had been narrated—'and am I the son of this wretched mother? Was I thus early doomed to misery?'

'It is too true,' replied my father; 'you are the child of whom I left Ellen pregnant when I departed on the ruinous errand besought by her seducer. When the fact of your mother's crime was made conviction to my senses, a thousand different modes of action poured in upon my brain; and, the creature more of impulse than of reason, I hurried to Ravenstoke to confront the adulterous pair. It was evening when I arrived—even such an evening as this—gloomy, dark, and cheerless,—yet in high accordance with the thoughts that urged me forward. As I hurried across the park that led to the mansion-house, a pony-chaise overtook me. I turned on its approach, and for a moment my senses forsook me at the sight of Ellen, who, with you for her only companion, was driving quickly homeward to avoid the threatening storm. My voice arrested her farther progress, as I groaned rather than uttered—"Ellen!" —"Wife!" At the summons she descended from the chaise, after wrapping you in her cloak as you lay along the seat, asleep and unconscious. What words I addressed to her I can hardly tell:—they were those which flowed at the dictation of a brain almost mad at the injury it had sustained; while her answer was none save tears and sobs of heaviness. At length she broke from the grasp with which, in my anguish, I had seized her—and then—then—Oh God, I cannot speak the words that should tell the rest!'

'For pity's sake, my father,' murmured I, sunk in the fearful interest of his story,—'for pity's sake, the end in a word—the end—the end!'

'Yes, yes!—the end, the end!' he echoed fiercely:—'it is one she earned, and it is wanting to make whole the frightful tale. Ambrose,—Ambrose,—she burst from my grasp, and rushed into a copse hard by. I pursued her, but in vain; for the momentary pause I had made in wonder at her meaning, had removed her from my sight, and I followed at random, guessing the direction she had taken as nearly as I might: after thus speeding for a few minutes, I reached the side of an ornamental lake that adorned the park, and there again caught glimpse of her by the dim light of a clouded moon, as she reached the opposite bank. Ambrose,—Ambrose,—cannot you imagine the rest?'

'Oh, father, was it so indeed?—And none to save her?'

'Was not I there, boy?—Thrice I dived into the bosom of the waters, after hurrying to the bank from which she had precipitated herself into destruction—thrice did I dive to the very depth of the pool—but in vain,—I could not find her— the circuit of the lake that I had had to make had afforded too much time to her fatal intention; and the attempt to find her body was fruitless. Mad with a thousand contending emotions, I returned to the chaise, and heard your little voice crying for your mother. It was then that I remembered my child, which the crime of its parent had made me forget. I took you in my arms; and as I gazed upon your innocence, my heart softened; and I resolved to put revenge aside for a while till I had secured you from peril. It was this that made me place you under the care of the old crone at the cottage in the fens.'

'But why was I kept there so long?'

'That remains yet to be told; and I shall have finished my narrative. As soon as you were safely provided for, the desire of vengeance again assumed its empire in my bosom; and I returned to Ravenstoke, hardly knowing what my purpose was, but whispering to myself, "Revenge! Revenge!" each moment of my journey. But even revenge had then for the season forsworn me. On my arrival at the village, the man who had so deeply injured me had the audacity to have me taken into custody on the charge—hear it, Ambrose, and help me to curse the villain—on the charge of having destroyed Ellen. I destroy Ellen!—Alas, alas, it was she who had destroyed me, if the banishment of peace, and of happiness, and of joy, for ever and for ever from my bosom, can be called by so poor a name as destruction. Of course, I need not tell you that when the matter came to trial I was instantly acquitted; but the event had given me timely warning of the extent to which the seducer of Ellen was able to carry his devilish contrivance to ruin the man he had already so deeply wounded; and I resolved to keep you—my only hope—in obscure concealment till the time should have arrived when I might call on you to join me in revenging my dishonour and Ellen's unhappy fate.'

'And has that time arrived?'

'It has, Ambrose!—And though we stalk on this dreary moor, the very outcasts of mankind, great and mighty is the revenge that is at hand for us.'

'Let us grasp it then,' cried I, fully wrought to the purpose,—'Let us grasp it then, and urge it to the quick.'

'Well said, well said, my son!—Oh, what years of labour has it not cost me to bring events to their present aspect! But the labour is well repaid. For the sake of revenge, I have consorted with villains of every description—I have sacrificed all and every thing to them, on the one sole bargain, that they should ruin my hateful foe; and well have they kept their word! The monster, a year or two after the death of Ellen, dared to marry. I was glad to the very heart when I heard of it; for I felt that the more ties he formed, the more ways there would be to pierce him to the heart. But his wife died too soon—before I had time to sacrifice her on the tomb of Ellen; and his son, the only offspring of the marriage, has as yet eluded my vigilance. But the father, Ambrose, the father! He is fast within my clutch! My emissaries taught him the art of throwing dice, and throwing away his estates—they inoculated him with the gambler's dreadful disease; and, for the last twelve months, he has been a ruined man in his fortunes. Desperate have been the efforts that he has made to redeem himself; but I was at hand, though never seen; and my mastermind, fraught to the very brim with his destruction, would not allow them to succeed. At length his despair was fed to its proper pitch, and I resolved to give the final blow, for which I had waited twenty long years with that exemplary patience which revenge only could bestow. I had it proposed to him, by his most familiar blackleg,* and on whom his only hopes of success rested, that they should proceed to Newmarket on a scheme, which, it was pretended, could not fail of realizing thousands. The only difficulty was, how they should get there, being at that time at Doncaster on a speculation that, through my interference, had utterly failed, and left my enemy altogether penniless; in which condition, the faithful blackleg also pretended to be. When his mind was sufficiently wrought upon by the picture of absolute and irremediable ruin that would happen, in the event of their not being able to reach Newmarket the very next evening, my agent, according to my instructions, proposed the only alternative—that of helping themselves to a horse a-piece out of the first field that afforded the opportunity, and by that means reaching the desirable spot that was to prove to them another *el Dorado*.* For a long while my enemy wavered, and I almost trembled for my scheme; but at length the longed-for thousands that flitted in fancy before his eyes, gilded the danger of the means of passage, and he consented. It was then, Ambrose, that I felt that revenge at length was mine, and I almost danced and sang in the ecstasy of my delight. Pursuant to my directions, my agent informed him who was so nearly caught within my meshes, that he had a companion to take with him, who would be absolutely necessary for the prosecution of the Newmarket scheme; and when the night for departing arrived, I was introduced as this third person. I had little fear of Edward's remembering me after a lapse of twenty years, each of which had added care, sorrow, and affliction to the lineaments of my countenance; but to guard against the possibility of danger, I muffled myself in a large cloak, and spoke the little that I uttered in a disguised voice. Every thing succeeded according to my wishes. After walking a couple of miles out of Doncaster, we came to a field where the cattle we needed were grazing; and each seizing his prize, and obtaining, with silence and caution, from the farmer's outhouse, the necessary harness, we soon found ourselves at full speed on the highway towards Newmarket. Edward was dreadfully agitated as he rode along; and once or twice I feared that he would fall from his seat— but worse evil awaited him. I will not, however, occupy our time by detailing all the minutiae of my scheme. Suffice it to say, that after giving the hint to my faithful agent to make his disappearance, I contrived that Edward and myself, on reaching the village of Stretton, should be apprehended on suspicion;

and that that suspicion should be made conviction by my volunteering as king's evidence. The rest you almost know. You yourself witnessed Edward Foster's committal to jail for horse-stealing, and my detention as the chief witness against him:—and most probably have heard, that on my evidence he was nine days ago convicted, and ordered for execution.'

'Conviction!—Execution!' exclaimed I. 'Then our revenge is indeed complete!'

'Not quite,' muttered my father; 'there is one other step to make it as perfect as my sweeping desire could wish.'

'Mean you a step beyond the grave? I know of none other—and only know that is impossible.'

'No, Ambrose, not beyond the grave, but the step to the grave!—Ask your heart! Does it feel hatred and disgust towards the man that has made wretched one parent, and scandalous the other?—that has condemned yourself to wander fortuneless and honourless over the cheerless face of the earth?—Ay, ay, boy; your gleaming eye and flushing cheek tell me the reply that your heart has already put forth. And I ask you, would it not be revenge's most glorious consummation, to repay your dreadful debt to Foster, by yourself dealing unto him that death which the law has awarded for his crime?'

'Father, father, what words are these?'

'Milk-livered boy! Why blanches your cheek, when I hold within your clutch the very satiety of vengeance? Why clench you not the precious boon? Or are you a man but in seeming, and a puling infant in resolve?'

'Speak on, father—speak on,—it seems to me as if each word you utter burns deeper and deeper into my brain—searing, as it goes, those doubtful agitations of my soul, that would raise a trembling opposition to your bidding. But they shall not! No, no! Down, down! Your wrongs shall answer the cry of humanity—my mother's fatal end the appeals of tenderness!'

'Now,' cried Lockwood, 'I know you for my son. But we have talked too much—action should be doing. The death of our foe is appointed for the third day from this; and I have learned, beyond doubt, that owing to there not having been an execution in Okeham for many years, the Sheriff finds great difficulty in procuring the proper functionary. It was this that stirred me to the hope that you would volunteer to the office; and I thank you that my hope has not been deceived. You must away to the Sheriff instantly, and get appointed; that attained, I trust to be able so to instruct you, that failure in the performance will be impossible.'

I obeyed—ay, I obeyed! I was successful! The honesty of human nature was scouted from my heart by the towering voice of the worst passion that ever cursed the breast of man.

The morning of execution arrived, and found me ready for my office. As the time had gradually grown nearer and nearer, my father had perceived, with dread, that misgivings, in spite of myself, shook my whole frame; and, in order to be more sure, he had kept me at carouse the whole of the previous night, in the miserable back street lodging that afforded us shelter.

The morning arrived; and, drunk with passion, vengeance, and brandy, it found me ready for my office.

The solemn tolling of the prison bell announced the hour of death to be at hand, as I awaited the coming of the prisoner in the outer cell. How I looked—how I acted—I know not; but, as well as I remember, it seems to me now as if I was awakened from a torpor of stupefaction on hearing the clanking of the chains that announced the approach of Foster; the sound reached my ear, more heart-chilling than the heavy tolling knell, that answered as if in echo; but I had not forgotten my lesson; I beat my hand against my brow, and whispered 'vengeance' to the spirit that was so ill at ease within. It was at that moment, that, for the first time, I beheld Edward Foster; he was not such as my soul had depicted. I pined for him to look hateful, ferocious, and bloody; but his aspect was placid, gentle, and subdued. I could have stormed in agony at the disappointment.

My first duty was to loosen his arms from the manacles that held them, and supply their place with a cord. As I fumbled at the task, I could feel myself trembling to the very fingers' ends; and it seemed as if I could not summon strength to remove the irons. My agitation must have attracted Foster's notice; for he looked at me, and gently sighed.

Gracious God, a sigh! I could as little have believed in Foster sighing as in a tigress dandling a kid. Was it possible that he was human after all? How frightfully was I mistaken! I had imagined that I had come to officiate at the sacrifice of something more infernal than a demon!

At length, with the assistance of a turnkey, every thing was prepared, and we mounted the scaffold of death. Short shrift was there; but it seemed to me as if the scene was endless; and when I looked around on the assembled multitude, I imagined that it was to gaze on me, and not on Foster, that they had congregated.

All was prepared. With some confused recollections of my father's instructions, I had adjusted the implement of death; and the priest had arrived at his last prayer, when the dying man murmured, 'I would bid farewell to my executioner.' The clergyman whispered to me to put my hand within those of Foster.

I did it! By Heaven, I did it! But it seemed as though I were heaving a more than mountain load, and cracking my very heart-strings at the task, as I directed my hand towards his. He gently grasped it, and spoke almost in a whisper.

'Young man,' said he, 'I know not how this bitter duty fell to your lot—yours is no countenance for the office; and yet it comes upon my vision as a reproach. God bless you, sir! This is my world-farewelling word; and I use it to say—I forgive you, as I hope to be forgiven.'

My hand, no longer held, dropped from his; and the priest resumed his praying. I could not pray! Each holy word that was uttered, seemed not for Foster, but for me—stabbing, not soothing.

At length the dread signal was given; and mechanically—it must have been, for the action of my mind seemed dead within me—mechanically I withdrew the bolt, and Foster was dead—swinging to the play of the winds—the living soul rudely dismissed, the body a lifeless mass of obliterated sensations.

A deep hoarse groan ran round the multitude—that groan was for me. It gave token of an eternal line of separation drawn between me and the boundaries of humanity.

Oh, that the groan had been all!—But there was one solitary laugh, too—dreadful and searching. It was my father that laughed, and it struck more horror to my soul than the groan of a myriad.

Oh, that the groan and the laugh had been all! As I crept away through the prison area, where each one shrank from me with disgust, I passed close to a youth deep bathed in tears, and some one whispered to another, 'It is poor Foster's son!' What devil tempted me to look in his face? I know not the impulse; but I know I looked—and he looked!—Oh, consummation of wretchedness, it was Foster's son—and it was he also who had offered to share with me his slender pittance on my first arrival at Okeham! As he gazed on me, a deep heavy sob seemed as though his heart was breaking.

I rushed from the spot like one mad. In all my misery, in all my wickedness, I had fondly clung to the recollection of that youth and his goodness, as the shipwrecked mariner to the creed-born cherub that he pictures forth as the guardian of his destiny. But this blow seemed to have destroyed my only Heaven. I had not even this one poor pleasurable thought left me to feed upon. His sob thrilled in my ear, as though it would never end; and the womanly sound was more overwhelming and more excruciating than the despising groan of the mob, or the atrocious laugh of Lockwood.

CHAPTER II

Many, many months have elapsed since the day on which the frightful event I have just recorded occurred; but the vision to my senses remains as perfect as if the scene was still enacting; and instead of there being for me a morrow, and a morrow, and a morrow, it seems as though my whole life was a mere repetition of one day's existence. I am built round, and confined to one abode of sensations, as Rome's offending Vestals* were encased for their unchasteness in the bondage of entombing bricks; and whatever outward events of variance occur, my heart is for ever reminding me that I am the executioner of Edward Foster. His care-worn dejected countenance flits for ever before my eyes: I meet him amid the desolateness of the far-extending moor; he walks by my side through the streets of the crowded city; and when I sleep he stalks before my fancy, dismal and enshrouded, the hero of my dreams.

But in the earlier days that followed that which ever haunts me, it was not my heart alone that reminded me of the hateful deed. I was the observed of all observers:—the rabble tracked my every footstep, and hooted me like some reptile, disgusting—not dangerous, back to my solitary den. I was the marked of men:—they almost disavowed my affinity to the species; and as I listened to their groans of execration, I began to feel as if that affinity was fast melting into air, and leaving me, in sooth, some monstrous thing that nature had created only to shew how beyond herself she had power to act.

My father very soon quitted me.—'We must part for a while,' said he to me on the second morning after that which had witnessed the close of Foster's life—'We must part for a while; for I have to provide the means of subsistence for us both— and perchance even a still further revenge. Here is such money as I can spare for the present; and this day six months we will meet again on this spot, that I may make farther provision for you.'

I was not sorry thus to part with him; for though he still retained his power over my mind, it was so united with fear and dread, that I rather looked upon him as a master than a friend, and felt that obedience to his will was something beyond choice or resistance. Besides, his presence was too intimately connected with the memory of my deed of death, to offer me any chance, while he remained, of being able to reject the painful burden from my mind; and I hoped that his absence would allow me to bury the hangman-image of my brain in the depths of forgetfulness.

But, as I have already said, the hope was vain. Though the author of the scene had departed, the scene itself was ever present; and after finding that I could not get rid either of my own reflections, or the insulting notice of the mob, I determined to quit Okeham, and not to return till my appointment with Lockwood demanded my reappearance there.

Once again, therefore, I became a wandering outcast, with none either to cherish or to pity me. Nay, I was in worse condition than when I first ventured to present myself to the mercy of the world on quitting the cottage in the fens. Then, though rejected by man, I had something within to support and assist in bearing me harmless against the attacks of misfortune. But now that single consolation had disappeared. I myself had struck down honesty in my heart, and had set up wickedness in its place. The death of Foster alone did not stand recorded there. The hatred of the multitude, expressed in no equivocal phrase whenever I appeared in the streets of Okeham, had driven me to the jail for refuge, where I learned to assort myself with those who set decency at defiance, and scouted morality as an intrusion upon their pleasures. I gazed upon these associates, and perceived that drink and debauchery were their prime pursuits; and when I remembered how brandy had helped me, on the night before the execution, to forget nature, and give strength to passion, I too resolved to pursue the gross luxuries taught by their brute-philosophy;— and the deeper I drank, the more firmly did I implant in my own system the wickedness of those, who, not being better, were worse than myself.

These were the changes, then, that had taken place within me since I first wandered from the cottage in the fens; and though I had not, as then, to beg for a miserable pittance, they were sufficient to make me feel that I was dragging on a useless existence with no object in view—with no remedy in prospect. I was like one of those unfortunates, who, in the olden time, had the choice given them to drown by water, or to burn at the stake; for I had but the alternative either to let the recollections of what had been wring my very heart, or to drown them in deep intoxicating draughts, from which, each time that I awoke from them, I was more and more hateful to myself.

The one small consolation that my departure from Okeham was intended to afford, was that of avoiding the sight of those who knew the guilty work in which these hands had been engaged, and who, in the exuberance of their feeling, hesitated not to let me know that they knew it. But this consolation was not of long continuance. After strolling for some days wherever chance directed, I reached the city of Peterborough, wet, tired, and in deep despondency at the forlorn abandonment which seemed to mark my destiny. It was in this state of feeling that I found myself at the door of a mean public-house, and the sight of it reminded me that there was still the pernicious refuge of brandy at my command. I entered, and called for liquor—drank, and called again. The fatigue that I had undergone gave additional strength to the potations in which I had indulged; and intoxication followed. What occurred during the stronger influence of the liquor I know not—but on my first beginning to regain possession of my senses, it seemed as if I had been wakened into consciousness by a severe blow on my forehead; but I had no time to ask myself any questions, for I found that I was surrounded by a mob of the lowest rabble,—pushed from side to side, with a blow from one and a kick from another—while universal execrations rang around. Oh, how well did I know those sounds!—and as they reached my ear I strained my heavy eyes to see whether some strange and unaccountable event had reconveyed me into the streets of Okeham. But no!—The houses and the streets were utterly unknown to me—it was the mob and their outcries alone that came familiar to my senses, and that reminded me of the foregone scene of my insults. It was long before I could escape their fangs, and when at last, through the humane exertions of a few, I succeeded in effecting a retreat, I still heard, as I crossed fields and sought infrequent places, the words,—'wretch,' 'villain,' 'hangman,' echoing in my ears. Hangman!—Aye, that was the word so uproariously dwelt upon.—Hangman!—Then I was discovered—traced!—Even in Peterborough—miles from the scene of my fatal revenge, the mob, as it were by instinct, had translated my character, and had joined their brethren of Okeham in expressing their abhorrence of it.

These thoughts urged me on with fearful speed; and after creeping, noiseless and stealthily, for another three or four days, by any path that seemed most desolate, I arrived at Bedford. As I beheld the tall spires of the town in the distance, I shuddered, and twice turned to avoid the place. But I was half dead with exhaustion; night was at hand; and with a kind of desperate resolution I slunk into the town, and dived into the first obscure street that presented itself. Each person that I met, I turned away my head, slouched my hat, and endeavoured to avoid his gaze. But no one seemed to notice me, and gradually I became more assured. My sinking strength warned me that I needed sustenance; and again, for the first time since my flight from Peterborough, I ventured into a public-house. Tempting brandy was at hand; I snuffed its seductive flavour as soon as I entered the place, and the recollection of its exciting, drowning, oblivious influence, infused itself with irresistible power over my spirit. Brandy was had. Glorious, destructive drink! I quaffed it, and it seemed to resuscitate me, heart and head. It was to me like the helm, and the buckler, and the coat of mail to the knight of crusade,— it armed me cap-à-pie,* and I staggered beneath the power of my panoply. Fresh draughts produced fresh intoxication, and again I was lost to all recollection of what was occurring. But—horror! horror!—again I was awakened from what I deemed my bliss by a repetition of the same scene that I had undergone at Peterborough—the same insults, the same buffeting, the same execration, awakened me from my drunkenness, and forced me to fly for my life.

What could it mean? Was I pursued through all my winding paths and labyrinth of ways by some treacherous spy, that only tracked me to betray, and hold me up to the detestation of mankind? I was bewildered by the confusion of ideas that my still half-intoxicated brain presented in solution of the riddle, when a few words that dropped from one of my groaning pursuers told me. Having launched after me a deep and ferocious shout, he exclaimed, 'Beast, be wise at least in future! If you must drink, do it where there are none to hear you blab your hangman secrets.'

Powers of hell, this, then, was the answer to the enigma that maddened me! I myself was the stupid spy that had discovered all, and roused the wrath of thousands against my guilty confessions. I was he that proclaimed to the world, 'Ambrose is an executioner!' And what urged me to such insane disclosure? Aye, aye—brandy, brandy! The only power to which I could fly to steep me in forgetfulness of myself, played the traitor game with me of bidding flow those words that betrayed me to the rest of the world.

Farewell, then, to all refuge against myself, and my own thoughts! Farewell to all oblivion of the thing that haunted me like a demon-spectre, each day presenting itself in more frightful guise than on the last! Farewell! farewell!—the deep potations for which my aching senses yearned must be forsworn; and for the sake of hiding my sin from the gaze of men, I must be content to expose it for ever and for ever to the galling of my own conscience, and the harrowing of my own recollections.

From the day of my exposure at Bedford, I looked upon myself as one for ever doomed to live apart, not only from the intercourse of men, but even from the very sight of them; and as I wandered through the country I was ready to fly, like a frighted deer, on the first glimpse of a human figure in the distance; till the all-subduing pangs of hunger forced me to encounter man, and even then I would purchase enough to last me for days, that I might not too soon again have to face my enemy.

Thus with various wanderings over the face of England I suffered the time to elapse till the day of my appointment with my father was drawing near. I had seen it gradually approaching, as the condemned prisoner counts the gliding hours that are slipping away between him and his fate; and it was with sensations of inexpressible disgust, that I contemplated the necessity of my once again appearing in Okeham, where my face and my crime were so well known. Compulsion, however, ruled my actions with a strong arm. My money was nearly exhausted; and my heart sickened at the thought of continuing to wander in dread and misery through the by-ways of the world. I resolved, therefore, to meet Lockwood as he had directed; I determined to detail to him all the horrors of thought and deed that I had undergone; and to implore him, by his paternal love for me, to make some arrangement by which I might be removed to another country, where all knowledge of me would be extinct.

These thoughts somewhat lightened my heart, as I turned my steps towards Okeham; and in obedience to its suggestions, I tried to persuade myself that there was only one more painful struggle to be undergone, and that after that there might be something—if not pleasurable—at least neutral and free from torture, about to fall to my lot. The same hope made me regard, with a more kindly aspect, the prospect of my reunion with my father. It was he, indeed, that had given action to my hatred for man, by moulding it into revenge towards one individual of the species; and it was through that revenge that the last six months of misery had been inflicted. But revenge was at an end—Foster was in his grave—Ellen's manes* were appeased—and I clung with inexpressible satisfaction to the hope that my father, when he should hear the details of my sufferings, would move heaven and earth to convey me from a land that seemed to have nothing but wretchedness to bestow on the most unfortunate of her children.

It was well for me that some such sensations as these stole upon me as I approached Okeham, or never should I have been able to have gathered sufficient courage within myself to enter that hated town. As it was, I lingered in the neighbourhood till the clouds of night collected thick and gloomy around, and even then did not venture amid the scenes that were too painfully inscribed on my memory ever to be forgotten, without affecting a change in my gait, and such alterations in my general appearance as seemed best calculated to spare me from recognition. At length, I arrived at the obscure lodging that had been appointed by my father for our rendezvous.— I was there to the very day,—almost to the very hour of the reckoning; and on finding that I had arrived at the goal of my expectation without discovery, or its accompanying shout of execration, such as had farewelled me from the place, I felt as if a huge load of bitterness had been subtracted from my bosom, and whispered to myself to welcome it as the forerunner of still better tidings.

On enquiring for my father, however, I found that he was not there; but in his stead was presented to me a letter which had arrived that morning. I opened it; and these were its contents:—

'Do you remember, Ambrose, the sentiment with which we parted six months ago?—"Perchance even a still further revenge is in preparation for us!" It is that chance that I have been watching. It has arrived—but I dare not quit my victim.

Come to me instantly, dear Ambrose. Come with gladness at your heart, and brightness in your eyes; for our mutual cup of vengeance will speedily be filled to the overflowing.'

The letter then went on to direct me to meet him at ——. But no, no!—I have already specified too many localities to trace my wretched progress; and I will not give utterance to that which will betray my present abode, and bring the callous and the curious to my receptacle for the purpose of comparing me with my distressful story, and so feeding their depraved and unfeeling appetite.

The few lines that Lockwood had thus penned, were read by me again and again, but it was vainly that I endeavoured to interpret their meaning. What further revenge my father had in store was a mystery beyond my solution, and seemed to belong to some portion of his story with which I was unacquainted. I only knew that the very mention of vengeance struck upon my heart with a pestilential sickness, such as can only be felt when the mind itself is in a state of utter loathing. That I still hated mankind, my bosom too keenly felt to admit of any question; but the sufferings that I had undergone, in answer to my claim for revenge, had been too acute and penetrating not to excite the deepest anguish when a second scene of the same order as the first was offered to my gaze.

Yet obey his letter I must!—Wellnigh penniless—entirely friendless,—it was to him alone that I had to look!

I set out, therefore, immediately upon the journey which he had prescribed; but it was with a fearful heaviness of spirit that I prosecuted my weary way thither. The gleam of happiness that had broken in upon me for a moment, was like the fitful bursting of the sun through a deep November gloom, coming but to disappear again, and to make the traveller still more conscious of the cheerless prospect that surrounded him.

After the lapse of some days, I reached the town to which my father had summoned me; and with no little difficulty discovered the lodging to which he had directed my steps.

He received me with almost a shout of delight; and as I gazed upon his countenance, all the past events that Okeham had witnessed crowded to my imagination with a frightful verity of portraiture.

'Ambrose, Ambrose,' he exclaimed, 'all is now complete. The death of Foster six months since was but a stepping-stone to this—the most glorious consummation of the most glorious passion that ever filled the heart of man. But you smile not, my son! I see not that glow of fervour that was wont to cross your brow when I whispered "revenge" in your ear, and pointed the certain road to its accomplishment.'

'I cannot smile,' returned I, with an inward groan, 'nay, I almost feel as if to expect it of me was an insult. I am not the same Ambrose that you knew six months ago.'

'Pshaw! you are a cup too low. Let us discuss a bottle of brandy, and I warrant there will be smiles enough dancing in your eyes.'

'No, no, no,' cried I with terror; 'No brandy! I have for-sworn the treacherous liquor that seduces only to betray.'

'Why, that is well too,' replied my father; 'I scorn to do that for brandy, which I dare not do without it. Besides, we have that within which soars high above the power of any mortal draught—We have revenge!'

'We have revenge!' I echoed, and the echo was in earnest, for the mention of brandy had reminded me of Peterborough and Bedford, and my disgraces there united with my disgraces at Okeham to make callous and inhuman my heart.

My father looked at me as I repeated the word 'revenge', as if he would search to my very soul for the key in which I had uttered it; and then, grasping my hand, he whispered, as if it was something too precious to be exposed to common parlance, 'It is ours! it is ours!'

I returned his pressure in token that the force of his words was acknowledged. But though my grasp was firm, my heart palpitated with uncertainty. I was all in all the creature of impulse, and was waiting for its full tide to direct me. At Okeham, at Peterborough, and at Bedford, I seemed ready to burst with hatred for the whole species; and felt as if no revenge could be sufficiently extensive to fill the measure of my rage. But since my exposure at the latter place, I had wandered about, solitary and unknown, now and then encountering an individual, but oftener creeping along in a country to me as blank as the South Sea Island to the shipwrecked Crusoe.

During this time my sensations had undergone a change. The vehemence of my wrath had been checked for want of fuel, and the innate propensity of my bosom to love my fellow-man had been struggling in spite of myself through the gloom of my more irritated feelings. But the hot fit was now again fast gaining on me, and I perceived that a second time I was about, through the intensity of my own sensations and the kindling of my father, to be plunged into the resistless flood of hot-blooded vengeance. As the suspicion of this reached my mind, my heart beat doubtfully, as if beseeching me to avoid that which in the end would again torture it so bitterly; but against the silent feebly-persuasive beating of that heart there was a fearful array urging me onwards—my father's looks and words—my now bad passions and man-hating recollections, were all united, strong, powerful, and headlong; and I felt as if nothing short of a miracle could save me.

I really believe that Lockwood chiefly interpreted the truth of the inward effort my heart was making to be released from its second thraldom of revenge; for as I was pausing after his last exclamation, he again interposed to hurry me on into the sea of passion.

'What,' cried he, 'will you echo my cry of "revenge," and then, when I exclaim "it is ours," do you desert me? Or is it true, that the fearful story of your parents' undoing, joined to that of the thousand world-heaped insults yourself have received, needs no further avengement? For shame, Ambrose, for shame!—Grasp that which I now offer; let this one week make all I desire complete, and the next shall bear us away from this cursed land for ever, to begin a new life, with new prospects and new happiness, in some country where justice yet lives, and has a practical acknowledgment.'

Yes, yes, my father must have read my thoughts; for if any thing could have confirmed me in the path that he was dictating, it was that last hope that he had presented to me; and I exclaimed, as I listened to his words, 'You have but to command, for me to obey. Let us fly this hateful England; and let us, ere we go, make a fearful reckoning for the injuries under which we have had to writhe.'

'My own Ambrose! now you have spoken words that make

me proud of my son. It only remains to put you in possession of my meaning to make you feel in your judgment, that which already has impress in your mind. When I related to you, six months since, the tale of the sufferings I had received at the hands of Foster, I was so wrapt in his crimes, that I forgot to advert to the only individual that he had made the sharer of his confidence and the upholder of his sins; for when the prime instigator of mischief is within our clutch, it is the nature of man to overlook the more humble accomplice. But no sooner had the monster suffered retribution by your hands, than my attention was directed to him, who, Foster being dead, stalked before my eyes like his ghost, mowing and chattering scornfully in my ears, as though he would say, "Foster in me lives again—lives to spurn at Ellen's tomb—to spit at and disdain your husband-sorrows.'"

'And what has become of this wretch?' demanded I, heated almost to fury by my father's words.

'Aye, aye,' replied Lockwood, 'I like that question;—it bespeaks a mind panting for justice. This miserable reflector of Foster's enormities is within our power; he lies hard by in one of the dungeons of the town-prison; he, too, has been caught in the fangs of the law, and execution three days hence is to be done upon him. Ambrose, do you understand me? Three days hence he is to be hanged; and you are in the town,—nay, within one little furlong of the jail! Do you not comprehend, dear Ambrose?'

'More blood for Ambrose, wherewith to stain his soul! Oh God, my father, I cannot do it!'

'Not do it!' shouted Lockwood; 'cry shame upon the puling words, and thank me for having thus a second time fostered your revenge, till it has arrived at full maturity. Think you I have worked only for myself? No; it was you that were the prime mover of all my efforts,—you, the only being in this world I have to love, to care for, or avenge. And will you now desert the glorious result that I tender ready to your hands?'

'And shall we, this accomplished, indeed quit England for evermore?'

'I swear it, Ambrose! It was for this last act alone that I have delayed our departure since Foster's death.'

'Then let us go this very day,' I cried. 'Is it not enough that we leave the wretch in the law's all-powerful grasp, but that I must again be its executioner?'

'There lies the sum of all!' vehemently exclaimed my father. 'I pine to stand below the gallows, even as I did at Okeham, and shout as I see the body of my foe swing nerveless in the air;—I long to be able to inform myself with endless repetition, "It was Ambrose that did this good deed."'

'No, no, no!' cried I; 'it will be that repetition that will kill me.'

'Not when you know all!'

'Know all, my father?'

'Aye,' returned he; 'You have not yet heard who this fresh victim of our hatred is. Did I not tell you, when first you heard my story, that it was with joy I learned that Foster had dared to marry, that all his ties of nature might be withered by my hand? His wife, alas, escaped me by dying too early for my schemes; but the boy she left behind—Foster's only son—his dear Charles—his pride Charles!—Ha, ha! it is he that is to suffer three days hence!—it is he that I call on you to immolate, for the sake of mine and your mother's wrongs!'

Oh God, how the words of Lockwood struck upon my soul! It seemed to me as if he had felled me with some mighty mental machine, and my whole brain staggered beneath the blow. Charles—the gentle, kind-hearted Charles,—he, the chosen single one of all the human race—the only being that had ever volunteered the wretched outcast Ambrose an act of grace—was to be the victim of my butchery! I verily believe, that had the mere recollection of the youth occurred while my father had been prompting me to fresh revenge, that alone would have been sufficient to have checked his weightiest word, to have brought from my lips a steady refusal to his plans.

And I was to be this angel's executioner!

'No, no, no!'—Aye, I screamed aloud with agony, as again I uttered, 'No, no, no!'

Lockwood appeared astounded at the sudden change I presented to his view. He gazed upon me as if to read my motive; and not meeting with the solution, he demanded sternly— 'What now, Ambrose?—what is this, boy?'

Again I shouted, 'No, no, no! I would not harm a hair of Charles's head to serve myself everlastingly!'

'And our revenge'——

'Talk not of revenge, father! It will be no revenge that Charles should die. Nay, for mercy's sake, as you have plotted his death—now at my entreaty, help to save him!'

'Save him!' exclaimed he; 'I would not save him if I had ten times the power to do it. But who is to save him? He is marked for execution!'

'I will save him, if Heaven will give me strength!'

'You, Ambrose!'—and, as he spoke, Lockwood put on those looks that once, at the cottage in the fens, had so overruled my words and very thoughts. 'You save him, Ambrose! Hark ye, boy; I know not what this change portends, but I command that here it cease. We have met for business, not for silly exclamations that want a meaning.'

But the reign of my father's power was fast growing to an end. Impulse, that till now had been in its favour, was at last arrayed against it. Nor was I still the unknowing child I had been when he had last resorted to the same means; and even were I, the image of Charles seemed to have a supernatural power over my every sensation. I had picked him, as it were, from the rest of mankind—divested him of his mortality—and enthroned him in my heart, the very god of my admiration.

It was under this influence that I replied—'They do not want a meaning, sir. On my soul, they mean, that if man can save Charles from execution, I will accomplish it. And you, too, must assist. When it was vengeance on Foster that you asked, I assisted you; now that it is mercy on his son that I require, you must assist me.'

Lockwood seemed wonderstruck at my manner; but the more he marvelled, the more was he enraged.

'Dog!' cried he, 'do you talk of mercy when I talk of vengeance? Down, sir, down on your knees, and swear to do my bidding; or I will curse you with news that shall make your heart sicken, and the very life shrink from your bosom.'

'You have cursed me with news,' I exclaimed, half mad; 'news more bitter than aught else could conjure into mischief. But Charles shall be saved. I will go to the magistrates and tell all I know.'

Lockwood absolutely foamed with passion at the audacity of my words; but at length he muttered, as though he were grinding the words between his teeth—'Yes, or no—will you do my office?'

'No, no!' I exclaimed, with a fierceness that seemed to excite him ten times more; 'No, no! I will have Charles's life saved, and his course made happy.'

'Then art thou utterly damned!' shouted Lockwood—'Listen, listen, while I curse you with words only exceeded in their sharpness by their truth—You are no son of mine!'

'For that I bless God,' was my answer. 'Say it again, that I may humble myself before Heaven in thanksgiving!'

'I do say it again; and this time I add the name of your real parent—It was Edward Foster!—Come with me, thou wretch, through the streets of this great town, that I may point out to the multitude aghast, the man that hanged his father!'

I gazed on him who had uttered these appalling words; or, rather, seemed to gaze on him; for my eyes, though there fixed, saw nothing. 'All my senses flocked into my ear,' which still rang with the dreadful sounds it had heard.

'Fool,' continued Lockwood, 'stand not staring there! But laugh—laugh, as I do, to think how deep in parricidal wickedness your soul is steeped.—Ha! ha! So the puler at last has qualms; and he who so blithely hanged his father, cannot fit the noose to his brother's neck! Well, well, poor wretch, the common hangman must do it instead; and you shall stand side by side with me below the gallows, and help me to count his dying agonies.'

The very excess of anguish that these words inflicted, forced me into motion. My limbs unlocked, and my tongue loosened, as I faltered in reply—'Monster beyond belief, why has this been done? How did I ever injure you, to be exposed to misery so unutterable?'

'Can you have heard my story,' replied Lockwood, 'and yet ask that question? Are you not the son of Foster? and did not Foster steal Ellen from her husband?'

'Oh! Lockwood,' I exclaimed, 'a minute since, in the folly of my heart, I blessed Heaven when you told me that I was not your son. Now, I will bless you—nay, on my bended knees, will pray God to bless you, if you will retract those words, and once more tell me that I am yours—or only that I am not Foster's child!'

'Then should I tell a lie!' replied the fiend—'Have you not had enough of those already from me? But you shall hear all, since this has turned out to be my day of truth-telling.— Foster, by all that is sacred, is your father; as for the rest of the story, I altered it a little to allow me to call you mine. It is true, that I left Ellen for two years—not exactly on your father's business, by the by—but I left no child; and you were not born till I had been absent a year. It was this, fool, and no silly dallying of parental nonsense, that made me steal you from the pony-chaise, and take such cunning steps that Foster, with all his anxious search, could never discover your retreat. All the rest is true. I watched him till the law better provided for him; and sent you as his executioner. The solitary life that you had led, and the insults you had received in your short progress towards Okeham, rendered you ripe for my scheme, which ever was to mingle you and Charles in Foster's ruin;—and if you do not recollect the rest, it shall be my daily delight to remind you of it; to'——

'Never, never!'

'To sit by your side, and tell how Foster died!'

'Oh God, spare me!'

'To cheer your spirits, by chuckling in your ear an echo of the glad laugh that burst from me when I saw his dead body dancing in the wind!'

'Wretch!—Monster!—Devil!'

'To wake you at night with an imitation of your father's groan;—and to welcome you in the morning with a copy of the execration that has since attended you.'

I could endure it no longer. I was mad—mad—mad! And, unwitting what influence ruled me, I rushed from the room, while he roared after me—'Stay, good father-killer, your brother Charles lies waiting for your further practice!'

From the moment that I thus extricated myself from the piercing words uttered by the wretch, who, under the name of father, had seduced me to my undoing, I seemed to be in that state of bewilderment, when to think would be as easy as to lift a mountain in my arms. I stalked along, without noticing aught of the outward objects that surrounded me, and was employed in the endless repetition of the words, 'good father-killer.' It was well that I could not think—it was well that I was so amazed and horror-struck, that my mind was incapable of reaching any conclusion; for, had it been otherwise, dreadful and instantaneous must have been the catastrophe. But, before I had really re-obtained the use of my reason, I had added to the words, 'good father-killer,' the rest of the demon's anathema—'your brother Charles lies waiting for your further practice.' Those words, intended to curse me beyond redemption, were my salvation.—He waited for my further practice.—Yes, for him I would practice; but it should be for his life, and not for his death; and if I failed, I swore by heaven and hell, that one hour should behold the end of both.

The thought of the possibility of my being able to save Charles, made me for the moment forget the crime that I had committed at Okeham; the hope of preserving his life spread over my brain as the influence of brandy had formerly done; and it was under a sort of mental intoxication that I addressed myself to the labour.

I cannot pause to detail all that passed. Even now that I write these events, instead of enacting them, my brain is on fire, and I am ready to rend my lungs with shouts of joy, or tear my hair for maddening grief, according as the alternate picture of my brother or my father flashes across my mind.

It was Lockwood's wicked counsel that helped me in my first progress. I succeeded in getting myself appointed executioner to my brother; and, subsequently, by dint of such bribes as my slender means would allow, and large promises to the extent of the credulity of my instrument, I obtained ingress to his dungeon by favour of one of the turnkeys. It was midnight when I entered, and found him gently slumbering on his miserable pallet. As I leaned over, to watch a sleep such as I could never hope to enjoy, the mould of his features brought back to my recollection, with irresistible force, the countenance of my father, when, at the last moment of his existence, he bestowed on me his forgiveness. The thought that rushed into my mind overcame me, and I burst into a passionate flood of tears.

One of those scalding drops fell upon the cheek of my brother, and roused him from his repose. He looked up, and gently cried—'Is the hour arrived? So be it. I am ready!'

Oh, merciful heaven! how his quiet accents ran through my blood!—I could not answer him.

As he perceived my agitation, he rose from his bed—'Who are you,' he cried, 'that come with tears of pity?—Let me gaze on one that speaks so comfortably to my spirit.'

I had turned away my head; but his words were all-persuasive; and, forgetting that my face was already too well known to him, I turned it towards him at his bidding. A shriek, that seemed to come from the bottom of his soul, told me how well I was recognised, and he, in his turn, averted his countenance, as if in disgust at my presence.

A minute, or perhaps more, elapsed before either of us uttered a word. But at length he cried,—'Why is this? Or is it necessary that the executioner should come to tell me that all is prepared?'

Words in seeming—daggers in sooth! The scathing scene of my father's death was again placed before me in all the horrid freshness of reality. But even that was softened by the influence of the errand that had brought me to my brother's dungeon; and I wept as if my heart would burst.

Charles seemed astonished; and the sound of my sobbing again induced him to turn his head towards me—'Yes, yes!' said he, after a second gaze,—'I cannot forget that face!—You do not come here to mock me?'

'To mock you, Charles?'

'Charles!'

'Dear Charles,' I replied, 'I have been praying that my tongue might have power to reveal to you the very truth of my soul. But it cannot be! It is beyond the reach of words; and I must be content to let my deeds stand alone. I have stolen hither to concert means by which you may be saved.'

'Saved!' he exclaimed:—'Who are you? Are you not he that'——

'Mercy! mercy!' I interrupted; 'do not you remind me of that, lest in my madness I should think that you were Lockwood, and forego my task.'

'Lockwood!' screamed my brother; 'aye, that is the villain's name, who, not content with robbing my father, stealing his child, and murdering Ellen, crowned all by a dreadful betrayal of him to the scaffold.'

I staggered with horror at the words that were uttered by Charles. Great God! could this be possible, after the story that Lockwood had narrated to me? At length I mustered words to exclaim—'Again,—again,—once more;—was Lockwood that villain?'

'Too surely,' replied Charles: 'he was tried for breaking open my father's escritoire, and stealing money to a considerable amount. His sentence was two years' imprisonment, at the expiration of which he waylaid his wife, who, ill-used beyond endurance, had yielded in the interim to my father's addresses, and the next morning she was found drowned in the park lake. The infant that was with her could not be traced; and though Lockwood was subsequently apprehended and tried, he met with an acquittal, from the absence of a link in the circumstantial evidence, that otherwise carried with it full moral conviction of his guilt!'

'And the child?'

'The child was never found! But my father to his dying day felt persuaded that the hour would arrive when he would be forthcoming; and in this belief he gave me, on his last farewell, the portrait of the mother set in diamonds, under a strict injunction to deliver it, with his blessing, to my brother, when that happy discovery should be made. Alas, alas! he has never been heard of:—and there will be no friend, no relation, to watch my last moments, when I am to undergo that death which has been unjustly awarded me.'

'Unjustly?'

'Aye, sir, unjustly,' returned my brother; 'I cannot expect you to believe it; but as there is truth in heaven, so is the truth on my lips, when I say—unjustly! Either by some extraordinary mischance, or inhuman conspiracy, the evidence that could have proved my innocence was withheld on the trial; and an ignominious death will be the result.'

'No, no!' I exclaimed;—'you shall live—live to bless—to curse your brother!'

And in very agony of spirit I clasped my hands, and sank on my knees before his feet.

He started, as if afraid to listen to my words, while I almost unconsciously ejaculated, 'Brother, brother!'

'Call me not by that name,' at length he said; 'I would not in these last moments be at enmity with any—even you I would forgive.—But do not insult me with that appellation, lest I forget my forbearance, and spurn you as the murderer of my father.'

'Yes, yes; I deserve even that—but not from you! Oh, Charles! if time permitted me to tell you how bitterly I have been deceived—how Lockwood has ever brought me up as his child, and roused me to the frightful stigma that has just escaped your lips by a thousand falsehoods, in the detail of my mother's miserable fate, you would not quite hate me, for the intervention of pity would prevent it. But the precious minutes fly! I have arranged a plan for your escape.'——

At this moment our conversation was interrupted by the friendly turnkey who had admitted me, shewing himself at the door, and exclaiming, in a low whisper, 'Come, come, my lad, your time is up. I dare not give you more for ten times the sum you have promised.'

'One minute, and I come,' I cried; and with a sort of growling assent he withdrew.

'I have not time,' I continued, turning to my brother, 'to explain. One word must do—sustain yourself even to the last moment; and when you get the signal from me, follow my bidding to the very letter! I shall be by your side!'

Charles looked at me doubtingly, and shook his head.

Again I kneeled—'Hear me heaven!' I exclaimed—'as I hope for mercy—as I do not expect it for the parricide—as I am a ruined, heart-riven man—I have not uttered one syllable that is not true! Farewell, dear brother—and—and do not refuse me the precious portrait of my mother, in token of your belief of my penitence.'

Charles turned from me, as he muttered, 'It cannot be.'

'If it cannot,' I replied, 'I will not again ask it. I deserve no consideration; and I am too guilty to dare to press for it.'

I was about to withdraw, when he called me back. His eyes were full of tears.

'I do believe your words,' he said; 'all of them, save those which would excite in me a hope that you can save me. Take the portrait. I am bound by my promise to our father to bestow it on you. I am more bound by the softening of my heart, which tells me that you have been the most unhappy victim of Lockwood's arts. He was wily enough to betray our father; how could your young untutored mind escape him! Brother, God bless you! If we should not meet again, remain in the assurance that that same "God bless you," shall be the last words these lips will utter.'

How I dragged myself away from him, I know not, but, under the turnkey's guidance, I soon found myself on the outside of the prison walls. Thus set free, I went forth into the open country, where none might spy my actions, and gave myself up to the recall of the scene I had just shared with Charles. A melancholy gladness crept into my soul at the recollection of his farewell words, and at the bold resolve with which I determined to effect his escape. I pressed my mother's portrait against my bosom, as I swore to save him, and it almost seemed to my disturbed fancy, as if the picture whispered to my heart, 'Save him!'

The rest of the day was spent in maturing my plans for the next coming morning, when I was again to figure on the public scaffold as an executioner. But I had thoughts, and hopes, and expectations, to cheer me onwards, and I felt as if I could submit to a thousand disgraces for the sake of adding one iota to the chance of my being able to preserve my brother's life.

The morning came. My plans were all well laid—I felt secure of success—and my heart was lighter than it had been since the day that the execrations of the mob drove me from Okeham to wander far a-field. Yes, even in spite of the action of each minute reminding me of the part that I had there performed, my thoughts refused to be checked in their ebullition. I stood within the dreary outer cell, awaiting the appearance of my brother—but the gloom of the dungeon had not power to overcast my soul. I heard the solemn tolling of the sullen bell—but to my ear it was hopeful music that spoke of Charles's freedom. I looked around, and the eyes of all men glouted* on me; yet, ere their gaze could reach me, it fell stillborn and impotent in the remembrance of the one cheering glance I was expecting from him for whom alone I lived. At length he approached from the inner prison: I heard the clanking of his chains, and the sound was welcomed by me with a smile; for I had strung my whole energies to the feat, and I was panting to be doing. But the look and the shudder of Charles, when he first beheld me with my hangman hands outstretched to knock away his fetters, nearly threw me from my balance; and I felt for a moment as if the better part of my strength had been suddenly plucked from me.

'What is this?' he murmured, as I leaned over him for the purpose of supplying the place of his irons with a cord—'What is this?—Have you spoiled my last moments and my last hope with a falsehood?—Speak, are you my brother, or are you my executioner?'

'Hush,' whispered I, while my whole frame shook with emotion—'I am true, as I hope for pardon.—Keep your energies bent to their highest pitch; the rest is for me to accomplish.'

He gazed on me as though he could hardly bring himself to the belief of my words; but I looked up from my odious task with such holy earnestness in his face, and his moistened eye so happily perceived that mine was ready to let fall a tear of reciprocity, that conviction in good time arrived, and I felt his tremulous fingers gently press my hand in token of his credence in my honesty.

All was arranged below; and under pretext of my office I mounted the scaffold that I might see that every thing accorded with the scheme I had previously formed in my own mind. The ascending of a score of steps placed me about ten or twelve feet above the level of the market-place, of which the jail formed one side; a narrow space of scarcely more than a yard in width, was railed off round the spot occupied by the platform for the reception of the posse comitatus,* and the barriers of that division were of sufficient strength to prevent the pressure of the crowd breaking in upon the constabulary arrangement. The moment that I reached the scaffold, I cast an anxious look around to see if every thing wore the aspect that I had prefigured to myself, and on which my plans were built. Every thing was as I could wish: the constables, by means of the barrier, were prevented from suddenly mingling with the mob, and could only reach the open space by coming quite back to the wall of the jail, and so passing through a wicket that formed the termination of the railing; and even the very execrations with which my presence was hailed, were pleasant to me, for I interpreted the public hatred towards me into sympathy towards Charles; and on the sudden evolving of that sympathy much of my success depended.

Thus reassured of the favourable appearance of the market-place, I descended again to the jail for the purpose of summoning the prisoner. Together we mounted the scaffold; and the execrations with which I had previously been greeted, were changed to sounds of pity and commiseration for my brother. They vibrated like heavenly music in my ears—they made my whole blood throb with the fever of excitement. I looked back to see how far distant we were from those who had to follow us to the platform. Fortune smiled upon me. The clergyman, who should have ascended next, was elderly and decrepit, and as he placed his foot on the first step he slipped, and seemed as if he had sprained some limb; at all events he paused, while those immediately behind gathered round him as if to afford assistance.

One glance told me all this. 'Now, Charles,' I whispered, 'this is the moment. Life or death, dear brother! Turn more towards the prison while I cut the cords that bind your hands— spring forward with a bold leap into the middle of the crowd, where you see the man with a red cap; he is placed there to make an opening for you—the multitude will be with you— they will favour your flight.—Rush through the opposite street which takes to the river, where awaits a boat—that once secured, there is none other to pursue you, and your escape to the opposite bank is certain.'

My brother listened attentively, and shewed by his eye that he comprehended all. Never, never was there such a moment in the life of man as that in mine when the last coil of the rope was cut, and my brother darted forward to the leap. As I had foretold to him, the man with the cap suddenly backed, and left an open space for him on which to alight, in addition to which he extended his arms round him so as to steady his descent. That was the great moment of my agitation, for had Charles come to the ground with a shock, his flight would have been hopeless. But it was but a moment, for in another he bounded forward through the crowd, which, with exhilarating cheers, opened on every side, and pursued his way with the speed of a greyhound towards the river. Meanwhile, my own blood refused obedience to my reason, and without plan or project, I too sprang from the scaffold, unable to resist the temptation of watching him to the consummation of his escape. But, as might well be expected, my motive was utterly misunderstood, and ten thousand groans saluted me as I darted through the passage made for Charles, and which by the suddenness of my pursuit had not yet had time to close; to groans succeeded blows—to blows missiles—but still I persevered, and exerting, as it were, a more than mortal speed, I was within a yard or two of Charles by the time he reached the river. When I perceived him thus far on the sure road to liberty, I could no longer restrain myself: I absolutely screamed with ecstasy; and what with my unintelligible shouts of delight, what with the streams of mud with which I had been assailed, and which ran down me on every side, what with my bleeding lacerated face, covered with wounds from the blows that I had received, I must have looked more like a mishapen lump of chaos than aught in human shape or bearing.

But all was not yet accomplished. Charles had reached the bank, which was some two or three yards above the level of the stream, and was turning to run down the hard way that led to the boat that lay ready for him, when a man suddenly made his appearance from behind a shed that stood in the angle formed by the bank and the jetty, and shewed by his actions that he was prepared to dispute my brother's passage.

Powers of hell! it was Lockwood!

Another moment, and he would have clutched Charles in his brawny arms, towards which my brother had unconsciously been running, not having perceived him till the very last moment. At the sight, my note of joy was changed to the yell of despair. It can hardly be said that I thought! No! It was as a mere act of desperation, that, still at the height of my speed, I rushed upon the villain, who had been too intent in his observations of Charles to notice me, or to prepare himself for the tremendous shock with which I assaulted him. I was in time—yes, even to a little instant, I was in time! Full with the rage of energy and speed, I drove against him, and together we toppled over the bank into the soft and oozy mud that the low-tided river had left behind. For myself I had no care; and even while in the act of falling, I shouted to my brother, 'Dear, dear Charles, to the boat—to the boat! Row with the strength of a thousand! Your demon foe is destroyed!'

Charles returned my shout with a heart-spoken blessing; and as I lay over Lockwood, who each moment, by his effort to disentangle himself from me, sank deeper and deeper into the suffocating mire, I could hear my brother ply the oars with desperate speed and vigour, while ever and anon his thanksgiving to the wicked Ambrose came on the wings of the wind, till struggling, exhaustion, and anxiety deprived me of all consciousness of existence, and left me lying senseless on the corpse of my arch-deceiver.

My story is told! My confessions are numbered! Why, I know not—but so it is; even as surely as I am now the inmate of a melancholy cell, and am counted by my fellow-men among the maniacs of the earth.—Mad! Oh no, I am not mad! Do I not remember too well the frightful scenes of Okeham—the dreadful cajolery of Lockwood, by which he has made my own thoughts my own hell?—Mad! Would I were mad; for then might these things be hidden in oblivion; and yet I would not forget all! It was I that saved the gentle Charles from execution; it was I that earned his blessings by deliverance; and though I weep when I put my hand into my bosom, and vainly seek my mother's portrait, the tears change into joyful drops when dear memory reminds me that it was to purchase his escape I sold the precious relic. No, no! I cannot be utterly mad, till I shall hear, which Heaven of mercy avert, that my brother is again within the peril of the law, as though the ghost of Lockwood, yet unsatiated, was still employed in hunting him into its toils.

A 'MAN ABOUT TOWN'

Samuel Warren

I HATE humbug, and would eschew that cant and fanaticism which are at present tainting extensive portions of society, as sincerely as I venerate and wish to cultivate a spirit of sober, manly, and rational piety. It is not, therefore, to pander to the morbid tastes of overweening saintliness, to encourage its arrogant assumptions, sanction its hateful, selfish exclusiveness, or advocate that spirit of sour, diseased, puritanical seclusion from the innocent gaieties and enjoyments of life, which has more deeply injured the interests of religion than any of its professed enemies; it is not, I repeat, with any such unworthy objects as these that this melancholy narrative is placed on record. But it is to shew, if it ever meet their eyes, your 'men about town,' as the *élite* of the rakish fools and flutterers of the day are significantly termed, that some portions of the page of profligacy are black—black with horror, and steeped in the tears, the blood of anguish and remorse wrung from ruined thousands!—that often the 'iron is entering the very soul'* of those who present to the world's eye an exterior of glaring gaiety and recklessness;—that gilded guilt *must*, one day, be stripped of its tinselry, and flung into the haze and gloom of outer darkness. *These* are the only objects for which this black passage is laid before the reader, in which I have undertaken to describe pains and agonies, *which these eyes witnessed*, and that with all the true frightfulness of reality. It has, indeed, cost me feelings of little less than torture to re-trace the leading features of the scenes with which the narra-tive concludes.

'Hit him—pitch it into him! Go it, boys—go it! Right into your man, each of you, like good ones!—Top sawyers these! —Hurra! Tap his claret-cask—draw his cork!—Go it—go it —beat him, big one! lick him, little one! Hurra!—Slash, smash—fib away—right and left!—Hollo!—Clear the way there!—Ring! ring!'

These, and many similar exclamations, may serve to bring before the reader one of those ordinary scenes in London—a street row; arising, too, out of circumstances of equally frequent recurrence. A gentleman(!) prowling about Piccadilly, towards nightfall in the month of November, in quest of adventures of a certain description, had been offering some impertinence to a female of respectable appearance, whom he had been following for some minutes. He was in the act of putting his arm round her waist, or taking some similar liberty, when he was suddenly seized by the collar from behind, and jerked off the pavement so violently, that he fell nearly at full length in the gutter. This feat was performed by the woman's husband, who had that moment rejoined her, having left her only a very short time before, to leave a message at one of the coach-offices, while she walked on, being in haste. No man of ordinary spirit could endure such rough handling tamely. The instant, therefore, that the prostrate man had recovered his footing, he sprung towards his assailant, and struck him furiously over the face with his umbrella. For a moment the man seemed disinclined to return the blow, owing to the passionate dissuasions of his wife; but it was useless—his English blood began to boil under the idea of submitting to a blow, and, hurriedly exclaiming, 'Wait a moment, sir,'—he pushed his wife into the shop adjoining, telling her to stay till he returned. A small crowd stood round. 'Now, by ——, sir, we shall see which is the better man!' said he, again making his appearance, and putting himself into a boxing attitude. There was much disparity between the destined combatants, in point both of skill and size. The man last named was short in stature, but of a square iron-build; and it needed only a glance at his posture to see he was a scientific, perhaps a thoroughbred, bruiser. His antagonist, on the contrary, was a tall, handsome, well-proportioned, gentlemanly man, apparently not more than twenty-eight, or thirty years old. Giving his umbrella into the hands of a bystander, and hurriedly drawing off his gloves, he addressed himself to the encounter with an unguarded impetuosity, which left him wholly at the mercy of his cool and practised opponent.

The latter seemed evidently inclined to play a while with his man, and contented himself with stopping several heavily-dealt blows, with so much quickness and precision, that every one saw 'the big one *had caught a Tartar*' in the man he had provoked. Watching his opportunity, like a tiger, crouching noiselessly in preparation for the fatal spring, the short man delivered such a slaughtering left-handed hit full in the face of his tall adversary, accompanied by a tremendous 'doubling-up' body-blow, as in an instant brought him senseless to the ground. He who now lay stunned and blood-smeared on the pavement, surrounded by a rabble jeering the fallen 'swell,' and exulting at seeing the punishment he had received for his impertinence, which the conqueror pithily told them, as he stood over his prostrate foe, was the Honourable St John Henry Effingstone, presumptive heir to a marquisate; and the victor, who walked coolly away as if nothing had happened, was Tom ——, the prize-fighter.

Such was the occasion of my first introduction to Mr Effingstone; for I was driving by at the time this occurrence took place; and my coachman, seeing the crowd, slackened the pace of his horses, and I desired him to stop. Hearing some voices cry, 'Take him to a doctor,' I let myself out, announced my profession, and seeing a man of very gentlemanly and superior appearance, covered with blood, and propped against the knee of one of the people round, I had him brought into my carriage, saying I would drive him to his residence close by, which his cards shewed me was in —— Street. Though much disfigured, and in great pain, he had not received any injury likely to be attended with danger. He soon recovered; but an infinitely greater annoyance remained after all the other symptoms had disappeared—his left eye was sent into deep mourning, which threatened to last for some weeks; and could any thing be more vexatious to a gay man about town? for such was Mr Effingstone—but no ordinary one. He did not belong to that crowded class of essenced fops, of silly coxcombs, hung in gold chains, and bespangled with a profusion of rings, brooches, pins, and quizzing-glasses, who are to be seen in fine weather glistening about town, like fire-flies in India. *He* was no walking advertisement of the superior articles of his tailor, mercer, and jeweller. No—Mr Effingstone was really a *man about town,* and yet no puppy. He was worse—an abandoned profligate, a systematic debauchee, an irreclaimable reprobate. He stood pre-eminent amidst the throng of men of fashion, a glaring form of guilt, such as Milton represents Satan—

'In shape and gesture proudly eminent,'*

among his gloomy battalions of fallen spirits. He had nothing in common with the set of men I have been alluding to, but that he chose to drink deeper from the same foul and maddening cup of dissipation. Their minor fooleries and 'naughtinesses,' as he termed them, he despised. Had he not neglected a legitimate exercise of his transcendent talents, he might have become, with little effort, one of the first men of his age. As for actual knowledge, his powers of acquisition seemed unbounded. Whatever he read he made his own; good or bad, he never forgot it. He was equally intimate with ancient and modern scholarship. His knowledge of the varieties and distinctions between the ancient sects of philosophers was more minutely accurate, and more successfully brought to bear upon the modern, than I am aware of having ever known in another. Few, very few, that ever I have been acquainted with, could make a more imposing and effective display of the 'dazzling fence of logic.' Fallacies, though never so subtle, so exquisitely *vraisemblant* to the truth, and calculated to evade the very ghost of Aristotle himself, melted away instantaneously before the first glance of his eye. His powers were acknowledged and feared by all who knew him—as many a discomfited sciolist* now living can bear testimony. His acuteness of perception was not less remarkable. He anticipated all you meant to convey, before you had uttered more than a word or two. It was useless to kick or wince under such treatment—to find your own words thrust back again down your own throat as useless, than which few things are more provoking to men with the slightest spice of petulance. A conviction of his overwhelming power kept you passive beneath his grasp. He had, as it were, extracted and devoured the kernel, while you were attempting to decide on the best method of breaking the shell. His wit was radiant, and, fed by a fancy both lively and powerful, it flashed and sparkled on all sides of you like lightning.

He had a strong bent towards satire and sarcasm, and that of the bitterest and fiercest kind. If you chanced unexpectedly to become its subject, you sneaked away consciously seared to your very centre. If, however, you really wished to acquire information from him, no one was readier to open the vast storehouses of his learning. You had but to start a topic requiring elucidation of any kind, and presently you saw, grouped around it, numerous, appropriate, and beautiful illustrations, from almost every region of knowledge. But then you could scarce fail to observe the spirit of pride and ostentation which pervaded the whole. If he failed anywhere—and who living is equally excellent in all things?—it was in physics. Yes, here he *was* foiled. He lacked the patience, perseverance, and almost exclusive attention, which the cold and haughty goddess presiding over them invariably exacts from her suitors. Still, however, he had that showy general intimacy with its outlines, and some of its leading features, which earned him greater applause than was doled out reluctantly and suspiciously to the profoundest masters of science.

Yet Mr Effingstone, though such as I have described him, gained no distinctions at Oxford; and why? because he knew that all acknowledged his intellectual supremacy; that he had but to extend his foot, and stand on the proudest pedestal of academical eminence. This satisfied him. And another reason for his conduct once slipped out in the course of my intimacy with him:—His overweening, I may say, almost unparalleled pride, could not brook the idea of the remotest chance of *failure*! The same thing accounted for another manifestation of his peculiar character. No one could conceive how, when, or where, he came by his wonderful knowledge. He never *seemed* to be doing any thing; no one ever *saw* him reading or writing, and yet he came into the world *au fait* at almost every thing! All this was attributable to his pride, or, I should say more correctly, his vanity. '*Results*, not processes, are for the public eye,' he was fond of saying. In plain English, he would shine before men, but would not that they should know the pains and expense with which his lamp was fed. And this highly-gifted individual, as to intellect, it was, who chose to track the waters of dissipation, to career among their sunk rocks, shoals, and quicksands, even till he sunk and perished in them! By some strange omission in his moral conformation, his soul seemed utterly destitute of any sympathies for virtue; and whenever I looked at him, it was with feelings of concern, alarm, and wonder, akin to those with which one might contemplate the frightful creature brought into being by Frankenstein.* Mr Effingstone seemed either wholly incapable of appreciating moral excellence, or wilfully contemptuous of it. While reflecting carefully on his ἰδιοσυγκρισία,* which several years' intimacy gave me many opportunities of doing, and endeavouring to account for his fixed inclination towards vice, and that in its most revolting form, and most frantic excesses, at a time when he was consciously possessed of such capabilities of excellence of every description;—it has struck me that a little incident, which came to my knowledge casually, afforded a clew to the whole—a key to his character. I one day chanced to overhear a distinguished friend of his father's lamenting that a man 'of Mr St John's mighty powers' could prostitute them in the manner he did; and the reply made by his father was, with a sigh, that 'St John was a *splendid* sinner, and he knew it.' From that hour the key-stone was fixed in the arch of his unalterable, irreclaimable depravity. He felt a Satanic satisfaction in the consciousness of being an object of regret and wonder among those who most enthusiastically acknowledged his intellectual supremacy. How infinitely less stimulating to his morbid sensibilities would be the placid approval of virtue—a commonplace acquiescence in the ordinary notions of virtue and religion! He wished rather to stand out from the multitude—to be severed from the herd. 'Better to reign in hell than serve in heaven,'* he thought; and he was not long in sinking many fathoms lower into the abyss of atheism. In fact, he never pretended to the possession of religious principle; he had acquiesced in the reputed truths of Christianity like his neighbours; or, at least, kept doubts to himself, till he fancied his reputation required him to join the crew of fools, who blazon their unbelief. *This* was *'damned fine.'*

Conceive, now, such a man as I have truly, but, perhaps, imperfectly, described Mr Effingstone—in the possession of

£3000 a-year—perfectly his own master—with a fine person and most fascinating manners—capable of acquiring with ease every fashionable accomplishment—the idol, the dictator of all he met—and with a dazzling circle of friends and relatives:—conceive for a moment such a man as this, *let loose upon the town*! Will it occasion wonder if the reader is told how soon nocturnal studies, and the ambition of retaining his intellectual character which prompted them, were supplanted by a blind, absorbing, reckless devotion—for he was incapable of any thing but *in extremes*—to the gaming-table, the turf, the cockpit, the ring, the theatres, and daily and nightly attendance on those haunts of detestable debauchery, which I cannot foul my pen with naming?—that a two or three years' intimacy with such scenes as these had conduced, in the first instance, to shed a haze of indistinctness over the multifarious acquirements of his earlier and better days, and finally to blot out large portions with blank oblivion?—that his soul's sun shone in dim discoloured rays through the fogs—the vault-vapours of profligacy?—that prolonged desuetude was gradually, though unheededly, benumbing and palsying his intellectual faculties?—that a constant 'feeding on garbage'* had vitiated and depraved his whole system, both physical and mental?—and that, to conclude, there was a lamentable, an almost incredible, contrast between the glorious being, Mr Effingstone, at twenty-one, and that poor faded creature—that prematurely superannuated debauchee, Mr Effingstone, at twenty-seven?

I feel persuaded I shall not be accused of travelling out of the legitimate sphere of these 'Passages,' of forsaking the track of professional detail, in having thus attempted to give the reader some faint idea of the intellectual character of one of the most extraordinary young men that have ever flashed, meteor-like, across the sphere of my own observation. Not that in the ensuing pages, it will be in my power to exhibit him such as he has been described, doing and uttering things worthy of his great powers. Alas, alas! he was 'fallen, fallen, fallen'* from that altitude long before it became my province to know him professionally. His decline and fall are alone what remain for me to describe. I am painting from the life, and those are living who know it: that I am describing the character and career of him who once lived,—who deliberately immolated himself before the shrine of debauchery; and they can, with a quaking heart, attest the truth of the few bitter and black passages of his remaining history, which here follow.

The reader is acquainted with the circumstances attending my first professional acquaintance with Mr Effingstone. Those of the second are in perfect keeping. He had been prosecuting an enterprise of *seduction*, the interest of which was, in his eyes, enhanced a thousandfold, on discovering that the object of his illicit attentions was—married. She was, I understood, a very handsome, fashionable woman; and she fell—for Mr Effingstone was irresistible! He was attending one of their assignations one night, which she was unexpectedly unable to keep; and he waited so long at the place of meeting, but slightly clad, in the cold and inclement weather, that when he returned home at an early hour in the morning, intensely chagrined, he felt inclined to be very ill. He could not rise to breakfast. He grew rapidly worse; and when I was summoned to his bedside, he exhibited all the symptoms of a very severe inflammation of the lungs. One or two concurrent causes of excitement and chagrin aggravated his illness. He had been very unfortunate in betting on the Derby, and was threatened with an arrest from his tailor, whom he owed some hundreds of pounds, which he could not possibly pay. Again—a wealthy remote member of the family, his god-father, having heard of his profligacy, altered his will, and left every farthing he had in the world, amounting to upwards of fifty or sixty thousand pounds, to a charitable institution, the whole of which had been originally destined to Mr Effingstone. The only notice taken of him in the old gentleman's will was, 'To St John Henry Effingstone, my unworthy god-son, I bequeath the sum of five pounds sterling, to purchase a Bible and Prayerbook, believing the time may yet come when he will require them.'—These circumstances, I say, added to one or two other irritating concomitants, such as will sometimes succeed in stinging your *men about town* into something like reflection, brief and futile though it be, contributed to accelerate the inroads of his dangerous disorder. We were compelled to adopt such powerful antiphlogistic treatment* as reduced him to within an inch of his life. Previous to, and in the course of, this illness, he exhibited one or two characteristic traits.

'Doctor—is delirium usually an attendant on this disorder?' he enquired one morning. I told him it was—very frequently.

'Ah! then, I'd better become ἄγλωσσος,* with one of old, and bite out my tongue; for, d—n it! my life won't bear ripping up! I shall say what will horrify you all! Delirium blackens a poor fellow sadly among his friends, doesn't it? Babbling devil—what can silence it? D—n, if you should hear me beginning to *let out*, suffocate me, doctor.'

'Any chance of my giving the GREAT CUT this time, doctor, eh?' he enquired the same evening, with great apparent nonchalance. Seeing my puzzled air—for I did not exactly comprehend the low expression, 'great cut'—he asked quickly, 'Doctor, shall I die, d'ye think?' I told him I certainly apprehended great danger, for his symptoms began to look very serious. 'Then the ship must be cleared for action. What is the best way of ensuring recovery, provided it is to be?' I told him that, among other things, he must be kept very quiet—must not have his mind excited by visitors.

'Nurse, please ring the bell for George,' said he, suddenly interrupting me. The man in a few moments answered the summons. 'George, d'ye value your neck, eh?' The man bowed. 'Then, harkee, see you don't let in a living soul to see me, except the medical people. Friends, relatives, mother, brothers, sisters, d—n, sirrah! shut them all out—And, harkee, duns* especially. If —— should come, and get inside the door, kick him out again; and if —— comes, and ——, and ——, tell them, that if they don't mind what they are about, d—n them! I'll die, if it's only to cheat them.' The man bowed and retired. 'And—and—doctor, what else?'

'If you should appear approaching your end, Mr Effingstone, you would allow us, perhaps, to call in a clergyman to assist you in your devo——'

'What—eh—a parson? Oh, —— it! no, no—out of the question—*non ad rem*,* I assure you,' he replied hastily. 'D'ye think I can't roll down to hell fast enough, without having my wheels oiled by *their* hypocritical humbug? Don't name it again, doctor, on any account, I beg.'

He grew rapidly worse, but ultimately recovered. His injunctions were obeyed to the letter; for his man George idolized his master, and turned a deaf ear to *all* applications for admission to his master's chamber. It was well there was no one of them present to listen to his ravings; for the disgorgings of his polluted soul were horrible. His progress towards convalescence was by very slow steps; for the energies of both mind and body had been dreadfully shaken. His illness, however, had worked little or no alteration in his moral sentiments—or, if any thing, for the worse.

'It won't do at all, will it, doctor?' said Mr Effingstone, when I was visiting him, one morning, at the house of a titled relation in —— square, whither he had been removed to prepare for a jaunt to the continent. 'What do you allude to, Mr Effingstone?—*What* won't do?' I asked, for I knew not to what he alluded, as the question was the first break of a long pause in our conversation, which had been quite of a miscellaneous character. '*What* won't do? Why, the sort of life I have been leading about town these two or three last years,' he replied. 'By G——, doctor, it has nearly wound me up, has not it?'

'Indeed, Mr Effingstone, I think so. You have had a very, very narrow escape—have been within a hair's breadth of your grave.'—'Aye,' he exclaimed, with a sigh, rubbing his hand rapidly over his noble forehead, ''twas a complete toss up whether I should go or stay!—But come, come, the good ship has weathered the storm bravely, though she *has* been battered a little in her timbers!' said he, striking his breast, 'and she's fit for sea again already, with a little caulking, that is. Heigho! what a d——d fool illness makes a man! I've had some of the strangest, oddest twingings—such gleams and visions!—What d'ye think, doctor, I've had dinging in my ears night and day, like a d——d church-bell? Why, a passage from old Persius,* and this is it (you know I was a *dab* at Latin once, doctor,) *rotundo ore,*

> "Magne Pater divum! saevos punire tyrannos
> Haud aliâ ratione velis, quum dira libido

> Moverit ingenium, ferventi tincta veneno;
> —Virtutem videant—intabescantque relictâ!"

True and forcible enough, isn't it?'

'Yes,' I replied, and expressed my satisfaction at his altered sentiments. 'He might rely on it,' I ventured to assure him, 'that the paths of virtue, of religion'—— I was going too fast.

'Pho, pho, doctor! No humbug, I beg—come, come, no humbug—no nonsense of that sort! I meant nothing of the kind, I can assure you! I'm a better Bentley* than you, I see! What d'ye think is my reading of "*virtutem videant?*"—Why—let them get wives when they're worn out, and want nursing—ah, ha!—curse me! I'd go on raking—ay, d—n it, I would, sour as you look about it!—but I'm too much the worse for wear at present—I must recruit a little.'

'Mr Effingstone, I'm really confounded at hearing you talk in so light a strain! Forgive me, my dear sir, but'——

'Fiddle-de-dee, doctor! Of course, I'll forgive you, if you won't repeat the offence. 'Tis unpleasant—a nuisance—'*tis*, upon my soul! Well, however, what do you think is the upshot of the whole—the practical point—the winding up of affairs—the balancing of the books'—he delighted in accumulations of this sort—'the shutting up of the volume, eh? D—e! I'm going to get married—I am, by ——! I'm at dead-low water-mark in money-matters, and, in short, I repeat it, I intend to marry—a gold bag! A good move, isn't it? But, to be candid, I can't take all the credit of the thing to myself, either, having been a trifle bored, bullied, *badgered* into it by the family. They say the world cries shame on me! simpletons, why listen to the world!—I only laugh, ha, ha, ha! and cry, curse on the world—and so we are quits with one another!—By the way, the germ of that's to be found in that worthy fellow Plautus!'*

All this, uttered with Mr Effingstone's characteristic emphasis and rapidity of tone and manner, conveyed his real sentiments; and it was not long before he carried them into effect. He spent two or three months in the south of France; and not long after his return to England, with restored health and energies, he singled out from among the many, many women who would have exulted in being an object of the attentions of the accomplished, the celebrated, Mr Effingstone, Lady E—— ——, the very flower of English aristocratical beauty, daughter of a distinguished peer, and sole heiress to the immense estates of an aged baronet in ——shire.

The unceasing exclusive attentions exacted from her suitor by this haughty young beauty, operated for a while as a salutary check upon Mr Effingstone's reviving propensities to dissipation. So long as there was the most distant possibility of his being rejected, he was her willing slave at all hours, on all occasions; yielding implicit obedience, and making incessant sacrifices of his own personal conveniences. As soon, however, as he had 'run down the game,' as he called it, and the young lady was so far compromised in the eyes of the world, as to render retreat next to impossible, he began to slacken in his attentions; not, however, so palpably and visibly as to alarm either her ladyship or any of their mutual relations or friends. He compensated for the attentions he was obliged to pay her by day, by the most extravagant nightly excesses. The pursuits of intellect, of literature, and philosophy, were utterly and apparently finally discarded—and for what? For wallowing swinishly in the foulest sinks of depravity, herding among the acknowledged outcasts, commingling intimately with the very scum and refuse of society, battening on the rottenness of obscenity, and revelling amid the hellish orgies celebrated nightly in haunts of nameless infamy. Gambling, gluttony, drunkenness, harlotry, blasphemy!

(I cannot bring myself to make public the shocking details with which the five following pages of Dr ——'s Diary are occupied. They are too revolting for the columns of this distinguished Magazine, and totally unfit for the eyes of its miscellaneous readers. If printed, they would appear to many absolutely incredible. They are little else than a corroboration of what is advanced in the sentences immediately preceding this interjected paragraph. What follows must be given only in a fragmentary form—the cup of horror must be poured out before the reader, only κατὰ στάγονα.)*

Mr Effingstone, one morning, accompanied Lady E—— and her mother to one of the fashionable shops, for the purpose of aiding the former in her choice of some beautiful Chinese toys, to complete the ornamental department of her boudoir. After having purchased some of the most splendid and costly articles which had been exhibited, the ladies drew on their gloves, and gave each an arm to Mr Effingstone to lead them to the carriage. Lady E—— was in a flutter of unusually animated spirits, and was complimenting Mr Effingstone, in enthusiastic terms, on the taste with which he had guided their purchases; and they had left the shop door, the footman was letting down the carriage steps, when a very young woman, elegantly dressed, who happened to be passing at that moment, seemingly in a state of deep dejection, suddenly started on seeing and recognizing Mr Effingstone, placed herself between them and the carriage, and lifting her clasped hands, exclaimed, in piercing accents, 'Oh, Henry, Henry, Henry! how cruelly you have deserted your poor ruined girl! What have I done to deserve it? I'm broken-hearted, and can rest nowhere! I've been walking up and down M—— street nearly three hours this morning to get a sight of you, but could not! Oh, Henry! how differently you said you would behave before you brought me up from ——shire!' All this was uttered with the impassioned vehemence and rapidity of highly excited feelings, and uninterruptedly; for both Lady E—— and her mother seemed perfectly petrified, and stood pale and speechless. Mr Effingstone, too, was for a moment thunderstruck; but an instant's reflection shewed him the necessity of acting with decision one way or another. Though deadly pale, he did not disclose any other symptom of agitation; and with an assumed air of astonishment and irrecognition, exclaimed, concernedly, 'Poor creature! unfortunate thing! Some strange mistake this!'—'Oh, no, no, no, Henry! it's no mistake! You know me well enough—I'm your own poor Hannah!'

'Pho, pho! nonsense, woman! *I* never saw you before.'——

'Never saw me! never saw me!' almost shrieked the girl, 'and is it come to this?'—— 'Woman, don't be foolish—cease, or we must give you over to an officer as an impostor,' said Mr Effingstone, the perspiration bursting from every pore. 'Come, come, your ladyships had better allow me to hand you into the carriage. See, there's a crowd collecting.'

'No, no, Mr Effingstone,' replied Lady E——'s mother with

excessive agitation; 'this very singular—strange affair—if it *is* a mistake—had better be set right on the spot. Here, young woman, can you tell me what is the name of this gentleman?' pointing to Mr Effingstone.

'Effingstone—Effingstone, to be sure, ma'am,' sobbed the girl, looking imploringly at him. The instant she had uttered his name, the two ladies, dreadfully agitated, withdrew their arms from his, and with the footman's assistance, stepped into their carriage and drove off rapidly, leaving Mr Effingstone bowing, kissing his hand, and assuring them that he should 'soon settle this absurd affair,' and be at —— street before their ladyships. They heard him not, however; for the instant the carriage had set off, Lady E—— fainted.

'Young woman, you're quite mistaken in me—I never saw you before. Here is my card—come to me at eight to-night,' he added, in an under tone, so as to be heard by none but her he addressed. She took the hint, appeared pacified, and each withdrew different ways—Mr Effingstone almost suffocated with suppressed execrations. He flung himself into a hackney-coach, and ordered it to —— street, intending to assure Lady E——, with a smile, that he had instantly 'put an end to the ridiculous affair.' His knock, however, brought him a prompt 'Not at home,' though their carriage had but the instant before driven from the door. He jumped again into the coach, almost gnashing his teeth with fury, drove home, and dispatched his groom with a note, and orders to wait an answer. He soon brought it back, with the intelligence that Lord and Lady —— had given their porter orders to reject all letters or messages from Mr Effingstone! So there was an end of all hopes from *that* quarter. This is the history of what was mysteriously hinted at in one of the papers of the day, as a 'strange occurrence in high life, which would probably break off a matrimonial affair long considered as settled.'—But how did Mr Effingstone receive his ruined dupe at the appointed hour of eight? He answered her expected knock himself.

'Now, look, ——!' said he sternly, extending his arm to her menacingly, 'if ever you presume to darken my doors again, by ——, I'll murder you! I give you fair warning. You've ruined me—you have, you accursed creature!'

'Oh, my God! What am I to do to live? What is to become of me?' groaned the victim.

'Do? Why go and be ——! And here's something to help you on your way—there!' and he flung her a cheque for £50, and shut the door violently in her face.

Mr Effingstone now plunged into profligacy with a spirit of almost diabolical desperation. Divers dark hints, stinging innuendoes, appeared in the papers, of his disgraceful notoriety in certain scenes of an abominable description. But he laughed at them. His family at length cast him off, and refused to recognise him till he chose to alter his courses—to 'purge.'

Mr Effingstone was boxing one morning with Belasco*—I think it was—at the latter's rooms; and was preparing to plant a hit which the fighter had defied him to do, when he suddenly dropped his guard, turned pale, and in a moment or two, fell fainting into the arms of the astounded boxer. He had several days previously suspected himself the subject of indisposition—how could it be otherwise, keeping such hours, and living such a life as he did—but not of so serious a nature as to prevent him from going out as usual. As soon as he had recovered, and swallowed a few drops of spirits and water, he drove home, intending to have sent immediately for Mr ——, the well-known surgeon; but on arriving at his rooms, he found a travelling carriage-and-four waiting before the door, for the purpose of conveying him instantly to the bedside of his dying mother, in a distant part of England, as she wished personally to communicate to him something of importance before she died. This he learnt from two of his relatives, who were up stairs giving directions to his servant to pack up his clothes, and make other preparations for his journey, so that nothing might detain him from setting off the instant he arrived at his rooms. He was startled—alarmed—confounded at all this. Good God, he thought, what was to become of him? He was utterly unfit to undertake a journey, requiring instant medical attendance, which had already been too long deferred; for his dissipation had already made rapid inroads on his constitution. Yet what was to be done? His situation was such as could not be communicated to his brother and sister-in-law—for he did not choose to encounter their sarcastic reproaches. He had nothing for it but to get into the carriage with them, go down to ——shire, and when there, devise some plausible pretext for returning instantly to town. That, however, he found impracticable. His mother would not trust him out of her sight one instant, night or day—but kept his hand close locked in hers; he was also surrounded by the congregated members of the family—and could literally scarce stir out of the house an instant. He dissembled his illness with tolerable success—till his aggravated agonies drove him almost beside himself. Without breathing a syllable to any one but his own man, whom he took with him, he suddenly left the house, and without even a change of clothes, threw himself into the first London coach—and by two o'clock the next day was at his own rooms in M—— street, in a truly deplorable condition, and attended by Sir —— and myself. The consternation of his family in ——shire may be conceived. He trumped up some story about his being obliged to stand second in a duel—but his real state was soon discovered. Nine weeks of unmitigated agony were passed by Mr Effingstone—the virulence of his disorder for a long time setting at defiance all that medicine could do. This illness, also, broke him down sadly, and we recommended to him a second sojourn in the south of France—for which he set out the instant he could undertake the journey with safety. Much of his peculiar character was developed in this illness; that haughty, reckless spirit of defiance, that contemptuous disregard of the sacred consolations of religion,—that sullen indifference as to the event which might await him, which his previous character would have warranted me in predicting.

About seven months from the period last mentioned, I received, one Sunday evening, a note, written in hurried characters; and a hasty glance at the seal, which bore Mr Effingstone's crest, filled me with sudden vague apprehensions that some misfortune or other had befallen him. This was the note:—

'Dear Doctor,—For God's sake come and see me immediately, for I have this day arrived in London from the continent, and am suffering the tortures of the damned, both in mind and body. Come—come—in God's name come instantly, or I shall go mad. Not a word of my return *to any one* till I have seen you. You will find me—in short, my man will accompany you. Yours in agony, St J. H. Effingstone. Sunday evening, November, 18—.'

Tongue cannot utter the dismay with which this note filled me. His unexpected return from abroad,—the obscure and distant part of the town (St George's in the East) where he had established himself,—the dreadful terms in which his note was couched, revived, amidst a variety of vague conjectures, certain fearful apprehensions for him which I had begun to entertain before he quitted England. I ordered out my chariot instantly; his groom mounted the box to guide the coachman, and we drove down rapidly. A sudden recollection of the contents of several of the letters he had sent me latterly from the continent, at my request, served to corroborate my worst fears. I had given him over for lost—by the time my chariot drew up opposite the house where he had so strangely taken up his abode. The street and neighbourhood, though not clearly discernible through the fogs of a November evening, contrasted strangely with the aristocratical regions to which my patient had been accustomed. —— row was narrow, and the houses were small, yet clean and creditable-looking. On entering No. —, the landlady, a person of quiet respectable appearance, told me that *Mr Hardy*,—for such, it seems, was the name he chose to go by in these parts—had just retired to rest, as he felt fatigued and poorly, and she was just going to make him some gruel. She spoke in a tone of flurried excitation, and with an air of doubt, which were easily attributable to her astonishment at a man of Mr Effingstone's appearance and attendance, with such superior travelling equipments, dropping into such a house and neighbourhood as hers. I repaired to his bedchamber immediately. It was a small comfortably furnished room; the fire was lit, and two candles were burning on the drawers. On the bed, the plain chintz curtains of which were only half drawn, lay—St John Henry Effingstone. I must pause a moment to describe his appearance, as it struck me at first looking at him. It may be thought rather far-fetched, perhaps, but I could not help comparing him, in my own mind, to a gem set in the midst of faded tarnished embroidery:

the coarse texture of the bed-furniture—the ordinary style of the room—its constrained dimensions, contrasted strikingly with the indications of elegance and fashion afforded by the scattered clothes, toilet, and travelling paraphernalia, &c.—the person and manners of its present occupant, who lay on a bed all tossed and tumbled, with only a few minutes' restlessness. A dazzling diamond ring sparkled on the little finger of his left hand, and was the only ornament he ever wore. There was something, also, in the snowiness, simplicity, and fineness of his linen, which alone might have evidenced the superior consideration of its wearer, even were that not sufficiently visible in the noble, commanding outline of the features, faded though they were, and shrinking beneath the inroads of illness and dissipation. His forehead was white and ample; his eye had lost none of its fire, though it gleamed with restless energy; in a word, there was that ease and loftiness in his bearing, that indescribable *manière d'être*, which are inseparable from high birth and breeding. So much for the appearance of things on my entrance.

'How are you, Mr Effingstone—how are you, my dear sir?' said I, sitting down by the bedside.

'Doctor—the pains of hell have got hold upon me. I am undone,' he replied gloomily, in a broken voice, and extended to me a hand cold as marble.

'Is it as you suspected in your last letter to me from Rouen, Mr Effingstone?' I enquired, after a pause. He shook his head, and covered his face with both hands, but made me no answer. Thinking he was in tears, I said in a soothing tone, 'Come, come, my dear sir, don't be carried away; don't'——

'Faugh! Do you take me for a puling child, or a woman, doctor? Don't suspect me again of such contemptible pusillanimity, low as I am fallen,' he replied with startling sternness, removing his hands from his face.

'I hope, after all, that matters are not so desperate as your fears would persuade you,' said I, feeling his pulse.

'Doctor, don't delude me; all is over, I know it is. A horrible death is before me; but I shall meet it like a man. I have made my bed, and must lie upon it.'

'Come, come, Mr Effingstone, don't be so gloomy, so

hopeless; the exhausted powers of nature *may* yet be revived,'
said I, after having asked him many questions.

'Doctor ——, I'll soon end that strain of yours. 'Tis silly—
pardon me—but it *is*. Reach me one of these candles, please.'
I did so. 'Now, I'll shew you how to translate a passage of
Persius.*

> "Tentemus fauces:—*tenero latet ulcus in ore*
> *Putre*, quod haud deceat plebeia radere beta!"

'Eh, you recollect it? Well, look!—What say you to this; isn't
it frightful?' he asked, bitterly raising the candle, that I might
look into his mouth. It was, alas, as he said! In fact, his whole
constitution had been long tainted, and exhibited symptoms
of soon breaking up altogether! I feared, from the period of
my attendance on him during the illness which drove him last
to the continent, that it was beyond human power to dislodge
the harpy that had fixed its cruel fangs deeply, inextricably in
his vitals. Could it be wondered at, even by himself? Neglect,
in the first instance, added to a persevering course of profligacy, had doomed him long, long before, to premature and
horrible decay! And though it can scarcely be credited, it is
nevertheless the fact; even on the continent, in the character of
a shattered invalid, the infatuated man resumed those disso-
lute courses which in England had already hurried him almost
to death's door!

'My good God, Mr Effingstone!' I enquired, almost
paralyzed with amazement at hearing him describe recent
scenes in which he had mingled, which would have made even
satyrs skulk ashamed into the woods of old, 'how *could* you
have been so insane, so stark staring mad?'

'By instinct, doctor, by instinct! The *nature* of the beast!'
he replied, through his closed teeth, and with an unconscious
clenching of his hands. Many enquiries into his past and present
symptoms forewarned me that his case would probably be
marked by more appalling features than any that had ever
come under my care; and that there was not a ray of hope that
he would survive the long, lingering, and maddening agonies,
which were 'measured out to him from the poisoned chalice'
which he had 'commended to his own lips.'* At the time I am

speaking of, I mean when I paid him the visit above described, his situation was not far from that of Job,* described in chap. xx. v. 7, 8.

He shed no tears, and repeatedly strove, but in vain, to repress sighs with which his breast heaved, nearly to bursting, while I pointed out—in obedience to his determination to know the worst—some portions of the dreary prospect before him.

'Horrible! hideous!' he exclaimed, in a low broken tone, his flesh creeping from head to foot. '*How* shall I endure it!—Oh, Epictetus,* how?' He relapsed into silence, with his eyes fixed on the ceiling, and his hands joined over his breast, and pointing upwards, in a posture which I considered supplicatory. I rejoiced to see it, and ventured to say, after much hesitation, that I was delighted to see him at last looking to the right quarter for support and consolation.

'Bah!' he exclaimed impetuously, removing his hands, and eyeing me with sternness, almost approaching fury, '*why* will you persist in pestering your patients with twaddle of that sort?—*eandem semper canens cantilenam, ad nauseam usque**—as though you carried a psalter in your pocket? When I want to listen to any thing of that kind, why, I'll pay a parson! Haven't I a tide enough of horror to bear up against already, without your bringing a sea of superstition upon me? No more of it—no more—'tis foul.' I felt roused myself, at last, to something like correspondent emotions; for there was an insolence of assumption in his tone which I could not brook.

'Mr Effingstone,' said I, calmly, 'this silly swagger will not do. 'Tis unworthy of you—unscholarly—ungentlemanly—you *force* me to say so. I beg I may hear no more of it, or you and I must part. I have never been accustomed to such treatment, and I cannot now learn how to endure it from you.—From what quarter can you expect support or fortitude,' said I, in a milder tone, seeing him startled and surprised at the former part, 'except the despised consolations of religion?'

'Doctor—you are too superior to petty feelings not to overlook a little occasional petulance in such a wretched fellow as I am! You ask me whither I look for support? I reply, to the energies of my own mind—the tried disciplined energies of my own mind, doctor—a mind that never knew what fear was—that no disastrous combinations of misfortune could ever yet shake from its fortitude! What but *this* is it, that enables me to shut my ears to the whisperings of some pitying friend, who, knowing what hideous tortures await me, has stepped out of hell to come and advise me to *suicide*—Eh?' he enquired, his eye glaring on me with a very unusual expression. 'However, as religion, that is, your Christian religion, is a subject on which you and I can never agree—an old bone of contention between us—why, the less said about it the better. It's useless to irritate a man whose mind is made up. D—n it! I shall *never* be a believer—may I die first!' he concluded, with angry vehemence.

The remainder of the interview I spent in endeavouring to persuade him to relinquish his present unsuitable lodgings, and return to the sphere of his friends and relations—but in vain. He was fixedly determined to continue in that obscure hole, he said, till there was about a week or so between him and death, and then he would return, 'and die in the bosom of his family, as the phrase was.' Alas, however, I knew but too well, that in the event of his adhering to that resolution, he was fated to expire in the bed where he then lay; for I foresaw but too truly that the termination of his illness would be attended with circumstances rendering removal utterly impossible. He made me pledge my word that I would not, without his express request or sanction, apprize any member of his family, or any of his friends, that he had returned to England. It was in vain that I expostulated, that I represented the responsibility imposed upon me; and reminded him, that, in the event of any thing serious and sudden befalling him, the censure of all his relatives would be levelled at me. He was immovable. 'Doctor, you know well I dare not see them, as well on my own account as theirs,' said he, bitterly. He begged me to prescribe him a powerful anodyne draught; for that he could get no rest at nights; that an intense racking pain was gnawing all his bones from morning to evening, and from evening to morning: and what with this and other dreadful concomitants, he 'was,' he said, 'suffering the tortures of the damned, and perhaps worse.' I complied with his request, and ordered him

also many other medicines and applications, and promised
to see him soon in the morning. I was accordingly with
him about twelve the next day. He was sitting up, and in his
dressing-gown, before the fire, in great pain, and suffering
under the deepest dejection. He complained heavily of the
intense and unremitting agony he had endured all night long,
and thought that from some cause or other, the laudanum
draught I ordered, had tended to make him only more acutely
sensible of the pain. 'It is a peculiar and horrible sensation;
and I cannot give you an adequate idea of it,' he said: 'it is
as though the marrow in my bones were transformed into
something animated—into blind-worms, writhing, biting, and
stinging incessantly'—and he shuddered, as did I also, at the
revolting comparison. He put me upon a minute exposition of
the *rationale* of his disorder: and if ever I was at a loss for
adequate expressions or illustrations, he supplied them with
a readiness, an exquisite appositeness, which, added to his
astonishing acuteness in comprehending the most strictly
technical details, filled me with admiration for his great powers
of mind, and poignant regret at their miserable desecration.

'Well, I don't think you can give me any efficient relief,
doctor,' said he, 'and I am therefore bent on trying a scheme
of my own.'

'And what, pray, may that be?' I enquired curiously.

'I'll tell you my preparations. I've ordered—by ——!—
nearly a hundredweight of the strongest tobacco that's to be
bought, and thousands of pipes; and with these I intend to
smoke myself into stupidity, or rather insensibility, if possible, till I can't undertake to say whether I live or not; and
my good fellow, George, is to be reading me Don Quixote,
the while.' Oh, with what a sorrowful air of forced gaiety was
all this uttered!

One sudden burst of bitterness I well recollect. I was saying, while putting on my gloves to go, that I hoped to see him
in better spirits the next time I called.

'Better spirits? Ha! ha! How the —— can I be in better spirits
—an exile from society—and absolutely *rotting* away here—
in such a contemptible hovel as this—among a set of base-
born brutal savages?—faugh! faugh! It *does* need something

here—here,' pressing his hand to his forehead, 'to bear it—
aye, it does!' I thought his tones were tremulous, and that for
the first time I had ever known them so—and I could not help
thinking the tears came into his eyes; for he started suddenly
from me, and affected to be gazing at some passing objects in
the street. I saw he was beginning to sink under a consciousness of the bitter degradation into which he had sunk—the
wretched prospect of his 'sun's going down in darkness!' I
saw that the strength of mind to which he clung so pertina-
ciously for support, was fast disappearing, like snow beneath
the sunbeam.

(Then follow the details of his disease, which are so shocking
as to be unfit for any but professional eyes. They represent all
the energies of his nature as shaken beyond the possibility of
restoration—his constitution thoroughly polluted—wholly
undermined. That the remedies resorted to had been almost
more dreadful than the disease—and yet exhibited in vain! In
the next twenty pages of the Diary, the shades of horror are
represented as gradually closing and darkening around this
wretched victim of debauchery; and the narrative is carried
forward through three months. A few extracts only, from this
portion, are fitting for the reader.)

Friday, January 5.—Mr Effingstone continues in the same
deplorable state described in my former entry. It is absolutely
revolting to enter his room, the effluvia are so sickening—so
overpowering. I am compelled to use a vinaigrette incessantly,
as well as eau de Cologne, and other scents, in profusion. I
found him engaged, as usual, deep in Petronius Arbiter!* He
still makes the same wretched show of reliance on the strength
and firmness of his mental powers; but his worn and haggard
features—the burning brilliance of his often half-frenzied
eyes—the broken, hollow tones of his voice—his sudden starts
of apprehension—belie every word he utters. He describes his
bodily sufferings as frightful. Indeed Mrs —— has often told
me, that his groans both disturb and alarm the neighbours,
even as far as over the way! The very watchman has several
times been so much startled in passing, at hearing his groans,

that he has knocked at the door to enquire about them. Neither Sir —— nor I can think of any thing that seems likely to assuage his agonies. Even laudanum has failed us altogether, though it has been given in unprecedented quantities. I think I can say with truth and sincerity, that scarce the wealth of the Indies should tempt me to undertake the management of another such case. I am losing my appetite—loathe animal food— am haunted day and night by the piteous spectacle which I have to encounter daily in Mr Effingstone. Oh, that Heaven would terminate his tortures—surely he has suffered enough! I am sure he would hail the prospect of death with ecstasy!

Wednesday, 10.—Poor, infatuated, obstinate Effingstone will not yet allow me to communicate with any of his family or friends, though he knows they are almost distracted at not hearing from him, fancying him yet abroad. Colonel —— asked me the other day, earnestly, when I last heard from Mr Effingstone! I wonder my conscious looks did not betray me. I almost wish they had. Good God! in what a painful predicament I am placed! What am I to do? Shall I tell them all about him, and disregard consequences? Oh—no—no;—how can that be, when my word and honour are solemnly pledged to the contrary?

Saturday, 20.—Poor Effingstone has experienced a signal instance of the ingratitude and heartlessness of mere men of the world. He sent his man, some time ago, with a confidential note to Captain ——, formerly one of his most intimate acquaintances, stating briefly the shocking circumstances in which he is placed, and begging him to call and see him. The captain sent back a *vivâ voce (!)* message,* that he should feel happy in calling on Mr Effingstone in a few days' time, and would then, but that he was busy making up a match at billiards, and balancing his betting-book, &c. &c. &c. This day the fellow rode up to the door, and—*left a card for Mr Effingstone, without asking to see him!* Heartless, contemptible thing! I drove up about a quarter of an hour after this gentleman had left. Poor Effingstone could not repress tears while informing me of the above. 'Would you believe it, doctor,' said he, 'that Captain —— was one of my most intimate companions—that he has won many hundred pounds of my money—and that I have stood his second in a duel?'—'Oh, yes—I could believe it all, and much more!'—'My poor man, George,' he resumed, 'is worth a million of such puppies! Don't you think the good, faithful fellow looks ill? He is at my bedside twenty times a-night! Do try and do something for him! I've left him a trifling annuity out of the wreck of my fortune, poor fellow!' and the rebellious tears again glistened in his eyes. His tortures are unmitigated.

Friday, 26.—Surely, surely I have never seen, and seldom heard or read, of such sufferings as the wretched Effingstone's. He strives to endure them with the fortitude and patience of a martyr—or rather is struggling to exhibit a spirit of sullen, stoical submission to his fate, such as is inculcated in Arrian's Discourses of Epictetus,* which he reads almost all day. His anguish is so excruciating and uninterrupted, that I am astonished how he retains the use of his reason. All power of locomotion has disappeared long ago. The only parts of his body he can move now are his fingers, toes, and head—which latter he sometimes shakes about, in a sudden ecstasy of pain, with such frightful violence as would, one should think, almost suffice to sever it from his shoulders! The flesh of the lower extremities—the flesh——Horrible! All sensation has ceased in them for a fortnight! He describes the agonies about his stomach and bowel to be as though wolves were ravenously gnawing and mangling all within.

Oh, my God! if 'men about town,' in London, or elsewhere, could but see the hideous spectacle Mr Effingstone presents, surely it would palsy them in the pursuit of ruin, and scare them into the paths of virtue!

Mrs ——, his landlady, is so ill with attendance on him—almost poisoned by the foul air in his chamber—that she is gone to the house of a relative for a few weeks, in a distant part of the town, having first engaged one of the poor neighbours to supply her place as Mr Effingstone's nurse. The people opposite, and on each side of the house, are complaining again, loudly, of the strange nocturnal noises heard in Mr Effingstone's room. They are his groanings!

Tuesday, 31.—Again I have visited that scene of loathsomeness and horror, Mr Effingstone's chamber. The nurse and

George told me he had been raving deliriously all night long. I found him incredibly altered in countenance, so much so, that I should hardly have recognised his features. He was mumbling, with his eyes closed, when I entered the room.

'Doctor!' he exclaimed, in a tone of doubt and fear, such as I had never known from him before, 'you have not heard me abuse the Bible lately, have you?'

'Not *very* lately, Mr Effingstone,' I replied, pointedly.

'Good,' said he, with his usual decision and energy of manner. 'There are awful things in that book—aren't there, doctor?'

'Many very awful things there are indeed.'

'I thought so—I thought so. Pray'——his manner grew suddenly perturbed, and he paused for a moment, as if to recollect himself—'Pray—pray'——again he paused, but could not succeed in disguising his trepidation—'do you happen to recollect whether there are such words in the Bible as—as— "MANY STRIPES?" '*

'Yes, there are; and they form part of a very fearful passage,' said I, quoting the verse as nearly as I could. He listened silently. His features swelled with suppressed emotion. There was horror in his eye.

'Doctor, what a—a—remark—able—nay, hideous dream I had last night! I thought a fiend came and took me to a gloomy belfry, or some other such place, and muttered "many stripes— many stripes," in my ear; and the huge bell almost tolled me into madness, for all the damned danced around me to the sound of it! ha, ha!' He added, with a faint laugh, after a pause, 'There's something, cu—cur—cursedly *odd* in the *coin- cidence*, isn't there? How it would have frightened *some* wise- acres!' he continued, a forced smile flitting over his haggard features, as if in mockery. 'But it is easily to be accounted for—the intimate connexion—sympathy—between mind and matter, reciprocally affecting each other—affecting each—— ha, ha, ha!—Doctor, it's no use keeping up this damned farce any longer, human nature won't bear it! D—n! I'm going down to HELL! I am!' said he, almost yelling out the words. I had never before witnessed such a fearful manifestation of his feelings. I almost started from the chair on which I was sitting.

'Why'—he continued, in nearly the same tone and manner, as if he had lost all self-control, '*what* is it that has maddened me all my life, and left me sober only at this ghastly hour—too late?' My agitation would not permit me to do more than whisper a few unconnected words of encouragement, almost inaudible to myself. In about ten minutes' time, neither of us having broken the silence of the interval, he said, in a calmer tone, 'Doctor, be good enough to wipe my forehead—will you?' I did so. 'You know better, doctor, of course, than to attach any importance to the nonsensical rantings extorted by deathbed agonies, eh? Don't dying people, at least those who die in great pain, almost always express themselves so? How apt superstition is to rear its dismal flag over the prostrate energies of one's soul, when the body is racked by tortures like mine! Oh, oh, oh, that maddening sensation about the centre of my stomach! Doctor, go home, and forget all the stuff you've heard me utter to-day—"Richard's himself again!"'*

Thursday, 2nd February.—On arriving this morning at —— row, I was shewn into the back parlour, where sat the nurse, very sick and faint. She begged me to procure a substitute, for that she was nearly killed herself, and nothing should tempt her to continue in her present situation. Poor thing! I did not wonder at it! I told her I would send a nurse from one of the hospitals that evening; and then enquired what sort of a night Mr Effingstone had passed. 'Terrible,' she said; 'groaning, shaking, and roaring all night long, "many stripes," "many stripes," "Oh God of mercy!" and enquiring perpetually for you.' I repaired to the fatal chamber immediately, though latterly my spirits began to fail me whenever I approached the door. I was going to take my usual seat in the arm-chair by the bedside.

'Don't sit there—don't sit there,' groaned, rather gasped, Mr Effingstone, 'for a hideous being sate in that chair all night long,' every muscle in his face crept and shrunk with horror, 'muttering, "*many stripes!*" Doctor, order that blighted chair to be taken away, broken up, and burnt, every splinter of it! Let no human being ever sit in it again! And give instructions to the people about me never to desert me for a moment—

or—or—carry me off!—they will! My frenzied fancy conjures up the ghastliest objects that can scare man into madness!' He paused.

'Great God, doctor! suppose, after all, what the Bible says should prove true!' he literally gnashed his teeth, and looked a truer image of despair than I have ever seen represented in pictures, on the stage, or in real life. 'Why, Mr Effingstone, if it *should*, it need not be to your sorrow, unless you choose to make it so,' said I, in a soothing tone.

'Needn't it, needn't it?' with an abstracted air—'Needn't it? Oh, good!—hope—There, there IT sate, all night long, there! I've no recollection of any distinct personality, and yet I thought it sometimes looked like—of course,' he added, after a pause, and a sigh of exhaustion—'of course these phantoms, or similar ones, must often have been described to you by dying people—eh?'

Friday, 3rd.—He was in a strangely altered mood to-day; for though his condition might be aptly described by the words 'dead alive' his calm demeanour, his tranquillized features, and the mild expression of his eye, assured me he believed what he said, when he told me that his disorder had 'taken a turn,'— that the 'crisis was past;' and he should *recover!* Alas, was it ever known that dead *mortified* flesh ever resumed its life and functions! To have saved himself from the spring of a hungry tiger, he could not have moved a foot or a finger, and that for the last week! Poor, poor Mr Effingstone began to thank me for my attentions to him during his illness; said, he 'owed his life to my consummate skill;' he would 'trumpet my fame to the Andes, if I succeeded in bringing him through.'

'It has been a very horrible affair, doctor—hasn't it?' said he.

'Very, very, Mr Effingstone; and it is my duty to tell you, there is yet much horror before you!'

'Ah! well, well! I see you don't want me to be too sanguine—too impatient—it's kindly meant—very! Doctor, when I leave here, I leave it an *altered man!* Come, does not that gratify you, eh?'

I could not help a sigh. He *would* be an *altered man*, and that very shortly! He mistook the feelings which prompted the sigh. 'Mind—not that I'm going to commence saint—far from it; but—but—I don't despair of being a Christian. I don't, upon my honour. The New Testament is a sublime—a—I believe—a true revelation of the Almighty. My heart is quite humbled; yet—mark me—I don't mean exactly to say I'm a believer—not by any means; but I can't help thinking that my enquiries might tend to make me so.' I hinted that all these were indications of bettered feelings. I could say no more.

'I'm bent on leading a different life to what I have led before, at all events! Let me see—I'll tell you what I've been chalking out during the night—I shall go to Lord ——'s villa in——, whither I've often been invited, and shall read Lardner, and Paley,* and get them up thoroughly—I will, by ——!'

'Mr Effingstone, pardon me'——

'Ah—I understand—'twas a mere slip of the tongue—what's bred in the bone, you know'——

'I was not alluding to the oath, Mr Effingstone; but—but it is my duty to warn you'——

'Ah—that I'm not going the right way to work—eh? Well, at all events, I'll consult a clergyman. The Bishop of —— is a distant connexion of our family, you know,—I'll ask his advice! Oh, doctor, look at that rich—that blessed light of the sun! Oh, draw aside the window-curtain, let me feel it on me! What an image of the beneficence of the Deity! A smile flung from his face over the universe!' I drew aside the curtain. It was a cold clear frosty day, and the sun shone into the room with cheerful lustre. Oh, how awfully distinct were the ravages which his wasted features had sustained! His soul seemed to expand beneath the genial influence of the sunbeams; and he again expressed his confident expectations of recovery.

'Mr Effingstone, do not persist in cherishing false hopes! Once for all,' said I, with all the deliberate solemnity I could throw into my manner, 'I assure you, in the presence of God, that, unless a miracle takes place, it is utterly impossible for you to recover, or even to last a week longer!' I thought it had killed him. His features whitened visibly as I concluded—his eye seemed to sink, and the eyelids fell. His lips presently moved, but uttered no sound. I thought he had received his death-stroke, and was immeasurably shocked at its having been from my hands, even though in the strict performance of my duty. Half an hour's time, however, saw him restored to nearly the same state in which he had been previously. I begged him to allow me to send a clergyman to him, as the best means of soothing and quieting his mind; but he shook his head despondingly. I pressed my point, and he said deliberately, '*No.*' He muttered some such words, as 'The Deity has determined on my destruction, and is permitting his devils to mock me with hopes of this sort—Let me go, then, to my own place!' In this awful state of mind I was compelled to leave him. I sent a clergyman to him in my chaise—the same whom I had called to visit Mr —— (alluding to the 'Scholar's Death-Bed;')* but he refused to see him, saying, that if he presumed to force himself into the room, he would spit in his face, though he could not rise to kick him out! The temper of his mind had changed into something perfectly diabolical, since my interview with him.

Saturday, 4th.—Really my own health is suffering—my spirits are sinking through daily horrors I have to encounter at Mr Effingstone's apartment. This morning, I sat by his bedside full half an hour, listening to him uttering nothing but groans that shook my very soul within me. He did not know me when I spoke to him, and took no notice of me whatever. At length his groans were mingled with such expressions as these, indicating that his disturbed fancy had wandered to former scenes.

'Oh!—oh!—Pitch it into him, Bob! Ten to two on Cribb!— Horrible!—These dice are loaded, Wilmington, by ——, I know they are!—*Seven's the main!*—Ha!—*done*, by ——! Hector, yes—(he was alluding to a favourite race-horse)—won't 'bate a pound of his price!—Your Grace shall have him for six hundred—Fore-legs, only look at them!—There, there, go it! away! away! neck and neck—In, in, by —— Hannah! what the ——'s become of her—drowned? No, no, no,—What a fiend incarnate that Bet —— is! Oh! horror, horror, horror! Rottenness! Oh, that some one would knock me on the head, and end me! Fire, fire! Stripes, many stripes—Stuff! You didn't fire fair. By ——, you fired before your time—(alluding, I suppose, to a duel in which he had been concerned)—d—— your cowardice!'

Such was the substance of what he uttered—it was in vain that I tried to arrest the torrent of vile recollections.

'Doctor, doctor, I shall die of fright!' he exclaimed an hour afterwards—'What d'ye think happened to me last night? I was lying here, with the fire burnt very low, and the candles out. George was asleep, poor fellow, and the woman gone out to get an hour's rest also. I was looking about, and suddenly saw the dim outline of a table, set, as it were, in the middle of the room. There were four chairs, faintly visible, and three ghostly figures came through that door and sat in them, one by one, leaving one vacant. They began a sort of horrid whispering, more like gasping—they were DEVILS, and talked about—*my* damnation! The fourth chair was for me, they said, and all three turned and looked me in the face. Oh! hideous—shapeless—damned!' He uttered a shuddering groan.

(Here follows an account of his interview with two brothers—the only members of the family—whom he had at last permitted to be informed of his frightful condition—who would come and see him.) He did little else than rave and howl, in a blasphemous manner, all the while they were present. He seemed hardly to be aware of their being his brothers, and to forget the place where he was. He cursed me—then Sir ——, his man George, and charged us with compassing his death, concealing his case from his family, and execrated us for not allowing him to be removed to the west end of the town. In vain we assured him that his removal was utterly impossible—the time was past; I had offered it once. He gnashed his teeth, and spit at us all! 'What! die—die—DIE in this damned hole?—I won't die here—I will go to —— street. Take me off!—*Devils*, then, do *you* come and carry me there!—Come—out, out upon you!—You have killed me, all of you!—You're twisting me!—You've put a hill of iron on me—I'm dead!—all my body is dead—George, you wretch! why are you ladling fire upon me?—Where do you get it?—Out—out—out!—I'm flooded with fire!—Scorched—Scorched!—Now—now for a dance of devils—Ha—I see! I see!—There's ——, and ——, and ——, among them!—What! all three of you dead—and damned before me?—W——! Where is your d——d loaded dice?—Filled with fire, eh?—So, YOU were the three devils I saw sitting at the table, eh?—Well, I shall be last—but, d——e, I'll be the chief of you!—I'll be king in hell!—What—what's that filthy owl sitting at the bottom of the bed for, eh?—Kick it off—strike it!—Away—out on thee, thou imp of hell!—I shall make thee sing presently!—Let in the snakes—let them in—I love them! I hear them writhing up stairs!' He began to shake his head violently from side to side, his eyes glaring like coals of fire, and his teeth gnashing. I never could have imagined any thing half so frightful. What with the highly excited state of my feelings, and the horrible scents of death which were diffused about the room, and to which not the strongest salts of ammonia, used incessantly, could render me insensible, I was obliged to leave abruptly. I knew the last act of the black tragedy was closing that night! I left word with the nurse, that so soon as Mr Effingstone should be released from his misery, she should get into a hackney-coach, and come to my house.

I lay tossing in bed all night long—my mind suffused with the horrors of the scene of which I have endeavoured to give some faint idea above. Were I to record half what I recollect of his hideous ravings, it would scare myself to read it!—I will not! Let them and their memory perish!—I fancied myself lying side by side with the loathsome thing bearing the name of Effingstone—that I could not move away from him—that his head, shaking from side to side as I have mentioned above, was battering my cheeks and forehead; in short, I was almost beside myself!—I was in the act of uttering a fervent prayer to the Deity, that even in the eleventh hour—the eleventh hour—when a violent ringing of the night-bell made me spring out of bed. It was as I suspected. The nurse had come—and, already, all was over. My heart seemed to grow suddenly cold and motionless. I dressed myself, and went down into the drawing-room. On the sofa lay the woman: She had fainted. On recovering her senses, I asked her if all was over;—she nodded with an affrighted expression!—A little wine and water restored her self-possession. 'When did it occur?' I asked. 'Exactly as the clock struck three,' she replied. 'George, and I, and Mr——, the apothecary, whom we had sent for out of the next street, were sitting and standing round the bed. Mr Hardy lay tossing his head about for nearly an hour, saying all manner of horrible things. A few minutes before three he gave a loud howl, and shouted, "Here, you wretches—why do you put the candles out—here—here—I'm dying!"

'"God's peace be with you, sir!—The Lord have mercy on you!"—we groaned, like people distracted.'

'"Ha—ha—ha!—D—n you!—D—n you all!—Dying?— D—n me! I won't die—I won't die!—No—no!—D—n me— I won't—won't—won't—" and made a noise as if he was choked. We looked—yes, he was gone!'—He was interred in an obscure dissenting burying-ground in the immediate neighbourhood, under the name of Hardy, for his family refused to recognise him.

So lived and died a 'man about town'— and so, alas, will yet live and die many another MAN ABOUT TOWN!

THE SPECTRE-SMITTEN

Samuel Warren

FEW topics of medical literature have occasioned more wide and contradictory speculation than that of insanity, with reference, as well to its predisposing and immediate causes, as its best method of treatment;—since experience is the only substratum of real knowledge, the easiest and surest way of arriving at those general principles which may regulate both our pathological and therapeutical researches, especially concerning the subtle, almost inscrutable disorder—*mania*—is, when one does meet with some striking, well-marked case, to watch it closely throughout, and be particularly anxious to seize on all those smaller features, those more transient evanescent indications which are truer characteristics of the complaint than perhaps any other. With this object did I pay close attention to the very singular and affecting case detailed in the following narrative. I have not given the *whole* of my observations— far from it; those only are recorded which seemed to me to have some claims to the consideration of both medical and general readers. The apparent eccentricity of the title will be found accounted for in the course of the narrative.

Mr M——, as one of a very large party, had been enjoying the splendid hospitality of Lady ——, and did not leave till a late—or rather, early, hour in the morning. Pretty women, music, and champaigne, had almost turned his head; and it was rather fortunate for him that a hackney-coach stand was within a stone's throw of the house he was leaving. Muffling his cloak closely around him, he contrived to move towards it in a tolerably direct line, and a few moments' time beheld him driving, at the usual snail's pace of those rickety vehicles, to Lincoln's-Inn; for Mr M—— was a law student. In spite of the transient exhilaration produced by the scenes he had just quitted, and the excitement consequent on the prominent share he took in an animated discussion, in the presence of about thirty of the most elegant women that could well be brought together, he found himself becoming the subject of a most unaccountable depression of spirits. Even while at Lady ——'s, he had latterly perceived himself talking often for mere talking's sake—the chain of his thoughts perpetually broken—and an impatience and irritability of manner towards those whom he addressed, which he readily resolved into the reaction following high excitement. M——, I ought before, perhaps, to have mentioned, was a man of great talent, chiefly, however, imaginative, and had that evening been particularly brilliant on his favourite topic—*diablerie* and mysticism; towards which he generally contrived to incline every conversation in which he bore a part. He had been dilating, in particular, on the power which Mr Maturin* had of exciting the most fearful and horrific ideas in the minds of his readers, instancing one of his romances, the title of which I have forgotten. Long before he had reached home, the fumes of wine had evaporated, and the influence of excitement subsided; and, with reference to intoxication, he was as sober and calm as ever he was in his life. *Why*—he knew not, but his heart seemed to grow heavier and heavier, and his thoughts gloomier, every step by which he neared Lincoln's-Inn. It struck three o'clock as he entered the sombrous portals of the ancient inn of court. The perfect silence, the moonlight shining sadly on the dusky buildings—the cold quivering stars—all these, together, combined to enhance his nervousness. He described it to me as though things seemed to wear a strange, spectral, supernatural aspect. Not a watchman of the inn was heard crying the hour—not a porter moving—no living being but himself visible in the large square he was crossing. As he neared his staircase, he felt his heart fluttering; in short, he felt under some strange unaccountable influence, which, had he reflected a little, he would have discovered to arise merely from an excitable nervous temperament, operating on an imagination peculiarly attuned to sympathize with terror. His chambers lay on the third floor of the staircase; and on reaching it, he found his door-lamp glimmering with its last expiring ray. He opened his door, and after groping some time in the dark of his sitting-room, found his chamber candlestick. In attempting to light it, he put out the lamp. He went down stairs, but found that the lamp of every landing had shared the fate of his own; so he returned, rather irritated, thinking to amerce the porter of his customary Christmas-box for his niggard supply of oil. After some time spent in the search, he discovered his tinder-box, and proceeded to strike a light. This was not the work of a moment. And where is the bachelor to whom it is? The potent spark, however, dropped at last into the very centre of the soft tinder. M—— blew—it caught—spread—the match quickly kindled, and he lighted his candle. He took it in his hand, and was making for bed, when his eyes caught a glimpse of an object which brought him senseless to the floor. The furniture of his room was disposed as when he had left it; for his laundress had neglected to come and put things in order; the table, with a few books on it, drawn towards the fire-place, and by its side the ample-cushioned easy-chair. The first object visible, with sudden distinctness, was a figure sitting in the arm-chair. It was that of a gentleman, dressed in dark-coloured clothes, his hands, white as alabaster, closed together over his lap, and the face looking away; but it turned slowly towards M——, revealing to him a countenance of a ghastly hue—the features glowing like steel heated to a white heat, and the two eyes turned full towards him, and blazing—absolutely blazing—he described it—with a most horrible lustre. The appalling spectre, while M——'s eyes were riveted upon it, though glazing fast with fright, slowly rose from its seat, stretched out both its arms, and seemed approaching him, when he fell down senseless on the floor, as if smitten with apoplexy. He recollected nothing more, till he found himself, about the middle of the next day, in bed, his laundress, myself, an apothecary, and several others, standing round him. His situation was not discovered till more than an hour after he had fallen, as nearly as could be subsequently ascertained, nor would it then, but for a truly fortunate accident. He had neglected to close either of his outer-doors, (I believe it is usual for chambers in the inns of court to have double outer-doors,) and a woman, who happened to be leaving the adjoining set, about five o'clock, on seeing Mr M——'s doors both open at such an untimely hour, was induced, by feelings of curiosity and alarm, to return to the rooms she had left for a light, with which she entered his chambers, after having repeatedly called his name without receiving any answer. What will it be supposed had been her occupation at such an early hour in the adjoining chambers? Laying out the corpse of their occupant, a Mr T——, who had expired about eight o'clock the preceding evening!

Mr M—— had known him, though not very intimately: and there were some painful circumstances attending his death, which, even though on no other grounds than mere sympathy, M—— had laid much to heart. In addition to this, he had been observed by his friends as being latterly the subject of very high excitement, owing to the successful prosecution of an affair of great interest and importance. We all accounted for his present situation, by referring it to some apoplectic seizure; for we were of course ignorant of the real occasion, fright, which I did not learn till long afterwards. The laundress told me that she found Mr M——, to her great terror, stretched motionless along the floor, in his cloak and full dress, and with a candlestick lying beside him. She at first supposed him drunk; but on finding all her efforts to rouse him unsuccessful, and seeing his fixed features and rigid frame, she hastily summoned to her assistance a fellow-laundress, whom she had left in charge of the corpse next door, undressed him, and laid him on the bed. A neighbouring medical man was then called in, who pronounced it to be a case of epilepsy; and he was sufficiently warranted by the appearance of a little froth about the lips—prolonged stupor, resembling sleep—and frequent convulsions of the most violent kind. The remedies resorted to produced no alleviation of the symptoms; and matters continued to wear such a threatening and alarming aspect, that I was summoned in by his brother, and was at his bedside by two o'clock. His countenance was dark and highly intellectual: its lineaments were naturally full of power and energy; but now overclouded with an expression of trouble and horror. He was seized with a dreadful fit soon after I had entered the room. Oh, it is a piteous and shocking spectacle to see the human frame subject to such demoniacal twitchings, and contortions, which are so sudden—so irresistible, as to give the idea of some vague, terrible exciting cause, which cannot be discovered: as though the sufferer lay passive in the grasp of some messenger of darkness *'sent to buffet him.'*

M—— was a very powerful man; and during the fits, it was next to impossible for all present, united, to control his movements. The foam at his mouth suggested to his terrified brother the harrowing suspicion that the case was one of hydrophobia. None of my remonstrances or assurances to the contrary sufficed to quiet him, and his distress added to the confusion of the scene. After prescribing to the best of my ability, I left, considering the case to be one of simple epilepsy. During the rest of the day and night, the fits abated both in violence and frequency; but he was left in a state of the utmost exhaustion, from which, however, he seemed to be rapidly recovering, during the space of the four succeeding days; when I was suddenly summoned to his bedside, which I had left only two hours before, with the intelligence that he had disclosed symptoms of more alarming illness than ever. I hurried to his chambers, and found that the danger had not been magnified. One of his friends met me on the staircase, and told me that about half an hour before, while he and Mr C—— M——, the patient's brother, were sitting beside him, he suddenly turned to the latter, and enquired, in a tone full of apprehension and terror—'Is Mr T—— dead?'

'Oh dear, yes—he died several days ago'—was the reply.

'Then it was he'—he gasped—'it was he whom I saw, and he is surely—*damned!*—Yes, merciful Maker!—he is!—he is!'—he continued, elevating his voice to a perfect roar—'and the flames have reduced his face to ashes!—Horror! horror! horror!'—He then shut his eyes, and relapsed into silence for about ten minutes: when he exclaimed—'Hark you, there—secure me! tie me! make me fast, or I shall burst upon you and destroy you all—for I'm going mad—I feel it!'—He ceased, and commenced breathing fast and heavily—his chest heaving as though under the pressure of enormous weight; and his swelling, quivering features, evidencing the dreadful uproar within. Presently he began to grind his teeth, and his expanding eyes glared about in all directions, as though following the motions of some frightful object, and muttering fiercely through his closed teeth—'Oh save me from him—save me—

save me!'—It was a fearful thing to see him lying in such a state—grinding his teeth as though he would crush them to powder—his livid lips crested with foam—his features swollen—writhing—blackening; and, which gave his face a peculiarly horrible and fiendish expression, his eyes distorted, or inverted upwards, so that nothing but the glaring whites of them could be seen—his whole frame rigid—and his hands clenched, as though they would never open again!—It is a dreadful tax on one's nerves to have to encounter such objects, familiar though medical men are with such and similar spectacles; and in the present instance, every one round the bedside of the unfortunate patient, stood trembling with pale and momentarily-averted faces. The ghastly, fixed, upturning of the eyes in epileptic patients, fills me with horror whenever I recall their image to my mind!

The return of these epileptic fits, in such violence, and after such an interval, alarmed me with apprehensions, lest, as is not unfrequently the case, apoplexy should supervene, or even ultimate insanity. It was rather singular that M—— was never known to have had an epileptic fit previous to the present seizure, and he was then in his twenty-fifth year. I was conjecturing what sudden fright or blow, or accident of any kind, or congestion of the vessels of the brain from frequent inebriation, could have brought on the present fit—when my patient, whose features had gradually sunk again into their natural disposition, gave a sigh of exhaustion—the perspiration burst forth, and he murmured—some time before we could distinctly catch the words—'Oh—spectre-smitten!—spectre-smitten!'—which expression I have adopted as the title of this paper—'I shall never recover again!'—Though sufficiently surprised, and perplexed about the import of the words, we took no notice of them; but endeavoured to divert his thoughts from the phantasy, if such there were, which seemed to possess them, by enquiring into the nature of his symptoms. He disregarded us, however; feebly grasped my hand in his clammy fingers, and looking at me languidly, muttered—'What—Oh, what brought the *fiend* into *my* chambers?'—and I felt his whole frame pervaded by a cold shiver—'Poor T——! Horrid fate!'—On hearing him mention T——'s name, we all looked simultaneously at one another, but without speaking; for a suspicion crossed our minds, that his highly-wrought feelings, acting on a strong imagination, always tainted with super-stitious terrors, had conjured up some hideous object, which had scared him nearly to madness—probably some fancied apparition of his deceased neighbour. He began again to utter long deep-drawn groans, that gradually gave place to the heavy stertorous breathing, which, with other symptoms—his pulse, for instance, beating about 115 a-minute—confirmed me in the opinion that he was suffering from a very severe congestion of the vessels of the brain. I directed copious venesection*—his head to be shaven, and covered perpetually with cloths soaked in evaporating lotions—and blisters behind his ears, and at the nape of the neck—and appropriate internal medicines. I then left him, apprehending the worst consequences: for I had once before a similar case under my care—one in which a young lady was, which I strongly suspected to be the case with M——, absolutely frightened to death, and went through nearly the same round of symptoms as were beginning to make their appearance in my present patient: a sudden epileptic seizure, terminating in outrageous madness, which destroyed both the physical and intellectual energies, and the young lady expired. I may possibly hereafter prepare for publication some of my notes of *her* case, which had some very remarkable features.

The next morning, about eleven, saw me again at Mr M——'s chambers, where I found three or four members of his family—two of them his married sisters—seated round his sitting-room fire, in melancholy silence. Mr ——, the apothec-ary, had just left, but was expected to return every moment, to meet me in consultation. My patient lay alone in his bed-room, asleep, and apparently better than he had been since his first seizure. He had had only one slight fit during the night; and though he had been a little delirious in the earlier part of the evening, he had been on the whole so calm and quiet, that his friends' apprehensions of insanity were beginning to subside; so he was left, as I said, *alone*; for the nurse, just before my arrival, had left her seat by his bedside for a few moments, thinking him 'in a comfortable and easy nap,' and was engaged, in a low whisper, conversing with the members of

M——'s family who were in the sitting-room. Hearing such a report of my patient, I sate down quietly among his relations, determining not to disturb him, at least till the arrival of the apothecary. Thus were we engaged, questioning the nurse in an under tone, when a loud laugh from the bed-room suddenly silenced our whisperings, and turned us all pale. We started to our feet, with blank amazement in each countenance, scarcely crediting the evidence of our senses. Could it be M——? It *must*; there was none else in the room. What, then, was he laughing about?

While we were standing silently gazing on one another, with much agitation, the laugh was repeated, but longer and louder than before, accompanied with the sound of footsteps, now crossing the room—then, as if of one jumping! The ladies turned paler than before, and seemed scarcely able to stand. They sunk again into their chairs, gasping with terror. 'Go in, nurse, and see what's the matter,' said I, standing by the side of the younger of the ladies, whom I expected every instant to fall into my arms in a swoon.

'Doctor!—go in?—I—I—I dare not!' stammered the nurse, pale as ashes, and trembling violently.

'Do you come *here*, then, and attend to Mrs ——,' said I, 'and I will go in.' The nurse staggered to my place, in a state not far removed from that of the lady whom she was called to attend; for a third laugh,—long, loud, uproarious,—had burst from the room while I was speaking. After cautioning the ladies and the nurse to observe profound silence, and not to attempt following me, till I sent for them, I stepped noiselessly to the bed-room door, and opened it slowly and softly, not to alarm him. All was silent within; but the first object that presented itself when I saw fairly into the room, can never be effaced from my mind to the day of my death. Mr M—— had got out of bed, pulled off his shirt, and stepped to the dressing-table, where he stood stark-naked before the glass, with a razor in his right hand, with which he had just finished shaving off his eyebrows; and he was eyeing himself steadfastly in the glass, holding the razor elevated above his head. On seeing the door open, and my face peering at him, he turned full towards me—(the grotesque aspect of his countenance denuded of so prominent a feature as the eyebrows, and his head completely shaved, and the wild fire of madness flashing from his staring eyes, exciting the most frightful ideas)—brandishing the razor over his head with an air of triumph, and shouting nearly at the top of his voice—'Ah, ha, ha!—What do you think of this?'

Merciful Powers! May I never be placed again in such perilous circumstances, nor have my mind overwhelmed with such a gush of horror as burst over it at that moment! What was I to do? Obeying a sudden impulse, I had entered the room, shutting the door after me; and, should any one in the sitting-room suddenly attempt to open it again, or make a noise or disturbance of any kind, by giving vent to their emotions, what was to become of the madman or ourselves? He might, in an instant, almost sever his head from his shoulders, or burst upon me or his sisters, and do us some deadly mischief! I felt conscious that the lives of all of us depended on my conduct; and I do devoutly thank God for the measure of tolerable self-possession which was vouchsafed me at that dreadful moment. I continued standing like a statue—motionless—silent—endeavouring to fix my eye on him, that I might gain the command of *his; that* successful, I had some hopes of being able to deal with him. He, in turn, now stood speechless—and I thought he was quailing—that I had overmastered him—when I was suddenly fit to faint with despair—for at that awful instant I heard the door-handle tried—the door pushed gently open—and the nurse, I supposed—or one of the ladies—peeping through it. The maniac also heard it—the spell was broken—and, in a frenzy, he leaped several times successively in the air, brandishing the razor over his head as before.

While he was in the midst of these feats, I turned my head hurriedly to the person who had so shamefully disobeyed my orders, and thereby jeopardied my life—whispered in low affrighted accents—'At the peril of your lives—of mine—shut the door, away—away, hush! or we are all murdered!' I was obeyed—the intruder withdrew, and I heard a sound as if she had fallen to the floor—probably in a swoon. Fortunately the madman was so occupied with his antics, that he did not observe what had passed at the door. It was the nurse who made the attempt to discover what was going on, I afterwards learnt—but unsuccessfully, for she had seen nothing. My injunctions were obeyed to the letter, for they maintained a profound silence, unbroken, but by a faint sighing sound, which I should not have heard, but that my ears were painfully sensitive to the slightest noise. But to return to myself, and my fearful chamber companion.

'Mighty talisman!' he exclaimed, holding the razor before him, and gazing earnestly at it, 'how utterly unworthy—how infamous the common use men put thee to!' Still he continued standing, with his eyes fixed intently upon the deadly weapon—I all the while uttering not a sound, nor moving a muscle, but waiting for our eyes to meet once more.

'Ha—doctor ——!—How easily I keep you at bay, though little my weapon—*thus*'—he exclaimed gaily, at the same time assuming one of the postures of the broadsword exercise—but I observed that he *cautiously avoided meeting my eye again*. I crossed my arms submissively on my breast, and continued in perfect silence, endeavouring, but in vain, to catch a glance of his eye. I did not wish to excite any emotion in him, except such as might have a tendency to calm, pacify, disarm him. Seeing me stand thus, and manifesting no disposition to meddle with him, he raised his left hand to his face, and rubbed his fingers rapidly over the site of his shaved eyebrows. He seemed, I thought, inclined to go over them a second time, when a knock was heard at the outer chamber door, which I instantly recognised as that of Mr —— the apothecary. The madman also heard it, turned suddenly pale, and moved away from the glass opposite which he had been stooping. 'Oh—oh!' he groaned, while his features assumed an air of the blankest affright, every muscle quivering, and every limb trembling from head to foot. 'Is that—is—is that T—— come for ME?' He let fall the razor on the floor, and clasping his hands in an agony of apprehension, he retreated, crouching and cowering down, towards the more distant part of the room, where he continued peering round the bed-post, his eyes straining as though they would start from their sockets, and fixed steadfastly upon the door. I heard him rustling the bed-curtain, and shaking it; but very gently, as if wishing to cover and conceal himself within its folds.

Oh, humanity!—Was *that* poor being—that silly slavering idiot—was *that* the once gay, gifted, brilliant M——?

To return. My attention was wholly occupied with one object, the razor on the floor. How I thanked God for the gleam of hope that all might yet be right—that I might succeed in obtaining possession of the deadly weapon, and putting it beyond his reach! But how was I to do all this? I stole gradually towards the spot where the razor lay, without removing once my eye from his, nor he his from the dreaded door, intending, as soon as I should have come pretty near it, to make a sudden snatch at the horrid implement of destruction. I did—I succeeded—I got it into my possession, scarcely crediting my senses. I had hardly grasped my prize, when the door opened, and Mr —— the apothecary entered, sufficiently startled and bewildered, as it may be supposed, with the strange aspect of things.

'Ha—ha—ha! It's *you*—, is it—it's you—you anatomy! You plaster! How dare you mock me this horrid way, eh?' shouted the maniac, and springing like a lion from his lair, he made for the spot where the confounded apothecary stood, stupified with terror. I verily believe he would have been destroyed, torn to pieces, or cruelly maltreated in some way or other, had I not started and thrown myself between him and the unwitting object of his vengeance, exclaiming at the same time, as a *dernier resort*, a sudden and strong appeal to his fears—'Remember!— T——! T——! T——!'

'I do—I—do!' stammered the maniac, stepping back, perfectly aghast. He seemed utterly petrified, and sunk shivering down again into his former position at the corner of the bed, moaning—'Oh me! wretched me! Away—away—away!' I then stepped to Mr ——, who had not moved an inch, directed him to retire instantly, conduct all the females out of the chambers, and return immediately with two or three of the inn-porters, or any other able-bodied men he could procure on the spur of the moment; and I concluded by slipping the razor unobservedly, as I thought, into his hands, and bidding him remove it to a place of safety. He obeyed, and I found myself once more alone with the madman.

'M——!—dear Mr M——!—I've got something to say to you—I have, indeed; it's very—very particular.' I commenced approaching him slowly, and speaking in the softest tones conceivable.

'But you've forgotten THIS, you fool, you!—you have!' he replied fiercely, approaching the dressing-table, and suddenly seizing *another razor*—the fellow of the one I had got hold of with such pains and peril—and which, alas, alas! had never once caught my eye! I gave myself up for lost, fully expecting that I should be murdered, when I saw the bloodthirsty spirit with which he clutched it, brandished it over his head, and with a smile of fiendish derision, shook it full before me! I trembled, however, the next moment, for himself, for he drew it rapidly to and fro before his throat, as though would give the fatal gash, but did not touch the skin. He gnashed his teeth with a kind of savage satisfaction at the dreadful power with which he was consciously armed.

'Oh, Mr M——! think of your poor mother and sisters!' I exclaimed, in a sorrowful tone, my voice faltering with uncontrollable agitation. He shook the razor again before me with an air of defiance, and really 'grinned horribly a ghastly smile.'*

'Now suppose I choose to finish your perfidy, you wretch! and do what you dread, eh?' said he, holding the razor as if he was going to cut his throat.

'Why, wouldn't it be nobler to forgive and forget, Mr M——?' I replied, with tolerable firmness, and folding my arms on my breast, anxious to appear quite at ease.

'Too—too—too, doctor!—Too—too—too—too!—Ha, by the way!—What do you say to a *razor hornpipe*—eh?—Ha, ha, ha—a novelty, at least!' He began forthwith to dance a few steps, leaping frantically high, and uttering, at intervals, a sudden, shrill, dissonant cry, resembling that used by those who dance the Highland 'fling,' or some other species of Scottish dance. I affected to admire his dancing, even to ecstasy—clapping my hands, and shouting, 'Bravo, bravo!—Encore!' He seemed inclined to go over it again, but was too much exhausted, and sate down panting on the window-seat, which was close behind him.

'You'll catch cold, Mr M——, sitting in that draught of air, naked, and perspiring as you are. Will you put on your clothes?' said I, approaching him.

'No!' he replied, sternly, and extended the razor threateningly. I fell back, of course—not knowing what to do, nor choosing to risk either his destruction or my own by attempting any active interference; for what was to be done with a madman who had an open razor in his hand?—Mr ——, the apothecary, seemed to have been gone an age; and I found even my *temper* beginning to fail me—for I was tired with his tricks, deadly dangerous as they were. My attention, however, was soon riveted again on the motions of the maniac. 'Yes— yes, decidedly so—I'm too hot to do it now—I am!' said he, wiping the perspiration from his forehead, and eyeing the razor intently. 'I must get calm and cool—and then—*then* for the sacrifice! Ah, ha, the sacrifice!—An offering—expiation—even as Abraham—ha, ha, ha!—But, by the way, how did Abraham do it—that is, how did he intend to have done it?—Ah, I must ask my familiar!'

'A *sacrifice*, Mr M——?—Why, what do you mean?' I enquired, attempting a laugh. I say, *attempting*—for my blood trickled chillily through my veins, and my heart seemed frozen.

'What do I mean, eh? Wretch! Dolt!—What do I mean?— Why, a peace-offering to my Maker, for a badly-spent life, to be sure!—One would think you had never *heard* of such a thing as religion—you sow!'

'I deny that the sacrifice would be accepted, and for two reasons,' I replied, suddenly recollecting that he plumed himself on his casuistry, and hoping to engage him on some new crotchet, which might keep him in play till Mr —— returned with assistance—but I was mistaken!

'Well, well, doctor ——!—Let *that* be, now—I can't resolve doubts, now—no, no,' he replied, solemnly,—''tis a time for action—for action—for action,' he continued gradually elevating his voice, using vehement gesticulations, and rising from his seat.

'Yes, yes,' said I, warmly; 'but though you've followed closely enough the advice of the Talmudist,* in shaving off your eyebrows, as a preparatory'——

'Aha! aha!—What! have *you* seen the Talmud?—Have you, really!—Well,' he added, after a doubtful pause, 'in what do you think I've failed, eh?'

(I need hardly say, that I myself scarcely knew what led me to utter the nonsense in question; but I have several times found, in cases of insanity, that suddenly and readily *supplying a motive for the patient's conduct*—referring it to a *cause*, of some sort or other, with steadfast intrepidity—even be the said cause never so preposterously absurd—has been attended with the happiest effects, in arresting the patient's attention—chiming in with his eccentric fancies, and *piquing* his disturbed faculties into *acquiescence* in what he sees coolly taken for granted, as quite true—a thing of course—mere matter-of-fact—by the person he is addressing. I have several times recommended this little device to them who have been intrusted with the care of the insane, and have been assured of its success.)

'You are very near the mark, I own; but it strikes me that you have shaved them off too equally—too uniformly. You ought to have left some little ridges—furrows—hem, hem!—to—to—terminate, or resemble the—the—the *striped stick* which Jacob held up* before the ewes!'

'Oh—aye—aye! Exactly—true!—Strange oversight!' he replied, as if struck with the truth of the remark, and yet puzzled by vain attempts to corroborate it by his own recollections. 'I—I recollect it now—but it isn't too late yet—is it?'

'I think not,' I replied, with apparent hesitation, hardly crediting the success of my strange stratagem. 'To be sure, it will require very great delicacy; but as you've not shaved them off *very* closely, I think I can manage it,' I continued, doubtfully.

'Oh, oh, oh!' growled the maniac, while his eyes flashed fire at me. 'There's one sitting by me that tells me you are dealing falsely with me—oh, you villain! oh, you wretch!' At that moment the door opened gently behind me, and the voice of Mr ——, the apothecary, whispered, in a low hurried tone, 'Doctor, I've got three of the inn-porters here, in the sitting-room.' Though the whisper was almost inaudible even to me, when uttered close to my ear, to my utter amazement, M—— had heard every syllable of it, and understood it too, as if some official minion of the devil himself had quickened his ears, or conveyed the intelligence to him.

'Ah—ha—ha!—Ha, ha, ha!—Fools! Knaves! Harpies!—and what are you and your three hired desperadoes, to *me*?—Thus—thus do I outwit you, fools—thus!' and springing from his seat, he suddenly drew up the lower part of the window-frame, and looked through it—then at the razor—and again at me, with one of the most awful glances—full of dark diabolical meaning, the momentary suggestion of the great tempter, that I ever encountered in my life.

'Which!—which!—which!' he muttered fiercely through his closed teeth, while his right foot rested on the window-seat, ready for him to spring out, and his eye travelled, as before, rapidly from the razor to the window. Can any thing be conceived more palsying to the beholders? 'Why did not you and your strong reinforcement spring at once upon him, and overpower him?' possibly, some one is asking.—Aha! and he armed with a *naked razor*? His head might have been severed from his shoulders, before we could have over-mastered him—or we might ourselves—at least one of us—have been murdered in the attempt. We knew not *what* to do! M—— suddenly withdrew his head from the window, through which he had been gazing, with a shuddering, horror-stricken motion, and groaned—'No! no! no!—I won't—can't—for there's T—— standing just beneath, his face all blazing, and waiting with outspread arms to catch me,' standing, at the same time, shading his eyes with his left hand—when I whispered,—'Now, now! go up to him—secure him—all three spring on him at once, and disarm him!' They obeyed me, and were in the act of rushing into the room, when M—— suddenly planted himself in a posture of defiance, elevated the razor to his throat, and almost *howled*—'One step—one step nearer—and I—I—I—so!' motioning as though he would draw it from one ear to the other. We all fell back, horror-struck, and in silence. What could we do? If we moved towards him, or made use of any threatening gesture, we should see the floor in an instant deluged with his blood. I once more crossed my arms on my breast, with an air of mute submission.

'Ha—ha!' he exclaimed, after a pause, evidently pleased with such a demonstration of his power, 'obedient, however!—come—that's one merit! But still, what a set of cowards—bullies—cowards you must all be!—What!—all four of you afraid of *one* man?' In the course of his frantic gesticulations, he had drawn the razor so close to his neck, that its edge had slightly grazed the skin under his left ear, and a little blood trickled from it over his shoulders and breast.

'Blood!—*blood*?—What a strange feeling! How coldly it fell on my breast!—How did I do it?—Shall—I—go—on, as I have made a beginning?' he exclaimed, drawling the words at great length. He shuddered, and—to my unutterable joy and astonishment—deliberately closed the razor, replaced it in its case, put both in the drawer; and having done all this, before we ventured to approach him, he fell at his full length on the floor, and began to yell in a manner that was perfectly frightful; but in a few moments, he burst into tears, and cried and sobbed like a child. We took him up in our arms, he groaning—'Oh, shorn of my strength!—shorn! shorn! like Samson!—Why part with my weapon?—The Philistines be upon me!'—and laid him down on the bed, where, after a few moments, he fell asleep. When he woke again, a strait-waistcoat put all his tremendous strugglings at defiance—though his strength seemed increased in a tenfold degree—and prevented his attempting either his own life, or that of any one near him. When he found all his writhings and heavings utterly useless, he gnashed his teeth, the foam issued from his mouth, and he shouted,—'I'll be even with you, you incarnate devils!—I will!—I'll suffocate myself!' and he held his breath till he grew black in the face, when he gave over the attempt. It was found necessary to have him strapped down to the bed; and his howlings were so shocking and loud, that we began to think of removing him, even in that dreadful condition, to a madhouse. I ordered his head to be shaved again, and kept perpetually covered with cloths soaked in evaporating lotions—blisters to be applied behind each ear, and at the nape of his neck—leeches to the temples, and the appropriate internal medicines in such cases—and left him, begging I might be sent for instantly, in the event of his getting worse.[†] Oh, I shall never forget this harrowing scene!—my feelings were wound up almost to bursting; nor did they receive their proper tone for many a week. I cannot conceive that the people whom the New Testament speaks of[*] as being 'possessed of devils,' could have been more dreadful in appearance, or more outrageous in their actions, than was Mr M——; nor can I help suggesting the thought, that, possibly, they were in reality nothing more than maniacs of the worst kind. And is not a man transformed into a devil, when his reason is utterly overturned?

On seeing M—— the next morning, I found he had passed a terrible night—that the constraint of the strait-waistcoat filled him incessantly with a fury that was absolutely diabolical. His tongue was dreadfully lacerated; and the whites of his eyes, with perpetual straining, were discoloured with a reddish hue, like ferrets' eyes. He was truly a piteous spectacle! One's heart ached to look at him, and think, for a moment, of the fearful contrast he formed to the gay Mr M—— he was only a few days before, the delight of refined society, and the idol of all his friends! He lay in a most precarious state for a fortnight; and though the fits of outrageous madness had ceased, or become much mitigated, and interrupted, not infrequently, with 'lucid intervals'—as the phrase is,—I began to be apprehensive of his sinking eventually into that hopeless, deplorable condition, idiotcy. During one of his intervals of sanity—when the savage fiend relaxed, for a moment, the hold he had taken of the victim's faculties—M—— said something according with a fact which it was impossible for him to have any knowledge of by the senses, which was to me singular and inexplicable. It was about nine o'clock in the morning of the third day after that on which the scene above described took place, that M——, who was lying in a state of the utmost lassitude and

---

[†] I ought to have mentioned, a little way back, that in obedience to my hurried injunctions, the ladies suffered themselves, almost fainting with fright, to be conducted silently into the adjoining chambers—and it was well they did. Suppose they had uttered any sudden shriek, or attempted to interfere, or made a disturbance of any kind—what would have become of us all?

exhaustion, scarcely able to open his eyes, turned his head slowly towards Mr ——, the apothecary, who was sitting by his bed-side, and whispered to him—'They are preparing to bury that wretched fellow next door—hush! hush!—one of the coffin-trestles has fallen—hush!' Mr ——, and the nurse, who had heard him, both strained their ears to listen, but could hear not even 'a mouse stirring'—'there's somebody come in—a lady, kissing his lips before he's screwed down— oh, I hope she won't be scorched—that's all!' He then turned away his head, with no appearance of emotion, and presently fell asleep. Through mere curiosity, Mr —— looked at his watch; and from subsequent enquiry ascertained that—sure enough—about the time when his patient had spoken, they *were* about burying his neighbour; that one of the trestles *did* slip a little aside, and the coffin, in consequence, was near falling; and finally, marvellous to tell, that a lady, one of the deceased's relatives, I believe, did come and kiss the corpse, and cry bitterly over it! Neither Mr —— nor the nurse heard any noise whatever during the time of the burial preparations next door, for the people had been earnestly requested to be as quiet about them as possible, and really made no disturbance whatever. By what strange means he had acquired his information—whether or not he was indebted for it to the exquisite delicacy, the morbid sensitiveness of the organs of hearing, I cannot conjecture; especially am I at a loss to account for the latter part of what he uttered, about the lady's kissing the corpse. On another occasion, during one of his most placid moods, but *not* in any lucid interval, he insisted on my taking pen, ink, and paper, and turning amanuensis. To quiet him I acquiesced, and wrote what he dictated; and the manuscript now lies before me, and is *verbatim et literatim* as follows:—

'I, T—— M——, saw—what saw I? A solemn silver grove— there were *innumerable spirits* sleeping among the branches —(and it is this, though unobserved of naturalists, that makes the aspen-tree's leaves to quiver so much—it is this, I say, namely, the rustling movements of the spirits,)—and in the midst of this grove was a beautiful site for a statue, and one there assuredly was—but *what* a statue! Transparent, of

stupendous size, through which (the sky was cloudy and troubled) a ship was seen sinking at sea, and the crew at cards; but
the *good spirit* of the HIM saved them; for he shewed them the
key of the universe, and a shoal of sharks, with murderous
eyes, were disappointed of a meal. Lo, man, behold—another
part of this statue—what an one!—has a FISSURE in it—it opens
—widens into a parlour, in darkness; and shall be disclosed
the *horror of horrors*, for, lo some one sitting—sitting—easy-
chair—fiery-face—fiend—fiend—oh, God! oh, God! save me,'
cried he. He ceased speaking, with a shudder—nor did he
resume the dictation, for he seemed in a moment to have forgotten that he had dictated at all. I preserved the paper; and
gibberish though it is, I consider it both curious, and highly
characteristic throughout. Judging from the latter part of it,
where he speaks of a '*dark parlour, with some fiery-faced fiend
sitting in an arm-chair;*' and coupling this with various similar
expressions and allusions which he made during his ravings, I
felt convinced that his fancy was occupied with some one
individual image of horror, which had scared him into madness, and now clung to his disordered faculties like a fiend. He
often talked about 'spectres,' 'spectral'—and uttered incessantly
the words, 'spectre-smitten.' The nurse once asked him what
he meant by these words; he started—grew disturbed—his eye
glanced with affright—and he shook his head, exclaiming,
'horror!' A few days afterwards he hired an amanuensis, who,
of course, was duly apprised of the sort of person he had to
deal with; and after a painfully ludicrous scene, he attempting
to beat down the man's terms from a guinea and a half a week
to *half-a-crown*—he engaged him for *three guineas*, he said,
and insisted on his taking up his station at the side of the bed,
in order that he might take down every word that was uttered.
M—— told him he was going to dictate a *romance!* It would
have required, in truth, the 'pen of a ready writer'* to keep
pace with poor M——'s utterance; for he raved on at a prodigious rate, in a strain, it need hardly be said, of unconnected
absurdities. Really it was inconceivable nonsense, rhapsodical
rantings in the Maturin style,* full of vaults, sepulchres,
spectres, devils, magic—with here and there a thought of real
poetry. It was piteous to peruse it! His amanuensis found it

impossible to keep up with him, and, therefore, profited by a hint from one of us, and, instead of writing, merely moved his pen rapidly over the paper, scrawling all sorts of ragged lines and figures, to resemble writing! M—— never asked him to read it over, nor requested to see it himself; but, after about fifty pages were done, dictated a title-page—pitched on publishers—settled the price and the number of volumes—*four!*—and then exclaimed—'Well!—thank God—*that's* off my mind at last!' He never mentioned it afterwards; and his brother committed the *whole* to the flames about a week after.

M—— had not, however, yet done with his amanuensis—but put his services in requisition in quite another capacity—that of reader. Milton was the book he selected—and actually they went through very nearly nine books of it—M—— perpetually interrupting him with comments, sometimes saying surpassingly absurd, and occasionally very fine, forcible things. All this formed a truly touching illustration of that beautiful, often quoted sentiment of Horace*—

> 'Quo semel est imbuta recens, servabit odorem
> Testa diu.'
>
> (*Epist. Lib. I. Ep. 2.* 69, 70.)

As there was no prospect of his speedily recovering the use of his reasoning faculties, he was removed to a private asylum, where I attended him regularly for more than six months. He was reduced to a state of drivelling idiotcy; complete fatuity! Lamentable! heart-rending! Oh, how deplorable to see a man of superior intellect—one whose services are really wanted in society—the prey of madness!

Dr Johnson was well known to express a peculiar horror of insanity.* 'Oh, God! afflict my body with what tortures thou willest; but *spare my reason*!' Where is he that does not join him in uttering such a prayer?

It would be beside my purpose here to enter into abstract speculations or purely professional details concerning insanity; but one or two brief and simple remarks, the fruits of much experience and consideration, may perhaps be pardoned me. It is still a *vexatu questio** in our profession, whether persons of strong or weak minds—whether the ignorant or the highly cultivated, are most frequently the subjects of insanity. If we are disposed to listen to a generally shrewd and intelligent writer, (Dr Monro, in his *'Philosophy of Human Nature,'*)* we are to understand, that 'children, and people of weak minds, are *never* subject to madness; for,' adds the Doctor, 'how can he despair, who cannot think?' Though the logic here is somewhat loose and leaky, I am disposed to agree with the Doctor, in the main; and I ground my acquiescence, first, on the truth of Locke's distinction, laid down in his great work,* (book ii. c. ii. § 12 and 13) where he mentions the difference 'between idiots and madmen,' and thus states the sum of his observations:

'In short, herein seems to lie the difference between idiots and madmen, that madmen put wrong ideas together, and do make wrong propositions, but argue and reason *right* from them; but idiots make very few or no propositions, and reason scarce at all.'

Secondly, On the corroboration afforded to it by my own experience. I have generally found that those persons who are most *distinguished* for their powers of thought and reasoning, when of sound mind, continue to exercise that power but incorrectly, and be distinguished by their exercise of that power—when of unsound mind—their understanding retaining, even after such a shock, and revolution of its faculties, the bent and bias impressed upon it before-hand; and I have found, further, that it has been chiefly those of such character—*i.e.* thinkers—that have fallen into madness; and that it is the perpetual straining and taxing of their strong intellects, at the expense of their bodies, that has brought them into such a calamity. Suppose, therefore, we say, in short, that *madness* is the fate of strong minds, or at least of minds many degrees removed from weak; and *idiotcy* of weak, imbecile minds. This supposition, however, involves a sorry sort of compliment to the fair sex; for it is notorious that the annual majority of those received into lunatic asylums, are *females*! I have found imaginative, fanciful people, the most liable to attacks of insanity; and have had under my care four such instances, or at least very nearly resembling the one I am now relating, in which insanity had ensued from sudden *fright*. And it is easily accounted for. The imagination—the predominant faculty—is immediately appealed to—and, eminently lively and tenacious of impressions, exerts its superior and more practised powers, at the expense of the judgment, or reason, which it tramples upon and crushes. There is then nothing left in the mind that may make head against this unnatural dominancy; and the result is generally not unlike that in the present instance. As for my general system of treatment, it may all be comprised in a word or two—acquiescence; submission; suggestion; soothing. Had I pursued a different plan with M——, what might have been the disastrous issue?

To return, however—The reader may possibly recollect seeing something like the following expression, occurring in 'The Broken Heart:'* 'A candle flickering and expiring in its socket, which suddenly shoots up into an instantaneous brilliance, and then is utterly extinguished.' I have referred to it, merely because it affords a very apt illustration—apter far than any that now suggests itself to me, of what sometimes takes place in madness. The roaring flame of insanity sinks suddenly into the sullen smouldering embers of complete fatuity, and remains so for months; when, like that of the candle just alluded to, it will instantaneously gather up and concentrate its expiring energies into one terrific blaze—one final paroxysm of outrageous mania—and lo! it has consumed itself utterly— burnt itself out—and the patient is unexpectedly restored to reason. The experience of my medical readers, if it have lain at all in the track of insanity, must have presented such cases to their notice not unfrequently. However metaphysical ingenuity may set us speculating about the 'why and wherefore' of it—the *fact* is undeniable. It was thus with Mr M——. He had sunk into the deplorable condition of a simple, harmless, melancholy idiot, and was released from formal constraint: but suddenly, one morning, while at breakfast, he sprung upon the person who always attended him—and, had not the man been very muscular, and practised in such matters, he must have been soon overpowered, and perhaps murdered. A long and deadly wrestle took place between them. Thrice they threw each other—and the keeper saw that the madman several times cast a longing eye towards a knife which lay on the breakfast-table, and endeavoured to swing his antagonist so as to get himself within its reach. Both were getting exhausted with the prolonged struggle—and the keeper, really afraid for his life, determined to settle matters as soon as possible. The instant therefore, that he could get his right arm disengaged, he hit poor Mr M—— a cruel blow on the side of the head, which felled him, and he lay senseless on the floor, the blood pouring fast from his ears, nose, and mouth. He was again confined in a strait waistcoat, and conveyed to bed—when, what with exhaustion, and the effect of the medicines which had been administered, he fell into profound sleep, which continued all day, and, with little intermission, through the night. When he awoke in the morning, lo! he was 'in his right mind!' His calmed, tranquillized features, and the sobered expression of his eyes, shewed that the sun of reason had really once more dawned upon his long benighted faculties. Aye—he was

—— 'himself again!'*

I heard of the good news before I saw him, and on hastening to his room, I found it was indeed so—his altered appearance at first sight amply corroborated it! How different the mild, sad smile now beaming on his pallid faded features, from the vacant stare—the unmeaning laugh of idiotcy—or the fiendish glare of madness!—the contrast was strong as that between the soft, stealing, expansive twilight, and the burning blaze of noonday. He spoke in a very feeble, almost inarticulate voice, complained of dreadful exhaustion, and whispered something indistinctly about 'waking from a long and dreary dream;' and said that he felt, as it were, only half awake—or alive. All was new—strange—startling! Fearful of taxing too much his new-born powers, I feigned an excuse, and took my leave, recommended him cooling and quieting medicines, and perfect seclusion from visitors. How exhilarated I felt my own spirits all that day!

He gradually, very gradually, but surely, recovered. One of the earliest indications of his reviving interest in life—

'And all its busy, thronging scenes,'

was an abrupt enquiry whether Trinity term had commenced—
and whether or not he was now eligible to be called to the bar.
He was utterly unconscious that *three* terms had flitted over
him, while he lay in the gloomy wilderness of insanity; and
when I satisfied him of this fact, he alluded with a sigh to the
beautiful thought of one of our old dramatists,* who, illustrating the unconscious lapse of years over 'Endymion'—makes
one tell him—

'Lo, the twig against which thou leantest when thou didst fall asleep,
is now become a tree when thou awakest!'

It was not till several days after his restoration to reason, that
I ventured to enter into any thing like detailed conversation
with him, or to make particular allusions to his late illness;
and on this occasion it was that he related to me his rencontre
with the fearful object which had overturned his reason—
adding with intense feeling, that not ten thousand a-year should
induce him to live in the same chambers any more.

During the course of his progress towards complete recovery, memory shot its strengthening rays further and further
back into the inspissated gloom in which the long interval of
insanity had shrouded his mind; but it was too dense—too
'palpable and obscure'*—to be ever completely and thoroughly
illuminated. The rays of recollection, however, settled distinctly
on some of the more prominent points; and I was several
times astonished by his sudden reference to things which he
had said and done, during the 'depth of his disorder.' He
asked me, once, for instance, whether he had not made an
attempt on his life, and with a razor, and how it was that he
did not succeed. He had no recollection, however, of his long
and deadly struggle with his keeper—at least he never made
the slightest allusion to it,—nor of course did any one else.

'I don't much mind talking these horrid things over with
you, Doctor—for you know all the *ins* and *outs* of the whole
affair; but if any of my friends or relatives presume to torture
me with any allusions or enquiries of this sort—I'll fight them!
they'll drive me mad again!' The reader may suppose the hint

was not disregarded. All recovered maniacs have a dread—an absolute horror—of any reference being made to their madness, or any thing they have said or done during the course of it; and is it not easily accounted for?

'Did the horrible spectre which occasioned your illness, in the first instance, ever present itself to you afterwards?' I once enquired. He paused and turned pale. Presently he replied, with considerable agitation—'Yes, yes—it scarcely ever left me. It has not always preserved its spectral consistency, but has entered into the most astounding—the most preposterous combinations conceivable, with other objects and scenes—all of them, however, more or less, of a distressing, or fearful character—many of them terrific!' I begged him, if it were not unpleasant to him, to give me a specimen of them.

'It is certainly far from gratifying to trace scenes of such shame and horror—but I will comply as far as I am able,' said he rather gloomily. 'Once I saw him,' meaning the spectre, 'leading on an army of huge speckled and crested serpents against me; and when they came upon me—for I had no power to run away—I suddenly found myself in the midst of a pool of stagnant water, absolutely alive with slimy shapeless reptiles; and while endeavouring to make my way out, *he* rose to the surface, his face hissing in the water, and blazing bright as ever! Again, I thought I saw him in single combat, by the gates of Eden, with Satan—and the air thronged and heated with swart faces looking on!' This was unquestionably some dim confused recollection of the Milton-readings, in the earlier part of his illness. 'Again, I thought I was in the act of opening my snuff-box, when *he* issued from it, diminutive, at first, in size—but swelling, soon, into gigantic proportions, and his fiery features diffusing a light and heat around, that absolutely scorched and blasted! At another time, I thought I was gazing upwards on a sultry summer sky—and in the midst of a luminous fissure in it, made by the lightning—I distinguished *his* accursed figure, with his glowing features wearing an expression of horror, and his limbs outstretched, as if he had been hurled down from some height or other, and was falling through the sky towards *me*. He came—he came—flung himself into my recoiling arms—and clung to me—

burning, scorching, withering my soul within me! I thought
further, that I was all the while the subject of strange, para-
doxical, contradictory feelings towards him;—that I at one
and the same time loved and loathed—feared and despised
him!' He mentioned several other instances of the confusions
in his 'chamber of imagery.'* I told him of his sudden exclamation concerning Mr T——'s burial, and its singular corroboration; but he either did not, or affected not to recollect any
thing about it. He told me he had a full and distinct recollection of being for a long time possessed with the notion of
making himself a 'sacrifice' of some sort or other, and that he
was seduced or goaded on to do so, by the spectre, in the most
dazzling temptations—and under the most appalling threats—
one of which latter was, that God would plunge him into hell
forever, if he did not offer up himself;—that if he did so, he
should be a sublime spectacle to the universe, &c. &c. &c.

'Do you recollect of dictating a novel or a romance?' He
started as if struck with some sudden recollection. 'No—but
I'll tell you what I recollect well—that the spectre and I were
set to copy all the tales and romances that ever had been written,
in a large, bold, round hand, and then translate them into Greek
or Latin verse!' He smiled, nay even laughed at the thought,
almost the first time of his giving way to such emotions since
his recovery. He added, that, as to the latter, the idea of the
utter hopelessness of ever getting through such a stupendous
undertaking, never once presented itself to him, and that he
should have gone on with it, but that he lost his inkstand!!

'Had you ever a clear and distinct idea that you had lost the
right use of reason?'

'Why, about that, to tell the truth, I've been puzzling myself a good deal, and yet I cannot say any thing decisive. I *do*
fancy that at times I had short, transient glimpses into the real
state of things, but they were so evanescent. I am conscious of
feeling at these times incessant fury arising from a sense of
personal constraint, and I longed once to strangle some one
who was giving me medicine.'

But one of the most singular of all is yet to come. He still
persisted *then*, after his complete recovery, as we supposed, in
avowing his belief that we had hired a huge boa serpent from

Exeter Change,* to come and keep constant watch over him, to constrain his movements when he threatened to become violent; that it lay constantly coiled up under his bed for that purpose; that he could now and then feel the motions—the writhing undulating motions of its coils—hear it utter a sort of *sigh*, and see it often elevate its head over the bed, and play with its soft, slippery, delicate forked tongue over his face, to soothe him to sleep. When poor M——, with a serious, sober, earnest air, assured me he STILL believed all this, my hopes of his complete and final restoration to sanity were dashed at once! How such an absurd—in short I have no terms in which I may adequately characterise it—how, I say, such an idea could possibly be persisted in, I was bewildered in attempting to conceive. I frequently strove to reason him out of it, but in vain. To no purpose did I burlesque and caricature the notion almost beyond all bounds; it was useless to remind him of the blank impossibility of it; he regarded me with such a face as I should exhibit to a fluent personage, quite in earnest in demonstrating to me that the moon was made of green cheese.

I have once before heard of a patient who, after recovering from all attacks of insanity, retained one solitary crotchet—one little stain or speck of lunacy—about which, and which alone, he was mad to the end of his life. I supposed such to be the case with M——. It was possible—barely so, I thought—that he might entertain his preposterous notion about the boa, and yet be sound in the general texture of his mind. I prayed God it might; I 'hoped against hope.'* The last evening I ever spent with him, was occupied with my endeavouring, once for all, to disabuse him of the idea in question; and in the course of our conversation, he disclosed one or two other little symptoms—specks of lunacy—which made me leave him, filled with disheartening doubts as to the probability of a permanent recovery.

My worst fears were awfully realized. In about five years from the period above alluded to, M——, who had got married, and had enjoyed excellent general health, was spending the summer with his family at Brussels—and one night destroyed himself—alas, alas, *destroyed* himself in a manner too horrible to mention!

THE THUNDER-STRUCK and THE BOXER

Samuel Warren

THE THUNDER-STRUCK

In the summer of 18—, London was visited by one of the most tremendous thunder-storms that have been known in this climate. Its character and effects—some of which latter form the subject of this chapter—will make me remember it to the latest hour of my life.

There was something portentous—a still, surcharged air—about the whole of Tuesday the 10th of July, 18—, as though nature were trembling and cowering beneath a coming shock. To use the exquisite language of one of our old dramatists,†* there seemed

> ——'A calm
> Before a tempest, when the gentle air
> Lays her soft ear close to the earth, to listen
> For that she fears steals on to ravish her.'

From about eleven o'clock at noon the sky wore a lurid threatening aspect that shot awe into the beholder; suggesting to startled fancy the notion, that within the dim confines of the 'labouring air' mischief was working to the world. The heat was intolerable, keeping almost everybody within doors. The very dogs, and other cattle in the streets, stood everywhere panting and loath to move. There was a prodigious excitement, or rather agitation, diffused throughout the country, especially London; for, strange to say, (and thousands will recollect the circumstance,) it had been for some time confidently foretold by certain enthusiasts, religious as well as philosophic, that the earth was to be destroyed that very day;

† Marlowe.

in short, that the awful JUDGMENT was at hand! Though not myself over credulous, or given to superstitious fears, I own that on coupling these fearful predictions with the unusual, or rather unnatural, aspect of the day, I more than once experienced sudden qualms of apprehension as I rode along on my daily rounds. I did not so much communicate alarm to the various circles I entered, as catch it from them. Then, again, I would occasionally pass a silent group of passengers clustering round a street-preacher, who, true to his vocation, 're- deeming the time,' seemed by his gestures, and the disturbed countenances around him, to be foretelling all that was fright- ful. The tone of excitement which pervaded my feelings was further heightened by a conversation on the prevailing topic which I had in the course of the morning with the distinguished poet and scholar, Mr ——. With what fearful force did he suggest probabilities; what vivid, startling colouring did he throw over them! It was, indeed, a topic congenial to his gloomy imagination. He talked to me, in short, till my dis- turbed fancy realized the wildest chimeras.

'Great God, Dr ——!' said he, laying his hand suddenly on my arm, his great black eyes gleaming with mysterious awe— 'Think, only think! What if, at the moment we are talking together, a comet, whose track the peering eye of science has never traced—whose very existence is known to none but God, is winging its fiery way towards our earth, swift as the light- ning, and with force inevitable! Is it at this instant dashing to fragments some mighty orb that obstructed its progress, and then passing on towards us, disturbing system after system in its way?—How—when will the frightful crash be felt? Is its heat now blighting our atmosphere?—Will combustion first commence, or shall we be at once split asunder into innumer- able fragments, and sent drifting through infinite space?— Whither—whither shall we fly! what must become of our species?—Is the Scriptural JUDGMENT then coming?—Oh, Doctor, what if all these things *are really at hand?*'

Was this imaginative raving calculated to calm one's feel- ings!—By the time I reached home, late in the afternoon, I felt in a fever of excitement. I found an air of apprehension throughout the whole house. My wife, children, and a young visitor, were all together in the parlour, looking out for me, through the window, anxiously—and with paler faces than they might choose to own. The visitor just alluded to, by the way—was a Miss Agnes P——, a girl of about twenty-one, the daughter of an old friend and patient of mine. Her mother, a widow, (with no other child than this,) resided in a village about fifty miles from town—from which she was expected, in a few days' time, to take her daughter back again into the country. Miss P—— was without exception the most charming young woman I think I ever met with. The beauty of her person but faintly shadowed forth the loveliness of her mind and the amiability of her character. There was a rich languor, or rather softness of expression about her features, that to me is enchanting, and constitutes the highest and rarest style of feminine loveliness. Her dark, pensive, searching eyes, spoke a soul full of feeling and fancy. If you, reader, had but *felt* their gaze—had seen them—now glistening in liquid radiance upon you, from beneath their long dark lashes—and then sparkling with enthusiasm, while the flush of excitement was on her beautiful features, and her white hands hastily folded back her auburn tresses from her alabaster brow, your heart would have thrilled as mine often has, and you would with me have exclaimed in a sort of ecstasy—'Star of your sex!' The tones of her voice, so mellow and various—and her whole carriage and demeanour, were in accordance with the expression of her features. In person she was a little under the average height, but most exquisitely moulded and proportioned; and there was a Hebe-like ease and grace* about all her features. She excelled in almost all feminine accomplishments; but the 'things wherein her soul delighted'* were music and romance. A more imaginative, etherealized creature was surely never known. It required all the fond and anxious surveillance of her friends to prevent her carrying her tastes to excess, and becoming, in a manner, unfitted for the 'dull commerce of dull earth!' No sooner had this fair being made her appearance in my house, and given token of something like a prolonged stay, than I became the most popular man in the circle of my acquaintance. Such assiduous calls to enquire after *my* health, and that of my family!—Such a multitude of men—

young ones, to boot—and so embarrassed with a consciousness of the poorness of the pretence that drew them to my house! Such matronly enquiries from mothers and elderly female relatives, into the nature and extent of 'sweet Miss P——'s expectations!' During a former stay at my house, about six months before the period of which I am writing, Miss P—— surrendered her affections—(to the delighted surprise of all her friends and relatives)—to the quietest, and perhaps worthiest of her claimants—a young man, then preparing for orders at Oxford. Never, sure, was there a greater contrast between the tastes of a pledged couple: she all feeling, romance, enthusiasm; he serene, thoughtful, and matter-of-fact. It was most amusing to witness their occasional collisions on subjects which brought into play their respective tastes and qualities; and interesting to note, that the effect was invariably to raise the one in the other's estimation—as if they mutually prized most the qualities of the other. Young N—— had spent two days in London—the greater portion of them, I need hardly say, at my house—about a week before; and he and his fair mistress had disputed rather keenly on the topic of general discussion—the predicted event of the 10th of July. If she did not repose implicit faith in the prophecy, her belief had, somehow or another, acquired a most disturbing strength. He laboured hard to disabuse her of her awful apprehensions— and she as hard to overcome his obstinate incredulity. Each was a little too eager about the matter: and, for the first time since they had known each other, they parted with a *little* coldness—yes, although he was to set off the next morning for Oxford! In short, scarcely any thing was talked about by Agnes but the coming 10th of July: and if she did not anticipate the actual destruction of the globe, and the final judgment of mankind—she at least looked forward to some event, mysterious and tremendous. The eloquent enthusiastic creature almost brought over my placid wife to her way of thinking!—

To return from this long digression—which, however, will be presently found to have been not unnecessary. After staying a few minutes in the parlour, I retired to my library, for the purpose, among other things, of making those entries in my Diary from which these 'Passages' are taken—but the pen

lay useless in my hand. With my chin resting on the palm of
my left hand, I sat at my desk lost in a reverie; my eyes fixed
on the tree which grew in the yard and overshadowed my
windows. How still—how motionless—was every leaf! What
sultry—oppressive—unnatural repose! How it would have
cheered me to hear the faintest 'sough' of wind—to see the
breeze sweep freshening through the leaves, rustling and stirring them into life!—I opened my window, untied my necker-
chief, and loosened my shirt collars—for I felt suffocated with
the heat. I heard at length a faint pattering sound among the
leaves of the tree—and presently there fell on the window-
frame three or four large ominous drops of rain. After gazing
upwards for a moment or two on the gloomy aspect of the
sky—I once more settled down to writing; and was dipping
my pen into the ink-stand, when there blazed about me, a
flash of lightning with such a ghastly, blinding splendour, as
defies all description. It was like what one might conceive to
be a glimpse of hell—and yet not a *glimpse* merely—for it
continued, I think, six or seven seconds. It was followed, at
scarce an instant's interval, with a crash of thunder as if the
world had been smitten out of its sphere, and was rending
asunder!—I hope these expressions will not be considered
hyperbolical. No one, I am sure, who recollects the occurrence I am describing, will require the appeal!—May *I* never
see or hear the like again!—The sudden shock almost drove
me out of my senses. I leaped from my chair with consternation; and could think of nothing, at the moment, but closing
my eyes, and shutting out from my ears the stunning sound
of the thunder. For a moment I stood literally stupified. On
recovering myself, my first impulse was to spring to the door,
and rush down stairs in search of my wife and children. I
heard, on my way, the sound of shrieking proceed from the
parlour in which I had left them. In a moment I had my wife
folded in my arms, and my children clinging with screams
round my knees. My wife had fainted. While I was endeavouring to restore her, there came a second flash of lightning,
equally terrible with the first—and a second explosion of thunder, loud as one could imagine the discharge of a thousand
parks of artillery directly over head. The windows—in fact

the whole house, quivered with the shock. The noise helped to recover my wife from her swoon.

'Kneel down! Love! Husband!'—she gasped, endeavouring to drop upon her knees—'Kneel down! Pray—pray for us! We are undone!' After shouting till I was hoarse, and pulling the bell repeatedly and violently, one of the servants made her appearance—but in a state not far removed from that of her mistress. Both of them, however, recovered themselves in a few minutes, roused by the cries of the children. 'Wait a moment, love,' said I, 'and I'll fetch you a few reviving drops!'—I stepped into the back room, where I generally kept some phials of drugs,—and poured out a few drops of sal volatile. The thought then for the first time struck me, that Miss P—— was not in the parlour I had just quitted. *Where* was she? What would *she* say to all this?—God bless me, where is she?—I thought with increasing trepidation.

'Edward—Edward,' I exclaimed, to a servant who happened to pass the door of the room where I was standing; 'where's Miss P——?'

'Miss P——, sir!—Why—I don't—oh, yes!' he replied, suddenly recollecting himself, 'about five minutes ago I saw her run very swift up stairs, and haven't seen her since, sir.'— 'What!' I exclaimed, with increasing trepidation, 'was it about the time that the first flash of lightning came?'—'Yes, it was, sir!'—'Take this in to your mistress, and say I'll be with her immediately,' said I, giving him what I had mixed. I rushed up stairs, calling out as I went, 'Agnes! Agnes! where are you?' I received no answer. At length I reached the floor where her bedroom lay. The door was closed, but not shut.

'Agnes! Where are you?' I enquired very agitatedly, at the same time knocking at her door. I received no answer.

'Agnes! Agnes! For God's-sake, speak!—Speak, or I shall come into your room!' No reply was made; and I thrust open the door. Heavens! Can I describe what I saw!

Within less than a yard of me stood the most fearful figure my eyes have ever beheld. It was Agnes!—She was in the attitude of stepping to the door, with both arms extended, as if in a menacing mood. Her hair was partially dishevelled. Her face seemed whiter than the white dress she wore. Her lips were of a livid hue. Her eyes, full of awful expression—of supernatural lustre, were fixed with a petrifying stare, on me. Oh, language fails me—utterly!—Those eyes have never since been absent from me when alone! I felt as though they were blighting the life within me! I could not breathe, much less stir. I strove to speak—but could not utter a sound. My lips seemed rigid as those I looked at. The horrors of night-mare were upon me. My eyes at length closed; my head seemed turning round—and for a moment or two I lost all consciousness. I revived. *There* was the frightful thing still before me—nay, close to me! Though I looked at her, I never once thought of Agnes P——. It was the tremendous appearance—the ineffable terror gleaming from her eyes, that thus overcame me. I protest I cannot conceive any thing more dreadful! Miss P—— continued standing perfectly motionless; and while I was gazing at her in the manner I have been describing, a peal of thunder roused me to my self-possession. I stepped towards her, took hold of her hand, exclaiming 'Agnes—Agnes!'—and carried her to the bed, where I laid her down. It required some little force to press down her arms; and I drew the eyelids over her staring eyes mechanically. While in the act of doing so, a flash of lightning flickered luridly over her—but her eye neither quivered nor blinked. She seemed to have been suddenly deprived of all sense and motion: in fact, nothing but her pulse—if pulse it should be called—and faint breathing, showed that she lived. My eye wandered over her whole figure, dreading to meet some scorching trace of lightning—but there was nothing of the kind. What had happened to her? Was she frightened—to death? I spoke to her; I called her by her name, loudly; I shook her, rather violently: I might have acted it all to a statue!—I rang the chamber-bell with almost frantic violence: and presently my wife and a female servant made their appearance in the room; but I was far more embarrassed than assisted by their presence. 'Is she killed?' murmured the former, as she staggered towards the bed, and then clung convulsively to me—'Has the lightning struck her?'

I was compelled to disengage myself from her grasp and hurry her into the adjoining room—whither I called a servant to attend to her; and then returned to my hapless patient. But what was I to do? Medical man as I was, I never had seen a patient in such circumstances, and felt as ignorant on the subject, as agitated. It was not epilepsy—it was not apoplexy—a swoon—nor any known species of hysteria. The most remarkable feature of her case, and what enabled me to ascertain the nature of her disease, was this; that if I happened accidentally to alter the position of her limbs, *they retained, for a short time, their new position*. If, for instance, I moved her arm—it remained for a while in the situation in which I had last placed it, and gradually resumed its former one. If I raised her into an upright posture, she continued sitting so without the support of pillows, or other assistance, as exactly as if she had heard me express a wish to that effect, and assented to it; but, the horrid vacancy of her aspect! If I elevated one eyelid for a moment, to examine the state of the eye, it was some time in closing, unless I drew it over myself. All these circumstances,—which terrified the servant who stood shaking at my elbow, and muttering, 'She's possessed! she's possessed!— Satan has her!'—convinced me that the unfortunate young lady was seized with CATALEPSY; that rare mysterious affection, so fearfully blending the conditions of life and death— presenting—so to speak—life in the aspect of death, and death in that of life! I felt no doubt that extreme terror operating suddenly on a nervous system most highly excited, and a vivid, active fancy, had produced the effects I saw. Doubtless the first terrible outbreak of the thunder-storm—especially the fierce splendour of that first flash of lightning which so alarmed myself—apparently corroborating and realizing all her awful apprehensions of the predicted event, overpowered her at once, and flung her into the fearful situation in which I found her— that of one ARRESTED in her terror-struck flight towards the door of her chamber. But again—the thought struck me—had she received any direct injury from the lightning? Had it blinded her? It might be so—for I could make no impression on the pupils of the eyes. Nothing could startle them into action. They seemed a little more dilated than usual, and fixed.

I confess that, besides the other agitating circumstances of the moment, this extraordinary, this unprecedented case too much distracted my self-possession to enable me promptly to deal with it. I had heard and read of, but never before seen such a case. No time, however, was to be lost. I determined to resort at once to strong antispasmodic treatment.* I bled her from the arm freely, applied blisters behind the ears, immersed her feet, which, together with her hands, were cold as marble, in hot water, and endeavoured to force into her mouth a little opium and ether. Whilst the servants were busied about her, undressing her, and carrying my directions into effect, I stepped for a moment into the adjoining room, where I found my wife just recovering from a violent fit of hysterics. Her loud laughter, though so near me, I had not once heard, so absorbed was I with the mournful case of Miss P——. After continuing with her till she recovered sufficiently to accompany me down stairs, I returned to Miss P——'s bedroom. She continued exactly in the condition in which I had left her. Though the water was hot enough almost to parboil her tender feet, it produced no sensible effect on the circulation or the state of the skin; and finding a strong determination of blood towards the region of the head and neck, I determined to have her cupped* between the shoulders. I went down stairs to drop a line to the apothecary, requesting him to come immediately with his cupping instruments. As I was delivering the note into the hands of a servant, a man rushed up to the open door where I was standing, and, breathless with haste, begged my instant attendance on a patient close by, who had just met with a severe accident. Relying on the immediate arrival of Mr ——, the apothecary, I put on my hat and great coat, took my umbrella, and followed the man who had summoned me out. It rained in torrents, for the storm, after about twenty minutes' intermission, burst forth again with unabated violence. The thunder and lightning were really awful!

THE BOXER

THE patient who thus abruptly, and under circumstances inopportunely, required my services, proved to be one Bill —— , a notorious boxer, who, in returning that evening from a great prize-fight, had been thrown out of his gig, the horse being frightened by the lightning, and the rider, besides, much the worse for liquor, had his ankle dreadfully dislocated. He had been taken up by some passengers, and conveyed with great difficulty to his own residence, a public-house, not three minutes' walk from where I lived. The moment I entered the tap-room, which I had to pass on my way to the staircase, I heard his groans, or rather howls, overhead. The excitement of intoxication, added to the agonies occasioned by his accident, had driven him, I was told, nearly mad. He was uttering the most revolting execrations as I entered his room. He damned himself—his ill-luck (for it seemed he had lost considerable sums on the fight)—the combatants—the horse that threw him—the thunder and lightning—every thing, in short, and every body about him. The sound of the thunder was sublime music to me, and the more welcome, because it drowned the blasphemous bellowing of the monster I was visiting. Yes— there lay the burly boxer, stretched upon the bed, with none of his dress removed, except the boot from the limb that was injured—his new blue coat, with glaring yellow buttons, and drab knee-breeches, soiled with the street mud into which he had been precipitated—his huge limbs, writhing in restless agony over the bed—his fists clenched, and his flat, iron-featured face swollen and distorted with pain and rage.

'But, my good woman,' said I, pausing at the door, addressing myself to the boxer's wife, who, wringing her hands, had conducted me up stairs; 'I assure you, I am not the person you should have sent to. It's a surgeon's, not a physician's case; I fear I can't do much for him—quite out of my way'——

'Oh, for God's sake—for the love of God don't say so!' gasped the poor creature, with affrighted emphasis—'oh, do *something* for him, or he'll drive us all out of our senses—he'll be killing us!'

'Do something!' roared my patient, who had overheard the last words of his wife, turning his bloated face towards me— *do* something, indeed? ay, and be —— to you! Here, here— look ye, Doctor—look ye, *here*!' He continued, pointing to the wounded foot, which, all crushed and displaced, and the stocking soaked with blood, presented a shocking appearance— 'look here, indeed!—ah, that —— horse! that —— horse!' his teeth gnashed, and his right hand was lifted up, clenched, with fury—'If I don't break every bone in his —— body, as soon as ever I can stir this cursed leg again!'

I felt, for a moment, as though I had entered the very pit and presence of Satan, for the lightning was gleaming over his ruffianly figure incessantly, and the thunder rolling close overhead while he was speaking.

'Hush! hush! you'll drive the doctor away! For pity's sake, hold your tongue, or Doctor —— won't come into the room to you!' gasped his wife, dropping on her knees beside him.

'Ha, ha! Let him go! Only let him stir a step, and lame as I am, —— me! if I don't jump out of bed, and teach him civility! *Here*, you doctor, as you call yourself! What's to be done?' Really I was too much shocked, at the moment, to know. I was half inclined to leave the room immediately—and had a fair plea for doing so, in the *surgical* nature of the case—but the agony of the fellow's wife induced me to do violence to my own feelings, and stay. After directing a person to be sent off, in my name, for the nearest surgeon, I addressed myself to my task, and proceeded to remove the stocking. His whole body quivered with the anguish it occasioned; and I saw such fury gathering in his features, that I began to dread lest he might rise up in a sudden frenzy, and strike me.

'Oh! oh! oh!—Curse your clumsy hands! You don't know no more nor a child,' he groaned, 'what you're about! Leave it—leave it alone! Give over with ye! Doctor, ——, I say—be off!'

'Mercy, mercy, Doctor!' sobbed his wife, in a whisper, fearing from my momentary pause, that I was going to take her husband at his word—'Don't go away! Oh, go on—go on! It *must* be done, you know! Never mind what he says! He's only a little the worse for liquor now—and—and then the *pain!* Go on, doctor! He'll thank you the more for it tomorrow!'

'Wife! Here!' shouted her husband. The woman instantly stepped up to him. He stretched out his Herculean arm, and grasped her by the shoulder.

'So—you ——! I'm drunk, am I? I'm *drunk*, eh—you lying ——!' he exclaimed, and jerked her violently away, right across the room, to the door, where the poor creature fell down, but presently rose, crying bitterly.

'Get away! Get off—get down stairs—if you don't want me to serve you the same again! Say I'm drunk—you beast?' With frantic gestures she obeyed—rushed down stairs—and I was left alone with her husband. I was disposed to follow her abruptly, but the positive dread of my life (for he might leap out of bed and kill me with a blow), kept me to my task. My flesh crept with disgust at touching his! I examined the wound, which undoubtedly must have given him torture enough to drive him mad, and bathed it in warm water; resolved to pay no attention to his abuse, and quit the instant that the surgeon, who had been sent for, made his appearance. At length he came. I breathed more freely, resigned the case into his hands, and was going to take up my hat, when he begged me to continue in the room, with such an earnest apprehensive look, that I reluctantly remained. I saw he dreaded as much being left alone with his patient, as I! It need hardly be said that every step that was taken in dressing the wound, was attended with the vilest execrations of the patient. Such a foul-mouthed ruffian I never encountered anywhere. It seemed as though he was possessed of a devil. What a contrast to the sweet speechless sufferer whom I had left at home, and to whom my heart yearned to return!

The storm still continued raging. The rain had comparatively ceased, but the thunder and lightning made their appearance with fearful frequency and fierceness. I drew down the blind of the window, observing to the surgeon that the lightning seemed to startle our patient.

'Put it up again! Put up that blind again, I say!' he cried impatiently. 'D'ye think *I'm* afear'd of the lightning, like my —— horse to-day? Put it up again—or I'll get out and do it myself!' I did as he wished. Reproof or expostulation was useless. 'Ha!' he exclaimed, in a low tone of fury, rubbing his hands together—in a manner bathing them in the fiery stream, as a flash of lightning gleamed ruddily over him. '*There* it is!—Curse it—just the sort of flash that frightened my horse— d—— it!'—and the impious wretch shook his fist, and 'grinned horribly a ghastly smile!'*

'Be silent, sir! Be silent! or we will both leave you instantly. Your behaviour is impious! It is frightful to witness! Forbear—lest the vengeance of God descend upon you!'

'Come, come—none o' your —— methodism *here!* Go on with your business! Stick to your shop,' interrupted the Boxer.

'Does not *that* rebuke your blasphemies?' I enquired, suddenly shading my eyes from the vivid stream of lightning that burst into the room, while the thunder rattled overhead— apparently in fearful proximity. When I removed my hands from my eyes, and opened them, the first object that they fell upon was the figure of the Boxer, sitting upright in bed with both hands stretched out, just as those of Elymas the sorcerer,* in the picture of Raphael—his face the colour of a corpse—and his eyes, almost starting out of their sockets, directed with a horrid stare towards the window. His lips moved not—nor did he utter a sound. It was clear what had occurred. The wrathful fire of Heaven, that had glanced harmlessly around us, had blinded the blasphemer. Yes—the sight of his eyes had perished. While we were gazing at him in silent awe, he fell back in bed, speechless, and clasped his hands over his breast, seemingly in an attitude of despair. But for that motion, we should have thought him dead. Shocked beyond expression, Mr —— paused in his operations. I examined the eyes of the patient. The pupils were both dilated to their utmost extent, and immovable. I asked him many questions, but he answered not a word. Occasionally, however, a groan of horror—remorse—agony—(or all combined) would burst from his pent bosom; and this was the only evidence he gave of consciousness. He moved over on his right side—his 'pale face turned to the wall'—and, unclasping his hands, pressed the fore-finger of each with convulsive force upon the eyes. Mr —— proceeded with his task. What a contrast between the present and past behaviour of our patient! Do what we would—put him to never such great pain—he neither uttered a syllable, nor expressed any symptoms of passion, as before. There was, however, no necessity for my continuing any longer; so I left the case in the hands of Mr ——, who undertook to acquaint Mrs —— with the frightful accident that had happened to her husband. What two scenes had I witnessed that evening!

I hurried home full of agitation at the scene I had just quitted, and melancholy apprehensions concerning the one to which I was returning. On reaching my lovely patient's room, I found, alas! no sensible effects produced by the very active means which had been adopted. She lay in bed, the aspect of her features apparently the same as when I last saw her. Her eyes were closed—her cheeks very pale, and mouth rather open, as if she were on the point of speaking. The hair hung in a little disorder on each side of her face, having escaped from beneath her cap. My wife sate beside her, grasping her right hand—weeping, and almost stupified; and the servant that was in the room when I entered, seemed so bewildered as to be worse than useless. As it was now nearly nine o'clock, and getting dark, I ordered candles. I took one of them in my hand, opened her eyelids, and passed and re-passed the candle several times before her eyes, but it produced no apparent effect. Neither the eyelids blinked, nor the pupils contracted. I then took out my penknife, and made a thrust with the open blade, as though I intended to plunge it into her right eye; it seemed as if I might have buried the blade in the socket, for the shock or resistance called forth by the attempt. I took her hand in mine—having for a moment displaced my wife—and found it damp and cold; but when I suddenly left it suspended, it continued so for a few moments, and only gradually resumed its former situation. I pressed the back of the blade of my penknife upon the flesh at the root of the nail, (one of the tenderest parts, perhaps, of the whole body,) but she evinced not the slightest sensation of pain. I shouted suddenly and loudly in her ears, but with similar ill success. I felt at an extremity. Completely baffled at all points—discouraged and agitated beyond expression, I left Miss P—— in the care of a nurse, whom I had sent for to attend upon her, at the instance of my wife, and hastened to my study to see if my books could throw any light upon the nature of this, to me, new and inscrutable disorder. After hunting about for some time, and finding but little to the purpose, I prepared for bed, determining in the morning to send off for Miss P——'s mother, and Mr N—— from Oxford, and also to call upon my eminent friend Dr D—— and hear what his superior skill and experience might be able to suggest. In passing Miss P——'s room, I stepped in to take my farewell for the evening. 'Beautiful, unfortunate creature!' thought I, as I stood gazing mournfully on her, with my candle in my hand, leaning against the bed-post. 'What mystery is upon thee? What awful change has come over thee?—the gloom of the grave and the light of life—both lying upon thee at once! Is thy mind palsied as thy body? How long is this strange state to last? How long art thou doomed to linger thus on the confines of both worlds, so that those, in either, who love thee may not claim thee! Heaven guide our thoughts to discover a remedy for thy fearful disorder!' I could not bear to look upon her any longer; and after kissing her lips, hurried up to bed, charging the nurse to summon me the moment that any change whatever was perceptible in Miss P——. I dare say, I shall be easily believed when I apprize the reader of the troubled night that followed such a troubled day. The thunder-storm itself, coupled with the predictions of the day, and apart from its attendant incidents that have been mentioned, was calculated to leave an awful and permanent impression in one's mind. 'If I were to live a century hence, I could not forget it,' says a distinguished writer. 'The thunder and lightning were more appalling than I ever recollect witnessing, even in the West Indies—that region of storms and hurricanes. The air had been long surcharged with electricity; and I predicted several days beforehand, that we should have a storm of very unusual violence. But when with this we couple the strange prophecy that gained credit with a prodigious number of those one would have expected to be above such things-neither more nor less than that the world was to come to an end on that very day, and the judgment of mankind to follow: I say, the coincidence of the events was not a little singular, and calculated to inspire common folk with wonder and fear. I dare say, if one could but find them out, that there were instances of people frightened out of their wits on the occasion. I own to you candidly that I, for one, felt a little squeamish, and had not a little difficulty in bolstering up my courage with Virgil's *Felix qui potuit rerum cognoscere causas*,' &c. *

I did not so much sleep as dose interruptedly for the first three or four hours after getting into bed. I, as well as my alarmed Emily, would start up occasionally, and sit listening, under the apprehension that we heard a shriek, or some other such sound, proceed from Miss P——'s room. The image of the blinded Boxer flitted in fearful forms about me, and my ears seemed to ring with his curses.—It must have been, I should think, between two and three o'clock, when I dreamed that I leaped out of bed, under an impulse sudden as irresistible—slipped on my dressing-gown, and hurried down stairs to the back drawing-room. On opening the door, I found the room lit up with funeral tapers, and the apparel of a dead-room spread about. At the further end lay a coffin on tressels, covered with a long sheet, with the figure of an old woman sitting beside it, with long streaming white hair, and her eyes, bright as the lightning, directed towards me with a fiendish stare of exultation. Suddenly she rose up—pulled off the sheet that had covered the coffin—pushed aside the lid—plucked out the body of Miss P——, dashed it on the floor, and trampled upon it with apparent triumph! This horrid dream woke me, and haunted my waking thoughts. May I never pass such a dismal night again!

I rose from bed in the morning feverish and unrefreshed; and in a few minutes' time hurried to Miss P——'s room. The mustard applications to the soles of the feet, together with the blisters behind the ears, had produced the usual local effects without affecting the complaint. Both her pulse and breathing continued calm. The only change perceptible in the colour of her countenance was a slight pallor about the upper part of the cheeks: and I fancied there was an expression about her mouth approaching to a smile. She had, I found, continued, throughout the night, motionless and silent as a corpse. With a profound sigh I took my seat beside her, and examined the eyes narrowly, but perceived no change in them. What was to be done? How was she to be roused from this fearful—if not fatal—lethargy?

While I was gazing intently on her features, I fancied that I perceived a slight muscular twitching about the nostrils. I stepped hastily down stairs (just as a drowning man, they say, catches at a straw) and returned with a phial of the strongest solution of ammonia,† which I applied freely with a feather to

_____
† Liquid smelling salts.

the interior of the nostrils. This attempt, also, was unsuccessful as the former ones. I cannot describe the feelings with which I witnessed these repeated failures to stimulate her torpid sensibilities into action: and not knowing what to say or do, I returned to dress, with feelings of unutterable despondency. While dressing, it struck me that a blister might be applied with success along the whole course of the spine. The more I thought of this expedient, the more feasible it appeared:—it would be such a direct and powerful appeal to the nervous system—in all probability the very seat and source of the disorder!—I ordered one to be sent for instantly—and myself applied it, before I went down to breakfast. As soon as I had dispatched the few morning patients that called, I wrote imperatively to Mr N—— at Oxford, and to Miss P——'s mother, entreating them by all the love they bore Agnes to come to her instantly. I then set out for Dr D——'s, whom I found just starting on his daily visits. I communicated the whole case to him. He listened with interest to my statement, and told me he had once a similar case in his own practice, which, alas! terminated fatally in spite of the most anxious and combined efforts of the *élite* of the faculty in London. He approved of the course I had adopted—most especially the blister on the spine; and earnestly recommended me to resort to galvanism— if Miss P—— should not be relieved from the fit before the evening—when he promised to call, and assist in carrying into effect what he recommended.

'Is it that beautiful girl I saw in your pew last Sunday, at church?' he enquired, suddenly.

'The same—the same!'— I replied with a sigh.

Dr D—— continued silent for a moment or two.

'Poor creature!' he exclaimed, with an air of deep concern, 'one so beautiful! Do you know I thought I now and then perceived a very remarkable expression in her eye, especially while that fine voluntary was playing. Is she an enthusiast about music?'

'Passionately—devotedly'——

'We'll try it!' he replied briskly, with a confident air—'We'll try it! First, let us disturb the nervous torpor with a slight shock of galvanism, and then try the effect of your organ.'[†] I listened to the suggestion with interest, but was not quite so sanguine in my expectations as my friend appeared to be.

In the whole range of disorders that affect the human frame, there is not one so extraordinary, so mysterious, so incapable of management, as that which afflicted the truly unfortunate young lady whose case I am narrating. It has given rise to almost infinite speculation, and is admitted, I believe, on all hands to be—if I may so speak—a nosological anomaly.* Van Swieten* vividly and picturesquely enough compares it to that condition of the body, which, according to ancient fiction, was produced in the beholder by the appalling sight of Medusa's head—

'Saxifici Medusae vultus.'*

The medical writers of antiquity have left evidence of the existence of this disease in their day—but given the most obscure and unsatisfactory descriptions of it, confounding it, in many instances, with other disorders—apoplexy, epilepsy, and swooning. Celsus,* according to Van Swieten, describes such patients as these in question, under the term '*attoniti*,' which is a translation of the title I have prefixed to this paper: while, in our own day, the celebrated Dr Cullen* classes it as a species of apoplexy, at the same time stating that he had never seen a genuine instance of catalepsy. He had always found, he says, those cases which were reported such, to be feigned ones. More modern science, however, distinctly recognises the disease as one peculiar and independent; and is borne out by numerous unquestionable cases of catalepsy recorded by some of the most eminent members of the profession. Dr Jebb,* in particular, in the appendix to his 'Select Cases of Paralysis of the Lower Extremities,' relates a remarkable and affecting instance of a cataleptic patient. As it is not likely that general readers have met with this interesting case, I shall here transcribe it. The young lady who was the subject of the

---

[†] I had at home,—being myself a lover, though not a scientific one, of music—a very fine organ.

disorder was seized with the fit when Dr Jebb was announced on his first visit.

'She was employed in netting, and was passing the needle through the mesh; in which position she immediately became rigid, exhibiting, in a very pleasing form, a figure of death-like sleep, beyond the power of art to imitate, or the imagination to conceive. Her forehead was serene, her features perfectly composed. The paleness of her colour—her breathing being also scarcely perceptible at a distance—operated in rendering the similitude to marble more exact and striking. The position of the fingers, hands, and arms was altered with difficulty, but preserved every form of flexure they acquired. Nor were the muscles of the neck exempted from this law; her head maintaining every situation in which the hand could place it, as firmly as her limbs.

'Upon gently raising the eyelids they immediately closed with a degree of spasm.† The iris contracted upon the approach of a candle, as in a state of vigilance. The eyeball itself was slightly agitated with a tremulous motion, not discernible when the eyelid had descended. About half an hour after my arrival, the rigidity of her limbs and statue-like appearance being yet unaltered, she sung three plaintive songs in a tone of voice so elegantly expressive, and with such affecting modulation, as evidently pointed out how much the most powerful passion of the mind was concerned in the production of her disorder; as, indeed, her history confirmed. In a few minutes afterwards she sighed deeply, and the spasm in her limbs was immediately relaxed. She complained that she could not open her eyes, her hands grew cold, a general tremor followed; but in a few seconds, recovering entirely her recollection and powers of motion, she entered into a detail of her symptoms, and the history of her complaint. After she had discoursed for some time with apparent calmness, the universal spasm suddenly returned. The features now assumed a different form, denoting a mind strongly impressed with anxiety and apprehension. At times she uttered short and vehement exclamations, in a

---

† This was not the case with Miss P——. I repeatedly remarked the perfect mobility of her eyelids.

piercing tone of voice, expressive of the passions that agitated her mind; her hands being strongly locked in each other, and all her muscles, those subservient to speech excepted, being affected with the same rigidity as before.'

But the most extraordinary—if not apocryphal—case on record, is one[†] given by Dr Petetin,[*] a physician of Lyons, in which '*the senses were transferred to the pit of the stomach, and the ends of the fingers and toes,* i.e. the patients, in a state of insensibility to all external impressions upon the proper organs of sense, were nevertheless capable of hearing, *seeing,* smelling, and tasting whatever was approached to the pit of the stomach, or the ends of the fingers and toes. The patients are said to have answered questions proposed to the pit of the stomach—to have told the hour by a watch placed there—to have tasted food—and smelt the fragrance of apricots touching the part, &c. &c.' It may be interesting to add, that an eminent physician, who went to see the patient, incredulous of what he had heard, returned perfectly convinced of its truth. I have also read somewhere of a Spanish monk, who was so terrified by a sudden sight which he encountered in the Asturias mountains, that, when several of his holy brethren, whom he had preceded a mile or two, came up, they found him stretched upon the ground in the fearful condition of a cataleptic patient. They carried him back immediately to their monastery, and he was believed dead. He suddenly revived, however, in the midst of his funeral obsequies, to the consternation of all around him. When he had perfectly recovered the use of his faculties, he related some absurd matters which he pretended to have seen in a vision during his comatose state. The disorder in question, however, generally makes its appearance in the female sex, and seems to be in many, if not in most instances, a remote member of the family of hysterical affections.—To return, however.

On returning home from my daily round—in which my dejected air was remarked by all the patients I had visited—I

[†] A second similar case, well authenticated, occurred not long afterwards, at the same place.—They are attributed by Dr P to the influence of animal electricity.

found no alteration whatever in Miss P——. The nurse had failed in forcing even arrow-root down her mouth, and, finding it was not swallowed, was compelled to desist, for fear of choking her. She was, therefore, obliged to resort to other means of conveying support to her exhausted frame. The blister on the spine, from which I had expected so much, and the renewed sinapisms* to the feet, had failed to make any impression! Thus was every successive attempt an utter failure! The disorder continued absolutely inaccessible to the approaches of medicine. The baffled attendants could but look at her, and lament. Good God, was Agnes to continue in this dreadful condition till her energies sunk in death? What would become of her lover? of her mother! These considerations totally destroyed my peace of mind. I could neither think, read, eat, nor remain anywhere but in the chamber, where, alas! my presence was so unavailing!

Dr D—— made his appearance soon after dinner; and we proceeded at once to the room where our patient lay. Though a little paler than before, her features were placid as those of the chiselled marble. Notwithstanding all she had suffered, and the fearful situation in which she lay at that moment, she still looked very beautiful. Her cap was off, and her rich auburn hair lay negligently on each side of her, upon the pillow. Her forehead was white as alabaster. She lay with her head turned a little on one side, and her two small white hands were clasped together over her bosom. This was the nurse's arrangement: for 'poor sweet young lady,' she said, 'I couldn't bear to see her laid straight along, with her arms close beside her like a corpse, so I tried to make her look as much asleep as possible!' The impression of beauty, however, conveyed by her symmetrical and tranquil features, was disturbed as soon as lifting up the eyelids, we saw the fixed stare of the eyes. They were not glassy or corpse-like, but bright as those of life, with a little of the dreadful expression of epilepsy. We raised her in bed, and she, as before, sate upright, but with a blank absent aspect that was lamentable and unnatural. Her arms, when lifted and left suspended, did not fall, but *sunk* down again gradually. We returned her gently to her recumbent posture; and determined at once to try the effect of galvanism upon her. My machine was soon brought into the room; and when we had duly arranged matters, we directed the nurse to quit the chamber for a short time, as the effect of galvanism is generally found too startling to be witnessed by a female spectator. I wish I had not myself seen it in the case of Miss P——! Her colour went and came—her eyelids and mouth started open—and she stared wildly about her with the aspect of one starting out of bed in a fright. I thought at one moment that the horrid spell was broken, for she sate up suddenly, leaned forwards towards me, and her mouth opened as though she were about to speak!

'Agnes! Agnes! dear Agnes! Speak, speak! but a word! Say you live!' I exclaimed, rushing forwards, and folding my arms round her. Alas, she heard me—she saw me—not, but fell back in bed in her former state! When the galvanic shock was conveyed to her limbs, it produced the usual effects—dreadful to behold in all cases—but agonizing to me, in the case of Miss P——. The last subject on which I had seen the effects of galvanism, previous to the present instance, was the body of an executed malefactor;[†] and the associations revived on the present occasion were almost too painful to bear. I begged my friend to desist, for I saw the attempt was hopeless, and would

---

[†] A word about that case, by the way, in passing. The spectacle was truly horrific. When I entered the room where the experiments were to take place, the body of a man named Carter, which had been cut down from the gallows scarce half an hour, was lying on the table; and the cap being removed, his frightful features, distorted with the agonies of suffocation, were visible. The crime he had been hanged for, was murder; and a brawny, desperate ruffian he looked! None of his clothes were removed. He wore a fustian jacket, and drab knee-breeches. The first time that the galvanic shock was conveyed to him will never, I dare say, be forgotten by any one present. We all shrunk from the table in consternation, with the momentary belief that we had positively brought the man back to life; for he suddenly sprung up into a sitting posture—his arms waved wildly—the colour rushed into his cheeks—his lips were drawn apart, so as to shew all his teeth—and his eyes glared at us with apparent fury. One young man, a medical student, shrieked violently, and was carried out in a swoon. One gentleman present, who happened to be nearest to the upper part of the body, was almost knocked down with the violent blow he received from the left arm. It was some time before any of us could recover presence of mind sufficient to proceed with the experiments.

not allow her tender frame to be agitated to no purpose. My mind misgave me for ever making the attempt. What, thought I, if we have fatally disturbed the nervous system, and prostrated the small remains of strength she had left? While I was torturing myself with such fears as these, Dr —— laid down the rod, with a melancholy air, exclaiming 'Well! what *is* to be done now? I cannot tell you how sanguine I was about the success of this experiment! Do you know whether she ever had a fit of epilepsy?' he enquired.

'No—not that I am aware of. I never heard of it, if she had.'—

'Had she generally a horror of thunder and lightning?'

'Oh—quite the contrary! She felt a sort of ecstasy on such occasions, and has written some beautiful verses during their continuance. *Such* seemed rather her hour of inspiration than otherwise!'

'Do you think the lightning itself has affected her?—Do you think her sight is destroyed?'

'I have no means of knowing whether the immobility of the pupils arises from blindness, or is only one of the temporary effects of catalepsy.'

'Then she believed the prophecy, you think, of the world's destruction on Tuesday?'

'No.—I don't think she exactly *believed* it; but I am sure that day brought with it awful apprehensions—or at least, a fearful degree of uncertainty.'

'Well—between ourselves,—there was something *very* strange in the coincidence, was not there? Nothing in life ever shook my firmness as it was shaken yesterday! I almost fancied the earth was quivering in its sphere!'

'It *was* a dreadful day! One I shall never forget!—*That* is the image of it,' I exclaimed, pointing to the poor sufferer—'which will be engraven on my mind as long as I live!—But the worst is, perhaps, yet to be told you: Mr N——, her lover—to whom she was very soon to have been married, HE will be here shortly to see her'——

'My God!' exclaimed Dr D—— clasping his hands, eyeing Miss P——, with intense commiseration—'What a fearful bride for him—'Twill drive him mad!'

'I dread his coming—I know not what we shall do!—And, then, there's her *mother*—poor old lady!—her I have written to, and expect almost hourly!'

'Why—what an accumulation of shocks and miseries! it will be upsetting *you!*'—said my friend, seeing me pale and agitated.

'Well!'—he continued—'I cannot now stay here longer— your misery is catching; and besides, I am most pressingly engaged: but you may rely on my services, if you should require them in any way.'

My friend took his departure, leaving me more disconsolate than ever. Before retiring to bed, I rubbed in mustard upon the chief surfaces of the body, hoping—though faintly—that it might have some effect in rousing the system. I kneeled down, before stepping into bed, and earnestly prayed, that as all human efforts seemed baffled, the Almighty would set her free from the mortal thraldom in which she lay, and restore her to life, and those who loved her more than life! Morning came—it found me by her bed-side as usual, and her, in no wise altered—apparently neither better nor worse! If the unvarying monotony of my description should fatigue the reader—what must the actual monotony and hopelessness have been to me!

While I was sitting beside Miss P——, I heard my youngest boy come down stairs, and ask to be let into the room. He was a little fair-haired youngster, about three years of age,— and had always been an especial favourite of Miss P——'s— her 'own sweet pet'—as the poor girl herself called him. Determined to throw no chance away, I beckoned him in, and took him on my knee. He called to Miss P——, as if he thought her asleep; patted her face with his little hands, and kissed her. 'Wake, wake!—Cousin Aggy—get up!'—he cried—'Papa say, 'tis time to get up!—Do you sleep with eyes open?†—Eh?— Cousin Aggy?' He looked at her intently for some moments and seemed frightened. He turned pale, and struggled to get off my knee. I allowed him to go—and he ran to his mother, who was standing at the foot of the bed—and hid his face behind her.

---

† I had been examining her eyes, and had only half closed the lids.

I passed breakfast time in great apprehension—expecting the two arrivals I have mentioned. I knew not how to prepare either the mother or the betrothed husband for the scene that awaited them, and which I had not particularly described to them. It was with no little trepidation that I heard the startling knock of the general postman; and with infinite astonishment and doubt that I took out of the servant's hand, a letter from Mr N——, for poor Agnes!—For a while I knew not what to make of it. Had he received the alarming express I had forwarded to him; and did he write to Miss P——! Or was he unexpectedly absent from Oxford, when it arrived?—The latter supposition was corroborated by the post mark, which I observed was Lincoln. I felt it my duty to open the letter. Alas! it was in a gay strain—unusually gay for N——; informing Agnes that he had been suddenly summoned into Lincolnshire, to his cousin's wedding—where he was very happy—both on account of his relative's happiness, and the anticipation of a similar scene being in store for himself! Every line was buoyant with hope and animation: but the postscript most affected me.

'P.S. *The tenth of July*, by the way—my Aggy!—*Is* it all over with us, sweet Pythonissa?—Are you and I at this moment on separate fragments of the globe? I shall seal my conquest over you with a kiss when I see you! Remember, you parted from me in a pet, naughty one!—and kissed me rather coldly! But that is the way that your sex always end arguments, when you are vanquished!'

I read these lines in silence;—my wife burst into tears. As soon as I had a little recovered from the emotion occasioned by a perusal of the letter, I hastened to send a second summons to Mr N——, and directed it to him in Lincoln, whither he had requested Miss P—— to address him. Without explaining the precise nature of Miss P——'s seizure, I gave him warning that he must hurry up to town instantly; and that even then, it was to the last degree doubtful whether he would see her alive. After this little occurrence, I could hardly trust myself to go up stairs again and look upon the unfortunate girl. My heart fluttered at the door, and when I entered, I burst into tears. I could utter no more than the words, 'poor—poor Agnes!'—and withdrew.

I was shocked, and indeed enraged, to find in one of the morning papers, a paragraph stating, though inaccurately, the nature of Miss P——'s illness. Who could have been so unfeeling as to make the poor girl an object of public wonder and pity? I never ascertained, though I made every enquiry, from whom the intelligence was communicated.

One of my patients that day happened to be a niece of the venerable and honoured Dean of ——, at whose house she resided. He was in the room when I called; and to explain what he called 'the gloom of my manner,' I gave him a full account of the melancholy event which had occurred. He listened to me till the tears ran down his face.

'But you have not yet tried the effect of *music*—of which you say *she* is so fond! Do not you intend to resort to it?' I told him it was our intention; and that our agitation was the only reason why we did not try the effect of it immediately after the galvanism.

'Now, Doctor, excuse an old clergyman, will you?' said the venerable and pious Dean, laying his hand on my arm, 'and let me suggest that the experiment may not be the less successful with the blessing of God, if it be introduced in the course of a religious service. Come, Doctor, what say you?' I paused.

'Have you any objection to my calling at your house this evening, and reading the service appointed by our church for the visitation of the sick? It will not be difficult to introduce the most solemn and affecting strains of music, or to let it precede or follow.' Still I hesitated—and yet I scarce knew why. 'Come, Doctor, you know I am no enthusiast—I am not generally considered a fanatic. Surely, when man has done his best, and fails, he should not hesitate to turn to God!' The good old man's words sunk into my soul, and diffused in it a cheerful and humble hope that the blessing of Providence would attend the means suggested. I acquiesced in the Dean's proposal with delight, and even eagerness: and it was arranged that he should be at my house between seven and eight o'clock that evening. I think I have already observed, that I had an organ, a very fine and powerful one, in my back drawing-room; and this instrument was the eminent delight of poor Miss P——. She would sit down at it for hours together, and her performance would not have disgraced a professor. I hoped that on the eventful occasion that was approaching, the tones of her favourite music, with the blessing of Heaven, might rouse a slumbering responsive chord in her bosom, an aid in dispelling the cruel 'charm that deadened her.' She certainly could not last long in the condition in which she now lay. Every thing that medicine could do, had been tried—in vain; and if the evening's experiment—our forlorn hope, failed—we must, though with a bleeding heart, submit to the will of Providence, and resign her to the grave. I looked forward with intense anxiety—with alternate hope and fear—to the engagement of the evening.

On returning home, late in the afternoon, I found poor Mrs P—— had arrived in town, in obedience to my summons; and heart-breaking, I learnt, was her first interview, if such it may be called, with her daughter. Her shrieks alarmed the whole house, and even arrested the attention of the neighbours. I had left instructions, that in case of her arrival during my absence, she should be shewn at once, without any precautions, into the presence of Miss P——; with the hope, faint though it was, that the abruptness of her appearance, and the violence of her grief, might operate as a salutary shock upon the stagnant energies of her daughter. 'My child! my child! my child!' she exclaimed, rushing up to the bed with frantic haste, and clasping the insensible form of her daughter in her arms, where she held her till she fell fainting into those of my wife. What a dread contrast was there between the frantic gestures—the passionate lamentations of the mother, and the stony silence and motionlessness of the daughter! One little but affecting incident occurred in my presence. Mrs P—— (as yet unacquainted with the peculiar nature of her daughter's seizure) had snatched Miss P——'s hand to her lips, kissed it repeatedly, and suddenly let it go, to press her own hand upon her head, as if to repress a rising hysterical feeling. Miss P——'s arm, as usual, remained for a moment or two suspended, and only gradually sunk down upon the bed. It looked as if she voluntarily continued it in that position, with a cautioning air. Methinks I see at this moment the affrighted stare with which Mrs P—— regarded the outstretched arm, her body recoiling from the bed, as though she expected her daughter were about to do or appear something dreadful! I learned from Mrs P—— that her mother, the grandmother of Agnes, was reported to have been twice affected in a similar manner, though apparently from a different cause; so that there seemed something like a hereditary tendency towards it, even though Mrs P—— herself had never experienced any thing of the kind.

As the memorable evening advanced, the agitation of all who were acquainted with, or interested in the approaching ceremony, increased. Mrs P——, I need hardly say, embraced the proposal with thankful eagerness. About half past seven, my friend Dr D—— arrived, pursuant to his promise; and he was soon afterwards followed by the organist of the neighbouring church—an old acquaintance, and who was a constant visitor at my house, for the purpose of performing and giving instructions on the organ. I requested him to commence playing Martin Luther's hymn*—the favourite one of Agnes—as soon as she should be brought into the room. About eight o'clock, the Dean's carriage drew up. I met him at the door.

'Peace be to this house, and to all that dwell in it!' he exclaimed, as soon as he entered. I led him up stairs; and, without uttering a word, he took the seat prepared for him, before a table on which lay a Bible and Prayer-Book. After a moment's pause, he directed the sick person to be brought into the room. I stepped up stairs, where I found my wife, with the nurse, had finished dressing Miss P——. I thought her paler than usual, and that her cheeks seemed hollower than when I had last seen her. There was an air of melancholy sweetness and languor about her, that inspired the beholder with the keenest sympathy. With a sigh, I gathered her slight form into my arms, a shawl was thrown over her, and, followed by my wife and the nurse, who supported Mrs P——, I carried her down stairs, and placed her in an easy recumbent posture, in a large old family chair, which stood between the organ and the Dean's table. How strange and mournful was her appearance! Her luxuriant hair was gathered up beneath a cap, the whiteness of which was equalled by that of her countenance. Her eyes were closed; and this, added to the paleness of her features, her perfect passiveness, and her being enveloped in a long white unruffled morning dress, which appeared not unlike a shroud, at first sight—made her look rather a corpse than a living being! As soon as Dr D—— and I had taken seats on each side of our poor patient, the solemn strains of the organ commenced. I never appreciated music, and especially the sublime hymn of Luther, so much as on that occasion. My eyes were fixed with agonizing scrutiny on Miss P——. Bar after bar of the music melted on the ear, and thrilled upon the heart; but, alas! produced no more effect upon the placid sufferer than the pealing of an abbey organ on the statues around! My heart began to misgive me: if *this* one last expedient failed! When the music ceased, we all kneeled down, and the Dean, in a solemn and rather tremulous tone of voice, commenced reading appropriate passages from the service for the visitation of the sick. When he had concluded the 71st psalm,* he approached the chair of Miss P——, dropped upon one knee, held her right hand in his, and in a voice broken with emotion, read the following affecting verses from the 8th chapter of St Luke:

'While he yet spake, there cometh one from the ruler of the synagogue's house, saying to him, Thy daughter is dead; trouble not the Master.

'But when Jesus heard it, he answered him, saying, Fear not; believe only, and she shall be made whole.

'And when he came into the house, he suffered no man to go in, save Peter, and James, and John, and the father and the mother of the maiden. And all wept and bewailed her: but he said, Weep not; she is not dead, but sleepeth. And they laughed him to scorn, knowing that she was dead.

'And he put them all out, and took her by the hand, and called, saying, *Maid, arise. And her spirit came again, and she arose straight way.*'

While he was reading the passage which I have marked in italics, my heated fancy almost persuaded me that I saw the eyelids of Miss P—— moving. I trembled from head to foot; but, alas, it was a delusion!

The Dean, much affected, was proceeding with the fifty-fifth verse,* when such a tremendous and long-continued knocking was heard at the street door, as seemed likely to break it open. Every one started up from their knees, as if electrified—all moved but unhappy Agnes—and stood in silent agitation and astonishment. Still the knocking was continued, almost without intermission. My heart suddenly misgave me as to the cause.

'Go—go—See if——'stammered my wife, pale as ashes— endeavouring to prop up the drooping mother of our patient. Before any one had stirred from the spot on which he was standing, the door was burst open, and in rushed Mr N——, wild in his aspect, frantic in his gesture, and his dress covered with dust from head to foot. We stood gazing at him, as though his appearance had petrified us.

'Agnes—my Agnes!' he exclaimed, as if choked for want of breath.

'AGNES!—Come!' he gasped, while a laugh appeared on his face that had a gleam of madness in it.

'Mr N——! what are you about? For mercy's sake, be calm! Let me lead you, for a moment, into another room, and all shall be explained!' said I, approaching and grasping him firmly by the arm.

'AGNES!' he continued, in a tone that made us tremble. He moved towards the chair in which Miss P—— lay. I endeavoured to interpose, but he thrust me aside. The Venerable Dean attempted to dissuade him, but met with no better a reception than myself.

'Agnes!' he reiterated, in a hoarse, sepulchral whisper, 'why won't you speak to me? what are they doing to you?' He stepped within a foot of the chair where she lay—calm and immovable as death! We stood by, watching his movements, in terrified apprehension and uncertainty. He dropped his hat, which he had been grasping with convulsive force, and before any one could prevent him, or even suspect what he was about, he snatched Miss P—— out of the chair, and compressed her in his arms with frantic force, while a delirious laugh burst from his lips. We rushed forward to extricate her from his grasp. His arms gradually relaxed—he muttered, 'Music! music! a dance!' and almost at the moment that we removed Miss P—— from him, fell senseless into the arms of the organist. Mrs P—— had fainted; my wife seemed on the verge of hysterics; and the nurse was crying violently. Such a scene of trouble and terror I have seldom witnessed! I hurried with the poor unconscious girl up stairs, laid her upon the bed, shut and bolted the door after me, and hardly expected to find her alive; her pulse, however, was calm, as it had been throughout the seizure. The calm of the Dead Sea seemed upon her!

I feel, however, that I should not protract these painful scenes; and shall therefore hurry to their close. The first letter which I had dispatched to Oxford after Mr N——, happened to bear on the outside the words 'special *haste!*' which procured its being forwarded by express after Mr N——. The consternation with which he received and read it may be imagined. He set off for town that instant in a post-chaise and four; but finding their speed insufficient, he took to horseback for the last fifty miles, and rode at a rate which nearly destroyed both horse and rider. Hence his sudden appearance at my house, and the frenzy of his behaviour! After Miss P—— had been carried up stairs, it was thought imprudent for Mr N—— to continue at my house, as he exhibited every symptom of incipient brain fever, and might prove wild and unmanageable. He was therefore removed at once to a house within a few doors off, which was let out in furnished lodgings. Dr D—— accompanied him, and bled him immediately, very copiously. I have no doubt that Mr N—— owed his life to that timely measure. He was placed in bed, and put at once under the most vigorous antiphlogistic treatment.

The next evening beheld Dr D——, the Dean of ——, and myself, around the bedside of Agnes. All of us expressed the most gloomy apprehensions. The Dean had been offering up a devout and most affecting prayer.

'Well, my friend,' said he to me, 'she is in the hands of God! All that man can do has been done; let us resign ourselves to the will of Providence!'

'Aye, nothing but a miracle can save her, I fear!' replied Dr D——.

'How much longer do you think it probable, humanly speaking, that the system can continue in this state, so as to give hopes of ultimate recovery?' enquired the Dean.

'I cannot say,' I replied with a sigh. 'She *must* sink, and speedily. She has not received, since she was first seized, as much nourishment as would serve for an infant's meal!'

'I have an impression that she will die suddenly,' said Dr D——; 'possibly within the next twelve hours; for I cannot understand how her energies can recover from, or bear longer, this fearful paralysis!'

'Alas, I fear so too!'

'I have heard some frightful instances of premature burial in cases like this,' said the Dean. 'I hope in Heaven that you will not think of committing her remains to the earth, before you are satisfied, beyond a doubt, that life is extinct.' I made no reply—my emotions nearly choked me—I could not bear to contemplate such an event.

'Do you know,' said Dr D——, with an apprehensive air, 'I have been thinking latterly of the awful possibility, that, notwithstanding the stagnation of her physical powers, her MIND may be sound, and perfectly conscious of all that has transpired about her!'

'Why—why'—stammered the Dean, turning pale—'what if she has—has HEARD all that has been said!'[†]

'Aye!' replied Dr D——, unconsciously sinking his voice to a whisper, 'I know of a case—in fact a friend of mine has just published it—in which a woman'—— There was a faint knocking at the door, and I stepped to it, for the purpose of enquiring what was wanted. While I was in the act of closing it again, I overheard Dr D——'s voice exclaim, in an affrighted tone, 'Great God!' and on turning round, I saw the Dean moving from the bed, his face white as ashes, and he fell from his chair, as if in a fit. How shall I describe what I saw, on approaching the bed?

The moment before, I had left Miss P—— lying in her usual position, and with her eyes closed. They were now wide open, and staring upwards with an expression I have no language to describe. It reminded me of what I had seen when I first

---

[†] In almost every known instance of recovery from Catalepsy, the patients have declared that they heard every word that had been uttered beside them!

discovered her in the fit. Blood, too, was streaming from her nostrils and mouth—in short, a more frightful spectacle I never witnessed. In a moment both Dr D—— and I lost all power of motion. Here, then, was the spell broken! The trance over!— I implored Dr D—— to recollect himself, and conduct the Dean from the room, while I would attend to Miss P——. The nurse was instantly at my side, shaking like an aspen-leaf. She quickly procured warm water, sponges, cloths, &c., with which she at once wiped away and encouraged the bleeding. The first sound uttered by Miss P—— was a long deep-drawn sigh, which seemed to relieve her bosom of an intolerable sense of oppression. Her eyes gradually closed again, and she moved her head away, at the same time raising her trembling right hand to her face. Again she sighed—again opened her eyes, and, to my delight, their expression was more natural than before. She looked languidly about her for a moment, as if examining the bed-curtains—and her eyes closed again. I sent for some weak brandy and water, and gave her a little in a tea-spoon. She swallowed it with great difficulty. I ordered some warm water to be got ready for her feet, to equalize the circulation; and while it was preparing, sat by her, watching every motion of her features with the most eager anxiety. 'How are you, Agnes?' I whispered, kissing her. She turned languidly towards me, opened her eyes, and shook her head feebly—but gave me no answer.

'Do you feel pain anywhere?' I enquired. A faint smile stole about her mouth, but she did not utter a syllable. Sensible that her exhausted condition required repose, I determined not to tax her newly-recovered energies; so I ordered her a gentle composing draught, and left her in the care of the nurse, promising to return by and by, to see how my sweet patient went on. I found that the Dean had left. After swallowing a little wine and water, he recovered sufficiently from the shock he had received, to be able, with Dr D——'s assistance, to step into his carriage, leaving his solemn benediction for Miss P——.

As it was growing late, I sent my wife to bed, and ordered coffee in my study, whither I retired, and sat lost in conjecture and reverie till nearly one o'clock. I then repaired to my patient's room; but my entrance startled her from a sleep that had lasted almost since I had left. As soon as I sat down by her, she opened her eyes—and my heart leaped with joy to see their increasing calmness—their expression resembling what had oft delighted me, while she was in health. After eyeing me steadily for a few moments, she seemed suddenly to recognise me. 'Kiss me!' she whispered, in the faintest possible whisper, while a smile stole over her languid features. I *did* kiss her; and in doing so, my tears fell upon her cheek.

'Don't cry!' she whispered again, in a tone as feeble as before. She gently moved her hand into mine, and I clasped the trembling, lilied fingers, with an emotion I cannot express. She noticed my agitation; and the tears came into her eyes, while her lip quivered, as though she were going to speak. I implored her, however, not to utter a word, till she was better able to do it without exhaustion; and lest my presence should tempt her beyond her strength, I once more kissed her—bade her good-night—her poor slender fingers once more compressed mine—and I left her to the care of the nurse, with a whispered caution to step to me instantly if any change took place in Agnes. I could not sleep! I felt a prodigious burden removed from my mind; and woke my wife, that she might share in my joy.

I received no summons during the night; and on entering her room about nine o'clock in the morning, I found that Miss P—— had taken a little arrow-root in the course of the night, and slept calmly, with but few intervals. She had sighed frequently; and once or twice conversed for a short time with the nurse about *heaven*—as I understood. She was much stronger than I had expected to find her. I kissed her, and she asked me how I was—in a tone that surprised me by its strength and firmness.

'Is the storm over?' she enquired, looking towards the window.

'Oh yes—long, long ago!' I replied, seeing at once that she seemed to have no consciousness of the interval that had elapsed.

'And are you all well?—Mrs ——,' (my wife,) 'how is she?'

'You shall see her shortly.'

'Then, no one was hurt?'

'Not a hair of our heads!'

'How frightened I must have been!'

'Pho, pho, Agnes! Nonsense! Forget it!'

'Then—the world is not—there has been no—is all the same as it was?' she murmured, eyeing me apprehensively.

'The world come to an end—do you mean?' She nodded, with a disturbed air—'Oh, no, no! It was merely a thunderstorm.'

'And is it quite over, and gone?'

'Long ago! Do you feel hungry?' I enquired, hoping to direct her thoughts from a topic I saw agitated her.

'Did you ever see such lightning?' she asked, without regarding my question.

'Why—certainly it was very alarming'—

'Yes, it was! Do you know, Doctor,' she continued, with a mysterious air—'I—I—saw—yes—there were terrible faces in the lightning'—

'Come, child, you rave!'

—'They seemed coming towards the world'—

Her voice trembled, the colour of her face changed.

'Well—if you *will* talk such nonsense, Agnes, I must leave you. I will go and fetch my wife. Would you like to see her?'

'*Tell N—— to come to me to-day*—I must see HIM. I have a message for him!' She said this with a sudden energy that surprised me, while her eye brightened as it settled on me. I kissed her, and retired. The last words surprised and disturbed me. Were her intellects affected? How did she know—how could she conjecture that he was within reach? I took an opportunity of asking the nurse whether she had mentioned Mr N——'s name to her, but not a syllable had been interchanged upon the subject.

Before setting out on my daily visits, I stepped into her room, to take my leave. I had kissed her, and was quitting the room, when happening to look back, I saw her beckoning to me. I returned.

'I MUST see N—— this evening!' said she, with a solemn emphasis that startled me; and as soon as she had uttered the words, she turned her head from me, as if she wished no more to be said.

My first visit was to Mr N——, whom I found in a very weak state, but so much recovered from his illness, as to be sitting up, and partially dressed. He was perfectly calm and collected; and, in answer to his earnest enquiries, I gave him a full account of the nature of Miss P——'s illness. He received the intelligence of the favourable change that had occurred, with evident though silent ecstasy. After much inward doubt and hesitation, I thought I might venture to tell him of the parting—the twice-repeated request she had made. The intelligence blanched his already pallid cheeks to a whiter hue, and he trembled violently.

'Did you tell her I was in town? Did she recollect me?'

'No one has breathed your name to her!' I replied.

'Well, Doctor—if, on the whole, you think so—that it would be safe,' said N——, after we had talked much on the matter—'I will step over and see her; but—it looks very—very strange!'

'Whatever whim may actuate her, I think it better, on the whole, to gratify her. Your refusal *may* be attended with infinitely worse effects than an interview. However, you shall hear from me again. I will see if she continues in the same mind; and, if so, I will step over and tell you.' I took my leave.

A few moments before stepping down to dinner, I sat beside Miss P——, making my usual enquiries; and was gratified to find that her progress, though slow, seemed sure. I was going to kiss her, before leaving, when, with similar emphasis to that she had previously displayed, she said again—

'*Remember!* N—— MUST be here to-night!'

I was confounded. What could be the meaning of this mysterious pertinacity? I felt distracted with doubt, and dissatisfied with myself for what I had told to N——. I felt answerable for whatever ill effects might ensue; and yet, what could I do?

It was evening,—a mild, though lustrous, July evening. The skies were all blue and white, save where the retiring sun-light produced a mellow mixture of colours towards the west. Not a breath of air disturbed the serene complacency. My wife and I sat on each side of the bed where lay our lovely invalid, looking, despite of her recent illness, beautiful, and in comparative health. Her hair was parted with negligent simplicity over her pale forehead. Her eyes were brilliant, and her cheeks occasionally flushed with colour. She spoke scarce a word to us, as we sat beside her. I gazed at her with doubt and apprehension. I was aware that health could not possibly produce the colour and vivacity of her complexion and eyes; and felt at a loss to what I should refer it.

'Agnes, love!—How beautiful is the setting sun!' exclaimed my wife, drawing aside the curtains.

'Raise me! Let me look at it!' replied Miss P—— faintly. She gazed earnestly at the magnificent object for some minutes; and then abruptly said to me—

'He will be here soon?'

'In a few moments I expect him. But—Agnes—Why do you wish to see him?'

She sighed, and shook her head.

It had been arranged that Dr D—— should accompany Mr N—— to my house, and conduct him up stairs, after strongly enjoining on him the necessity there was for controlling his feelings, and displaying as little emotion as possible. My heart leaped into my mouth—as the saying is—when I heard the expected knock at the door.

'N—— is come at last!' said I, in a gentle tone, looking earnestly at her, to see if she was agitated. It was not the case. She sighed, but evinced no trepidation.

'Shall he be shewn in at once?' I enquired.

'No—wait a few moments,' replied the extraordinary girl, and seemed lost in thought for about a minute. 'Now!' she exclaimed; and I sent down the nurse, herself pale and trembling with apprehension, to request the attendance of Dr D—— and Mr N——.

As they were heard slowly approaching the room, I looked anxiously at my patient, and kept my fingers at her pulse. There was not a symptom of flutter or agitation. At length the door was opened, and Dr D—— slowly entered, with N—— upon his arm. As soon as his pale, trembling figure was visible, a calm and heavenly smile beamed upon the countenance of Miss P——. It was full of ineffable loveliness! She stretched out her right arm: he pressed it to his lips, without uttering a word.

My eyes were riveted on the features of Miss P——. Either they deceived me, or I saw a strange alteration—as if a cloud were stealing over her face. I was right!—We all observed her colour fading rapidly. I rose from my chair; Dr D—— also came nearer, thinking she was on the verge of fainting. Her eye was fixed upon the flushed features of her lover, and gleamed with radiance. She gently elevated both her arms towards him, and he leaned over her.

'PREPARE!' she exclaimed, in a low thrilling tone;—her features became paler and paler—her arms fell. She had spoken—she had breathed her last. She was dead!

Within twelve months poor N—— followed her; and, to the period of his death, no other word or thought seemed to occupy his mind but the momentous warning which issued from the expiring lips of Agnes P——, PREPARE!

I have no mystery to solve, no denouement to make. I tell the facts as they occurred; and hope they may not be told in vain!

BIOGRAPHICAL NOTES

Patrick Fraser-Tytler (1791–1849), an Edinburgh lawyer and historian, was joint founder with Walter Scott of the Bannatyne Club, and is best known for his *History of Scotland* (1828–43). He contributed to the early numbers of *Blackwood's*, but left in 1818 because of the magazine's sometimes scurrilous tone. See John Burgon, *The Portrait of a Christian Gentleman: Memoir of Patrick Fraser-Tytle*r (London, 1859).

John Galt (1779–1839), a native of Ayrshire, is best known for *Annals of the Parish* (1821), *The Provost* (1822), *The Entail* (1823), and *The Life of Lord Byron* (1830). Galt was a frequent contributor to *Blackwood's* for nearly fifteen years and two of his novels, *The Ayrshire Legatees* (1821–2) and *The Steamboat* (1822), were serialized in the magazine. See Ian Gordon, *John Galt: The Life of a Writer* (Toronto, 1972).

William Godwin the Younger (1803–32) was the only son of the philosopher William Godwin and his second wife Mary Clairmont. He was a reporter on the *Morning Chronicle* from 1823 until his death from cholera. He published a few essays in the *Weekly Examiner*, as well as three in *Blackwood's*. A posthumously published novel, *Transfusion* (1835), contains a memoir by his father.

James Hogg (1770–1835) was born in Ettrick Forest, and spent some of his youth as a shepherd before joining the literary life of Edinburgh in 1810. He settled as a farmer at Yarrow from 1816. His principal works include *Confessions of a Justified Sinner* (1824), *Songs by the Ettrick Shepherd* (1831), and *The Domestic Manners and Private Life of Sir Walter Scott* (1834). He was a key contributor to *Blackwood's* from the start, and the originator of the notorious 'Chaldee Manuscript' (1817). See Lewis Simpson, *James Hogg: A Critical Study* (Edinburgh, 1962).

John Howison (1797–1859) was born in Edinburgh and seems to have received some training as a doctor. He travelled in Canada from 1818 until 1820, and in 1821 was posted by the East India Company's military service to Bombay, where he spent twenty years travelling extensively through Africa, India, and the Arctic. His travel books include *Sketches of Upper Canada* (1821) and *European Colonies* (1834). Between May 1821 and July 1822 he contributed eight pieces of fiction to *Blackwood's*. See *Dictionary of Canadian Biography* (13 vols; Toronto, 1985), viii. 409–11.

William Maginn (1793–1842) was a graduate of Trinity College Dublin, and a formidable linguist: by 20 he had mastered the classical and Celtic tongues, and was able to speak and write with ease in French, German, Spanish, and Italian. He was author of the satiric novel *Whitehall* (1827), and the first editor of *Fraser's Magazine* (1830–6), in which he published his 'Illustrious Literary Characters' (1830–8) and 'Homeric Ballads' (1838–42). Maginn was a voluminous contributor to *Blackwood's* throughout the early years, and is thought to have suggested the idea for the *Noctes Ambrosianae* series. See M. M. H. Thrall, *Rebellious Fraser's* (New York, 1934).

William Mudford (1782–1848), a London journalist, novelist, and historian, was editor of the *Courier* (1817–28) and the *John Bull* (1841–8), and author of several books, including *The Maid of Buttermere, A Domestic Tale* (1803), *The Five Nights of St. Albans* (1829), and *Stephen Dugard* (1840). In *Blackwood's* he published a number of tales, as well as a popular series of political papers under the pseudonym of 'The Silent Member'. See *DNB*.

Daniel Keyte Sandford (1798–1838), a native of Edinburgh, was from 1821 Professor of Greek at Glasgow University. He was awarded a knighthood in 1830 and in 1834 was briefly Member of Parliament for Paisley. He was author of numerous Greek translations and an *Introduction to the Writing of Greek* (1826). He contributed several articles to *Blackwood's* at the end of his career, including a series of dramatic sketches on the Athenian politician and general Alcibiades. See *DNB*.

Michael Scott (1789–1835) was born at Cowlairs and attended Glasgow University before leaving for Jamaica in 1806, where he ran a series of successful businesses and travelled a great deal. He returned to Scotland permanently in 1822, and became a partner in his father-in-law's firm. Scott wrote two immensely popular novels, *Tom Cringle's Log* (1829–33) and *The Cruise of the Midge* (1834–5), both of which were serialized in *Blackwood's*. He concealed his activities as a writer so well that he was dead before his authorship of *Cringle* was known. See George Douglas, *The Blackwood Group* (Edinburgh, 1897), 134–50.

Walter Scott (1771–1832) was educated at Edinburgh University and published his first book, a translation from Bürger, in 1796. In addition to his phenomenal success as a poet and then a novelist, he assisted in the founding of the *Quarterly Review* (1809), produced important editions of Dryden (1808) and Swift (1814), and wrote a good deal of perceptive criticism, a *Life of Napoleon* (1827), and a *History of Scotland* (1829–30). Scott was a significant contributor to *Blackwood's*, though an often ambivalent supporter. He published over a dozen articles in the magazine, including reviews, tales, and historical essays, the majority of them in 1817–18. See A. Wood, 'Sir W. Scott and "Maga"' in *Blackwood's Magazine*, 232 (1932), 1–15.

Catherine Sinclair (1800–64), a native of Edinburgh, was for many years secretary to her father, Sir John Sinclair, who organized the first *Statistical Account of Scotland*, before turning to children's fiction with the successful *Holiday House* (1839). Her many novels for adults include *Modern Flirtations* (1841) and *Sir Edward Graham; or Railway Speculators* (1849); her non-fictional writings include *Scotland and the Scotch* (1840) and *Popish Legends, or Bible Truth* (1852). As a local philanthropist, she established soup kitchens and drinking fountains in Edinburgh. Her sole contribution to *Blackwood's* was 'The Murder Hole' (1829). See *DNB*.

Henry Thomson: nothing is known of this contributor.

Samuel Warren (1807–77), the son of a Methodist preacher from Manchester, studied medicine at Edinburgh before taking up a literary career. He was the author of many legal textbooks and an early detective novel, *Now and Then* (1847). His most popular works, *Passages from the Diary of a Late Physician* (1830–7) and *Ten Thousand a Year* (1839–41), were serialized in *Blackwood's*. He served briefly as Member of Parliament for Midhurst (1856–9), and was later appointed Master in Lunacy (1859–74). See *DNB*.

John Wilson (1785–1854) was born at Paisley and educated at Glasgow University and Magdalen College Oxford, where he won the first Newdigate Prize. In 1802 he wrote Wordsworth an enthusiastic letter of admiration and in 1807 he moved to the Lake District, where he was for a time intimate with the Wordsworths, contributed to Coleridge's weekly *The Friend* and became De Quincey's closest friend. A financial crisis forced him to Edinburgh in 1815, where he was called to the Bar before becoming Professor of Moral Philosophy at the University in 1820, a position he held until 1851. As a poet he produced *The Isle of Palms* (1812) and *The City of the Plague* (1816), and as a novelist *The Trials of Margaret Lyndsay* (1823) and *The Foresters* (1825). Under the pseudonym of 'Christopher North' he was the mainstay of *Blackwood's* for over three decades, contributing hundreds of articles, including most of the *Noctes Ambrosianae* (1822–35). See Elsie Swann, *Christopher North [John Wilson]* (Edinburgh, 1934).

EXPLANATORY NOTES

Attributions for the tales are based on A. L. Strout, *A Bibliography of Articles in Blackwood's Magazine . . . 1817–1825*; *Wellesley Index to Victorian Periodicals*, ed. W. Houghton, *et al.* (5 vols; Toronto, 1966–89), i. 7–209; and Brian Murray, 'The Authorship of Some Unidentified or Disputed Articles in *Blackwood's Magazine*' in *Studies in Scottish Literature*, 4 (1967), 144–54.

Sketch of a Tradition Related by a Monk in Switzerland

Published in the June 1817 issue (1/3, 270–3), over the initials 'P.F.' This tale by Patrick Fraser-Tytler suggested that there was a striking similarity between a Swiss legend and Byron's Gothic drama *Manfred* (1817). Byron responded curtly: 'the Conjecturer is out—& knows nothing of the matter—I had a better origin than he can devise or divine for the soul of him' (*Byron's Letters and Journals*, ed. L. A. Marchand (12 vols; London, 1973–82), v. 249). The best account of Byron's relationship with *Blackwood's* is in A. L. Strout's edition of Lockhart, *John Bull's Letter to Lord Byron* (Norman, Okla., 1947).

  3 *Altorf*: town in central Switzerland. Tell is said to have been born in nearby Bürglen.

    Having just read . . . 'Manfred': *Manfred* was published on 16 June 1817; Fraser-Tytler's tale appeared only four days later.

  5 *'The silence . . . hills'*: Wordsworth, 'Song at the Feast of Brougham Castle', 163–4.

  6 *'into their airy elements resolved, were gone'*: slightly misquoted from Robert Southey's *Roderick, The Last of the Goths*, conclusion to part XXI.

  7 *'glory beyond all glory ever seen'*: Wordsworth, *Excursion*, ii. 832.

  8 *'The sounding cataract haunted him like a passion'*: Wordsworth, 'Tintern Abbey', 76–7.

Narrative of a Fatal Event

Published in the March 1818 issue (3/12, 630–5), under the signature 'TWEEDSIDE'. This tale of remorse is by Walter Scott, whose review of *Frankenstein* appeared in the same issue (A. Wood, 'Sir W. Scott and "Maga"' in *Blackwood's Magazine*, 232 (1932), 1–15).

10 *Knapdale*: area in the south-west Highlands.

Cannach: cotton-grass.

11 *point of Cantyre*: Kintyre, the peninsula south of Knapdale.

below his tree ... his own discoveries: the tree presumably refers to the legend of Newton under the apple tree evolving his laws of gravity. Among other achievements, Newton invented the practical reflecting telescope and calculated the approximate weight of the sun.

15 *Cowal ... Lochfine*: Loch Fyne separates Knapdale from Cowal.

'Forthwith this ... me free': slightly misquoted from Coleridge, *Rime of the Ancient Mariner*, 578–81.

Extracts from Gosschen's Diary

Published anonymously in the August 1818 issue (3/17, 596–8). This cruel tale by John Wilson suggested the central incident in B. W. Procter's 'Marcian Colonna' (1820), and is a probable source for Robert Browning's 'Porphyria's Lover' (1836) (R. W. Amour, *Barry Cornwall* (Boston, 1935), 148–51; and Michael Mason, 'Browning and the Dramatic Monologue' in *Writers and their Background: Robert Browning*, ed. I. Armstrong (Athens, Oh., 1975), 255–66). Although Wilson promised further 'extracts', the Gosschen series did not continue.

A Night in the Catacombs

Published in the October 1818 issue (4/19, 19–23). This tale of internment by Daniel Keyte Sandford was submitted in the form of a letter from 'E.——'.

27 *peace of Amiens*: a fourteen-month cessation of hostilities between Britain, France, Spain, and the Netherlands during the Napoleonic Wars. The Treaty of Amiens was signed on 27 March 1802.

Catacombs: a vast system of underground stone quarries dating back to Roman times. Toward the end of the eighteenth century they were converted into a charnel-house for bones removed from disused Paris graveyards. Victims of some of the bloodiest days of the Revolution are also deposited here.

Barrière d'Enfer: a gate in the southern section of the Paris city wall which houses the principal entrance to the Catacombs; now the site of the Place Denfert-Rochereau.

28 *described so often*: see, for example, John Scott, 'Original Description of the Catacombs' in *A Visit to Paris in 1814* (London,

1815), pp. lxii–lxviii: 'In one chamber bones were laid out in shelves on the walls; and in others, small altars of thigh bones were surmounted by solitary skulls. The minutes lengthened out as I walked through the extended series of passages and apartments.'

'*Felix qui potuit . . . Acherontis avari!*': 'Blessed is he who has been able to win knowledge of the causes of things, and has cast beneath his feet all fear and unyielding Fate, and the howls of hungry Acheron' (Virgil, *Georgics* ii. 490–2). Acheron is a river in Hades, the Grecian underworld.

32 *stile*: antiquated form of style, here meaning designation.

The Buried Alive

Published anonymously in the October 1821 issue (10/56, 262–4). This tale by John Galt forms part of a chapter of his novel *The Steamboat* (1822), and is a probable influence on several Poe stories (J. Gerald Kennedy, 'Poe and Magazine Writing on Premature Burial' in *Studies in the American Renaissance*, ed. Joel Myerson (1977), 165–78). In Poe's 'How to Write a Tale for Blackwood', Mr Blackwood refers to this tale as 'a capital thing!—The record of a gentleman's sensations, when entombed before the breath was out of his body—full of taste, terror, sentiments, metaphysics, and erudition' (*Collected Works of Edgar Allan Poe*, ed. T. O. Mabbott (3 vols; Cambridge, Mass., 1978), ii. 339).

37 *galvanic experiment*: in 1791 Luigi Galvani concluded that animal tissue contained a previously unnoticed innate vital force which he called 'animal electricity'. Galvani used frogs to test his theory, but his followers routinely experimented upon stolen corpses and recently hanged criminals.

The Floating Beacon

Published anonymously in the October 1821 issue (10/56, 270–81). This tale is one of eight by John Howison that appeared in *Blackwood's* between May 1821 and July 1822, making Howison the magazine's main contributor of fiction at this time. 'The Floating Beacon' was adapted for the stage by the popular dramatist Edward Fitzball in 1824 and again by an unknown hand in 1829 (Allardyce Nicoll, *A History of English Drama* (6 vols; Cambridge, 1952–9), iv. 312, 462, 584; and Robert Morrison, 'John Howison of *Blackwood's Magazine*' in *Notes and Queries*, NS 42 (June 1995), 191–3).

39 *Bergen to Christiansand*: cities on the south-west and south coasts of Norway respectively.

The Man in the Bell

Published anonymously in the November 1821 issue (10/57, 373–5), this unusual tale by William Maginn is a probable source for the last stanza of Poe's 'The Bells', and for a number of his tales (see Mabbott, *Collected Works*, ii. 359; Michael Allen, *Poe and the British Magazine Tradition* (Oxford, 1969)).

64 *the fate of the Santon Barsisa*: the devil twice betrays the Santon Barsisa, and then spits in his face and leaves him to hang ('The History of Santon Barsisa' in *The Guardian*, ed. J. C. Stephens (Lexington, Ky, 1982), 483–5).

The ancients . . . annihilate him: Tartarus is a section of Hades reserved for the punishment of the wicked. In Graeco-Roman myth, the punishment of the descending rock is usually meted out to Tantalus. See, for example, Lucretius, *De Rerum Natura*, iii.

65 *electric jar*: Leyden jar, a device that can be made to store static electricity and then deliver a shock.

66 *Alexander Selkirk, in Cowper's poem*: 'Verses, Supposed to be Written by Alexander Selkirk, During his Solitary Abode in the Island of Juan Fernandez.' In the poem, Selkirk laments that 'the sound of the church going bell | These vallies and rocks never heard' (29–30).

Mahometan hatred . . . Muezzin: the Commander of the Faithful can refer to either the Prophet Muhammed or to the ruling Ottoman Caliph of the time, Mahmud II. Muslims are called to prayer by the human voice, not by a bell.

The Last Man

Published in the March 1826 issue (19/110, 284–6). The author of this tale has not been identified. Byron's 'Darkness' (1817) concerns the theme of 'the last man' and, between 1823 and 1826, Thomas Campbell, Thomas Lovell Beddoes, Mary Shelley, and Thomas Hood all produced works with this title (Arthur McA. Miller, *The Last Man: A Study of the Eschatological Theme in English Poetry and Fiction From 1806 Through 1839*, unpub. thesis (Duke University, 1966); and A. J. Sambrook, 'A Romantic Theme: The Last Man' in *Forum for Modern Language Studies*, 2 (1966) 25–33).

67 *ether*: in the nineteenth century, it was believed that this transparent, undetectable, universal substance permeated all matter and space, including the void.

68 *There was . . . their being*: this passage, and the tale as a whole, reflects the Ptolemaic geocentric cosmology, disproved by Copernicus in 1543, in which the universe is composed of a number of concentric spheres, at the centre of which is the earth.

As it was . . . wonder: by the early nineteenth century, the use of telescopes, by scientists such as Sir William Herschel (1738–1822), had revealed the barrenness of the moon's surface.

Le Revenant

Published anonymously in the April 1827 issue (21/124, 409–16). When it appeared, this tale by Henry Thomson was 'talked of by every body I know', Thomas Hood told William Blackwood. Charles Lamb wrote to his editor and friend William Hone: 'There is in Blackwood this month an article MOST AFFECTING indeed called Le Revenant . . . I beg you read it and see if you can extract any of it. *The Trial scene in particular.*' Poe is indebted to 'Le Revenant', as is Dickens, particularly for the trial scene in the penultimate chapter of *Oliver Twist* (1839) (*The Letters of Thomas Hood*, ed. Peter Morgan (Toronto, 1973), 78; *The Letters of Charles and Mary Lamb*, ed. E. V. Lucas (3 vols; London, 1935), iii. 78; Margaret Alterton, *Origins of Poe's Critical Theory* (Iowa, Ia., 1925), 7–45; and H. P. Sucksmith, 'The Secret of Immediacy: Dickens' Debt to the Tale of Terror in *Blackwood's*' in *Nineteenth-Century Fiction*, 26 (Sept. 1971) 151–7).

73 *Le Revenant*: the ghost, or someone who returns from the dead.

75 *Newgate*: the main prison in London from the thirteenth till the nineteenth century.

The Murder Hole

Published anonymously in the February 1829 issue (25/149, 189–92). This tale by Catherine Sinclair was told to Walter Scott by Sinclair's mother, Lady Diana, in March 1828. Scott noted that 'the whole legend is curious. I will try to get hold of it' (*The Journal of Sir Walter Scott*, ed. W. E. K. Anderson (Oxford, 1972), 441–2).

89 *Collins*: 'Ode to Fear', 5–8.

'lonesome desert': possibly misquoted from Byron's 'Morgante Maggiore' (1823), 'An abbey which in a lone desert lay, | 'Midst glens obscure, and distant lands' (158–9).

'blasted heath': *Macbeth*, I. iii. 77.

90 *'I will . . . storm'*: adapted from Isaiah 32: 2: 'And each shall be as an hiding-place from the wind, and a covert from the tempest;

as rivers of water in a dry place, as the shadow of a great rock in a weary land.'

92 *'steep themselves in forgetfulness'*: slightly misquoted from *King Henry IV*, pt. II, III. i. 8.

Heat and Thirst

Published anonymously in the June 1830 issue (27/167, 861–3). This tale by Michael Scott eventually formed part of a chapter of his popular novel *Tom Cringle's Log*, serialized in *Blackwood's* from September 1829 to August 1833. De Quincey admired Tom Cringle 'greatly', Coleridge declared the sketches 'most excellent', and Lockhart thought *Cringle* 'perhaps the most brilliant series of Magazine papers of the time'. *Cringle* is a probable influence on the Brontës, including the West Indian scenes in *Jane Eyre* (1847), and the episode of Jackoo's death in 'Heat and Thirst' was borrowed by Richard Hughes for his *A High Wind in Jamaica* (1929) (H. Eaton, *Thomas De Quincey* (Oxford, 1936), 354; *Table Talk*, ed. Carl Woodring (2 vols; Princeton, NJ, 1990), ii. 278; *Quarterly Review*, 50 (Jan. 1834), 377; Tom Winnifrith, *The Brontës and their Background* (London, 1973), 91–2; and Ian Milligan, 'Richard Hughes and Michael Scott: A Further Source for *A High Wind In Jamaica*' in *Notes and Queries*, NS 33 (June 1986), 192–3).

97 *floated double . . . of the poet*: Wordsworth's 'Yarrow Unvisited'. 'The Swan on still St. Mary's Lake', writes Wordsworth, 'Float double, Swan and Shadow!' (43–4).

98 *junk . . . taffril*: rope hanging from the stern railing of a ship.

Corromantee: Coromantee or Coromantine; a slave from Africa's Gold Coast.

gammoning: the lashing of ropes by which the bowsprit is made fast to the hull.

100 *'El muchacho . . . Aqua.'*: 'The boy is dying of thirst—water.'

'El hijo . . . verlo': 'My son—water for my son little Peter—Don't worry about me—Oh last night, last night! . . . Let me see him then, oh God, let me see him'.

The Iron Shroud

Published in the August 1830 issue (28/170, 364–71), as 'by the author of "First and Last"' and under the signature 'M'. Written by William Mudford, this ingeniously claustrophobic tale appealed strongly to Poe, who used the idea in 'The Pit and the Pendulum' (1843) and a number of other tales (see Allen, *Poe*). Mudford told

Blackwood that this tale 'came into my head in a strange & original way. I have bestowed too more than ordinary labour to make it striking in execution' (National Library of Scotland MS.4028).

101 *rock of Scylla . . . its grandeur*: headland projecting into the Strait of Messina from the coast of southern Italy.

The Mysterious Bride

Published in the December 1830 issue (28/174, 943–50), as 'BY THE ETTRICK SHEPHERD'. This tale by James Hogg is, in effect, an addition to his *Shepherd's Calendar*, a series of tales and essays contributed by Hogg to *Blackwood's* between April 1819 and April 1828. Like many of Hogg's tales for *Blackwood's*, 'The Mysterious Bride' draws on Border folklore of brownies, ghosts, and witches (see *James Hogg: Selected Stories and Sketches*, ed. Douglas Mack (Edinburgh, 1982), pp. ix, 202–3).

115 *Even Sir Walter . . . renegade*: Hogg is thinking in particular of 'My Aunt Margaret's Mirror', published in the annual *Keepsake* (London, 1829), 1–44, where the narrator comments that nowadays the only people who believe in supernatural stories are 'fools and children'.

Nathaniel Gow: (1766–1831), a Scottish violinist and composer.

St Lawrence's Eve: 9 August; St Lawrence was one of the most venerated Roman martyrs, celebrated for his Christian valour.

curtch: Hogg seems to mean the pommel or horn of the saddle.

116 '*Let me in this ae night*': a version of this song appears in David Herd's collection of *Ancient and Modern Scottish Songs* (1776); Burns published two versions of this song.

laughing at the catastrophe: Herd's version of the song concludes:

> But ere a' was done, and a' was said,
> Out fell the bottom of the bed;
> The lassie lost her maidenhead,
> And her mither heard the din, jo.
> O the devil take this aw night, this ae, ae, ae night,
> O the devil take this ae night, that ere I let you in, jo.

120 '*Of fancy . . . wind*': Hogg slightly misquotes his own *The Queen's Wake*, 'Dumlanrig, The Sixteenth Bard's Song', 508–9.

125 '*The Fourfold State of Man*': *Human Nature in its Fourfold State* (1720), a popular work of Calvinist theology by Thomas Boston (1677–1732).

125 *callant*: a boy or young man.

126 *'Elegit'*: he/she has chosen.

128 *the last of his race*: cf. Wordsworth's 'The Brothers': 'they two | Were brother Shepherds on their native hills. | They were the last of all their race' (71–3).

129 *cushats biggit*: pigeons built.

howk: dig.

The Executioner

Published in the February and March 1832 issues (31/191–2, 306–19, 483–95), over the signature 'SYPHAX'. This tale by William Godwin the Younger is notable for its resemblances to the fictions of the author's father, especially to the prison scenes and episodes of solitary flight in *Things as They Are, or The Adventures of Caleb Williams* (1794). The gloom of the outcast hero also has some echoes of *Frankenstein* (1818) by Mary Shelley, the author's elder half-sister. In a larger context, the tale looks back to *Oedipus the King* and forward to *Great Expectations*. In a letter to Blackwood, Godwin described the tale as 'descriptive of extraordinary passions & extraordinary situations'. Later he told Blackwood: 'The hint that you have afforded me about my style of writing shall not be lost—that it will affect a change, I cannot yet promise, for [I] may safely assert that my manner is hardly so much formed on my father's publications, as on my general intercourse with him—a source, I apprehend, much more difficult to be turned aside.' There was some discussion about the title of the tale. Godwin suggested 'The Confessions of an Executioner' and 'The Web of the Wicked', but left the matter 'entirely' in Blackwood's hands (National Library of Scotland, MS.4029, 4033).

134 *ignes fatui*: will o'the wisp.

141 *Rutlandshire*: an eastern English county, later absorbed into Leicestershire. The county town is usually spelt 'Oakham'.

142 *Dogberry*: the self-important constable in Shakespeare's *Much Ado About Nothing*.

143 *custos*: guardian, custodian.

144 *'peach*: informer.

151 *blackleg*: swindler (here, a criminal accomplice).

152 *el Dorado*: the fabled city of gold sought by early explorers in South America.

156 *Rome's offending Vestals*: the Vestal Virgins who tended the sacred flame in the temple of Vesta were punished by being

entombed alive if they broke their vow of chastity. A case of this punishment being meted out is recorded in Book 4, letter 11 of the *Letters* of the Younger Pliny.

160 *cap-à-pie*: head to toe.

162 *manes*: ancestral spirits.

176 *glouted*: frowned.

posse comitatus: company of constables.

A 'Man About Town'

Published anonymously in the December 1830 issue (28/174, 921–38), as the main part of Chapter 5 of Samuel Warren's immensely popular *Passages from the Diary of a Late Physician*, serialized in *Blackwood's* from August 1830 to August 1837. Henry Crabb Robinson characterized the series as 'of considerable power, and deserved popularity, but in bad taste, full of exaggerations and over-dosing the reader with horrors'. In 1839 Douglas ('Delta') Moir wrote that 'the *Physician's Diary* . . . was truly a hit' and extended Warren's reputation 'not only through France and Germany, but, as a lady from Moscow informed me, to the most northern extremities of Europe. The instant his separate tales came out in *Blackwood's*, translators both at St Petersburg and Moscow were at their tasks; and all the theatres strove which to be first to have him on the stage.' When 'A "Man About Town"' appeared Warren wrote to Blackwood that it was 'exciting a sensation among the Clubs, and elsewhere. "Horrible", "ghastly", "frightful", "lamentable", are some of the expressions to which I have listened.' Certain parts of this tale may have been used as the basis for the deathbed scene of Arthur Huntingdon in Anne Brontë's *The Tenant of Wildfell Hall* (1848) (Henry Crabb Robinson, *On Books and their Writers*, ed. E. J. Morley (3 vols; London, 1938), ii. 453; 'Memoir' in *The Poetical Works of David Macbeth Moir*, ed. Thomas Aird (Edinburgh, 1852), p. lxiv; Mrs Oliphant, *Annals of a Publishing House* (3 vols; Edinburgh, 1897), ii. 31; Winnifrith, *The Brontës*).

181 *'iron is entering the very soul'*: adapted from the Anglican *Book of Common Prayer*, Psalm 105: 18.

184 *'In shape and gesture proudly eminent'*: Milton, *Paradise Lost*, i. 590.

sciolist: a smatterer; one who pretends to knowledge.

186 *the frightful creature brought into being by Frankenstein*: the monster created from parts of corpses by the medical student

Victor Frankenstein in Mary Shelley's novel *Frankenstein; or the Modern Prometheus* (1818).

186 ἰδιοσυγκρισία: idiosyncrasia: peculiarity of temperament or of constitution.

'Better to reign in hell than serve in heaven': Milton, *Paradise Lost*, i. 263.

187 *'feeding on garbage'*: probably misquoted from *Hamlet*, I. v. 57–9: 'So lust, though to a radiant angel link'd, / Will sate itself in a celestial bed / And prey on garbage.'

'fallen, fallen, fallen': Dryden, 'Alexander's Feast', 77.

189 *antiphlogistic treatment*: treatment to counteract inflammation, e.g. by cupping, bleeding, or blistering.

ἄγλωσσος: aglossos: dumb, speechless.

duns: impatient creditors.

non ad rem: irrelevant, not to the point.

190 *a passage from old Persius!*: from the third Satire of the Roman poet Persius Flaccus (AD 34–62): 'May it be your will, great father of the gods, to punish cruel tyrants, whose characters are perverted by the raging intoxication of terrible lust, in just this way: that they may see virtue, and waste away for the loss of it.'

191 *a better Bentley*: i.e. a better scholar of Latin. Richard Bentley (1662–1742) Royal librarian and Master of Trinity College Cambridge, was the leading classical scholar of his day.

that worthy fellow Plautus!: Titus Maccus Plautus (c.250–184 BC), Roman comic playwright.

192 κατὰ στάγονα: kata stagona: drop by drop.

195 *Belasco*: not identified—possibly a real boxer or coach of the times, although not listed in the standard histories.

199 *a passage of Persius*: from Persius' third Satire, 113–14: 'If we looked into your tender throat, would we not find a sore place that must not be scraped by plebeian beet?'

'measured out . . . his own lips': adapted from *Macbeth*, I. vii. 10–12: 'this even handed justice | Commends the ingredients of our poisoned chalice | To our own lips'.

200 *situation . . . of Job*: 'Yet, he shall perish for ever like his own dung' (Job 20: 7).

Epictetus: the Stoic philosopher of the first century AD, who preached indifference to fate.

eandem semper canens... usque: 'always singing the same old song until it makes us sick'—partly adapted from Terence's play *Phormio*, iii. 496.

203 *Petronius Arbiter!*: the first-century Roman novelist, presumed author of the *Satyricon*, which portrays some of the decadent excesses of Roman society.

204 *'a vivâ voce (!)' message*: here, just a message by word of mouth rather than in writing; literally 'by living voice'.

205 *Arrian's Discourses of Epictetus*: Flavius Arrianus, a historian and political administrator in the second century AD, had been a student of Epictetus (see note to p. 200 above) and preserved his master's writings for publication.

206 *'MANY STRIPES'*: Luke 12: 47: 'And that servant, which knew his lord's will, and prepared not himself, neither did according to his will, shall be beaten with many stripes.'

207 *'Richard's himself again!'*: from Colley Cibber's adaptation of Shakespeare's *Richard III* (1700), V. iii. 119.

209 *Lardner, and Paley*: Nathaniel Lardner (1684–1768) and William Paley (1743–1805) each wrote a standard defence of Christian belief. Lardner was the author of the seventeen-volume work *The Credibility of the Gospel History* (1727–57). Paley wrote the more popular *A View of the Evidences of Christianity* (1794).

210 *alluding to the 'Scholar's Death-Bed'*: an editorial reference back to another story, 'A Scholar's Death-Bed', published three months previously in the same series.

The Spectre-Smitten

Published anonymously in the February 1831 issue (29/177, 361–75), as the seventh chapter of Warren's *Passages*. Dickens may have borrowed from this tale for his 'A Madman's Manuscript' in *Pickwick Papers* (1837) (Sucksmith, *Secret of Immediacy*).

216 *Mr Maturin*: Charles Robert Maturin (1780–1824), Anglo-Irish clergyman and novelist, whose most famous and fearful work was the Gothic novel *Melmoth the Wanderer* (1820).

221 *venesection*: the cutting open of veins.

226 *'grinned horribly a ghastly smile'*: misquoted from Milton, *Paradise Lost*, ii. 846.

228 *the Talmudist*: the supposed author of the Jewish body of law governing correct ceremonial practice.

the striped stick which Jacob held up: Genesis 30: 37–43.

231 *the people whom the New Testament speaks of*: Matthew 4: 24; also Mark 1: 32.

233 *'pen of a ready writer'*: Psalm 45: 1: 'my tongue is the pen of a ready writer.'

rantings in the Maturin style: see note to p. 216 above.

234 *often quoted sentiment of Horace*: from Book I of Horace's *Epistles*, 2. 69–70: 'The jar will long keep the fragrance of what it was once steeped in when new.'

Dr Johnson . . . horror of insanity: the quotation here is very loosely based on Johnson's letter of 19 June 1783 (shortly after his stroke) to Mrs Thrale, as recorded in Boswell's *Life of Johnson*.

vexatu questio: troublesome question.

235 *Dr Monro, in his 'Philosophy of Human Nature'*: not identified. There was a dynasty of Monro doctors in the eighteenth and early nineteenth centuries, several of them occupying successively the post of physician to Bedlam, the notorious London lunatic asylum.

Locke's . . . great work: John Locke (1632–1704), English philosopher; his great work, quoted here, is the *Essay Concerning Human Understanding* (1692).

236 *'The Broken Heart'*: an earlier story by Warren, published in the same series in October 1830.

237 *'himself again'*: see note to p. 207 above.

238 *one of our old dramatists*: John Lyly (?1554–1606), whose play *Endymion* (V. i. 51–2) is misquoted here, from a scene in which Endymion has awoken from a sleep of forty years.

'palpable and obscure': misquoted from Milton, *Paradise Lost*, ii. 406.

240 *'chamber of imagery'*: Ezekiel 8: 12: 'every man in the chambers of his imagery.'

241 *Exeter Change*: a building on the Strand in London, partly devoted to the exhibition of exotic animals. It was demolished in 1830.

'hoped against hope': Romans 4: 18: 'Who against hope believed in hope.'

The Thunder-Struck and The Boxer

Published anonymously in the September 1832 issue (32/198, 279–99), as the thirteenth chapter of Warren's *Passages*. The tale has been suggested as a source for Poe's 'The Fall of the House of Usher' (1839) (Alterton, *Poe's Critical Theory*).

243 *one of our old dramatists*: not identified; the attribution to Marlowe appears to be mistaken.

245 *Hebe-like ease and grace*: in Greek mythology, Hebe is the daughter of Hera and Zeus, noted for her beauty.

'*things wherein her soul delighted*': possibly from Isaiah 42: 1: 'in whom my soul delighteth.'

251 *antispasmodic treatment*: treatment to counteract spasms or convulsions.

have her cupped: bled by means of a cupping-glass.

254 '*grinned horribly a ghastly smile!*': see note to p. 226 above.

255 *Elymas the sorcerer*: in Acts 13, Elymas is a false prophet who obstructs the mission of Paul and Barnabas in Paphos and is punished by being blinded. This incident was chosen for one of a series of tapestries in the Vatican's Sistine Chapel, designed by Raphael in preliminary cartoons in 1515–16. The cartoon, with others in the series, was acquired by Charles I of England, and is now in the Victoria and Albert Museum, London.

257 *Virgil's 'Felix qui potuit . . . causas'*: see note to p. 28 above.

260 *nosological anomaly*: i.e. something outside the known classification of diseases.

Van Swieten: Gerard van Swieten (1700–72), Dutch physician, Professor of Medicine at Leiden and Vienna. His *Commentaries* (1743) on the medical doctrines of his former teacher Herman Boerhaave were widely translated and consulted. He also published in 1759 a treatise on the diseases prevalent in armies.

'*Saxifici Medusae vultus*': misquoted from Ovid's *Metamorphoses*, v. 217: 'the petrifying face of Medusa.'

Celsus: Aulus Cornelius Celsus, author of an important medical encyclopedia in the first century AD.

the celebrated Dr Cullen: William Cullen (1710–90), Scottish physician, pillar of the Edinburgh medical school, and author of the standard textbook *First Lines of the Practice of Physic* (1776–84).

Dr Jebb: John Jebb (1736–86); his work *Select Cases of Paralysis of the Lower Extremities* appeared in 1782.

262 *Dr Petetin*: Jacques-Henri-Désiré Petetin (1744–1808) of Lyons published a number of works on catalepsy, galvanism, and similar

topics, including *Mémoire sur la découverte des phénomènes que présentent le catalepsie et le somnambulisme* (Lyons, 1787), and *Théorie du Galvanisme* (Paris, 1803).

263 *sinapisms*: mustard plasters.

270 *Martin Luther's hymn*: Luther composed many popular hymns, but it is likely that the hymn referred to here is his best loved 'Ein' feste Burg ist unser Gott' (1528), which is based on the 46th Psalm, and rendered into English as 'A safe stronghold'.

271 *the 71st psalm*: 'In thee, O Lord, do I put my trust.'

the fifty-fifth verse: 'And her spirit came again, and she arose straightway: and he commanded to give her meat.'

THE WORLD'S CLASSICS

A Select List

HANS ANDERSEN: Fairy Tales
Translated by L. W. Kingsland
Introduction by Naomi Lewis
Illustrated by Vilhelm Pedersen and Lorenz Frølich

ARTHUR J. ARBERRY (Transl.): The Koran

LUDOVICO ARIOSTO: Orlando Furioso
Translated by Guido Waldman

ARISTOTLE: The Nicomachean Ethics
Translated by David Ross

JANE AUSTEN: Emma
Edited by James Kinsley and David Lodge

Northanger Abbey, Lady Susan, The Watsons,
and Sanditon
Edited by John Davie

Persuasion
Edited by John Davie

WILLIAM BECKFORD: Vathek
Edited by Roger Lonsdale

KEITH BOSLEY (Transl.): The Kalevala

CHARLOTTE BRONTË: Jane Eyre
Edited by Margaret Smith

JOHN BUNYAN: The Pilgrim's Progress
Edited by N. H. Keeble

FRANCES HODGSON BURNETT: The Secret Garden
Edited by Dennis Butts

FANNY BURNEY: Cecilia
or Memoirs of an Heiress
Edited by Peter Sabor and Margaret Anne Doody

THOMAS CARLYLE: The French Revolution
Edited by K. J. Fielding and David Sorensen

TOBIAS SMOLLETT: The Expedition of Humphry Clinker
Edited by Lewis M. Knapp
Revised by Paul-Gabriel Boucé

ROBERT LOUIS STEVENSON:
Treasure Island
Edited by Emma Letley

ANTHONY TROLLOPE: The American Senator
Edited by John Halperin

GIORGIO VASARI: The Lives of the Artists
Translated and Edited by Julia Conaway Bondanella and Peter Bondanella

VIRGINIA WOOLF: Orlando
Edited by Rachel Bowlby

ÉMILE ZOLA: Nana
Translated and Edited by Douglas Parmée

A complete list of Oxford Paperbacks, including The World's Classics, OPUS, Past Masters, Oxford Authors, Oxford Shakespeare, and Oxford Paperback Reference, is available in the UK from the Arts and Reference Publicity Department (BH), Oxford University Press, Walton Street, Oxford OX2 6DP.

In the USA, complete lists are available from the Paperbacks Marketing Manager, Oxford University Press, 200 Madison Avenue, New York, NY 10016.

Oxford Paperbacks are available from all good bookshops. In case of difficulty, customers in the UK can order direct from Oxford University Press Bookshop, Freepost, 116 High Street, Oxford, OX1 4BR, enclosing full payment. Please add 10 per cent of published price for postage and packing.